Star Gazer

Book Two

The Twelve Tribes

The Second Tales in the Chronicles of

Jack Barleycorn

by

John Morris

Charlotte Greene
Dorset, England

Copyright © 2020 by John Morris

First Edition

Printed in the United Kingdom (or country of purchase)

This is a work of fiction. Names, characters, places and incidents
are the product of the author's imaginations or are used
fictitiously. Any resemblance to actual persons living or dead is
entirely coincidental.

Published by Charlotte Greene, Dorset, England

Editor: Susan Dewey http://beeberrywoods.com/FiberEtc/

Cover: Boris Junkovic   http://www.charlotte-
greene.co.uk/Agents_BorisJunkovic.htm

Maps, Illustrations and website graphics: Boris Junkovic

Acknowledgements: Melissa Felton, Terry Dickerson, Ian Brown,
Jim Bayliss, Mike Cheek

Dedicated to my Father, Jack Morris

Official Star Gazer website: http://www.star-gazer.co.uk

Official author website: http://www.john-morris-author.com

ISBN Print: 9781910711057
ISBN eBook: 9781910711088

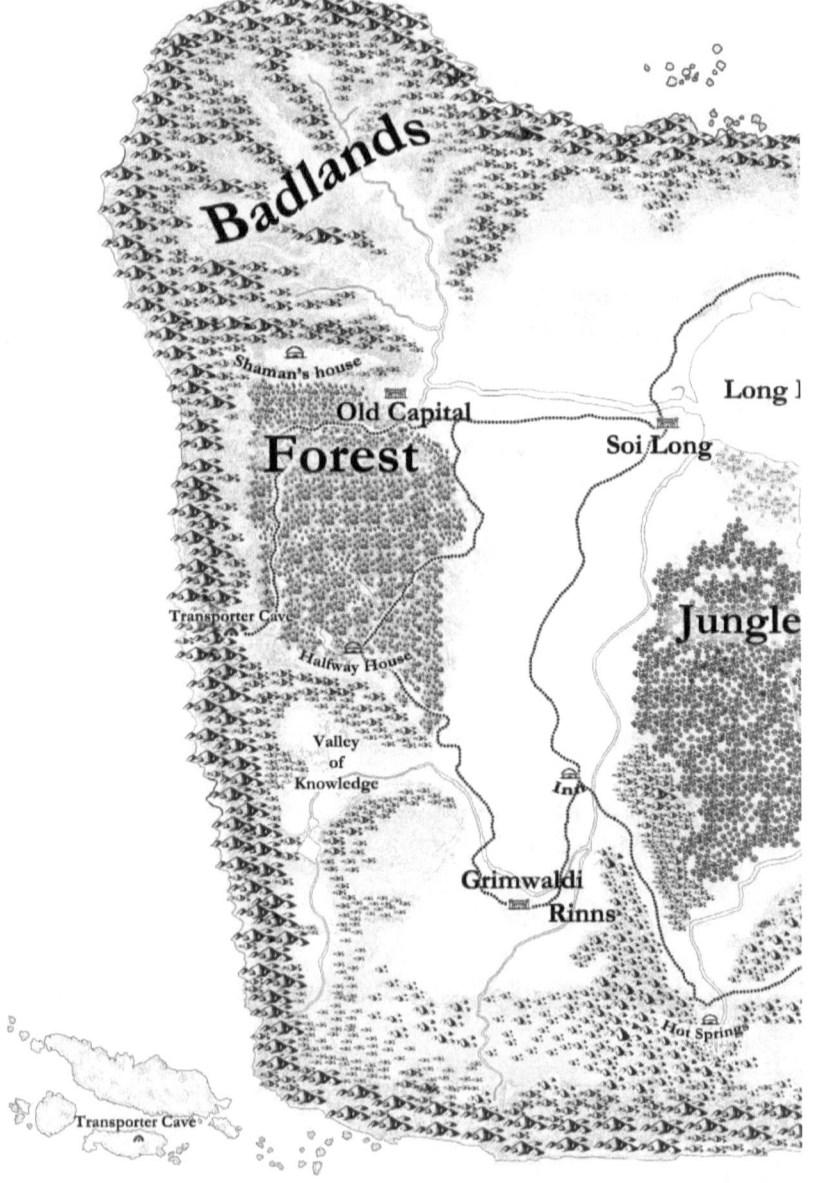

Island

— 1 mile

Gu Long Dux

Lake

Lagoon

Meade Lake

Village

Transporter Cave

Forest Meade

Outlands

N
nw · ne
W · E
sw · se
S

v

Table of Contents

Main Characters

Jack Barleycorn (homo sapiens or Last). The Guardian. Although married to Jien Noi, he chose not to become Emperor.

The Second (homo erectus)
Jien Noi. The Empress and Gatekeeper. She is the ultimate power; the Second are a matriarchal society. Jack calls her Jinnie.
Ræm, firstborn of Jack and Jinnie, Empress and Gatekeeper elect.
The Shaman, an enlightened, and possibly elemental being.
n'Gnung. First Warrior of the Second, and Jack's closest friend.
n'Gue. Prime Messenger of the Second, n'Gnung's elder brother.
Gung Loi. Second Warrior, leader of the Second's Special Forces, and senior control room operator, marries n'Gnung.
Barph. General of the Second's army.
§
Horovitz (homo sapiens). Captain of the Second's Blitzkrieg forces, Sergeant ex-mercenary who changed sides.

The Seventh, Ddwyrth, or Dwarves (homo neanderthalensis).
King Owain a'y Brenin
Llwydd the Bold, First Warrior of the Ddwyrth.
Aroweena (female), Second Warrior of the Ddwyrth. Known as the Keeper of Hearts, and not because of her beauty.

The Eleventh or Elves
Ælthrelntheine, High Queen of the Eleventh, High Lord Protector of Gaia, mother of Kay.
Kay (Ælkræleinnoire), High Lord of Destiny, Queen of the Eleventh Elect.

The Twelfth or Giants
King Rambling Longshanks.
Gangling Shortfalls, learned sage and translator.

The Tenth or Ogres
The Great Ogre – arch villain.
The Trolls, slaves of the Great Ogre; some liberated as the New Tenth.

Villains from Book 1
Theodosius Quinn, Ogre clone who invaded the Island.
Sar Tan, two clones responsible for allowing Quinn access.

Notable characters

The Last
Dawn, Jack's oldest friend
Neal Podmore, Jack's very good friend
John, leader of the Island research facility and University.
Penelope [Peni] Pendleton, eminent sub-nuclear particle physicist.

The Second
The Seer, Won Long.
Weid Noi, Won Long's daughter and trainee Seer.
Lo Si, Keeper of Ancient Knowledge, Druid, husband of the Seer, father of Weid Noi and Sun Kist.
Ju Lo, Lo Si's understudy, and senior control room operator.
Da Phai Nai, mother of Sun Kist; forbidden to marry Lo Si by a previous Empress.
Sun Kist, daughter of Da Phai Nai and Lo Si, High Priestess, later Shaman Supplicant.
Langnor and her husband Bufor, senior control room operators.

Jack's larger team includes: Xi Xah, Xi Sai (the girls), To Mo and To Ma (the twins). They are always nearby and working in the background, but seldom mentioned by name.

Non-human Entities
The Core, computer in control of the spacecraft; thinks it is Captain Taris.
Matron, leading robotic medic who shows her humanity in Book Three.

Recap

In *The Gatekeeper and the Guardian*, Jack was lost at sea, and washed ashore, half dead, on an uncharted South Pacific island in August 2010. There he discovered an impossibly advanced science, operated by a stone-age culture, one that had lost the use of fire and the wheel. It was inhabited by people, but not by *homo sapiens*.

The first person he met was Jien Noi, (Jinnie), the Empress Elect of the matriarchal, *homo erectus* colony. She also held the position of Gatekeeper, which was a rare combination.

His best friend to be was introduced next, n'Gnung, one with whom he shares a brotherly understanding. Jack marries Jien Noi, and n'Gnung is forever by his side. With others, they defeat an Ogre invasion led by Quinn and his band of clones and mercenaries, .at the end of Book One.

But the threat posed by the Great Ogre remains; a menacing despot who demands all sentient life on Gaia, (as Earth is known), bow to him, or be exterminated.

The Twelve Tribes introduces the enigmatic Kay (Ælkræleinnoire), or Dark Elf. And Owain, King of the Ddwyrth or Neanderthals, comes more into the plot. Other characters are added as the tale unwinds, something Jack is opposed to, and tries to limit.

The story picks up directly from the last lines of book one, and finds the Second assessing damage and rebuilding after the Ogre invasion. Will they have enough food to last until the next harvest? Will they have enough people to restore their civilisation?

These questions and more are answered in book two, but even more are asked concerning the evolution of humankind, and the role of the Ancestors. Meanwhile the Great Ogre awakens and wages war, as Gaia amasses Earthly powers to wipe humanity from the face of the globe.

Chapter 1 ~ Ruins and Renewal

Jack

It was the dawn of a new day, yet the world looked bleak; desolation lay all around. Of our once grand Imperial Palace, only short stumps of support columns remained, hiding with intent to trip the unwary. The remainder was a mangled mass of charcoal and smouldering debris.

With our trusted, we had moved the Imperial safe and hidden it deep within the storeroom at the rear of the ancient church. Neither were manmade. Despondent, we trudged towards the stone steps leading down to the city proper. The buildings were gone, replaced by charred remnants obscured by clouds of ash that billowed in the breeze.

I looked to where our large storage sheds had stood; "Do you think we'll have enough food for the coming year," I asked the Empress. I looked up at the cloudy and darkening sky.

Jien Noi became thoughtful before replying, "I have tasked the Provost with making a daily count. Yesterday he told me we had lost half of our harvest. We do not even have the bare minimum, and this does not allow for wastage and spoiling. Even losing workers from the fields for training in the army, we were quite comfortable, until the enemy burned most of our storage here at Grimwaldi Rinns. The towns and hamlets are well stocked, but half of our people live in this city."

"Every person not engaged in rebuilding is now in the fields," I stated, before looking at the heavens once more. "The skies grow heavy. The storms will come before we have finished the harvest, or rebuilt people's homes after the Ogre invasion. We must also rebuild our storage sheds, or find an alternative. Let me think on it some."

She rested her hand on my arm, "Do not worry, Jackie. I do not yet smell rain, so there is still time to work the fields. The Seventh [Ddwyrth or Dwarves], have offered to send temporary shelters if we need them. The Eleventh [Elves] have offered us food. I would prefer not to take their kindness because it is charity, and we are a proud people."

I nodded my head and patted her hand. I was about to speak when n'Gue, the head messenger, hurried up to us, "Empress, I have news about our population after the invasion by the Ogre clones of the Last. It is not good news, Your Highness."

Her eyes turned to him in dismay, "How bad is it?"

n'Gue spoke with reticence, "We lost the lives of more than one fifth of the population. The final figure will be more than one and a half thousand. Many were women and children."

The Empress visibly shook and wailed, "So many innocent lives lost. They did not deserve to be mown down by the modern weapons of your kind Jackie. There is no honour in the Last massacring peasants armed only with wooden spears and stone daggers, hoes and cooking pots. Oh my poor people..." Her thoughts trailed off, lost within loss. I put my arm around her shoulder to comfort her, as she leaned into me.

A short while later her indomitable spirit returned. She gathered herself, pulled her shoulders back and moved away. Standing tall once more, she said, "My duty is to the living. There may be enough food for this year with so many fewer mouths to feed. Husband, ensure we have enough food and use any means available.

"We will bury the dead on the Hill of Hallows with full honours, although I am sure some families will use their personal burial grounds.

"n'Gue, please send Dan Sek, the Master of Stone to me at once. I will commission a large cenotaph in memory of all those that fought so bravely in our cause. Guardian, do you know of a fitting design?"

I made several suggestions and explained the significance of each in my world. She settled on a Celtic cross and seemed slightly heartened.

Owain, the King of the Ddwyrth was still with us, and we asked if he could spare some men with metal shovels to help dig many burial plots. He sent off small army armed with shovels and pickaxes, instead of claymores. The work was hard, but completed before nightfall.

I had intended to dump the bodies of the mercenaries that attacked us way out over the sea, but Horovitz petitioned me, so they too were buried, although in a different place and without honour. Sergeant Horovitz and the forty mercenaries who changed sides and fought with us, said a few words for their former colleagues.

Later we spoke, "Guardian, I know you cannot return us, but we are glad to still be alive. We can help train your army, and I hope you will allow our wives and families, girlfriends to come and join us."

I studied him for some seconds before I replied, "I understand and will consider it. Do not expect this to happen for some time, if at all. Prove yourselves to us first and we will see what the Empress decides."

Some of his men grumbled, but he said, "Guardian, I expected as much. In time things may be different, but I accept your concerns. We will also need something else to do, as killing has been our life."

"Work with our builders where your skills are of most value. Impress and please the Empress and she may grant your wishes. As well as dwellings and public buildings, I need mass storage sheds for any harvest we gather. Make that your priority and improvise. Speed is of the essence as the rains will soon be here.

"In the long-term, you will train our troops in modern warfare, and prepare for war. The Eleventh and Seventh are adamant the Great Ogre, leader of the Tenth Tribe, will reawaken and lay siege to our shores."

"Thank you, Guardian. Some of us were engineers so we have expertise at hand. We will need a base and labourers."

I turned to n'Gnung, my second and always by my side. "Go with Horovitz and see to his needs. Come to me when you are done."

I spoke to the Seventh later that day, and they told of atrocities the Ogres had committed in the past, mostly centuries before. Owain worked to convince me of the threat, "Guardian, the Ogres are utter evil incarnate. We believe they turned on their creators and murdered them. They have sworn to exterminate or subjugate all the tribes of humanity; this is the only thing they live for: total control of all sentient beings."

My day was busy and flashed past in a blur of crisis. The town of Soi Long had lost its main storage sheds, but much of the harvest already gathered could be saved. Replacement sheds were under construction.

The Provost was slowly delivering precise information regards quantities of goods stored to the Empress, while I needed quick and rough estimates. I sent out the twins with orders to check on all our storage facilities and estimate what we had left and needed most.

To Mo reported, "Guardian, cotton and coffee are untouched and we have full stocks as before. There are no problems with livestock."

To Ma added, "We are short of barley for beer, wheat for bread, and low on oats, rye, and flax. Most of our jute was destroyed, Guardian."

I said, "Jute, what we may need most of immediately, n'Gnung?"

"Without it we will be short of sacks, rope, and twine. We also need it for stout clothing, nets, and carryalls. I will make it a priority."

I agreed as Horovitz appeared nearby; "Guardian, we have our base set just north of the city and I have production lines ready to make prefabricated building panels. The builders will work to our templates. I need wood and straw, plus the manpower to make full use of it."

I took a moment to review progress on my screen before stating, "Good work, Sergeant. Set out areas for each crop and I will deliver the stalks direct from the fields. They will have to dry in situ.

"To Mo, set up a jute processing area nearby and work as directed by Horovitz. The panels he makes need to be tied together.

"To Ma, gather as much bamboo as quickly as you can. We'll use that to frame the panels. Again, set this up nearby so all prefabrication is contained within a small area. Any questions...?"

Horovitz spoke for all, "Excellent. Once this is set up and running smoothly, I'll look at grain and other storage. I wish we had tarpaulin or similar for waterproofing, but we'll do our best with what we have."

My day continued in similar vein, although the problems, locations, and associated people changed with alarming frequency. The Empress and I, n'Gnung and n'Gue saw it through until the day was done.

That evening the Empress spoke from the Imperial Mount. "My people, we mourn the loss of so many loved ones. many of whom now lie at peace on the Hill of Hallows. They showed true heart and are sorely missed. They fell protecting us, so that we may live to enjoy our lives. Join with me for a minute's silence in memoriam…

"To honour their ultimate sacrifice, I urge you to bring forth new life to replace that which was lost. Our newborn will turn our sorrow of the moment, into bright new hopes for the future. The recent war has left us with orphans who should be brought here to the Imperial Mount, or taken to the palace of their home town. They will be cared for by the Imperial housemaids and Royal staff until either claimed by relatives, or adopted by other families. Anyone wishing to adopt should speak to the Provost at once. This also applies to the aged and infirm, anyone who is incapable of looking after themselves.

"We owe a deep debt of gratitude to Ælthrelntheine and the Eleventh, Owain and the Seventh for coming to our aid in such desperate times. Without them, we would now be dead or enslaved.

"Owain and the Ddwyrth have toiled to lift a heavy burden from us this day and I thank you brothers and sisters. Owain, I would ask you and your party to stay and enjoy our hospitality. My people, please make our new friends welcome.

"Food and shelter are now available on the Imperial Mount behind me, please follow me, eat your fill, and rest in safety."

The Empress led the way and we assembled to eat with the common people in the new building. Since our victory, talk had been about the war, the Elves and Dwarves, and on rebuilding. That evening our thoughts turned to food, or the lack thereof, and our efforts to make good the shortfall. Our labours that day were tremendous, but lay open to the vagaries of the elements. One storm or heavy downpour could yet undo all our great work.

Ale flowed as we discussed and debated plans and priorities for the coming days. Food was provided from our rebuilt Imperial kitchen, the only building on the Imperial Mount to be refurbished. A new dining hall was nearing completion, which we and those still homeless were already using for food. This would continue until their own homes were rebuilt. It would also provide communal shelter and sleeping accommodation for those that had lost everything.

Celebrations were well under way, when I was unexpectedly joined by Bufor. After being caught unaware by the invasion, we had asked for volunteers with keen night vision. A woman called Langnor and her husband Bufor had been selected, and now worked every evening until dawn. They relieved one another, and it fit the needs of the moment.

Chapter 2 ~ The Dark Elf

Bufor came to me and asked I attend the control centre. I drew him into my embrace and using my return bracelet, immediately transported us to the control centre. I was greeted by the confused stare of Langnor. I looked up at the screen and welcomed Ælthrelntheine, "Queen of the Eleventh, what an unexpected pleasure. How can I assist you? Please forgive our new night staff; they have never seen your kind before."

Her laughter trickled like a babbling mountain brook, and she replied, "Guardian, that is not necessary, thank you. It is not you that can help me, but I that can help you. Our librarian, linguist, and historian will all arrive tomorrow. However, my daughter has finished her work on the interstellar threat she has been monitoring, and is eager to come to you at once. I presume it is night there."

It was my turn to laugh, and I responded, "Owain and Aroweena are still with us. Today he provided a small army of men to help us bury the dead. We finished a short time ago and at this moment, they are all socialising in what remains of our capital city. Your daughter is most welcome, but the place is still a building site."

A voice spoke to her side, and the Elf Queen deferred before she turned back to look at me, "Ælkræleinnoire is ready to leave right now, and I will send her just as soon as we finish. You remember how to lock on to our exchange of course, Guardian?"

"There will be no problem, and I'll show the new staff what to do."

She smiled for a moment before continuing, "I have warned you that my daughter is regarded as *unusual*. As you will have noticed, our kind have blonde hair, and blue or green eyes with golden flecks, yes?"

I nodded and confirmed, "You have been warned. Until we meet again, Jack Barleycorn."

The screen went dead, and I showed the two new operators how to receive incoming transportation from the control centre of the Eleventh. I let Langnor make the transfer, and went to greet our latest guest. The doorway to the transporter room opened, and a figure appeared before my eyes. I stopped in awe as before me stood a young woman of great aura and beauty. What transfixed me was the sight of her tumbling black hair, and penetrating white eyes.

Her laughter was a little deeper than her mother's was. She glided towards me and held out her hand in friendship. I shook myself and took her hand, turning it to brush the back with my lips. Rising I said, "Ælkræleinnoire, Queen of the Eleventh Elect, High Lord of Destiny, welcome to the home of the Second. It's my pleasure to meet you"

Her eyes were surreal. I tried not to peer at them. She knew well the effect she had on me, probably on everyone she met, and glossed over my astonishment, "Guardian, know the pleasure is all mine."

She smiled beguilingly, before adding, "Our home lands can get so boring at times, and Owain is a lot of fun, isn't he. I look forward to seeing him again, but first, show me around this control room, tomorrow I will begin working with you."

I turned aside and waved my arm with a flourish, entreating her with knightly chivalry. The night crew dropped to their knees, but Ælkræleinnoire bade them rise, taking both their hands in friendship, and helped them stand. They, too, stared at the form before them, before remembering their manners and mumbling in their amazement.

The woman laughed, and I saw a chance to redeem myself, "Apologies, you look so unworldly, so stunning. I bet this happens all the time. I hope our uncouth reaction has not offended you."

This time her laughter was more of a rumble, and she turned to look me in the eye, "It is nothing, merely a compliment. 'Stunning', why thank you kind sir. Now, where do we begin?"

There was a flash in the transfer circle and Jinnie appeared, "Jackie, I was worried about you, what's keeping you away so long…"

Her words died as she spotted Ælkræleinnoire. I introduced them, and although clearly surprised, Jien Noi found words of welcome at once, "Ælkræleinnoire, I am so happy to finally meet you; this is such a lovely surprise. I hope my husband is not boring you to death."

"Quite the contrary, Empress of the Second, and Gatekeeper. Those twin roles must be a heavy burden upon you, how do you cope?"

We toured the room and came to the door of the stairway. I asked Ælkræleinnoire, "Have you ever walked through solid rock before?"

She beamed back, "No Guardian. They say there is a first time for everything. Let's do it now."

Her surreptitious smirk and goading demeanour led me to believe she may have been alluding to something completely different. She flicked her head and winked back at Jien Noi. I replied in good humour, "No. Let us see what wonders await through this doorway instead."

Her smile grew larger, and she responded, "A man after my own heart." Again, I heard the double entendre in the timbre of her words, but let it pass as she continued to taunt me, "So, Guardian. How do we do this thing then?"

I gave her a stern look, before smiling magnanimously. I inserted my ring finger, and drew her in front of me so she could pass through. She tittered aside, "Ooh! This could be interesting." She smiled playfully at me, and then my wife. Jinnie took her proffered hand and followed her through to the staircase that led to a physical means of entry. It consisted of a few steps, a landing, and repeat. The walls were lined with panels sporting ancient, rune-like symbols on either side.

Ælkræleinnoire briefly read the first panel facing her, before moving down to the next. She said, "This script I have never seen before. It is remarkable, and quite modern. I can read the majority of it, but the higher meanings and sub-texts will require greater study."

She went down all the way before stopping at the central panel at the foot of the staircase and pointed, "This is a doorway, no doubt how you found your way inside. What lies on the other side?"

"It lies at the bottom of a large pool, beneath a waterfall, in the Valley of Knowledge, near where we have built our home."

"Interesting, the Ancestors always hid their secrets many levels deep. I suspect this writing, and the control centre are similar in nature. I have always wanted to see the Valley of Knowledge, they say it is exceptionally beautiful."

The Elf Queen Elect scanned every panel coming back up the stairs on the other side, and the one at the top, before returning to one and stated, "Mother was correct. This tells us the place we are in is special. But, where is the rest of it? Gatekeeper, Guardian, tomorrow we must try to discover where it is. Before we meet Owain and the Ddwyrth, may I be allowed to sit at the main control console?"

Ælkræleinnoire continued to familiarise herself. In time she took my seat, and said, "This is extremely powerful as one would expect, but there is so much more to it. Guardian, this is no normal control centre. It is much too big. What is its real purpose? Wait, there is more…"

Her open eyes glazed, and we stood watching in wonder. Some seconds later her gaze cleared, and she said a strange thing, "I saw something, heard something more like. Yes, an entity was definitely trying to interface mentally with me in the language of the Ancestors. Guardian, have you ever tried talking to the machine? Has it ever spoken to you inside your head?"

"I have felt the urge, but did not get anywhere with it. Why?"

Ælkræleinnoire looked at us and said, "I have the strongest feeling that the buttons and controls we see are all for show. This may respond to direct telepathic communication. I just tried in the Ancestor's language, but nothing happened. It's another mystery for us to unlock. Perhaps we need to activate other control systems first. I would stay here all night, but I must see Owain, so let us leave this for now."

We transported to the Imperial Mount where festivities were progressing heartily. Owain was in fine form, but stopped in mid sentence when his eyes lit our new arrival. He rose and stomped to greet her, his arms spread wide with welcome, "Ale kray lean wah…"

Ælkræleinnoire put her finger to his lips, silencing the verbal assassination of her given name. She filled her mug with Ddwyrthen beer and announced, "I know some of you find my name impossible to pronounce. Those of us here can call me Kay, cheers!"

The toast complete, Owain continued, "Kay me wee darlin', it has been far too long. My, but you look more beautiful than ever. Tell me if you ever have need of a good husband and I will come a-running."

She hugged the Dwarf, and his face was red by the time she let go of him. She said, "You old goat, you know that if I ever have need of a man, you will be the first I call upon, although this Guardian offers you serious competition."

She gave Jien Noi a conspiratorial smirk, before laughing. Once calm she took the Empress' arm in her own, leading them away for introductions to the rest of our friends and nobility.

We watched them leave, and Owain said, "That there wee lassie is not only the most beautiful woman I have ever met, but also the most unavailable. She is the staunchest friend any man or woman could wish for. We are blessed with her presence."

I put my arm around his shoulders in manly sharing, and guided us in the direction of the table. As we walked he admitted, "She is one hell of a woman, but too good for the likes of you or I."

An hour or so later, before the hearty celebrations began to become more boisterous, Owain followed me to the latrine. He said, "This has been a great party, but we all know what will happen next. Do you mind if I transfer to the shore on the Outlands, I prefer it there, it agrees with me and offers a great sense of freedom."

I chuckled, "Me also, although this has been fun. The shore has enough beds for us all. When we return to the table, I will propose we leave and toast in farewell, agreed?"

That was what transpired, although it took longer than either of us expected. The Empress, Aroweena, and all our usual cohort departed with us, including the provocative dark Elf.

Kay drank like the rest of us, unlike the majority of her own kind. It was not long before Aroweena, Second Warrior of the Ddwyrth, challenged Gung Loi, Guerrilla General of our armies, to a bout of play-fighting. Kay watched for some minutes before she enquired, "What are the rules?"

n'Gnung, sitting at my right hand, said, "Kay, there are none. Hand to hand combat, overpower your opponent by any means you can."

She beamed within mischievous delight, and challenged the pair of them, two upon one, "Catch me if you can girls."

I had never seen a being move so quickly, or deceptively. She evaded the girls' strikes, and encouraged them to come at her from opposite sides. Her speed was tremendous. At one point, the girls collided quite badly, and ended up flat out on the ground. Kay went to them full of concern, "Are you all right?" and bending, soon found herself on her back, being attacked by two aggressive female warriors. I do not know how she did it, but one second Kay lay open and vulnerable, the next she had twisted free and countered the attack. She threw them in tandem, standing over two surprised girls.

She held up her hand, and stated, "Thank you girls, this has been great fun, but should we continue, I fear this will become serious. Let us drink in new friendship instead, and save our wrath for the enemy."

She bowed to them, and gracefully withdrew. Her challengers took her proffered helping hands with enthusiasm, and brought her back to the safety of our round table. We all knew Kay had won, especially the two she bested. Later all three talked together about technique, and their real friendship began.

Chatter was witty and we learned the Seventh, like the Last were a patriarchal society, which brought Aroweena great honour. The Second were matriarchal. Kay surprised us all, "The Eleventh are a uniarchal society. Neither male nor female holds power because of their sex, and in most respects we are quite egalitarian. Each individual is judged personally upon their worth, although, the odds are stacked slightly towards the female, if only because of where we live."

I looked at her deeply and said, "Lake Titicaca, the centre of the female world."

Her eyes seared into mine once more, and she elucidated, "Correct, Guardian. We live nearby, where the true centre of the female power of this world originates. The force of focus fluctuates over a period of one thousand years, between our homelands, and that of the Twelfth, or Giants. Our land appears to others like a mountain, which they can climb. It is like your island shield here, but realistically physical. Just before the end of your last millennia, Guardian, the power centre of the world changed from the Himalayas, and swung back to the Andes."

Her eyes clouded for a moment, before she added, "It is said the Giants are extinct, but I am not so sure. After my latest star gazing, I felt a ripple in the fabric of space and time. That would have been the Shaman ... you have met her?"

Jien Noi responded in awe, "Yes, she blessed our wedding. You know, she spoke into the minds of each of us at the same time, but we each heard different words, and then she disappeared into thin air."

Talk batted back and forth, before Kay told us all a secret, "You are aware the Shaman is considered to be an elemental being, aren't you? She is regarded as the foremost ambassador of Gaia, and as such, commands our utmost respect. The Wrath of Gaia will soon be upon us, but with the Shaman on our side, I feel sure we will survive."

Our meal that evening was a casserole served with potatoes greens, and bread. The gravy was delicious and I commented when Da Phai Nai was near. She thanked me and went to summon her daughter.

Sun Kist came to me and said, "Do you like the meal, Guardian?"

"Yes, it is delicious. What is different?"

"As you are aware, between meals we often try out new recipes. I have been experimenting with herbs and spices, and this mixture was liked best of all. I'm glad you like it."

"I do, very much so. Where did you get the idea?"

"Many are combinations known to my mother or other cooks. Some I thought would work well together so just tried them to see what they would taste like when cooked."

"You have proved this to me, please continue. Oh, there are many recipes shown in the Corridor of Knowledge. n'Gnung, I think we should show those to Sun Kist, what do you think?"

"Certainly, Guardian, I will take her tomorrow, and show her where the torches are kept and how to use them. This meal is so tasty; another helping, Guardian?"

"Yes please..."

Some time later, Owain began singing, "Old MacDonald..."

We were already in fits of giggles when Kay said, "Jackie, you recall that weird dance thing your kind do, the Okay Pokey or something?"

I stood and we formed a circle, before I sang out and actioned, "Put your left arm in, your left arm out, in, out, in, out, shake it all about..."

We soon ended up in a right mess and laughing hysterically. And that is how the Hokey Cokey got added to our list of favourite, drunken pastimes.

Chapter 3 ~ The Core

The following morning I sat at my console as Ælkræleinnoire studied the writing on the staircase in greater detail. I had loaned her my ring so she could come and go as she pleased, because only the Ring of the Ancestor would allow a person passage through that particular doorway. Meanwhile, I ran my usual checks, and looked for my close friend Dawn. My note to her remained unopened on her kitchen table at the cottage in Wales. I knew she only used the place at weekends, and that sometimes weeks passed if her life was busy. I felt frustrated, but could do nothing until she returned.

I was surprised when Kay rushed in and stated, "I need to speak to my mother at once. Do not transfer the other Eleventh here until I return. Allow me to set the co-ordinates if you will."

I stood and watched as she worked my console, and for the first time saw snatches of the Elven home world. It was mystical, and appeared to be enchanted. The land showed little sign of husbandry, being covered with an alluring pastiche of trees and shrubs, many heavily laden with fruit, nuts, and berries. Impossible crenulated castles and towers dotted the landscape, interspersed with thatched cottages and arboreal homes. The view focused on Romanesque pillars surrounded an open-air forum, in the centre of which stood an impossibly large tree, the like I had never seen before. Kay offered, "That is The One Tree, the symbol of our nation, and so named because it is the only one of its kind."

I was perplexed and said, "If there is only one then what happens when it dies. How does it reproduce?"

"That is a great secret, Guardian. Even most Eleventh do not know the answer to that riddle. Desist and let me find my mother."

Ælthrelntheine was studying parchment in what appeared to be a room created inside another impossibly large tree nearby. "Guardian, please send me there at once, I will explain all when I return. May I borrow your return bracelet just in case? I'll swap it for your ring, here."

I handed her the wristlet and sent her to her mother as soon as she reached our transfer circle. They spoke briefly before Kay's arms encircled her mother, and moments later they were both standing in our transporter. I rose to greet the Queen of the Eleventh, and it was clear she was puzzled. Kay returned my bracelet, and they headed towards the stairway, leaving me wondering what all the fuss was about.

Beside me, n'Gnung cocked his eyebrow and as we followed, he spoke into our bewilderment, "Guardian, it appears that the ways of the Eleventh are even stranger than the ways of women."

"You are correct. A double-whammy, they are both women of the Eleventh. Let's discover what they are about."

Chapter 3

I guided them through the door as Jien Noi joined us. Soon the Eleventh were studying a short line of writing. Their words in the Elven tongue flowed quickly, as if exchanging bursts of machine gun fire.

I wanted to know what the problem was, but was loath to interrupt their obvious deep concentration. We murmured quietly amongst ourselves as we watched.

The Eleventh seemed to reach an agreement, and Ælthrelntheine turned towards us. I immediately asked, "What is it? What have you discovered that is so important?"

"We cannot be sure without further study, but if my daughter is correct, a small but important part of the history of the Eleventh is incorrect. Jien Noi, as Empress you will be aware that some things should remain privy to the eyes and ears of the nation's leader, or possibly shared with only the most trusted of companions."

She looked at the Gatekeeper, who nodded her head in understanding, and I did likewise as her eyes fell on me. "Even you n'Gnung, First Warrior of the Second, will appreciate the significance of this. Rest assured there are no secrets between us standing here, but I would prefer to shelter my own people from this knowledge until the time is ripe. I will leave at once to cancel the party of our learned due here today. Daughter, you will remain here until all the secrets of the Ancestor have been revealed. Excuse me if you will, as I must depart before I am missed."

Ælthrelntheine was duly returned to the library, and her daughter instigated a training session for all staff, but some things were explained only to the Gatekeeper and I. Kay took over my station several times as she came to familiarise herself with the system and controls, before passing knowledge on.

During the afternoon, I was becoming quite familiar with the console. I felt a mental tug on a couple of occasions, but it was fleeting, too brief to define. Later, Kay tried to unlock the mental communication system, but made little progress. She said to me, "Guardian, try talking mentally to the machine, come and sit in the Captain's chair, and see what happens."

I did as she asked, but only felt a barrier in the way. I told her what I felt, and she enquired, "What language are you thinking in?"

"Why, my own English of course." My thoughts morphed, but she beat me to the words, "Try it again, this time in the language of the Second."

I did as instructed, and for the very first time managed to link directly with the Core. It was tentative at best. I felt quite drained within moments, and quickly broke the communication. I managed to say, "It worked a little bit. I am dreadfully tired. I need to lie down."

Apparently, I collapsed at the console and was immediately transferred to my home. I woke as shadows lengthened in the world outside. Jinnie was at my side, bathing my forehead. The Keeper of Life, as the head healer was known, was in close attendance. My eyes opened and Jinnie gave a cry of joy, before engulfing me in her arms.

"Jackie, never do that again. You have no idea just how worried I have been. The same thing happened to Kay a short time later, and she is in our guest room asleep."

Jinnie helped me to sit up, and asked me how I felt. I was not sure, so told her the truth, "I'm OK. That was a bit weird though. I spoke mentally to the Core in your language, but briefly. Abruptly I felt tired and broke the connection."

I stood up and realised my strength was returning quickly. I also felt as if a veil had been lifted. My eyes seemed more alert than before. I walked outside and said to Jinnie and n'Gnung, "I feel fine actually, better than ever. I think we should remain here tonight though, just to be sure, and also tend to Kay."

My brother bowed his head, and left to make arrangements, although I noticed Sun Kist was already preparing the evening meal in our kitchen. I was about to go and sit at the head of our table, when Gung Loi called from the depths of the home, "Gatekeeper, Kay is waking."

We raced to Ælkræleinnoire, and found her sitting up, looking confused. A wall of concerned words greeted her, and she smiled, although for that moment, laughter remained beyond her. She took several deep breaths, and shook her head, as if trying to clear it of mental cobwebs. In time she said, "Wow! That was strange. I feel as if my brain just got bigger."

I spoke up, "Me too. And my senses seem more aware. Is it the same for you?"

She did not reply. I presumed she needed a little more time to fully recuperate.

Jien Noi said, "Please drink this herbal tonic our healer has prepared for you, it is of Elven design."

The healer offered her the tonic, as Jien Noi enquired, "Is there anything you need, anything I can get for you?"

Kay declined and asked, "Where am I?"

I replied, "You are in our home."

This time her smile was more responsive, "In that case, could I have a tumbler of water from the falling waters nearby?"

Gung Loi grabbed a beaker and left at once, returning a minute later dripping wet, and proffered the liquid. Kay said with alarm, "Thank you, but there was no need to drench yourself on my account."

Chapter 3

Gung Loi bowed to her and replied, "Think nothing of it, High Lord. It is my pleasure. I am so happy to see you well again. Would you like another?"

As with me, Kay's strength returned quickly, and she walked outside with us. She stopped in the doorway and gazed about, a look of rapture on her face. "The Valley of Knowledge. It is beautiful. How wise you are to make your home here. I am so pleased to be amongst the first of my kind to witness this wonder. Perfect, just perfect."

I thought she would sit with us at the table, but instead she strolled down to the pool, and cast her eyes around, clearly besotted. We watched as she skipped onto a small ledge and drank directly from the fall, before immersing her head in the cascading waters. She sprang down like a faery, and shook her mane, before wiping her face and eyes. Moments later, she ambled amongst the grass, gazing out along the valley towards the setting sun.

In time she returned to us, speaking openly, "That was such a rush, both here and within the Core of the machine. I discovered something, so it was worth it. To get anywhere, we need to mind-link with the Core in the language of the Ancestors. To make any changes, you have to do it, Guardian, because you are the accepted bearer of the Ring of the Ancestor."

I was about to say how impossible that was, before she silenced me with a knowing look and raised finger. "There is a language training program referenced. Tomorrow we should try to unlock it, bring it online. I also believe, the more we interface with the Core, the greater will be our learning, and the less dramatic the side effects."

"Like a toddler taking its first steps you mean."

"Exactly, but hopefully our progress will be a lot quicker." Her words trailed off as the air shimmered behind me.

A Ddwyrthen voice boomed out, "I be thinking, lads and lassies, that thou mightst be in need of some ale and the company of friends, on this special eve."

I rose to greet Owain, noticing n'Gnung had brought along Aroweena carrying a mountain of food, and Da Phai Nai. The latter hollered, "Come, Keeper of Hearts, my daughter needs assistance in the kitchen, and we require the food you carry."

Owain said to nobody in particular, "Tis such a bonnie wee glen. It has an elusive, exquisite beauty unique." He wandered away to absorb the wonder, just before the last of the sun's rays disappeared.

Lo Si and Won Long apparated nearby and came to sit with us, and later when the shift changed in the control room, n'Gue, Ju Lo, and Weid Noi appeared to complete our party. We did not drink long or late because we had much to do the next day. Instead, we made plans and discussed priorities, our focus on renewal and making good our harvest.

Llwydd the Bold, First Warrior of the Seventh arrived during breakfast in the cockcrow of following day. We were not surprised when the leading Ddwyrth departed after a short meeting, Owain promising to return in the near future. Most others of our party returned to the control room, although Lo Si went back to the Outlands.

Da Phai Nai and Sun Kist sat to eat when the kitchen work was done. The latter finished her meal and remarked, "I don't know which place I prefer more, here or the village on the shore. Both are magical in their own way."

We murmured in agreement, before she asked, "Guardian, where will you be this evening, as I should prepare if you again choose to come here."

I did not know, so looked to Jinnie for a cue. The Gatekeeper considered options for a moment, before stating, "With the Ddwyrth gone. At least for now, I think it best we centre ourselves here. I worry these two," she stopped to indicate Ælkræleinnoire and I, "will become lost within the Core once more and this is the place for recuperation. That aside, I also want to make it feel like home, as so far it is more of a lodge we occasionally stay at."

I agreed at once, knowing she was correct, but added, "When the rebuilding work is complete, I think we should add some guest quarters. Winter is coming, and I can smell rain in the air today. The clouds are heavier, darker than ever, the rainy season will be with us at any moment."

I had hardly finished speaking, before the first drops of rain fell, and whilst few in number, the portent was ominous. "We must not tarry here in that case as there I still much to do. I'll take review in the control room and set the day's priorities under your direction, Empress."

Minutes passed while we assessed the current situation. Jien Noi said, "It is better than I feared, it seems many worked late last night. Although Owain has gone, he left us groups of Ddwyrth to continue the rebuilding. By day's end, we will have communal kitchens and separate dormitories finished and ready for occupation across the land. The new storage sheds will be completed by midday, so our most urgent needs will be met. Tomorrow our focus will be on rebuilding people's homes.

"Guardian, later today we must ensure time to discuss my ideas for changing the layout of the city. I want it to be more people friendly, more accessible, and with open spaces where people can gather"

"I have some ideas regards grouping of homes near work areas, parks for leisure and sports. We'll speak of it later, Empress."

"Thank you. Now I need to speak with all team leaders before I task my father, the Emperor, and the other royal houses of their forthcoming duties. We will start today and hone our plans for tomorrow."

There followed a procession of people entering our control room for instructions, which were often mapped out on our screens. In less than one hour we were done and the Empress readied to depart. I left instructions for our control room team to follow, although most already knew what needed to be done.

I turned to Kay and said, "I am free, what should we do today?"

Kay spoke her thoughts aloud, "In that case, I would walk the valley today. I need to relate the physical with the theory. There are caves of great knowledge here I need to see, and I believe that time is now."

I said, "n'Gnung, please prepare torches so we can see inside the caves, and also the underground paths to Corridor of Knowledge."

Jien Noi added, "I would love to go with you, but I need to be with my people and order the rebuilding. We will not be ready in time before the rains come, but I need to make it as close as possible. They are all depending upon me. n'Gue, Gung Loi, you are both with me today. n'Gnung, it is your responsibility to ensure that the High Lord of Destiny and the Guardian do not get into any more mischief. Inform me at once when they do."

With her words spoken, she rose to leave. I looked at Kay, before turning my gaze towards my brother. He raised an enquiring eyebrow, and we three burst out laughing.

When settled, we three transported to the valley. n'Gnung left, and returned from my storeroom a short time later with a carrier of our best grass torches.

Kay looked at them with alarm, and asked to see one. As soon as it was handed to her she said, "You cannot be serious! I will return for my staff at once. I also need to read a scroll in the library, and pack a bag for a longer stay. I won't be long. The sooner I leave, the sooner I return."

Chapter 4 ~ Greater Understanding

Kay had said she would only be a moment, but she was away for some time. Between helping with transfer logistics, I interfaced with the Core. I was trying to expand my knowledge and how long I could stay in direct mental communication. n'Gnung counted to five seconds the first time, and ten the next. With breaks in between each attempt, I almost got to one minute before I felt tired, and immediately withdrew.

I was delighted, felt OK, if slightly hung-over, and took a power nap. Kay returned as I resurfaced, and congratulated me on extending my tolerance to the effects of the Core. I asked Da Phai Nai for a coffee, which was served extra sweet and black.

Kay watched me drink the hot liquid, "What is that?"

"Coffee. Would you like to try some?"

"I'll try a sip only."

Her face contorted. n'Gnung added, "It is better with milk, Kay. Da Phai Nai, ask the dairymaid to provide us with milk."

Kay took another sip, "Wow! This stuff has a rush to it. It's unlike any coffee I have ever drunk before. Is it hallucinogenic?"

"Unfortunately not. It seems our local coffee beans have higher caffeine content than normal. Are you sure you won't take a mug?"

"No, tomorrow at breakfast with cream and sugar. The day is passing quickly. We should leave as soon as you finish."

She insisted on walking. She wanted to explore the seventeen caves of the Second, but they were full of produce. She did visit the standing stones and stone circles we came across.

Soon we arrived at the first Cave of the Ancestor. She flicked a button on her staff, and the head erupted in a blaze of white light. We started at the first cave, ending with the fourth one. The last picture drew her attention, and disbelieving, she turned to look at me, then flicked her eyes back to the image of the spacecraft, my head showing clearly. She muttered, "That is impossible, isn't it?"

"The impossible is only just beginning. Let me lead the way into greater understanding. Kay, mind your step, and your head."

We clambered down to the underground cavern, and stopped at the foot of the bridge we had built across the subterranean river. I was sure her eyes bugged-out when her light fell on the picture of me. We crossed the bridge in silence, as these things take us by surprise, and we react in our own ways. Kay quickly regrouped her sensibilities, and touching the depiction, said, "The flowing white robes suit you, Guardian. I will have some made of the finest Elven gossamer for you. Now explain how this picture of you was painted thirty-odd thousand years ago?"

n'Gnung and I both chuckled and shrugged our shoulders. "The truth is, we don't know. But there is more."

We moved quickly along the passageway, but Kay stalled where the corridor branched off; "Guardian, what lies down this route?"

"Why nothing. A rock fall blocks the way a little further on. I think it was a project that was never completed, why do you ask?"

Kay seemed unsure, and followed, stalling once more when she saw the third picture of me. She shook her head, as if ridding her mind of the distraction, and followed us down the Corridor of Knowledge. She turned off the light of her staff when my ring empowered the sectioned lighting of the corridor. She became fascinated with the ancient script, "I will need some time to study these properly, but everything is recorded here, it is absorbing. The history of our people and the Ancestors is all here. Nevertheless, I am sure time passes quickly without. Let's check out the rest of this corridor quickly, I will read each panel, and return to study tomorrow. That OK with you?"

I was sure many more hours passed, before we reached the doorway at the end, and motif. I said, "We can go through, but there is only a small room on the other side and nothing else."

n'Gnung said, "Guardian, the last time was before we discovered the true Ring of the Ancestor. I think we should check again."

"Thank you brother, you are quite correct, as usual. Let's see if we can finally unlock this puzzle. Try it with your ring first."

He did, and soon disappeared from view. I inserted my ring finger in the centre of the motif and enfolded Kay. I had wondered if she would follow with more innuendo, but concluded she perhaps used mild flirtation as a shield when facing unknown situations. That day she was work-like and not in a playful mood. That was a relief, but curiously, I felt slightly rebuffed. We passed through to the other side. Immediately n'Gnung spoke, "Guardian, the moment you inserted your finger into the lock, this appeared."

He pointed at a motif that was not there before. He said, "This is a major discovery. Try it with your ring, Guardian."

I did as he urged, and poked my head through into another chamber. I was greeted by virtual darkness, but sensed a large space. I took a breath, but there was no air. I pushed back immediately to prevent the others following me through, and explained. "There is a large room, but it has no light and there is no air. What does this mean?"

There were no answers. A secret revealed, and a new puzzle waiting to be resolved. With our motivation sapped, we returned to my home for sustenance.

We gathered around the dining table we preferred, and when Jien Noi joined us we spoke first of our day, before talk turned to planning and layout of our main city. I mentioned zoning and altering the standard gazebo hut design to include a second level. "It will save space," I elucidated. "A shop can be below with living or storage space above. It was a simple adaption of the existing template."

As others joined our party, they also added ideas to the discussion, some stressing the need for green spaces and a park with shallow lake for children to enjoy. The new layout was swiftly agreed on, which the Empress would action beginning the next day.

Early the next morning, Kay, n'Gnung and I transported in and resumed discoveries at the strange doorway where we finished the night before. We this time walked away from the source. Kay said, "It all reads so much better, and deeper this way round. It is clear to see the Ancestor began at the doorway, and worked outwards."

n'Gnung was thoughtful; "That means, the Ancestor began here. He must have been able to come from that room, but how?"

We had no answers, just more questions. We worked forwards, passing most panels quickly, but examining some more thoroughly. When we reached the last, I said, "That's about it, Kay, unless you want to go back and recheck a panel. What do you want to do?"

"It is time to return. Today, I would like to walk the Valley of Knowledge once more. Please indulge me, because I suspect there is more here than we realise."

Without comment, she lit her staff and walked forward. We followed in her wake, unsure just where this most unpredictable creature was leading us. We came to the tee junction where she went right towards the wall of rock. "There's nothing there."

She ignored us, and reaching the barrier, she held her staff high, "If this is a rock fall, then why is the ceiling smooth?"

I cursed aloud. The Ancestor had duped me again. I could not believe I had not seen this ploy the second time around, but there it was confronting me once more, the same deception in a different place. As we stared befuddled at the ceiling, Ælkræleinnoire scrambled up the rocks and called out, "There is a passageway beyond. Give me a hand here guys. Why is it whenever you need a Ddwyrth there isn't one, and when you don't there are several?"

We got stuck-in and moved rock. It did not take long before Kay dove through a small gap, one we had to enlarge for ourselves — Elves may be tall, but they are also slender and willowy. Minutes later we joined her on the other side, her staff glowing brightly in the distance. We ran to catch up with her, as the corridor slowly turned northeast. We walked for twenty minutes, before we reached a dead end.

I said, "My intuition tells me we are not far away from where we were at the depths of the other corridor."

n'Gnung replied, "That is my feeling also, Guardian. But this time we have walked on the flat, not headed on a gentle down slope. What can it mean?"

I repeated what was becoming an all too familiar explanation of what we did not understand, "The secrets of the Ancestors lie hidden three and four levels deep. This is the end of level two. Where have they secreted level three? Look for the shadow doorway of a cave, or anything that appears odd."

I walked back and forth using spectral vision. n'Gnung did likewise to his own pattern and predilection. Ælkræleinnoire stayed where she was, and scrutinised the end of the tunnel. It was just a wall of rock, and I wondered why she became so engrossed with it. We drew a blank and were ready for going home. As we approached, Kay said, "Good timing Guardian. My intuition tells me this is the same style of shielding we use. Place your ring finger right here, and let's see what happens."

Unconvinced, I did as instructed, and I felt an intangible shimmy. I don't know how else to describe it. Kay's eyes at once came to focus on me, but I moved my ring slightly, and reached a point that had a great pull. I pressed my ring finger into solid, mortal rock. Instantly the phoney stone wall disappeared, and I watched as my ring finger slid and locked with a motif.

I turned in amazement. Kay said, "Thank you for revealing level three of this conundrum, Guardian. Let us see if this is the end, or if there is a level four, 'lay on MacBarleycorn'"

The room we entered was a box about eight feet square and remarkably similar to the other entry nearby. Apart from the doorway, there was nothing else of any note. The air was stale, but we stayed inside long enough to examine the room, before leaving. The others passed through as I held the door open using my ring, but my eye caught something to the side. I pulled back and looked closely at the spot. I determined a panel, as the surface was completely black, not starlit like every other face. There was another on the other side at chest height, a foot high, and several inches wide.

I stood back and said to myself, "This is a lift." I looked around and became sure of my conjecture. The only problem was, the power was turned off. My deliberations were disturbed by the telling fact the air had a nasty tang to it. I left at once, rejoined my companions, and we returned to our known world.

Chapter 5 ~ A New Dawn

The next morning Kay continued to familiarise herself with the control centre, while I helped with the harvest home. A great deal had been accomplished and little remained to be gathered. The Empress was on site ensuring adequate stores, kitchens, and shelter were completed before the main storms arrived. So far we had been lucky, the ominous skies depositing brief showers only.

Once my assistance was no longer needed, I checked upon my dear friend Dawn. I found there had at last been some activity at her cottage in Wales. My note lay opened on the table, and my mobile phone had been taken to pieces. The excellent news lightened my spirits and I left the image of her living room on my screen, I sat back in thought. I decided to monitor the display for a few hours and in the meantime, composed another note, borrowing paper and pen from her table.

Hello you,

I hope everything is all right and you are having fun! It's been ages since I sent you my last message and mobile phone. I see you have returned at last and have had a look at the phone.

I would love to see you again, so please humour me.

It's dinner time in Blighty, and you have no idea how much I'd love to complete our deal from before I left, and demolish a bag of fish and chips. After you read this, return with one for each of us, and I'll come knocking on your door.

Luv'n'stuff

Jackie xxxxxxxxx

I was not sure if my return bracelet would work so far away, so Kay was conscripted to respond appropriately. I knew I would not be staying long, but this was a needful, if dangerous move.

Dawn reappeared with wet hair, a towel wrapped around her; she froze when she saw the new note. Tentatively she opened it, and shook her head, obviously in disbelief. She looked around as if searching for me, before reading the note and throwing it dismissively on the table, hurrying away. I wanted to follow her, but this was already an invasion of her privacy, one I felt compelled to make for the greater good.

She had changed into street clothes when she returned, and seemed to swear into the air. She grabbed her bag, and headed out into the night. I checked her walking up the street, before returning to view her kitchen table. Sometime later she reappeared, and put two wrappers on the table. Finding a marker pen, she wrote 'Jackie' on one.

Chapter 5

I signalled Ælkræleinnoire to cover me, transported, and moments later I knocked on Dawn's door. It opened in seconds, and tentatively a head poked out. She flew into my arms. The babble of words between us was lost in the moment, but I do remember her saying, "Jackie, it really is you. I don't believe it. You're supposed to be dead you know. Thank you for coming back to haunt me. Come in, I have the meal already ... but I guess you already know that?"

I moved forward, and once secure inside, opened my arms for a proper cuddle. Just before she was about to break away, I flicked the return bracelet, and it worked. 'In for a penny, in for a pound'. Dawn whirled on me when we arrived, and asked, "What have you done Jackie? ... Where am I?"

I replied with my most convivial smile, "You are in the middle of the South Pacific ocean somewhere near the Tropic of Capricorn. You are inside a massive and extinct volcano about thirty miles in diameter. Most of the people you will soon meet are descendants of a tribe of humanity that have been here undisturbed for around thirty thousand years, at least until my arrival some years ago.

I took her hand and led her through to our control room, where she stopped to gaze. The people she saw were not any form of humanity she had ever seen before. I introduced her to several, and was surprised when n'Gnung remembered a few words of English, "Hello, how do you do? Knife, water, sun, moon."

She smiled and said, "Hello yourself, thank you good man."

I saved Kay for last, and said, "It is my pleasure to introduce Ælkræleinnoire, Queen Elect of the Eleventh. Please call her Kay"

Ælkræleinnoire spoke to her in English, welcoming Dawn to the homeland of the Second. Although clearly shocked, Dawn replied in good voice, "My pleasure to meet you. Your eyes are fascinating. Are you an Elf?"

Ælkræleinnoire laughed and said, "Yes, my people are called the Elves, but we usually consider that term to be disrespectful. Correctly, we are known as the Eleventh. You did not know, so there is no harm done. Thank you for being up front. My eyes are quite special. Most people simply try to pretend they have not noticed, thank you also for being so honest."

I showed Dawn my screen, where she saw her home and stared at it in amazement. She turned to me and said, "If this device fell into the wrong hands it would change the world."

"Yes, I agree. I intend to keep this place secret, except for my most trusted." I transported the fish and chips to us, and I took her through to the transfer circle to collect them. On my signal, n'Gnung transferred us to the shore. I knew she loved the outdoors, especially beaches and mountains.

We strolled along the nearby strand, ate perched upon nearby rocks, and chatted; "I built my first home up there…"

Time flew by as she told me of her life, and I detailed how I had survived after the accident, and remained unaware that the island was inhabited.

After I had told of my survival, she said, "My mind is warped already, yet you survived alone, and also learned their language, you clever man. The ancient technology is astounding. You said it is at least thirty thousand years old. Yet the people are from the Stone Age, who, what are they Jackie?"

"This is most interesting, and I wish I could research it properly. Their man of knowledge, Lo Si, has informed me their forefathers knew of a race of people we identified as Denisovans, or possibly Maori by evolution. In those times they occupied related territory in north and southeast Asia, and given the date, I would assume all were being driven south by the last Ice Age. The last Ancestor brought these people here to save their race, and stayed until he died. Kay and I are trying to unravel his legacy. Regards the inhabitants, I have been told they are *homo erectus.*"

Dawn gaped at me, and I shrugged my shoulders. I needed her to put things in perspective, "Kay and Lo Si have told me the Ancestors arrived here from the stars, and they created all the races of humanity, including us. They both maintained the Ancestors arrived here in a spaceship a very long time ago, perhaps millions of years, who knows? That in turn means this technology is also that old.

One spaceship landed intact, and we are currently trying unravel what our control centre is. We believe there is a lot more of it, or related parts lying around the island. However, we are still trying to understand how to operate it, and find the rest of it."

She turned to the sea and stared into the distance. I left her to her thoughts, and when she spoke, her eyes held a look of confusion and wonder. "I would have ended up in an asylum by now Jackie. This is incredible. Thank you for showing me; had you tried to tell me, I would have had you locked up."

I laughed and we talked a little more of other matters, "You still dating?"

"Yes, I'm seeing a wonderful man, but he is beginning to get serious about us, so he will soon be history. You know how I feel about being independent."

"You were gone a long time, I thought you had eloped."

Chapter 5

"No, silly. My brother Ali was back in England for a couple of weeks leave. You remember he's working on deep water oil exploration platforms based off the Japanese coast. His long-term relationship just ended due to his being away for so long, and I got him interested in life again. He was very upset to hear of your death, and recalled the happy times we all shared."

Timely, n'Gnung appeared nearby. Dawn jumped, but I cautioned, "You get used to it."

"Come Guardian, it is lunch time and you are missed. Dawn."

The Empress welcomed her to the restaurant in the village. I introduced Dawn to my friends and translated as she met and talked with them. As the meal drew to a close I enquired, "What would you do? It must be midnight back in Wales. You are most welcome to stay, or leave whenever you wish."

She answered immediately, "I'd love to stay and see more. This place is so amazing. These people are wonderful. Where did our kind go so wrong, Jackie?"

She looked at me for an answer before continuing, "You know, they remind me so much of when I first met our Nepali friends." She kissed me on the cheek whispering, "Thank you."

"They do not have money, and crime is virtually unheard of. They call us *the clever people*. I consider them to be *the wise people*, as their knowledge of the needs of each other far outstrips our own insular and personalised worlds, where we have made ourselves the centres of our individual humanity."

She relaxed into our camaraderie, and although inquisitive, enjoyed herself. My friend stayed until the following evening and left promising to return soon with tents and tarpaulins. We devised a simple signalling system, a hoop she would place on a nail outside her back door, and she asked me what else I needed bringing back.

Bless her, when she returned the next weekend, she had a large pile of marquees and tarpaulins set aside, and brought with her not only rechargeable torches and solar power supply, but also a few small gifts for the islanders. She also brought her camera, and a smart phone that could store an amazing amount of snapshots and video.

I knew the grapevine had been busy and said, "I am not sure, but I suspect you will meet your first Dwarf this evening. They call themselves 'The Ddwyrth', and are also known as The Seventh; they are *homo neanderthalensis*. Be warned, they greatly enjoy the pleasures of life and bring with them fun in abundance."

As we settled for dinner that evening, Owain and Aroweena arrived. We greeted in boisterous renewal of friendship. I introduced them to my friend, "Dawn, this is my dear friend Owain a'y Brenin, King of the Ddwyrth. Please call him Owain."

Her surprise turned to astonishment as he stole the moment, "Tis all my pleasure, me wee lassie," before striding forward and sweeping her up in his bear hug. He pulled back with their faces almost touching and asked, "Can ye drink young lady?"

I presumed it was his endearing and infectious smile that got to her, just as it always did me. She was quick to respond, "I'm ready for a pint now, and challenge you to drink it quicker than I."

I thought to caution her, that being one of the worst things one could ever say to a Ddwyrth. Doubtless, she would learn … come time.

The next morning I found her collapsed at the dining table, and I had to chuckle. Owain was snoring peacefully on the earth nearby, and I noticed Da Phai Nai bustling over. "This one is as bad as you Guardian. Are all your kind like this?"

"No, wise Mother, neither my kind, nor Dawn, usually. Last night was special for her and I'm pleased she enjoyed herself and made new friends. Please prepare some of your elixir of life for her, if you would be so kind."

I awakened Dawn slowly and coaxed her to drink Da Phai Nai's concoction. When she reanimated, I showed her the deeper workings of the control room and, after a brief tour, the door to the stairway. I placed my ring finger in the centre of the motif, and we both watched as the ring locked into place. She gasped as my hand began to disappear through solid rock. She uttered, "That is impossible. Can we go through?"

"Yes, let's go, you first," I replied, encircling her within my arms.

"Incredible!" She turned to stare at the other side of the door, touching it before hitting it. She shook her head as if to clear the impossibility, and looked to me for support.

"This stairway is lined with panels of ancient writing. See these marks and squiggles, they are runes. Kay and her mother can read them to a great extent, but not completely."

Dawn ran her hands over them and said, "This rock is warm, and it is all cast in one piece. How can that be?"

"I do not think it is rock, but some sort of plasma that takes the form of rock. The control panels are made of the same substance and can change shape. The light in here activates when a ring of power is inside. I presume the doorway has a camera, but we have not discovered that yet. We are like toddlers who have discovered how to turn an electric light switch on and off, but with no idea of how or why it works. It is a steep learning curve, as it appears the Core—the main computer of this place, works in the language you see written on the walls."

Chapter 5

She looked once more before saying, "Jackie. The only way you could have kept your sanity is to see all this through the eyes of a child. Well done you! Is there anything more tangible, as this all leaves me disconcerted and confused? You mentioned a war yesterday, show me."

We returned to the control room, and I led her to the room where we kept the possessions of the mercenaries. I let her rummage through their clothing and paraphernalia. Many of the weapons were state of the art. They included night-sighted radio headsets, other gismos neither of us understood, and a pile of personal items such as dog tags and wallets. She spent time with those as the cruelty of death came to haunt her.

I placed a hand on her shoulder. "Have no sympathy. These mercenaries killed many of the islanders with their modern weapons. The defenders were armed only with stone-age knives, wooden spears, and a few long bows with arrows that I had tried to reinvent and return from their ancient society and lost knowledge."

To heighten the spell, I added, "That was about ten or twelve thousand years ago. The Ancestor had long since departed, and these people were reduced to a few hundred in number. I believe our stories of the Bible, myth and legend, would make that the era of Noah and the Ark. The Second survived all of that, only to be confronted with this."

I swept my arm around, sometimes pointing at light machine guns or RPG, the remains of the mercenary's weapons. "The invasion by several hundred highly trained mercenaries was so unfair..."

My words trailed off, as bitter memories of battle resurfaced to gnaw away at my equilibrium. Dawn drew close to comfort me, and changed the subject as a distraction by asking, "What about the Second? You won, right."

I smiled ruefully and replied, "Yes we won. I am sure we would all be dead now if it were not for the Eleventh and Seventh. They came willingly to assist us in our hour of greatest need, and by so doing, changed the battle, and with losses of their own, we prevailed. That is why there is such a deep bond between us all. Ælthrelntheine, Owain, and their armies saved us from certain annihilation. Come, I will show you. Be warned, this is not a pretty sight."

Returning to my station, I showed her the fresh graves of our fallen, changing the view from town to village, to hamlet by turns. I said, "These hundreds are lain to rest publicly, but others were taken by family or friends, and interred nearby their own homes."

Dawn looked, and tried to count our fallen, but there were too many. Her voice was cracking as she said, "This is horrendous."

I replied, "There is a more, but perhaps it would be wise if you do not see the worst of it?"

Dawn begged me to continue, and so I duly showed her the Hill of Hallows. She became frozen, like a sculpture left staring at the screen — row upon row of fresh graves covering an area the size of a football pitch. They were set slightly to one side, and marked by a second cenotaph in the form of a Celtic cross. Relatives were planting flowers, and some interments had been adorned with grass weavings of highest artisanship. One old widow was sobbing prostate on top of the graves of her entire family, all now resting at peace. Sprinkled between, were graves that had not been tended, perhaps the cruellest indication of all, the entire family line having been murdered. In time she managed to utter a few broken words, "H, h ... how many?"

Her eyes remained riveted on the graves. I replied, "One thousand, six hundred and thirty seven. Owain sent an army of Ddwyrth to help us bury them all. And all because of one man's lust for power over us, we lost so many of this irreplaceable population."

Tears came to her eyes and she flew into my arms, trying to hide her eyes and babbling almost incoherently. Jinnie picked that precise moment to enter the room, and I nodded to my wife, beckoning her come to me with looks alone. Jinnie had a puzzled expression on her face, until she saw what was on my screen. Instantly her demeanour changed, and she moved towards Dawn with newfound understanding and empathy for sharing our loss.

After a few moments, Dawn became aware, and turned to embrace Jien Noi, tears running freely down her cheeks. Dawn's face seemed to quail with implosion, as she dramatically surged to hug the Empress, as if their lives depended upon the sharing.

Dawn left us some days later. She was on a fact-finding mission to shed light on the history of the people she had met. Her priority was the last known archaeological evidence regarding *homo erectus*, especially in Southeast Asia.

Meanwhile, Kay and I worked in the control room, our quest for hidden knowledge taking up hours of our days. As our comprehension grew, we found we could spend tens of minutes connected to the Core.

At times, I felt like we were chipping away at a granite mountain with tools such as a feather, or ice cream cornet. Slowly understanding came, but it was a trial of endurance. It sometimes felt as if the Core was waiting for us to come of age, to reach a minimal level of enlightenment before it would allow us to progress.

One thing we did accomplish was to turn on sound capability for our search screens — a bit like hitting the mute switch, so easy, once you knew how. It was not perfect by any means. The Core informed us, "The scanners are able to detect slight vibrations, such as on a pane of glass, or water in a bottle. These are translated into sounds, isolating speech patterns being one of the parameters."

We also discovered that we were making so little progress, because there was no dedicated interface. After probing, Kay stated, "The interface we are looking for is located in 'The Captain's Quarters'."

"The Core told me I need to reinstate the Captain's 'ready room'. I have no idea where that has gone, why it disappeared, or how to find it again. Our only clue is the word 'Captain'."

"Captain as in the leader of a ship, in this case I would presume a spaceship. Can it be?"

"It is the only thing that makes any sense. Your mother…"

"Yes. Your ring of power is not from the same set as ours; remember the ring of the warrior?"

"I'd prefer to forget all about that evil thing. But yes, agreed. Remind me."

"The Ancestors came to Earth in three spaceships. According to our known history, only one of those landed intact, and that is where our rings of power came from. The other two spacecraft were destroyed upon entry."

"My ring proves that at least one of those other two spaceships arrived on this planet. Are we thinking that this control room is the bridge of whatever remains of one of those other craft?"

"I believe we are, Jackie, and that it was under the control of Captain Taris. I move we accept that as a working hypothesis, at least until proven or otherwise."

"Agreed. Well then, we better try to find this Ready Room."

We tried to locate the missing room, or identify a means to do so, but fatigue quickly took its toll. All too soon, we were forced to retire each evening before the breakthrough came. It was most frustrating.

Chapter 6 ~ The Creation Myth

The time came when we completed our rebuilding program. A new Imperial palace stood proudly on the Imperial Mount. True to her word, Jien Noi ensured it was the last building to be completed. By putting her people's needs before her own, she garnered their deepest respect.

The new palace was unlike the old. Jinnie and I had worked on the design and layout, making it an integrated and useful building. It was also far grander and more imposing, with several storeys and interlinking passageways for use by both Royalty and staff

Ælthrelntheine came to visit after the rains had passed, and just before the first chills of winter raked their icy draft amongst us. The meeting took place at our home, and coincided with the immanent winter solstice of the southern hemisphere. Three of each tribe were present, and Da Phai Nai attended our needs of table.

We were about to begin, when Dawn appeared nearby, having received the message I left for her. She was known to many of the delegates, but not the Eleventh. I introduced Ælthrelntheine, who replied, "I am delighted to make your acquaintance, First Light of the New Day. The Second and Ddwyrth have told me many interesting things about you. Please be welcome, come hither and join us."

Dawn replied graciously, as she was adept, and sat within my party. Ælthrelntheine opened as she had called the meeting. She stood and looked at everyone before speaking; "Sisters and brothers, thank you all for attending. The time approaches when we must prepare to face The Wrath of Gaia. Our great mother Earth still slumbers, but in a short while, possibly only a few years, she will awaken to rid the world of the infestation known as the Last. I pray we will all survive.

"We also face a second threat. The Great Ogre is driven by one obsession, to enslave, or murder, all who do not bow to him. Our sources inform us he still hibernates, but when he awakens, he will surely use The Wrath of Gaia to try to enchain any of the tribes that remain. His captains may try sooner of course, but this is how my senior advisors believe the most likely scenario to evolve.

"I remind you all of what is to come. We also await the birth of your daughter with great anticipation, Gatekeeper, Guardian. Her destiny cannot be foreseen, and oddly, is shielded from us. This is most unusual, and bodes well or woe, depending upon the omens at the moment of her birth.

"To survive The Wrath of Gaia, and prove victorious over the Great Ogre, we must reunite the Twelve Tribes with The One. Because the Tenth, led by the Great Ogre, are one of these tribes, this creates a conundrum, one we should all consider deeply."

29

Chapter 6

"The One?"

"The Ancestors, their heritage, and the Twelve Tribes. To this end, we have been searching for any sign of the other tribes thought to be extinct. I have great pleasure in announcing that we have at last made provisional contact with the Fourth. They are few in number, and exist in two small communities in Southeast Asia. Laos, and Flores Island in Indonesia is named after them—or was it the other way around? Anyway, I expect to meet their leader in a few days."

A buzz of excitement swept those at the table, although I still wondered who, or what, all these Tribes of Humans were. As if reading my thoughts, Lo Si sitting nearby whispered, "Guardian, I will explain all later, and probably after our guests have departed."

Over to my right, Kay added, "I will also share what I know, and of what is written in the Corridor of Knowledge. I must study those panels in much greater detail, but the revelations to date are amazing."

Before our mutterings could continue, Ælthrelntheine spoke up, "The Fourth told our contact, they had received word from the Eighth some millennia ago and I believe they may still survive. We also know the Third are alive and well. With them, our only problem lies with locating the true line, not the modern people or mixed-blood descendants. One of them must still carry the Ring of Power given to their people by the Ancestors. That person may not realise the significance of what they wear. Guardian, I may need to call on you, as you may speak a language they may know."

From that point forwards, the assembly turned into a general discussion. Jinnie announced we would all remain and share food where we sat. Owain immediately called for a barrel of ale and was summarily cussed by Da Phai Nai.

I waited until after we had eaten, but before the boisterous Ddwyrth embarked upon their seemingly never-ending campaign to drink us dry. They had not succeeded thus far, although we had come close on occasions. Choosing my moment I spoke up, "Kay, Lo Si, anyone, pray tell about the Twelve Tribes. You all appear to know far more than I."

Lo Si smiled and nodded in appreciation. However, he surprised me by saying, "Ju Lo, please have your children join us. They, as the next Keepers of Knowledge, should hear this first hand. This night, greater wisdom may be forthcoming from those more learned than I."

Our sage began as soon as Ju Lo returned with his family. "It is said the Ancestors arrived here from the stars in the far distant past. The planet where they lived was under threat, and but a few fled to our great Mother Earth. We believe that only three groups managed to escape, and two were destroyed. Only one of their craft landed intact.

30

"Their number was twelve, plus their leader; thirteen. It is said that leader was a female called Oma, but the Ancestor we know of was called Taris, a man, and yet he wore the Thirteenth Ring, that of the Captain. I cannot understand this contradiction, but this is what I was taught. They were highly advanced, and able to fly in the sky above, and ride on, or beneath the waters below. The Last can also do these seemingly impossible things."

I nodded in confirmation, and he continued, "Be that as it may, know in time the Ancestors became lonely and needed companions. They created the first three tribes, the Twelfth—Giants, the Eleventh— Elves, and the Tenth—Ogres. I do not know how they did this, but from you, Guardian, I have learned that your kind can almost do the same thing today. You call it genetic engineering I remember, cloning also.

"Imagine, another thousand years of research and development, Guardian. Would not the Last develop these same powers, similar to those of the Ancestors? Your Tribe, Guardian, would probably be able to create advanced forms of your kind, ones with special skills or resilience. It is thought that this is how the Ancestors themselves lived to extreme old age, and reproduced; although I fail to understand why they should wish to miss all the fun of begetting?"

Chortles abounded, but Ælthrelntheine interrupted before the mothers of his known children, Da Phai Nai and Won Long responded.

"Our understanding is that the Ancestors were not suited to living on a planet so close to the sun. To solve their problems, the crew of Oma's ship took an early and advanced form of hominina, and through trial and error, developed their first successful prototype, *homo sapiens habilis*. Using this DNA base, they mixed in sections of their own DNA, perfecting their design over millennia. Their goal was to create a perfect form of themselves, one that was suited to life on Gaia. The first beings created as a template were *homo sapiens ergaster*, although a second template soon followed—*homo sapiens erectus*. We usually drop the central 'sapiens', but this is the full title of our joint heritage.

"The template complete, the Ancestors created all twelve tribes, one led by each specialist crew member. The Twelfth were created first, and a long time later, so were we, the Eleventh. The Tenth were infused with initiative and assertiveness, as becomes a soldier, but they displayed controlling aggression instead. This tells me the Ancestors were fallible. During trials, the Ogres mutinied and some escaped unto the wild. They have sought to enslave or obliterate all sentient life ever since.

"Unfortunately, the Ancestors created them as ultimate and most fearsome warriors, and we believe this is why in turn, the Ogres were driven to create the Trolls, as slaves in their own image. It is rumoured the Ogres turned on their creators and tried to enslave them also. But we

31

know not what became of the Ancestors, except for Taris, who died naturally on this island many millennia ago."

Even though I had heard some of this story before, I was deeply unsettled, my anxiety showed as ill-disguised rage. "You can't just create people in a test tube, can you?"

Dawn placed a soothing hand on my shoulder, and I grimaced back at her. She said, "Actually Jackie, we've been doing that since the Seventies. Today's scientists can alter genes to prevent things like cystic fibrosis, a disease that is now being treated with gene therapy."

I answered back, "Yes I know that, but this is far more insidious. Cloning, gene manipulation, and DNA enhancement. We are talking about Creation, godlike powers over life and death."

n'Gnung said, "Jackie, we are what and whom we are. Accept this as fact, and let's move on. I find this extremely interesting, and remember, we are all related by our humanity. Cheers!"

His humour was infectious, and the beer I raised in salute, morish. However, the Queen of the Eleventh fired back, "Really? You mean reports of the Last creating a prototype super-soldier in a laboratory are wrong. I do not think so Guardian. They are trying to include infra-red, snake-like, enhanced vision in their design, although strange your kind would create soldiers first, do you not think?"

I knew Ælthrelntheine was correct. I just did not want to admit that creation by the omnipotent being called God was a fallacy, a lie. That this god, these gods were simply advanced human beings called The Ancestors. Murmurs flitted in the round, and fluttered within my mind. Timely, Lo Si resumed, "Thank you High Lord, if we may continue.

"The Ancestors created the Twelve Tribes over myriad of millennia. After their mistakes with the Tenth, the Twelfth helped create the Ninth and Eighth. The Eleventh joined them to create the next tribe, and I thank you for the likes of Owain, Llwydd, and Aroweena."

A cheer rose and people toasted, led by a chorus of the Seventh. The forum could easily have dissolved into the raucous banter of a back-street bar, but Ælthrelntheine stood stolid to quell the burgeoning merriment. "Thank you most learned one, you are correct. Owain, later you may drink your fill, but not now.

"Guardian, you should know the Ninth are *homo sapiens antecessor*, and the Eighth *homo sapiens heidelbergensis*. The Seventh are *homo sapiens neanderthalensis*, and were made hardy, because Gaia became colder. Leaner peoples like the Giants and ourselves suffered unduly. Fortunately, we both had homelands with shields."

Dawn rose to ask a question, "High Queen, how do you know so much about our ways, our technology and terminology? Many of our own kind do not understand what you speak about."

Ælthrelntheine's trickling laughter cracked the moment, but her reply tore it asunder. "First Light, as your name implies, those that open their eyes early learn to see. I received my Doctorate from Harvard. My daughter mastered sciences in Oxford, and Doctored Cosmology with applied mathematics at Cambridge. Then she went to Yale to study…"

Kay wafted her hand dismissively and interjected, "It was no big deal mother, covering my ears was the most serious problem I had. As for the thesis, it was mainly made up of equations, although the greater part of my real learning entailed practicable physics and associated biological studies, such as punting on the Cam."

Ælthrelntheine's eyes burned towards her daughter, who smirked distractedly askance, followed by her taking a long drink of ale.

Dawn stifled a grin and said, "Thank you High Queen. This is fascinating; please continue telling us about the Twelve Tribes."

Ælthrelntheine pursed her lips, her eyes became orbs of inquiry, and her eyebrows rose, before she shook the moment away and continued as if nothing had intervened.

"Development became polarised with the Sixth, who had abundant body hair, unlike any other race. They were created as a prototype of modern humans, the precursors of your kind, Guardian. They were the formative *homo sapiens sapiens*, but are generally referred to as Cro-Magnon, immediate forerunners of the Last. They were cautious, and are known by many names; Bigfoot, Yeti, and Sésquac come to mind.

"The Fifth *homo sapiens rhodesiensis*, and the Fourth *homo sapiens floresiensis*, were likewise created to perform specific functions in other parts of our world. You should consider this to be testing creation in real life." Ælthrelntheine could not stifle a titter, which spread quickly as her unintended pun took hold and she shook with half-stifled mirth.

Lo Si, aware of the changing mood, quickly rose and spoke, "Sisters and brothers, it is the held belief that the Third were not created, but allowed to develop independently. I do not believe this. It does not make any sense. Neither does it fit with the history of the Second."

Ælthrelntheine quieted, turned and said, "Apologies Lo Si, I was taken by the moment. What happened was that the Ancestors were closing on their goal of recreating themselves on this planet, Gaia. Understand, they had been working continuously. They kept improving and recombining DNA segments. The Third should rightly be regarded as representing different aspects of continued honing and development. They should be cited as the first truly modern *homo sapiens sapiens*.

"My understanding of the ancient texts is that the Ancestors finally unlocked the secret of their creations' self-improvement. The key was being self-aware as fully sentient individuals.

"With Cro-Magnon they had enlarged the cerebral cortex, but not the neurotransmitters and associated synaptic connections, neurons were associated with few axons, and dendritic connectors; let alone equivocal neurotransmitter receptors. The key was cranial capacity, and especially, interconnectivity of the base neurons.

"These elements were added to all the tribes as on ongoing process, thus empowering our process of thought, and creating reason. Many of these experiments were actually conducted on the Twelfth and Eleventh primarily, which is perhaps why we possess the gift of telepathy, as did the Ancestors.

"The true Third are what you know of as Denisovans. They developed in eastern China and intermixed with the existing homo erectus and Neanderthals of that region. The last ice age drove all humanity south where they dispersed far and wide.

"The Denisovans mixed too well and were forerunners of many disparate races, such as the Australian Aborigines, New Zealand Maori, and most New World Indians. But yes Lo Si, they were of slightly differing DNA combinations and developed in their own ways.

"The mixing and matching of DNA was endless Guardian. Even your modern historic myths tell of tall, white people, with long white hair and blue eyes. These were the Ancestors. They were probably checking up on how their creations were doing out in the real world.

"We believe the Third gave the Ancestors the breakthrough they had been seeking for hundreds of thousands of years; the means to create life in their own image. Guardian, you do not think your image on the walls of ancient caves is of the slightest co-incidence, do you?"

Kay interrupted, "Mother, our history is wrong, but I will speak of Taris another time. Guardian, I was waiting for the right time to tell you and I guess this is it. The pictures are not of you, but of Taris.

"I found it written in the Corridor of Knowledge on my last visit a few days ago. However uncanny the likeness, it is co-incidence."

With those words spoken, I felt the yoke of paranoia lifted from me, and jumped up to punch the air in unbridled delight. I felt animated with the knowledge, and clanged pots with Owain, but saw Da Phai Nai give us a stern and disapproving look, before she shook her head and returned to her conversation with Lo Si.

Ælthrelntheine shouted, "Jack Barleycorn! Will you please wait your beer one moment. We are almost done, and you may learn more."

Duly reprimanded, but personally empowered, I turned to look at her, nodded my head respectfully, and retook my seat. I did not want to miss a word of anything that could be important.

I expected the Queen of the Eleventh to finish the tale, but Lo Si came to the fore. With a nod to Ælthrelntheine, he filled in the missing pieces, "Yes, this is our understanding also. I like the term *cousins*, because that is what we feel we are to the Third, and the Last.

"In essence, the Second are the alternative to the Last. The Ancestors work was irregular and haphazard, but consistent over time. They were always empowering us in new ways, and as with the other tribes, making us more clever over æons of time. We became adaptable, and perhaps in our case, more fallible, trusting, socially aware, and caring. There can be no doubt the Second, Third, and Last are closely related..."

His words were cut off as Ælthrelntheine resumed, "Yes, Lo Si. You are correct. Presumably, because of mistakes with the Tenth, the Ancestors hedged their bets, creating two lines in tandem, the product of perhaps different teams or templates. Of this we may never know."

Kay confirmed, "This is as good as stated in the Corridor of Knowledge, Mother. Two options, same goal. My reading tells me the Second have the emotional and social traits of the Ancestors, the Last, their physical form and ingenuity." She smiled mischievously and added, "I wonder how we could recreate the Ancestors?"

She left her curious statement to hang, but her mother quickly returned to the conversation. "Thank you Daughter. This is indeed good news. Two paths, one goal. So finally, we come to the Last, the product of the final combining of DNA from Cro-Magnon and other tribes, and most especially the Second. Some would have us believe, Guardian that you represent the consummate perfection of the Ancestors will, the pinnacle of their achievements. You represent a tribe able to replace them, and replicate as in their own image, as their own reincarnation. One ideally suited to life on Earth, and beyond. Often, I do not see it.

"What I consider to be the ultimate potential of evolution has already been given life, although one not birthed as yet, Gatekeeper. By combining your two lines of hereditary, I believe you have succeeded where the Ancestors failed. It will be interesting to see what develops from this union. Perhaps the new Thirteenth..."

An unnatural hush fell, as the High Queen's words trailed off, overtaken by her inward musings. Lo Si responded before any other, "Yes, you may well be correct Ælthrelntheine. To create new life in your own image is an awesome undertaking. Your daughter would give birth to a renewed Thirteenth Tribe, Empress. the ultimate product of the combining of the Second and the Last. It would be most fitting."

Lo Si looked across to his first girlfriend and nodded. "Ye Gads!" erupted from Da Phai Nai's lips, as she marched towards me, brandishing a new broom with wanton intent.

"Don't you get it yet? We all carry the creator's spark of life within us, the common heritage of the Ancestors' benediction, humanity. It is just our outer packaging that is different. Don't you see, we are all made from bits of each other? Composite strands of creation. DNA shared between all of us, brothers and sisters of the greater plan. It is like conjuring the perfect meal, adding more or less of one thing or the other, to create the ultimate dish."

Da Phai Nai's outburst gave rise to cheers and shared communal understanding. The meeting did not break up when the telling curtailed, but flourished as a little more detail, and greater amity prevailed.

I asked an open question, "Anyone, there is still one point that niggles me. Why are the tribes numbered backwards? Lo Si, I remember you once explained the Ancestor's intention was to make only twelve tribes, but this still does not explain the why of it. Why not begin at number one?"

Lo Si considered for a moment, but Ælthrelntheine answered, "The Tribes are regarded as the Twelve and the One. Thirteen is a magical number. It is the first prime number to be composed of two different prime numbers, the first two primes. Therein lies analogy with the Last and the Second.

"The Ancestor's believed the number thirteen as more than just lucky. It is a number of greatest power, although there are others, not all of them prime numbers, or odd numbers either. The power of numbers can be used for either good or bad, right or wrong. This represents one of the keys of knowledge.

"Guardian, the answer to your question is simple. The Ancestors considered the number thirteen to be all-powerful, sacred. They considered themselves to be The First of the Thirteen Tribes, the highest ranking, the Creators. All crew wanted to become the thirteenth member, their leader, the Captain, and aspired to this end with their life's work. Therefore, the next most senior and twelfth Ancestor created the twelfth Tribe, the Giants. This continued as the Eleventh crewmember created us, the Eleventh, and so on.

"The Ancestors were the First Tribe, so your kind is the Last. That is our shared creation myth. I told you it was easy to understand."

Finally I had satisfaction, an answer I could accept. My mind greatly eased, and I accepted the Ancestors created all genus of *homo sapiens* in their own image.

Chapter 7 ~ Wake of the Giants

The seasons changed through Winter to Spring. The Island New Year approached, and Jien Noi grew heavy with our child. Dawn came to join us a few days before the expected birth. She was never a baby-person; she was there solely to support me.

The Moon rose overly large in the heavens above and seemed unearthly close to Gaia, as she appeared to chase the Sun from the sky. Our group were settled on the shore early one evening, when there came a scream.

We looked where people pointed. Three whirlpools were steadily advancing underwater towards us. My mind immediately flipped to old Godzilla movies: the three-headed monster, King Ghidorah. I grabbed my weapons and raced down to the shoreline to confront the fiend. n'Gnung was at my side, as were Ælkræleinnoire. Curiously, Da Phai Nai, who had raised the alarm, planted the handle of her broom steadfastly in the sands of our shore, as if to confirm ownership, and that none would pass. We were reinforced moments later by every other person present, n'Gue already gone to summon reinforcements.

The large head of a man broke the surface, followed by that of a woman, and an extremely large adolescent. They continued to walk directly towards us, and Ælkræleinnoire shouldered arms, "These are the Twelfth, the last remaining Giants. We all thought they were dead, extinct. Quickly, Jackie, prepare a celebration."

I immediately drew n'Gnung and Ælkræleinnoire into my encircling arms, looked at Jinnie for approval, and she nodded consent. I pressed my transfer bracelet, and we arrived in the control room, instantly communicating with the Eleventh and Seventh simultaneously. There was no time to tarry. Kay and I returned directly to the shore, to welcome our most unexpected guests, n'Gnung being left with a list of instructions.

Within moments, Ælthrelntheine and Owain were standing at our side, their cohort mustering to greet the presumed extinct, but now very much and visibly alive, Twelfth. The oldest race of humanity appeared incredibly large. I considered the Eleventh tall, but the Giants strode towards us seemingly twice as high.

As they came upon the shore Jien Noi warmly greeted them, "Lord of the Twelfth, welcome to our home. Know that you honour us with your presence."

The Empress bowed formally, and rose to introduce the three other representatives of the races in order: Ælthrelntheine, Owain, and myself. Each of us bowed in our traditional way, as platitudes of friendly exchange and genuine warmth filled the evening air.

Chapter 7

We stood aside as Barph led the guard of honour to perform our traditional welcome Haka. Once completed, they cheered wildly, before closing ranks, and leading our group towards the village. During this honour, others from all the races came hurriedly to form a celebration corridor. All bowed in turn as the Twelfth passed serenely by, and the crowds fell in behind us.

Gung Loi brought some ill-prepared dancers and musicians to us in the few minutes we had at our disposal. Meanwhile, Bu Te was hurriedly arranging a selection of snacks, juices, and liquors.

The Giants were too large to sit at our tables, but appeared happy to sit on the earth nearby and enjoy their interaction with our leaders and most learned. Jien Noi wanted to hold a proper reception at the capital, but the Giants preferred to remain with our small group that first evening. We agreed that tomorrow they would receive an official reception in Grimwaldi Rinns.

We were on tenterhooks, wondering why these genial people had unexpectedly come to us. Nevertheless, decorum and etiquette concerning how to treat an unknown race of humanity, resulted in a gentle introduction to the real issues of this portentous day.

We learned the King of the Giants was named Rambling Longshanks, his wife Fleetfoot Fourgay, and their son Leaping Longshanks, normally called Junior. I looked up into the eyes of someone twice my height and fifty years older, and acknowledged that calling him *Junior* told me a lot about this self-deprecating race.

Given their natural longevity, in the region of three hundred years, they were in no hurry to get to their reason for appearing. For the overly efficient Eleventh, this was mildly irritating, but the Seventh soon found good drinking partners who could match them.

While Owain and his trusted were happy to pass the time of day, as was their wont, Ælthrelntheine kept gently probing for information in most discreet ways. Finally, she got a titbit, when Rambling informed her, "Tomorrow will be our Harvest Moon, and the First day of the New Beginning."

It was our Spring Festival, with holiday fiesta well planned. I looked into Rambling's eyes and nodded in understanding. His great smile turned into thunderous laughter and we toasted to bond in the moment. The Giants appeared to be passing time in genial company, without becoming otherwise involved with their true motives for being with us. We knew that tomorrow was a most important day, but the *why* of it escaped almost everybody.

At length, Ælthrelntheine's gentle coercion elicited a response to her enquiry, "Why didn't you transport from your homeland?"

With his father's approval, Leaping began to recount a sad tale of betrayal and deceit, and one that irrevocably altered the lives of the Twelfth forever. He began, "In ancient times our home was dedicated to knowledge and learning. We worked with the Ancestors to create new and improved beings, as we are nowhere near perfect as a race. The Eleventh..."

Junior confirmed all we knew about the creation of humanity, adding little that was not discussed at our previous meeting. He turned and looked directly into my eyes, my heart with the most unexpected and penetrating gaze, "Guardian, I exclude you and a few others of your kind from this observation, but know the Last and the Tenth are extremely similar. This is one of the reasons why we came here today. But it is not the most important reason, of which you will all learn of tomorrow, so please be patient.

"Of the two factions of the Tenth, the Ogres were by far the stronger. Their smaller and meeker cousins were the Trolls, created as slaves. One day, the Trolls sent an emissary to befriend our King in order to seek assistance. At length this was refused, primarily because they would not halt their interminable civil wars with the Ogres.

"Our King of the time, Furlong Fourgay, and direct ancestor of my mother, was tricked by the Ogres who also befriended us. He was offered a fine draught of the rarest wine, and encouraged to seal an alliance, despite the Great Ogre of the day, being told there would be none forthcoming, as we are a peaceable people.

"King Fourgay drank, and was overcome. The wine had been tainted with a substance that rendered him paralysed, but fully alert. He was bound to his throne, as his court around him was killed by troops of the Ogres.

"Furlong was forced to witness the torture and lingering deaths of all of his companions in the high place, as he watched as his life's work come to a most barbaric demise. I will not dwell upon how his wife, the Queen, was invasively humiliated, although the Ogres later fought over who would eat the unborn girl child they cruelly ripped from her belly, mere weeks before birth. The Queen was still alive as they ripped the baby to pieces and ate it. It is said that in abject horror, she screamed herself to death.

"It is told, that after witnessing this malevolent desecration of human life, King Fourgay's wrist was cut, his blood being drained into tankards that the Ogres drank in celebration, before he was finally allowed to die. There are no words of forgiveness that could ever be uttered, to assuage these most heinous crimes against the living, our forefathers. The Ogres are utterly evil."

Chapter 7

I looked over at my wife's swollen belly, and could not conceive of how Furlong must have felt. My eyes were open and wet with tears, as were most others. Some showed anger instead, and cursed, before vowing the unreserved destruction of the Ogres, and extinction of their kind. Their iniquity was beyond contempt, and unbefitting sentient beings. In time we rallied, and offered our unfettered empathy, promised to stand with the Twelfth, and eviscerate the Tenth from existence.

The emotions Leaping conveyed within his tale were heart-rending, to the point we were all crying and in need of a break. However, despite their tears it was also plain to see Junior's parents were exceedingly proud of their son's storytelling skills.

An emotional weir enveloped us, and I felt we needed more beer to break its morbid hold. As I ordered a new barrel, n'Gnung said, "Junior, this is the most distressing tale I have ever heard, and yet your species still survives. How do you know what was said and done that day?"

Rambling thanked n'Gnung for his insight, before whispering to his son. Leaping took a long swallow of ale, before finishing the most harrowing of tales. "Our memories are overly long, as are our bodies, and lifespan. However, we still honour our forefathers to this day.

"Furlong managed to preserve our line, devising to send his male son, Footsure Fourgay, on a long errand. When the son returned, he found himself to be the new King, his parents and all his kith and kin slaughtered mercilessly. He searched, at last finding a sole serving girl still clinging to life. He sustained her, her injuries severe, and slowly she physically healed. By playing dead, she was able to witness the atrocity through shuttered eyes.

"The couple fled as soon as the wench, Temerity Shortfalls, could walk, and between them they gave new life to our species. In time, they found succour with other Giants, clans living apart from our ancestral homeland. The Twelfth have never forgotten this atrocity, and this is one reason why we left the known world. I propose a toast to Footsure Fourgay and Temerity Shortfalls."

He stood to honour his forefathers, and we all touched beakers, and drained our tankards supportively. Leaping continued quickly, lest the hiatus return to dwarf our spirits once more; replacing loss with rebirth is one art of the accomplished storyteller.

"Brothers and sisters, be aware, our inheritance from the Ancestors, the Ring of Power we hold dear, disappeared. Most believe the Great Ogre took it, but he has never used the Ring of the True Heart throughout millennia. Surely, if it were in his possession, he would have usurped it to do his bidding. This has never happened. I believe King Furlong secreted the true Ring of Power before that fateful meeting with the Great Ogre. As to where it resides, we know not, yet we all yearn for the return of our rightful heritage. Thank you, let us toast in friendship."

That evening we discovered. the demise of the Twelfth at the hands of the Great Ogre. That their Ring of Power was missing, hidden perhaps. And that Rambling was not named because of his physical dexterity, but because of his unquestionable gift for telling long, and compellingly engaging stories. Neither was Leaping named for his jumping ability, but because he was given to leaps of logic.

Unsought, the Eleventh and Seventh had sent messengers to brim our larders full with finest ales and culinary delicacies. In a quiet moment, I sought the answer to a troublesome fact of my life, and enquired of Rambling, "How did you manage to get through our shield tonight, because it repels all outside circumvention?"

Rambling's smile was all-knowing, encompassing parental intrigue and dispensation, "Guardian, how did you arrive here on these shores, because I am sure your way was as our own. I cannot tell you of why we came here today, but I think you already know. I can either tell you about how we came to be here tonight, or how we passed like fishes through your shield. Which do you choose?"

I wondered what game they were playing. In truth, I felt like an inquisitive kid who had removed the light switch from its housing, and was left staring at wires with pretty colours. What did they all mean?

I felt tugs to my brain, and turned instantly to look at Kay. She was staring intently at me, as if willing me to take the next small step towards greater enlightenment. I was floundering, but somehow opened my mind, and her words came unbidden, "If you do not know the answer to a question, reply with a better question."

"Junior, if I were to ask you to tell me about these things, which do you know best?"

Rambling fell about in laughter, accompanied by his family, and also more demurely, the Eleventh. The hilarity passed the Seventh by and they refilled their tankards. Fleetfoot chided her menfolk for being too obscure, and hastily brought them to attention.

Junior replied, "We came through your shield, as you yourself did, because it allows fish in and out. It really is that simple. The size of the fish is not restricted, which is why there are so many sharks in these waters. Any who approach under water are seen as being no threat, merely fish."

I cursed, already knowing some of the mercenaries had entered by the same way, Sar Tan left and returned using the same means, but I appreciated the independent confirmation. "Rambling, tell me about 'Why you are here tonight?'"

Chapter 7

He looked at me forlornly and answered the question, but not the implied one I had asked. "We have wandered aimlessly for æons, but desperately seek to return to our homeland, the high place. One reason we are here is to ask for assistance."

Owain stood tall and raised his tankard, "Brothers, Sisters all. Today we will enjoy the company of the Twelfth. Tomorrow, we will retake their lands. Drink with me to seal our blood-bond."

Ælthrelntheine added, "We will also stand with you Rambling, and assist your return, but it will not be tomorrow Owain. First, we must welcome a new Empress Elect amongst our number, and then we must prepare. I have to leave now, because there are urgent matters I must attend to. I will return tomorrow with a great surprise for you all."

Chapter 8 ~ The Work of Women

The next day found us enjoying the festival of the Spring Moon. Being so near the Tropic of Capricorn, our fields were already planted. New shoots of life had developed into a verdant blaze of established growth. The city was a buzz of expectation. The new sun calendar would begin in three days' time, at the autumnal equinox, as I knew of it, and five days holiday would follow.

However, the whole island was already on holiday due to the immanent birth of their future Empress. People travelled from the towns and hamlets to enjoy the festivities, the evening's Mardi Gras, and were expectant of change.

n'Gue had already ensured the people knew of a special parade to welcome new friends, and as midday drew near, his messengers obliquely let slip the visitors were not of a known race, and were exceptionally tall. As prearranged, Ælthrelntheine and her representatives returned to be a part of the honour guard.

The procession began, as was customary, to the west of the city, and comprised the usual musicians, dancing girls, jugglers, and general mayhem I was now accustomed to. The Empress waited on the platform before the palace, her labour immanent. The Giants found their celebrity status a little overpowering. It was obvious they were unused to being the centre of attention for hundreds of people. Once the shock of seeing such tall people passed, the crowd rushed to speak with, and touch the strangers. The throng massed and Barph had to summon extra troops in order to clear a passage for us, and keep the procession moving. In time the Giants reached the Imperial Mount, acclimatised, and took it all in their gigantic strides, showing a brave face and typical serene smiles.

As events progressed, I felt a tug to my conscious, and was sure Kay was speaking into my mind, repeating the phrase, "Guardian, come to me." I looked around and she was standing nearby with her mother, and both of them had their eyes closed, as if in inner commune. I began to walk towards them, but stalled, I considered it would be rude of me to interrupt. The voice came again, more distinct this time, "That's it Jackie, come to me now."

I walked up to the pair and enquired, "Excuse me ladies, but did you just call me? I know it sounds stupid."

Kay's eyes flew wide open and she flung her arms around me and gave me a brief hug, before turning to Ælthrelntheine. "See mother, I told you he could do it. Please help us, because we need to penetrate the Core."

I said incredulously, "You mean you may be able to help us understand the control centre?"

Chapter 8

The Queen of the Eleventh looked at me as if I were an uncouth brat she had decided to indulge just once, along the road to greater understanding. "Guardian, you are stupid, then wise by equal measure. We love you for it all the same, and just the way you are, Jack Barleycorn."

Interacting with the Eleventh was a bit like a youthful suitor trying to understand females: squared. Ælthrelntheine bent as if to kiss my worried brow, but locked her forehead to mine instead—instantly my comprehension exploded.

I remember her laughter trickling like a moonlit fountain beneath the enormity of heaven, whirling, joining, and evolving into a gigantic splendour within my comprehension. I gave thanks for her presence within my heart and soul, and knew those feelings mattered.

I came around to voices in the distance asking if I was all right. As my ears cleared and senses focused, I realised Jinnie was holding me tightly, her physical presence helped me to earth once more. Weid Noi was watching me intensely, as Won Long came to my side and smoothed my brow. She said, "It is always like this the first time with the Eleventh. It gets easier, and more different also over time."

Ælthrelntheine spoke up as soon as she could see I was OK, "Guardian, the gift I gave your mind should help you during your quest for knowledge. It is but a small help along the way, a bridge at best. I must depart once more, for there is a task of great import I must complete before the Moon is full."

We bid her farewell, and I quickly recovered. I felt elated and grasped the air, knowing this was a turning point for me, for all of us. I rounded on my friends with great enthusiasm, "This is a momentous breakthrough. I hope that now I'll be able to link deeply with the Core, and we can begin to make real progress by unlocking the Ancestor's secrets. Yes!"

I wanted to go directly to the control room and try out my new powers, but we had guests to attend, and my wife needed my support. I noticed a maid was in close attention, and later a healer appeared by her side. Jinnie said, "It has begun. Our daughter will be with us soon, but there is still time to wait, many hours I am told."

Despite my distracted concerns, the afternoon passed in congenial company, as five races of the Twelve Tribes combined in friendship and shared understandings. The giants became inquisitive, and went amongst our people. They delighted in the small and normal things they did as a part of their everyday lives.

Jinnie's labour grew heavy, and she rested in her private chambers as the afternoon became evening. We knew the birth was imminent, as we discussed our chosen name, before confirming our previous decision. It was a most unusual choice, but one we both felt comfortable with, and laden with deeper layers of meaning and significance.

Jinnie said she needed to rest, so I went outside looking for a purpose. n'Gnung was waiting for me at the door as I left the Empress' chambers, and he steered me to the company of my closest: Kay, Gung Loi, and Dawn.

As shadows lengthened, Jinnie sent for me, "Husband, the time grows near. Every Empress to date has been born on the Imperial bed, in the Empress's chambers. Take me to our home. We begin a new dynasty this day, and I will have our daughter born in the Valley of Knowledge, as that is her destiny to fulfil."

"Jinnie, I know this is the right thing to do. It had been on my mind to suggest it, but preparations were well advanced here, and I thought this was what you wanted."

She drew me down to kiss her, before I picked her up and carried her outside. An air of expectancy enveloped all around us, and she whispered to my ear, "I have never been so happy, nor known so much pain. Stay with me now to welcome our daughter into this world, my love."

I thought wild horses could not drag me away, nor giants even; the act of childbirth is truly a miracle. Her contractions had begun, as the Moon became ever more present, rising fully into the edge of evening sky, bathing us in her bountiful magnificence.

As soon as the Seer heard about the change of venue, she left at once for the control room taking Weid Noi with her. Moments later, we were transported to our home. I carried my wife to our marital bed and laid her gently to rest. No sooner had I wiped her brow with a moist cloth, than other women joined us.

Da Phai Nai stood near at hand to offer a potion, different from the ones she usually proffered, this one to ease the passage of childbirth. Jinnie gratefully accepted, and I stayed to comfort her, until a woman's voice commanded, "Jack Barleycorn, will you please leave this poor girl alone and find something useful to do.

"You are cluttering up the place and getting in our way. This is woman's work, and you have no place here. Look at what he has done to the poor girl, made her with child. Sun Kist, fetch my best broom so I can chase this wastrel out of here!"

We started to laugh, before another contraction stymied Jinnie's mirth. I stood my ground as Da Phai Nai chased interloping Ladies in Waiting and Imperial physicians out of our bedroom. Gung Loi took control of the confused hangers-on, and cleared them out of our home.

I knew that Da Phai Nai had not forgotten about me, and that my turn would come, but for the interval, I held Jien Noi's hand, and wiped her brow in simple sharing of togetherness and compassion. Somehow, n'Gnung had managed to dodge the matron's broom, and having infiltrated the heart of this exclusively female domain, uttered hurriedly, "Empress, Guardian, everybody is coming here."

"What? Festivities have already begun in Grimwaldi Rinns."

"Guardian, when you departed, so did they. Every single person of our nation is coming here to witness the birth of their new Empress. Come, we need to manage this."

Jinnie spoke up, "Husband, *Daddy*." She smiled as she patted her stomach. "We must share this moment, it is the most important moment in the lives of our people. Bring them all here, and bring our restaurants and kitchens too if you can find a way, because only you can do this. Bring everything you can think of, tables, chairs, and have builders standing by just in case things don't quite work out as planned. Hurry, my contractions come closer together, our daughter will be with us soon."

I kissed her lips, and rose to leave, placing my hand on her swollen belly for the last time. My eyes were bewitched by the love and understanding of creation. My wife whispered into my distraction, "Send Weid Noi to me, I have need of her. She must witness the birth — it is something I do not understand."

I began to reply, when a voice boomed nearby. "Ahha! There you are Guardian. I knew you would be lurking somewhere nearby. Be gone with you, and take this wiseacre with you."

She swung her broom, almost catching me on the arm with a stout blow. I ran for cover, n'Gnung leading the way to safety. We ran for the door. Da Phai Nai charged after us, her broom casting pre-emptive strikes against our behinds, occasionally connecting, as we began to find the situation ludicrously hilarious.

She continued hollering as she chased us away, "What would you two likely lads be doing loitering here, if not up to some kind of mischief? Be off with you," swoosh, "for you have guests to entertain," swish, "a kingdom to run," slap, "and a world to save!"

We made it just outside the entrance, and doubled over in fits of laughter. Our arms interlocked upon the other's back, before the swoosh of practised broom caned our backsides. We ran a few more paces before turning.

Her rant continued unabashed, "That should be enough, but oh no. Instead, I find you whispering in secret about *girls*. Don't even bother to deny it, for I know you both well — one of them your as yet unborn daughter, Guardian. The good Lord preserve us."

Her eyes were telling a very different story. n'Gnung spoke into my thoughts, "You said many weeks ago, Da Phai Nai is a person who changes your perspective, and brings laughter in her wake — once you understand her and her true intentions of course."

We looked back at her in admiration. Da Phai Nai was standing resolute in the middle of the doorway to my home, the upright broom in her hand a fearsome weapon. We stood before her formidable demeanour and bowed to her, thanking her for her understanding. She dropped her mask for a moment, and bowed back, her smile, that of a small sun upon our countenance.

We had not been aware, but Lo Si had been hovering in the shadows nearby, waiting for his moment to enter. He told me later that night, "I watched you both disappear, and thought it all quite funny, and also quite right of my childhood sweetheart. She can be a contrary woman, but one with a sense of fair play.

"As you disappeared, I followed her inside. Her eyes cast sideways to look at the Empress, so deeply happy in anticipation, awaiting her offspring. Jien Noi asked for Weid Noi to be present, the offspring of my genes of course, and my official wife. That is something neither woman has never quite managed to put behind her heart, nor forgiven me for.

"Da Phai Nai was slow to react when my arm went around her, and she cried deeply. I was reading her thoughts closely and knew she needed a distraction, so I spoke my mind. I said, 'Think of our child, for she is a clever one, knows the ways of plants and the earth. She should hold higher station.'

"I felt her nod into my chest, so spoke boldly, 'Several times on my better days, I have accompanied her to examine the Caves of the Ancestor. She has expressed a wish to spend time with the Shaman and study her ways. I fully support her in this, if that is your wish also, dearest one? Let us see what the Shaman determines of this.'

"My words seemed to pull her back from an emotional abyss. She said, 'Thank you Deru. Sun Kist studies plants and potions, and is quite adept; make this so. It would give me great heart, and break it also'.

"Sun Kist of course, was the always and only constant in her life. But to train as the next Shaman, this was madness, wasn't it? The midwife returned just then with a tonic, and I made a hasty exit to avoid her broom, as you will appreciate and understand."

There is an exceptionally special moment only almost-fathers understand and are bewildered by. Women have absolutely no idea what wrings through their husbands minds at the time of birth. It is a time of impotence and empowerment, a time of wonder and wishful thinking, and a time of almost understanding the greater workings of this curious thing we call life. It is one men tend to cope with badly, first-time fathers worst of all.

Often, the least useful person at a wedding is the groom. So, it proved to be, that the least useful person at a birth, was the first-time father. Fortunately, my brother was beside me always in support. I wondered if I was worthy of being a father? Could I guide my daughter to become more than she would otherwise be? Keep her from making the mistakes I had made? But most of all, I worried that one day she would have no need of me.

Being active helped, because as soon as preparations nearby and at Grimwaldi Rinns were complete, we went to the control room. I brought buildings, people, and wherewithal to nearby our home. The builders checked the structures were stable before anybody used them.

Transferring kept us busy until most of the population were moved and the last buildings were awaiting inspection. n'Gnung acted as liaison and kept me busy with transfer logistics and puzzles.

In rare quiet moments my mind wandered to thoughts of my wife and soon to be daughter.

Time moved on.

Chapter 9 ~ One Plus One Equals Three

Eventually I sat back in the Captain's chair to bask knowing our job was done and a crisis averted. I was waiting for word from my home, but nothing was forthcoming. Then I remembered Jinnie's request and asked Weid Noi to join my wife for the birth of our child.

Won Long spoke up, "Guardian, I will send her shortly, but first I need her here with me."

"What is wrong Seer?"

"Usually the future is plain to see, especially when the time is so close. Normally each event is a choice between two alternatives, and we build our reading from this source, even as the continual choices augment. The Empress choosing to deliver your baby at home was never considered, because it has never been known before. Therefore we need to recheck how the future will become."

I raised an enquiring eyebrow in n'Gnung's direction, and he replied in kind. I wanted to return to our home as quickly as possible, but had to wait for the builders to complete their inspection. Finally, word came to us that the buildings had survived the move remarkably well.

n'Gnung and I were preparing to leave, when Won Long shrieked, "Oh my good Lord! They have chosen the third and windy way."

We turned to her with concern, before she said to Weid Noi, "Compared with the two paths I know of, this will turn quickly, either tomorrow or the day after, when one of our number either stays or goes, but I cannot see which one of us it will be. Neither can I see if the going or staying of this person leads to the good path or the wrong path, because the mysteries of time enshroud it before my comprehension. The third path is unpredictable, and commits all our futures to the whim of destiny.

"Destiny is a real concept, you do remember? The Three Ladies always watch over us, play games within the ether, and cede our souls with diversions and mischief. To side with either: Luck, Fate, or Serendipity — within lies torment."

I asked what she meant, and she regained her senses enough to say, "Guardian, you and your wife have chosen the third way, and it is obscured. We cannot see the future."

"Then you are now like the rest of us Seer. I am sure everything will work out just fine."

"It is of utmost importance, Guardian. Without knowing what is due to occur, we cannot prepare for it."

"That may be, Seer. But it seems to me the future has already changed from the one you foresaw. Come Weid Noi, the Empress asked for you specifically to attend the birth, and I worry it will not be long."

Chapter 9

"Take her if you must, but it will be hours yet. I remember my own time much too well."

We three departed for my home and n'Gnung called on Barph to provide troops as a precaution. We worried people would become overly excited when the news of the birth reached them. We merely needed a demarcation line between public and more private space. Horovitz was acting as Barph's First Lieutenant, and quickly implemented a suitable cordon.

In one way, the Seer proved to be correct, the waiting was interminable. I distractedly sipped the beer my brother urged me to swallow. I felt out of it. My mind and consciousness somewhere my physical body was not allowed to go. My worries needed abandon, but not within the beckoning betrayal of booze. A new life would soon be depending upon me. That was an exceedingly heavy thought.

In all honesty, my about-to-be daughter would probably not need me at all to begin with. She would depend upon her mother's milk for survival. My role was to make their arbour a secure place for both of them. In those minutes, I grew into manhood, and accepted my fate as the responsibility of caring after others. I was already doing so as Guardian of my adopted people, but this time it was personal.

Above the Moon rose to her imperious majesty. Her womanly beauty and fullness captured all our hearts. I was staring at her, when I felt the need to glance about. There was something, but nothing. My eyes strayed to a vacant chair sometimes, but there was never anybody sitting there. The company of my friends was beguiling, and in time, I raised my beaker, drinking slightly deeper than before.

Sun Kist came rushing up to me and said a curious thing, "Guardian, there is one here that would speak with you. Please pay her the courtesy of your attention."

I looked over to where she pointed, and saw a woman I had never seen before, sitting in the place my eyes had wandered back to, repeatedly. She appeared to be almost Caucasian, and looked about mid-thirties. She was attractive, without being overly so, and seemed to be apart from everyone else. No one spoke to her, or even acknowledged her presence. Intrigued, I downed my ale, and went to discover what she was about — my mind was already running the chances of probability; there was only one explanation.

Before I could speak, the newcomer uttered:

"One plus one is nearly three,
Thus, creation will envelop thee.
From cauldron of the womb set free,
Honey'd fruit of bird and bee."

I heard her words, and looked at her, only she was gone. A voice at my shoulder added in parting,
"Seer between the worlds is one,
Another reckless, aims a gun.
The third, a child completes the sum,
Her majesty yet ne're begun."

I was left staring into space. The person who had spoken to me, was gone. I gaped around. Sun Kist was still nearby, "I know that was the Shaman. How did you see her? Nobody else did. She wasn't an old crone, and I don't understand that."

The girl shifted uneasily on her feet, as if her jittery arms and legs could conjure an answer. I tried to calm her, but her personal understanding lay beyond her ability of rational explanation.

She stated simply, "The Shaman is what she is, Guardian. She is of this world, and she is not. That's all I understand, but I like her very much. She was kind to me, and asked me 'what I would be'. I think she meant, 'what I wanted to do in life', but she speaks weirdly you know."

I comforted her by sharing my bewilderment, and she drew reassurance from the fact that I was as perplexed by the Shaman as she was. The main evening entertainment began a short way down the valley, and many rose to enjoy the carnival. We that remained stilled to watch as the heavenly Lady came towards the pinnacle of her majesty. I pondered upon our own insignificance within the cosmic balance of Space and Time. Yin and Yang. Male and Female.

Hours seemed to float by on her whim and forbearance. Finally, word came; the time was nigh. The air shimmered nearby, and Ælthrelntheine appeared. With her were a retinue of quite differing peoples. At my nod and n'Gnung's instruction, Barph immediately mustered a small honour guard, and they performed a welcome Haka.

The Maori were delighted and replied in kind with their own version. Friendships were already made, and their King was soon in agreeable conversation with Lo Si. The other race were a curious folk. I could never have imagined they existed outside of Gaelic legends. They stood a mere three feet tall, dressed all in green, and were immediately into the blarney, singing, dancing, and general mischief.

Our introductions to the Fourth and Third were welcoming, if brief. Ælthrelntheine was aware of the hour at hand, and quickly took our guests to enjoy the hospitality of the Second.

I stood alone, but for n'Gnung, as we watched the festivities enjoyed by others. n'Gnung glanced up and said, "Guardian, I know this sounds strange, but I am sure the Moon will be full, and at mid-heaven at midnight. That is when she will be born. This is a rare event indeed."

Chapter 9

The celestial orb was almost directly overhead as we ambled in the general direction of our home. We arrived to find the way blocked by Gung Loi. "Guardian, know I cannot stop you from entering, but please show respect and wait for them to call for you. It will be but a moment."

She made an official bow to me, and I thanked her for her timely advice. I stood aside in jitters of ready expectation. The ways of womenfolk are many and mysterious to a multitude of men. It was simply the same in the Stone Age. The Moon came to her zenith, and within that moment, we heard a baby cry. I clasped n'Gnung to me in unbridled joy, his own delight obvious, Gung Loi joining us.

Seconds later, the contrary voice of Da Phai Nai boomed out. "Where is that useless husband of yours? Drinking and gallivanting with his friends most likely, whilst we poor women labour to create new life within and without our being. Guardian!"

Many would think this a rebuke, except it was anything but. Da Phai Nai had a way with words to confound the best. I already knew our daughter was born healthy, as the matron bustled towards us enquiring, "Why are you loitering outside?"

The three of us at the door could not help from giggling at the absurdity of her entreaty, which she compounded by adding. "You better bring that useless oaf with you as well."

I ran, and within moments was at my wife's side. She offered our daughter for me to hold and behold. Jinnie's wondrous and beseeching eyes elucidated her words; "I gift new life for you, Daddy."

I was beside myself with wonder at this small miracle, as every father will know. My eyes were also for my 'Genie'. I asked if she was all right, and said some stupid male things the womenfolk pretended to think were of little worth.

I looked around momentarily, and near the midwife, saw Da Phai Nai crying with joy, and if that wasn't startling enough, she was being comforted against Weid Noi's breast. I think that was probably the most bizarre thing I had ever seen in my whole life.

I stole a second glance, only for the next Seer's eyes to indicate what we *boys* should be doing already. n'Gnung chucked my daughter under the chin and made smiling faces at her. She cried. I did not have a clue what to do with her.

My devoted eyes rested on this most fragile of creations, my mind blown away. I had no words to describe the feeling. My first child. Oh so wondrous to behold, to carry, and to touch. Tears of happiness rolled down my cheek, and nobody paid me any heed. I raised her and bent to kiss her for the first time. Our bond was sealed. Now I had to try to work out just how to hold a baby, it appeared to be extremely difficult. Her crying increased in volume.

I held her tightly with both arms, rapt within my own insecurity. I bent to kiss her again, and her face turned deepest red, almost purple. Da Phai Nai was there in an instant, swinging the child into the crook of her arm, against her breast. She stopped crying immediately, resumed her normal colour, and was handed gently back to her mother. I looked to n'Gnung for help, but realised this was traumatic for him, remembering he had lost both his wife and child during childbirth. I rested my hand on his shoulder in genuine empathy. He grimaced, but smiled wryly.

The Shaman materialised, interrupting us, and bestowed the baby with flowers and herbs, followed by a short chant. She cast hand-written parchment runes into the air, that magically burst into flame, and disappeared. She gave an imperceptible bow of her head, as if to say *get on with it.*

Jinnie nudged me, and as I bent to her, she whispered, "Pick us up and carry us outside. Our people, our guests need to see her."

I did as instructed, and the Shaman led us out of our home, casting sweetly scented water, flowers, and seeds around arbitrarily to her unfathomable will and dispensation. Our small party emerged to great cheers, a host gathered before us. It seemed *the world and his wife* had arrived to share our private happiness. Behind us, n'Gnung and Weid Noi were our best once more, whilst Da Phai Nai had recovered her equilibrium and took rear guard with Gung Loi.

We presented the newly born babe to the Emperor, our other leading figures, and the representatives of the Twelve Tribes by turn. As we wended our way, the Shaman led our party unerringly; lit by the light of the closest and fullest Moon I had ever known in all my years.

By degrees, we came to the pool, where the Shaman walked around casting spells and magic from her runed yew staff and willow wand. The clearing of the waters complete, she beseeched the Moon's grace to come amongst the waters, as the ultimate and time-sworn image of purity and blessed womanhood.

Her pool for a cauldron purified, the Shaman produced a large leaf from her carrier, and blessed it with the waters of the nearby fall. She placed our baby upon it, and flicked the impossible raft out into the pond, like a gambler might shoot craps, a destiny to see.

I was alarmed and made ready to dive into the water to save our child, but my concerns proved groundless. I watched stupefied, as the wanded hand of the Shaman, guided the miraculous cockleshell of wonderment. A hush fell upon us all. We bore witness, as we watched the impossible craft slowly revolve before coming to rest in the exact centre of the lake, and in the middle of the Moon's reflected image.

Chapter 9

The Shaman produced an ancient challis evolved from a conch shell, and mixed the aerated fall waters with some secret preparations from within her sack, and readied a potion of most propitious welcome. I did not watch everything she did, because my eyes, like everybody else's, were fixated upon the child in the leaf, adrift on the pool. We moved around, at first by chance, and later by purpose, and always, the small raft appeared to be in the middle of the image of the Moon as reflected upon the pool, and that was crazy. It seemed like time stood still.

What occurred next was the stuff of wild imaginations. Rambling leant down to whisper, "May we?"

I had no idea what he is talking about, but I trusted him. His great smile broke the moment, and no sooner did he straighten and gesture, than an Elven ensemble broke into the most elaborate and unearthly dance, both beside, and seemingly above the waters of the small lake.

It was as if they sprinkled faery dust upon the waters, because within moments the small leaf protecting our new born twirled, and took the reflection of the Moon to the shore. The Shaman bathed our daughter in the Moon's lake-light, washing her clean with the prepared potion. I swear I witnessed the tears of the Moon falling upon our child's naked body, so deeply significant was the moment.

The hundreds of watchers could have been as a blade of grass on a still day, so little noise was made. The Shaman had one thing left to say before she departed,

"Born at midnight of the world were thee,
A gift of love from brethren free.
Our Lady Moon comes close to see,
This Wonder of the World to be."

As she finished, the new life was returned to her mother. The Shaman stilled, her work done. She mused a distracted thought into the ether,

"I doubt this ceremony of welcome's worth,
ne'er before performed upon *this* Earth."

She did not say it aloud, but that is what I know I heard her say.

Chapter 10 ~ Child of the Windy Way

That night a Mardi Gras erupted as people enjoyed the festivities. Jinnie insisted we tarry with our esteemed guests, because Seven Tribes were sharing our table, our present and our futures together.

Da Phai Nai presented my wife with a feast: a bowl of plain chicken noodle soup, and a small amount of steamed oily fish set on a bed of rice with a little lettuce, and only hot water to drink.

Excepting medicinal tonics, this was all she would eat and drink until the next full moon. The reason for this was simple. The mother's milk would contain traces of things she consumed. Strictly controlling what the mother ingested was critical to our baby's development.

As we settled, I was encouraged by n'Gnung to wet the baby's head. I did not need the distraction of drinking in celebration of the baby's birth. I wanted to be with my wife and child and enjoy their being.

Ælkræleinnoire and Owain put paid to my best intentions. I told Jien Noi of my heart's desire, but she bade me celebrate with our guests.

I felt the yoke of the new Father settle on my shoulders, but that was brushed aside by the arm of n'Gnung, who replaced it with a tankard of ale. After several toasts, I noticed the Emperor talking aside with Ælthrelntheine, and knew a scheme was afoot.

My eyes looked over the celebrations down the valley and I felt sure every citizen was with us that night. I also noticed the Shaman had retaken her seat, completely alone and ignored by everybody around. As I watched her, trying to fathom her reason for staying, welcome though she was, her eyes fixed mine briefly, and a curious smile played around her lips. I felt like I had been hit in the head and noticed her cackle. My mind seemed to expand, but my thoughts felt normal. I looked back for her, but the Shaman was gone. I noticed nobody ever sat in that seat the entire evening.

n'Gnung's voice broke the Shaman's spell, "Guardian. The question upon everybody's lips is what will you name the baby?"

I helped Jinnie to stand and supported her, as she in turn swaddled our baby. She spoke proudly to our close companions at the table, "Esteemed visitors; dearest friends. We are delighted to present your future Gatekeeper and Empress in Waiting, Zhao Ræm Mooyi."

The assembled cheered and raised goblets in toast, Ælthrelntheine asked of the naming significance. Jien Noi said, "Zhao is the name of the Imperial family, which has remained unbroken since before we came to this island. Ræm was the name of our greatest leader in prehistory, the Empress who guided us here. It is a very rare name, but fitting. Mooyi means 'our personal daughter', as of ourselves and of the Second. It is a familiar name shared by my sister and aunt."

Chapter 10

Over time, she was to become renowned as Ræm. We toasted the newborn many times, as each Tribe offered a salutation, followed by a small gift. It was unexpected and I was sure none of us were worthy of such honour. We were helped by the ebullient presence of the Emperor, who took it upon himself to act as the master of ceremonies. It also explained what he and the Queen of the Eleventh had been plotting.

The giants began the audience with fine words spoken by Rambling Longshanks, "Gatekeeper. Guardian. Child of the Moon. We give thanks this day for your coming amongst us, and know in time you will lead us on a new path through dark and dangerous times ahead, until the world is reborn anew and whole once more. Thank you for permitting us to attend this most auspicious moment. The True Heart of the Twelfth stand beside you during the trials to come."

He bowed, before reaching forward to hand Jien Noi a small package that contained a cloak of finest, filigree gossamer. It had only one fastening that clasped at the collar. He smiled and said, "This is called the Ægis and will bring protection to the pure and true of heart."

We thanked him, knowing this was a priceless gift. Kay whispered, "Jackie, the Ægus, as we call it, is the most powerful gift of protection, if used wisely. Oma gifted it to the Eleventh, and we in turn passed it on to the Twelfth in a dark hour of prehistory. Its revelation and passing to another Tribe, a new generation is most propitious."

The Emperor was magnanimous as his words flowed. The Giant retreated and Ælthrelntheine took his place. The Queen of the Eleventh did not speak, but sang a haunting melody that was unworldly in its beauty and complexity. Others of the Eleventh joined her as voices burst and swooped, and I would swear they painted a picture in the night. At length she rested and bowed before us. She offered the baby a delicate bracelet of friendship, similar to the ones she had previously gifted to Jien Noi and I. This was the fairest of them all and crafted with exquisite detail. "Child of the Windy Way, wear this and know that if you have need, call and we will be standing with you."

We had tears in our eyes but the Emperor's banter was long enough for us to recover and receive the Ddwyrth. In contrast to the Eleventh, they sang a song of valour and victory that was more suited to a bawdy sailor's bar. Their revelry and antics made a most gripping musical tale. As they sang, they acted respective rolls within the unfolding drama.

Finally, Owain was the only one left standing, and he came to us, crossing his right fist to his heart. "Gatekeeper, Guardian, Child of the Earth. Please accept this token of our undying bond." He presented a finely crafted dagger encrusted with runes, it felt alive.

"This blade was made by our ancient Master of master craftsmen. The runes were given life by the Eleventh during the final casting. Know it can never be broken, blunted, nor taken from the hand of its rightful owner. I now command this blade to answer only to this new life before us. Dearest child, if you ever have cause to wield this short sword in warfare, know the Seventh stand by your side until death do us part!"

I had read of magical blades, as surely Excalibur was one. To hold such a blade, if only for a moment, was breathtaking. It felt alive, a part of my body. I passed it on to Jien Noi, who let our daughter hold it. Meanwhile the Emperor was introducing the Fourth.

Ruaidhrí Ó Riáin, Red King of the Fourth came before us in his mischievous manner, as his partners stood beside him. At his nod, one began playing a pennywhistle, whilst the others sang, and they all skipped around in circles of interactive mayhem. Their antics had us all laughing again. Once finished, the King searched his pockets bringing out keepsakes of others he had *found*, before discovering his gift still in his companions mouth—such are the ways of the Fourth.

He leaned forward with a twinkle in his eyes and said, "Child of the Waters of Life, this bonnie wee whistle is made from a branch of the One Tree. Play it at your leisure for fun, and play it in the deepest recess of hell to lighten your spirits and cast the shadows from your heart."

I accepted this gift, as the Emperor sought to move on. Instead, Cayden came forward and presented a short twig saying, "Be pleased to accept this lowly gift, for it is a *twiddling stick*. If ever thy mind goes blank and the way forward is unclear, simply *twiddle* with it, and in due course, a new path will come to you."

He bowed and stepped back as Cayleigh replaced him. She said, "Bonnie wee babe, we will know if either are used in time of need, and will assemble at your side. This is our pledge to you."

Stepping away the Fourth resumed their jig, and enchanted the crowd as they mingled amongst them to delight in their laughter. The Emperor was clearly smitten with affection, but recovered in time to introduce the Third. King Burnam, Prince Gelar, and Princess Myuna came to us and bowed in their way, before offering a Haka of welcome. I thought they were too few for a show, but they were a remarkable sight, as they chanted and moved in perfect synchronicity.

When they finished, Burnam said, "Guardian, Gatekeeper, Child of Life, of Creatures and Plants. We offer ourselves to work with you to understand the lost time, and renew the Earth in time of peril. Our brothers in Australia, New Zealand, our cousins in the Americas and arctic wastes, may have forgotten our more ancient lineage, but together we wish to change this for the good of all humankind. With your permission, my son and daughter would stay and work under your most revered of teachers, Lo Si and Won Long. We would rekindle the flame of unity and brotherhood lost over oceans and æons.

"Cousins, thirty thousand years have passed since our forefathers went their separate ways. The time is long overdue for us to renew our bonds of friendship and common heritage. The Third are dedicated to supporting the Second whilst the breath of life remains within us."

They stood proud, as a tear formed in Jinnie's eye. She nodded in acceptance, she was so moved that words failed her. Burnam took a pendant from around his neck and presented it to our daughter. He bowed and stood back as Gelar presented a similar pendant to Jien Noi as Mother and Sovereign, while Myuna presented another to me.

Burnam said, "These gifts are symbolic of our greater nation. These hand-carved bone pendants are known as 'The Triple Twist'. They depict two new shoots growing together, which represent the joining of our cultures, the bonding of friendship, and love between our people."

The Third bowed and retired, and Horovitz stepped forward. "Permission to speak on behalf of the Last, Guardian?"

I was greatly intrigued. "Granted."

"We are not gifted with the power of fine words, but with the skills of war. Child of those born free, whenever you have need, know we will be standing with you, even unto the depths of hell."

He saluted, and led his men in chorus, "hip-hip," "Hurrah!" "Hip-hip," "Hurrah!" "Hip-hip," "Hurrah!"

I cheered with them and nodded in thanks for a perfect delivery that brought balance to proceedings. The Emperor took the front once more and called for quiet amongst the cheering crowd.

Jien Noi's eyes were shining as she rose unsteadily upon her feet. I reached out to support her, Weid Noi doing likewise on her other side. The crowd stilled when the Empress stood proud before our people.

"True friends, Sisters and Brothers all. Know we were unprepared and are humbled by your bounteous kindness and humanity. This enriches all of us in every aspect of our lives, knowing that somebody cares." She paused to squeeze my hand, which did not go unnoticed.

"Know from this day forth, the Second stand proudly together with all Tribes here today. Whatever the danger we face, however fearful the foe, the Second will be at your side through whatever may come."

She paused, taking time to look directly at each of our guests in turn.

"Know that from this moment onwards, the Tribes of the Ancestors are committed to an unshakable bond for the betterment of us all, and the protection of our great Mother Earth."

Jien Noi finished and we assisted her to sit, as the crowd erupted in wild celebration. Unexpectedly the ground shook as a tremor ran through the earth. People stilled to wonder, but were distracted as a meteorite shower flooded the heavens above. Swiftly, a gust of wind blew, followed by the boom of the ocean upon the volcano walls.

All eyes turned once more to the heavens and we were stargazers all. At length the murmur of voices broke the stillness as the Earth resumed its natural metre. I glanced at the chair and wondered if the Shaman was responsible, there had to be a rational explanation.

Weid Noi encouraged Jien Noi to place the pipe at our baby's lips, and a soft note was heard. The Eleventh reacted immediately and their harmonies increased the sound. The Fourth picked up the tune, and the Twelfth add their bass. We applauded as musicians of the Second spontaneously improvised. Meanwhile, dancers weaved to new threads of artistic interpretation amongst the boundless rhythms of goodwill.

Just then, Dawn came to me with her video camera recording the magic for posterity. Once the impromptu musical ended, she showed me the recording. I was stunned. Dawn had captured the presentation from the moment we emerged from our home.

Dawn said, "I would not have missed this night for the world. It is incredible. Thank you for being you and bringing me here."

Jien Noi refused to leave our guests, stating our child would not approve. Instead, a bed was brought for her and our baby so they might both retire, yet remain a part of the celebrations.

The festivities continued and I found myself in company with the Fourth. I said, "Are your tribe related to Leprechauns?"

Ruaidhrí replied, "To be sure now, me young fella."

In that instant, I saw before me a mischievous leprechaun clad in green, so replied in kind, "Wouldst that be the pot of gold thee offer I?"

"Bejabbers, that lies at the end of the rainbow. Any of the line of Fionn mac Cumhaill would know this truth. He was the greatest Giant that ever walked the Earth, for he stood as tall as the stars above."

Upon hearing this, the Giants roared with laughter, which became exacerbated when Ruaidhrí strutted over to the shaking King of the Twelfth, and admonished him, "Look here me young laddie. Know ye're not too big for me to put across me knee and give a good hiding!"

Rambling was laughing uncontrollably as his hand crashed down upon the earth, narrowly missing the King of the Fourth – who leapt sideways for his life. This had us all in stitches, as the banter continued between the two for some time; Ruaidhrí leaping around to miss the flailing limbs of the Twelfth. Eventually he clambered up on the Giant's chest to admonish him. Finally, Ælthrelntheine came to the rescue.

The Queen of the Eleventh appeared beside the King, and lifted him by the scruff of his neck. Bringing him before her eyes she enquired, "Ruaidhrí Ó Riáin, you would not want to upset me now, would you?"

Ruaidhrí stilled immediately, stating, "Never O great and wondrous lady. I was merely answering the great Guardians question, your greatness of ladyships and all things fair."

She held out her hand, and somewhat regretfully, he placed a small object in the High Queen's hand, adding, "It was so beautiful I only wanted to look at it for a moment."

Ælthrelntheine thanked him for returning her favourite keepsake, before flipping him in the air. She caught him by the silver buckles of his tall black boots, and shook him upside down. All manner of items fell from his green tunic and landed by her feet. She said, "If you have *mislaid* something, think to ask the Fourth if they have *found* it for you."

I looked at hundreds of items on the ground, and said to n'Gnung, "If we go to war, we will send the Fourth to aid the enemy."

I would swear the Fourth were ignorant of all the items they added to the pile before Ælthrelntheine. At last, the Queen of the Eleventh appeared happy, and set the wee man down on his feet.

It was clear Ælthrelntheine found it highly amusing. She whispered to us, "I should not have done that, but it was so very funny, wasn't it?"

I could only agree, as I was still chuckling at the Fourth's expense. Ælthrelntheine, continued, "I scanned them before they came and they will leave with nothing that does not belong to them. I will show you how to do this, as you will need this skill every time you meet them.

"Please accept them for who they are, because they are not bad people at all. It is simply their way. Foremost, they are fierce allies in times of need, and that time is approaching us all quickly."

The party continued until daybreak, when we stood to toast and bid them farewell. Everyone responded in genuine friendship because, if forgiven their foibles, the Fourth were true brethren of us all, and great entertainers.

The Eleventh rose to leave, chaperoning the Fourth like sheepdogs patrolling a flock. I accompanied them to the control centre where we learned the secrets of ensuring nobody entered or left our transporter with more than we acknowledged. This turned out to be a sub-routine of the detection of weapons programme.

No sooner was everything set, than Ælthrelntheine and the Fourth were gone. My constant companion n'Gnung checked the transfer circle immediately, retrieving several trinkets, which we would endeavour to reunite with their rightful owners.

The eventual daylight did not dilute our happiness and shared carnival. As the Moon's beams weakened, so the sun rose and came to renew and sustain life. Our people continued to arrive to look at our daughter. Later the queue subsided; Jinnie retired to our home, and people sought succour in the lazy embrace of Hypnos and his son, Morpheus.

Chapter 11 ~ The Shaman's Apprentice

The first day in the life of Ræm saw me waking next to her, with her mother to her other side. I lay there and watched her for a long time, until at length she stirred, and shortly started to cry. Jinnie was immediately awake, and quickly silenced her with a supply of mother's milk. We shared these magical moments, as looks of love, unbridled happiness, and gentle whispers passed between us.

Weid Noi came to us. She had slept in our spare bedroom, and sat on the bed to watch this wonder of new life. It was obvious to me, she was becoming broody herself, a fact not lost on my wife either. When the baby had taken her fill, Weid Noi took Ræm, saying she would tend to her ablutions. Jinnie whispered, "Her maternal urges are getting stronger. She needs a husband and child of her own. I wonder who she will choose?"

We shared feelings of wonder about our creation—our daughter, and later shared afternoon breakfast on our balcony overlooking the valley, and the remnants of last night's festivities.

I had stayed late, but not as late as most. Weid Noi returned to us in due course, in company with n'Gnung, Ælkræleinnoire, and Dawn, who in turn broke their fast, as Jinnie resumed her role as mother. I watched the radiance of her face, the healthy glow that only accompanies newly birthed mothers. Those moments I treasured.

Jien Noi was conscious of my looking, but ignored it for a while, before turning and catching my eyes directly, "Husband, today I must return to Grimwaldi Rinns. The people expect to see their next Empress. I must formally present her to them." I opened my mouth to protest, but she raised a finger to silence me.

"I need to be at the Palace where staff are ready and waiting to perform their duty, and help look after our daughter. Also, know that if I do not go there, then the people will come here, or not leave. You have much work to do, as the Third are here to stay for a while. Ah-Weid, know I would have you involved with them also, because they want to check on their distant cousins in the worlds of the Last."

Weid Noi acknowledged her, being something they appeared to have already spoken about at length. It made a lot of sense when taken within the greater scheme of things. However, n'Gnung and I cast a look at each other, mouthed to confirm the familiarisation, "ah-Weid?"

Jinnie continued, "Guardian, this is what I need you to do…"

My first duty was to return the buildings we had borrowed, but I had to wait for the remaining citizens to be fed, which delayed my plans, but not my wife's. Again, the buildings survived the transit surprisingly well, and I followed them as soon as the people had been returned to the city, and the builders had confirmed they were serviceable.

The late afternoon was devoted to Imperial duty, followed by a formal reception, and it was late before we were finally able to relax. Later, as I drifted into the welcoming sleep, I sensed, felt, Ræm's small fingers grasp my index finger, and her touch soothed my passage into dreams of the brightest future for us all.

The following day, many again rose late. I awoke to find the familiar warmth of my wife as she slumbered, and watched both her and our child wrestle within their dreams. At length they both came awake and included me in their shared feeding. Oh such a joy for a newly father to behold. That morning I returned to the control room with my closest companions, where we resumed our normal daily activities.

After luncheon, I was sitting with Ælkræleinnoire, discussing our understanding of the Core. Nearby Ju Lo spoke to Da Phai Nai, we being aware Lo Si had suggested Sun Kist offered her services as trainee to the Shaman. The mother replied, "Although I would miss her terribly, she is gifted with the ways of plants, and I am sure she would make an excellent student. What we do not know is if the Shaman wants an apprentice, or if Sun Kist is suitable."

My thoughts turned to the girl herself, as people seemed to be deciding this for her, without her input. I strolled over to the kitchen, seeking a word with Sun Kist alone. When I mentioned the matter, it quickly became obvious she was aware of the proposal, and she had dropped hints to stimulate her parent's interest.

I took her for a walk, just the two of us, to ensure her privacy. She chatted about the baby, our visitors, and said she would love to learn more about the strange beings.

I asked, "What about your own culture and interests? What are your dreams and aspirations?"

"Well, Guardian, I am extremely interested in nature and I spend much of my free time in the Caves of the Ancestor

This in turn drew us into a new line of conversation, as I was letting her lead the direction of our tête-à-tête, and only prompting occasionally.

She said, "Guardian, I am fascinated by the old ways as depicted upon the cave walls. I have spent many hours thinking about what they mean. I have also studied the cooking pictures in great detail, and tried some of the recipes, I doubt you know that."

We had been walking away from the others, not intentionally towards the caves themselves. On the spur of the moment, I asked her to show me what she had learned, and our previously meandering steps took on purpose. Just before we reached the caves, n'Gnung joined us.

He must have read my mind, because he had brought with him one of Dawn's rechargeable flashlights.

Sun Kist went directly to the cave that fascinated her most, the fourth one, and delighted in showing us the drawings that obviously thrilled her the most. With the torch, she was able to go much deeper, and was soon explaining the deeper significance of pictures, elaborating on the recipes and remedies shown.

n'Gnung and I both knew there were many others in the Corridor of Knowledge, and I looked at him quizzically. His eyes tilted towards the rear of the cave, before he flicked his brow upwards. When we reached the back of the cave, she saw the picture of my face in the flying machine, and her brow immediately furrowed, but she remained silent.

With a flick of my eyes towards n'Gnung, I said, "There is more, but it is a secret. If we show you, I need you to promise never to speak of this to anyone, other than my closest companions, the people who are regular diners at my table."

She readily agreed, and we negotiated the drop, and entered the cavern below. When she saw the painting of me on the wall opposite, she said, "Guardian, that is you. How? What is…?"

She was lost for words, and we tried to explain, before crossing the bridge and heading onwards to distract her astonishment. We spent most of the afternoon there, and she pointed out several plants that only she and her mother knew the location of, telling us what they were used for. Her knowledge was extremely good, and she was in her element.

By the time we had visited most of the nature and cooking panels, I had no qualms about her joining the Shaman as her apprentice, if the old crone wanted her. I did not know how we could even contact her, let alone ask her diplomatically.

It was already evening by the time we emerged from the underworld. The moon lighted our way back to the hamlet my home had become. People watched us questioningly, as we returned to their company, many hours having elapsed. It was late as I sat down to eat, so late that only we remained to be served. Da Phai Nai told us she would cook, allowing Sun Kist unexpected respite from the labours of the kitchen.

Da Phai Nai joined us after we had eaten. I said, "Sun Kist was extremely interested in the Caves of the Ancestor, and has visited them many times. Her knowledge of plants is exceptional, and she explained several pictures we did not understand. In view of this, we also showed her the Corridor of Knowledge. Da Phai Nai, I suggest you accompany her next time she goes, but remember, without a true ring bearer, the passageway will be dark, so take some of these new torches with you and do not use the ones that smoke. I will see if Princess Siu Mooyi would care to join you, I have a feeling she will be delighted. Sun Kist, tell us what you discovered."

Sun Kist was instantly talking a'gabble, relating plants she knew of, and ones she did not. Clearly, her eyes had been opened, and her enthusiasm was contagious. Da Phai Nai showed great interest when her daughter described one medicinal preparation depicted in the Corridor of Knowledge, seeming to know the whereabouts of the plant concerned, but not its use. At once, Kay offered to translate the panel, and take her staff to light the way.

As the evening progressed, I cast a glance over to the chair no one had sat in the previous night, unsure if I detected a presence, but there was never anything I could define. Sun Kist was in her element, and noticed nothing, even when she looked in that direction, so I concluded my mind was playing tricks on me.

However, the suspicion had turned my thoughts, and judging the moment, I asked, "Was there anything else that was special for you alone?"

"Yes Guardian, it was the Shaman, because she was able to do things no one else could."

"Go on."

"Guardian, from since I was a little girl, my mother taught me all her skills. I know you may think me a simple cook, but I have also learned much about the way she uses herbs and medicinal plants. I find this fascinating, and have knowledge of this as deep as her now.

"The night of Ræm's birth, the Shaman made a potion that was exceptional and I would love to learn more about what else she can do with other recipes. But my life is that of a simple cook, so this is what I will do, if you will allow me to continue."

She rested. Her dreams confronted with her reality, and I had the distinct impression she thought herself unworthy. My friends and I set about buffing her confidence and self-worth, as Da Phai Nai left to bring nibbles and more beer.

We made a great play of her excellence, and soon her disconsolate look disappeared, being replaced by the Sun as it appeared in her radiant smile, doubtless why she was thus named. Within moments she appeared years younger, her enthusiasm returned to brighten our table.

Sun Kist was animated, and soon ran off to tell her mother the good news—that she could continue to be a cook, and also learn the secrets of plants.

In the meantime, a movement to my left attracted my attention. Turning, I noticed the Shaman in the valley, wearing her guise as an old crone. She was walking towards us with a large and unwieldy bag borne on her back. I rushed to meet her and bowed, thanking her for her efforts of the previous evening, and offered to carry the bag.

She cocked a snoop at me with searing eyes and cackled, before setting down her load, and walked onwards without a backward glance. I may not have been the world's strongest man, but I was physically fit, yet it was all I could do to lift the sack. It felt as if it was full of heavy rocks, a ton of iron perhaps. I just about managed to lift it off the ground and move it a stride, and I was done.

n'Gnung came rushing to me, and together we took a handle each, and this time we managed to move it two paces, before having to put it down. My brother tried to move it on his own, with similar results to my first effort. We looked inside, and all there appeared to be, were a few herbs gathered from the riverbank, and a scattering of leaves. We sat and stared at one another in disbelief; "There's nothing of any weight inside."

The cackle rang louder as we struggled once more to move it, and Dawn came to assist, but we got no farther with our next try. She also looked inside as we sat to rest, and was as confused as we were. We muttered about improbabilities, but in the meantime, Sun Kist came running over to assist our distress.

Arriving she said, "The Shaman told me to help you."

n'Gnung told her to try lifting the bag, which she somehow managed to pick up on her own, without much difficulty. She set it down again and looked at us, before hefting it on her back and carrying it all the way back to the Shaman in one unbroken walk.

We sat and watched, as she stood for a moment before the Shaman, who within a word, turned and left. Sun Kist followed behind, still carrying the bag. As if waiting for Sun Kist to catch up with her, she turned one last time, and reaching for the east wind, struck her gnarled and warped staff to the ground.

Deep within her thrall we heard her words cast upon the whispers of the breeze, which were lost amongst most others:

"Ye sins lie heavy: mortal woe,
Bag but empty, lest thee know,
Weight of dally, heavy though,
For those that feign, but cease to grow."

We all looked at one another, but it was Dawn who finally broke the silence by saying "That was fucking heavy you know?"

"The bag," I enquired, "or the words?"

We could not help but laugh aloud, as the situation was ludicrous. In good spirits, we wandered slowly towards Kay, she alone waiting for our return.

Chapter 11

As we approached the table, Dawn said, "This was a test of the worthy. I guess the Shaman read our thoughts. Perhaps she looked into the future and took matters into her own hands, and this is how it should be?"

We dallied for a time, twenty paces from our table, discussing how heavy the bag was for us all. Da Phai Nai walked over to where we were, and was animated with wonder and pride of knowing her daughter had been chosen to be the next Shaman. It seemed to us, her life's work resulted in that one moment. Her only child had found her true calling in life, and left her maternal refuge.

We talked quietly, leaving Da Phai Nai to watch, as her daughter trudged after her new vocation, with the weight of a neophyte on her shoulders. We all knew that in time this would lighten, and judging the moment n'Gnung and I turned simultaneously to put an arm around each of her shoulders. We had not planned this, and acted independently, but it was no surprise to either of us, that we acted in tandem.

Her shoulders relaxed as she sank into our brotherly hold, and she struggled to say thank you, which we were unworthy of. We held her between us for a minute or so, as the shapes receded into the distance, and then they were gone.

It was in that instant that Da Phai Nai realised her life's travail had left the nest, and was now her own woman in the making. The success of her enduring motherhood collided head-on with the loss of her daughter.

Her shoulders heaved, and she convulsed one last time. Within that moment, she was renewed, her heart firmed. Shaking herself free of our support, she rounded on us in her familiar way, "Now just what do you two, good-for-nothings want with an old woman? I would tan your hides before I let you take advantage of me."

We each kissed our belligerent friend on the cheek; it was so good to have her thoughts back with us. She proceeded to chase us away, trying successfully to beat our behinds with her punishing slaps of broom. We made it back to the safety of the restaurant before she calmed and said, "Four beers it is then."

Dawn said, "She gives off this persona of being such a mother hen, when underneath her cacti-like barbs, she is really a little girl inside. Her offensive words are the opposite of what she really means. Well done you two, and you Kay. Now I begin to properly understand her. This is her proudest day as a mother, it's obvious."

We lingered out of respect, as Da Phai Nai lumbered over to us with four fresh beers in her one hand, for such are the dextrous wiles of practiced innkeepers. Placing them on the table before us, she sought to turn, but I called her to wait and rising to stand, said, "Da Phai Nai, we toast your daughter Sun Kist." I raised my tankard to her. n'Gnung stood likewise and confirmed, "I toast the wise mother of Sun Kist, our next Shaman."

Da Phai Nai stilled, as Dawn also stood and picked up her beaker of ale and joined the toast, "I would drink to a fine mother and daughter. To a new woman who will have need of her own wise mother's counsel along the path her life has now chosen."

Kay also stood, but was more enigmatic, "Here's to the future, whatever that may hold."

We shouted "Cheers, to Da Phai Nai! God's blessing's to Sun Kist!" Clashing our breakers together, we drank down the beer and slammed the empties back onto the table. Without waiting, we bowed to her in unison and retook our seats

Tears fell once more from the old woman's eyes, as she slumped into a vacant chair. Having lost her daughter to her chosen future moments earlier, she realised she now had four more children to look after. In time, her heart stilled, and was at peace once more. The emotion diminished, and she smiled again.

She spoke aloud, "You children are indeed my truest brothers and sisters. I know deep within my heart, I will never be alone within your company."

I knew she was on the verge of saying more, but within a breath, her old fire re-ignited, as if to cover her wound. "Ahha! I know your games. You are trying to drink me out of house and home, just like a mess of Ddwyrth. I better get you a large barrel."

n'Gnung rose first, a fraction before I did, our thoughts aligned. We bade her stay with us at table, and brought a small barrel of beer for ourselves, and the best wine for her. n'Gnung departed at once, and returned with Lo Si.

The five of us offered him implausible explanations of what had just taken place. I was not sure any of us truly understood the Shaman at all, but we gallantly evocated our best of discourse. In time, Da Phai Nai rejoined us in the spirit of the moment, drinking the wine at her leisure. Lo Si encouraged her, his eyes shining with obvious pride.

We knew she kept this elixir for special occasions, and as her tongue loosened, so she added her own thoughts on what had come to pass. "I miss her so badly already, yet I know I must let her go. I must allow her the freedom to become something far more than I, we," she gripped Lo Si's hand before finishing her sentence, "can imagine her being.

Chapter 11

"I already did that with Lo Si. Is this to be the sum of my life? Giving the heart of me away for others' benefit, and now my Daughter also?"

Kay comforted Da Phai Nai, gentled her to stand, and cocooned her away, her words becoming lost as they left us. "There is a special technique I know of, one that calms the wrought heart, soothes the spirit, and massages the flesh, the mind. Come, you are in need of Elven Healing. You must feel so proud, yet heartbroken…"

Chapter 12 ~ Awakening Ancient Powers

Over breakfast, Ælkræleinnoire and I discussed our strategy regards unlocking the secrets of the Core. I was not sure how my interaction with the Shaman had affected me; perhaps my thoughts were clearer.

Notwithstanding, since the Queen of the Eleventh had touched my brow, I had a far greater grip on the complexities of mental communication. I was not all that good at it, but I could speak to Kay most of the time.

She clarified, "We cannot invade another person's mind with our thoughts without permission. That's the problem with Quinn. He is highly resistant of our probing, and he is also adept at probing others.

"Jackie, between family and close friends, telepathy can seem like an automatic process, and the other's thoughts simply appear in the mind. But I cannot reach you, or you I, if say one of us is totally distracted, or refuses contact. All Ælthrelntheine did was to show you where this mental doorway is, you still have to learn to use it properly."

"Surely you could have done the same thing?"

"Not so Guardian, that is a power of the Ring of the Protector. My own ring is almost as powerful, but not quite, like the ring the Gatekeeper wears it has restrictions. Sometimes only the ultimate ring of power will suffice."

n'Gnung interrupted us, "Guardian, Kay, are you all right? Why are you staring at one another?"

Kay's smile broke with jubilant release. I had not realised we had been communicating without using words. It came as a great shock to me, something she gently teased me about, before using spoken words, "Jackie. You have made brilliant progress. I think that today we should focus both our minds, together, let's reinstate the Captain's day room. That is where the interface we need to use should be located."

We began work with a rush of expectant intensity, but soon discovered we hit the same old problem, we could not complete the command telepathically with the Core. She said, "This is an enigma. I have enough knowledge of the Ancestor's language, but wear the wrong ring. You wear the right ring, but do not have the language. Let us merge minds as best we can, and see if this gives us the breakthrough."

We tried several times, until Kay received a message back, which she spoke aloud, although I had already heard it echo into my own mind in translation, "Security override. Hostile environment. Operator error. Unknown subject."

I had good knowledge of computer systems, something I knew Ælkræleinnoire and n'Gnung did not. I sat back and clasped my hands behind my head deep in thought. In time I spoke into their murmuring, "We have the correct access thoughts, the key if you prefer. This must be you, Kay, as I do not have the language skills. What I believe is happening, is that although I do have the correct power to open the lock, the security system is picking up the command comes originally from you. Does that make any sense?"

We discussed the matter briefly, and arrived at a consensus; Kay needed the correct authority, and it should work. We tried again, using all combinations of rings and workstation, but the message from the Core came back the same. In frustration, I decided to break for early lunch, and unusually, ordered a beer. n'Gnung joined me when I stated, "I need to look at this problem from a different perspective, and the alcohol may give me a whiff of intuition."

Da Phai Nai overheard my remark, and scolded, "Whatever will you think of next! Any excuse to drink when you should be working." The resultant laughter brought us release, and others joined our table. We were first to arrive, and last to leave.

When we were alone once more, we returned to discussing our problem with the Core. The beers had loosened our imaginations, and tongues. This provided many implausible resolutions, none of which upon considered examination, made complete sense.

There were a few ideas we considered worth trying, but when we did, the Core responded the same as usual. n'Gnung usually added brief insights as we worked, but this time he remained silent and watched. After our last failed attempt, I was feeling irritated, testy, and hauled myself to my feet with a groan of a sigh. I walked away, seeking to divine inspiration from the walls around.

I knew we were so close, but a whisker away. n'Gnung spoke into the ether, "You have tried it with my ring, and also the Ring of the Ancestor, yet the Core rejects one or both of you. I believe it is Kay. We are no longer certain your Elven ring was used in this control room, ever. There can only ever be one accepted Captain. Have you tried using the ring Jien Noi wears?"

"The ring of the First Officer. Brilliant — that must be it."

Jien Noi attended our call, with Ræm clutched to her bosom. The results were the same. Eventually insight hit me, "Kay, you have never been accepted by our transporter, have you?"

She looked at me strangely, as I explained about the induction process, "Why, no, never." That she already had access was a problem I did not wish to consider.

We went through the acceptance procedure; Ælkræleinnoire stood in the transfer circle, and used the Gatekeeper's ring. Nothing happened. We were rocked by disappointment and surprise. Our minds were slow to return to the problem at hand.

n'Gnung said, "Guardian, there can only be one resolution. What is different about the Queen of the Eleventh Elect?"

Our eyes searched his, discarding the obvious instantly. I raised an eyebrow in his direction, and he smiled, "What if the ring Ælkræleinnoire wears does not belong here, but is recognised?"

He was referring to her Elven ring of power, and I said to her, "Kay, take off your ring and try placing it in the centre of the transporter circle."

Her reply was instant, "I cannot, only my mother's ring can remove it. Our rings work that way, it cannot be removed."

"Kay, at least try. What have we got to lose?"

She was correct, the ring would not come off. Perplexed, I said offhand, "Try placing your ring finger in the centre of the circle."

Verging on a fit of temper, the first I had ever noticed, she jabbed her finger at the centre point, grabbed her ring, and pulled, saying, "See, I told you so, this ring won't…"

Her words faltered, as her gaze moved to her finger and thumb. Within was held her ring. Her face contorted in astonishment, the first time she had ever been able to remove the ring since she became Queen Elect. She tried to speak, but her thoughts and words had already left her. I said, "Slide it down into the centre, and let us solve this riddle, and be done with it."

She obeyed, almost without a thought of her own, and moments later, Jien Noi shouted from the control room. "Guardian, you are needed at the Captain's console."

I raced back, and pressed the rune I knew to mean accept. The transporter lit up and Kay disappeared into the acceptance procedure, before reanimating seconds later.

I hurried back to her, and she was amazed. Her mind appeared slightly clouded, but she put on her ring once more, and even still standing within the transport, could not remove it again. She looked up, clearly confused and said, "I need to be at peace for a while. Later you will find me at the old banyan tree near the village on the shore."

Her head drooped as she tried to recover her known reality. n'Gnung said, "I will attend her, and ensure she is not disturbed."

I sent my closest on their way, and felt like I needed another drink. This was so frustrating. My mind filled with selfish thoughts, as I twiddled my wife's ring of power, and handed it back to her. The thought of being with her, and Ræm, gave me impetus.

We transported at once, and after dinner, I lay beside them, careful not to disturb our daughter. As if sensing my presence, Ræm reached out and gripped my little finger in her hand, wrapping her fingers around it. She was so small and fragile. I drifted off to sleep, waking periodically when Jinnie and Ræm did, our family complete.

The next morning, I did not see either Ælkræleinnoire or n'Gnung, until the latter arrived to warn me, "Kay is in a strange mood."

We left for the control centre, and she appeared moments later. I was about to speak, when she cast a determined look at me, "It is time to finish this thing. Come Guardian, let's unlock the mystery."

Kay was all business and totally preoccupied. We went through the same procedures we had been through many times before, and with Kay's mental assistance, initiated reinstatement the Captain's day room in place of the larger meeting room. There was no rejection, and I felt elated, but there was no acceptance either. I was aware Ælkræleinnoire was speaking through my mind, direct to the Core, and felt her weaken. I was about to break the connection, when the room swirled about us. n'Gnung gawped.

Moments later, reality returned, and everything looked the same, except Kay was keeled over at her console. I ran to her, and noted she had a pulse, but was unconscious. I took her in my arms and hollered for us to be sent to a healer. n'Gnung took control, and sent us to the room she used in our house. The Keeper of Life appeared at her side moments later, with my brother as shepherd.

Physically she was fine, and breathing regularly. However, she appeared to be comatose. Our staff would watch over her and attend to her needs, but apart from rest, there was little we could do for her. We considered sending her to the Eleventh, but her relationship with them seemed to be strained. Regardless, we doubted they could do anything we could not.

n'Gnung and I returned to the control room, and went directly to inspect the new room. The large meeting room had morphed into a new purpose, some items we had left inside were resting on the floor. The door could be locked from either side, or left open, and the area reminded me of a Captain's cabin on an old galleon. There was a meeting table to one side, and behind where my console in the main room would be. Beyond was a small kitchenette, fronting a bathroom. On the other side of the room were two large workstations that faced each other. The second was bigger, and faced towards the door. The 'L' shaped layout continued behind the consoles, with a relaxation area, and through another door, a bedroom. It was all neatly arranged and ideal for work, or a power nap.

n'Gnung did not understand everything, and I was about to show him what I had deduced, when he thumped the wall where the 'L' extended towards the bedroom. "What do you think may be on the other side of this wall, Guardian?"

"Let's see if we can find out."

We checked out the control room, and everything was as was, all except that adjacent to the door to the stairs, a new door had appeared on the back wall. The new doorway was typically framed and arched, but unusually, a motif was set to the side of the door, not within it. I pushed my ring finger into the motif, and the door vanished. Before us lay a short corridor, about the same length as the Captain's ready room, which ended at a blank wall. As if a continuation of the staircase top landing, the doors on our left opened to reveal storerooms. The opposing wall was blank, except for a door nearest the control room.

This had a rune that was not glowing, and a motif, again set to the side. I pressed my ring into the depression, and the rune lit. I pressed the mark, and the door disappeared.

n'Gnung and I walked into a small box of a room, about eight feet square. Immediately recalling another of similar specifications and size, we went inside, and turning, smiled. A strangely familiar panel was set to both sides of the door, echoing another I had seen once before. It was set horizontally, five layers high, and many widthways. Two runes were glowing, and many others were not. Premonition gripped us, n'Gnung pressed the upper rune, there was a flash, just like a transportation, and we were in the same, but different room, a motif in front of us, and another behind. We passed through the one in front, and came into a corridor.

There was no light, not even when our eyes acclimatized. By feel, we made it back to where we thought we had arrived, after establishing it was an underground corridor. Once again, a wall of rock greeted us, a dead end. This time we did not have Kay's staff to see by. n'Gnung said, "In future, I'm always carrying a torch."

We spent many minutes trying to determine where the motif was. It had to be central in the facing wall, and at about eye level. By linking arms we arrived at the general location, and by the feel of pull on my ring, we eventually got back inside the box.

I was not surprised to find three runes glowing beside the door, only the bottom one was in the same position as before. I pressed it, and moments later we apparated in another small room. Gingerly we poked our heads outside, and found ourselves at the beginning of the Corridor of Knowledge. We 'high-fived'. Now it all made sense.

Retreating, n'Gnung pressed the top, glowing rune. We found ourselves, as expected, back in the corridor next to our control room. We were making progress, but it felt as if we were trapped within a bowl of setting porridge, battling to take the next step.

Chapter 12

After a brief check of operations, we retired to my new day room. It took short shrift to find the direct interface with the Core. I had to try. We had searched for this for what felt like æons.

I was amazed by what I discovered, confirmation this was the remains of a spacecraft. I knew my mind was overloading with information, and tried to rip the headphone-like appendages away. I remember shouting to n'Gnung, "We have to repair the ship."

My world went blank.

Chapter 13 ~ Death Becomes Us

I came back to life one day later than Ælkræleinnoire. Most were delighted and celebrating our return, but some admonished us for doing what we did. My bond with Kay deepened. I could not explain—it was extra-worldly. Only we knew, understood implicitly what we had endured, and we had both come out the other side. Despite our promises to behave and not take risks in future, we both acknowledged it was bound to happen again, many times. We were both driven to understand the all of it.

Kay and I returned to the control room in the afternoon, chaperoned by n'Gnung. We spent a while catching up with the controllers, but had missed little, despite being comatose for two days. I showed Kay the new transport lift, and we soon confirmed it gave access to the corridors we had discovered, one to the Corridor of Knowledge, the other adjacent. When we assembled to return, Kay stopped me pressing the rune, and said, "Control room," in the Ancestor's language. We arrived at once, and now knew systems could also be voice activated.

We moved on and toured the new day room. It was not long before I sat at the Captain's console, with Kay opposite. n'Gnung sat at the meeting table keeping an eye on us. I showed her the interface device, and we both used it momentarily, simply passing the headset from one to the other, before discovering a second set.

I looked at Kay "You were correct. Before I stayed under too long, I confirmed this is a spacecraft, and it needs repairing. That's what the Core told me. I have no idea how to find the rest of the craft, never mind how to restore it. I think this is where we begin."

Our first break came towards the end of the week, when we discovered the entire spacecraft had emergency landed, and had remained virtually in the condition of its arrival on planet Earth. The Ancestor had made repairs enough to maintain the crafts integrity, shut down all systems, except to reinstate the control room and access corridor to the pool. We presumed he had become reconciled to living on Earth for the remainder of his years.

The next week the Core informed us the craft was currently powered by gamma rays from the sun, which the shield fed to the Core. Presumably, there was some sort of energy conversion and advanced battery system. That was the best analogy I could comprehend. I knew the process and technology used was alien, and perhaps impossible for me to understand. We also discovered the language training program, which we both studied.

During the following week, we each concentrated on different aspects, and made steady progress. One afternoon I was monitoring

Kay, when she refused to come out of the Core at the allotted time. I stayed with her mind, ready to physically break the connection by removing the headset, when she did so herself.

She was groggy, n'Gnung bringing her a glass of water. We all knew she would soon need to lie down and recuperate properly. Before we left for my home, she gathered herself and said, "This place is divided into areas, based upon sections, a bit like a modular design, but quite complex. Apart from the Core not having processed me, there was a second reason we could not bring this room back. It was not fit for human habitation."

"Damn! You are right. I remember one new room at the end of the Corridor of Knowledge, it had no light or air. There could also have been contamination, perhaps radioactive or biological. This fits perfectly. Systems needed to be restored, the area or module made safe, before it can be remoulded. Once that is done, we are allowed to incorporate it. I have no idea how this works, but that explains the unexpected delay we experienced."

Kay agreed and added, "One more thing before I lie down. The entire ship needs to be remodelled in this way. To do that, we need to turn the power storage capacity to maximum. I have no idea how it is possible to store gamma ray energy, but I have the feeling we will find out. This is so exciting, but I must sleep at once."

We saw her to her room, but quickly returned to the Captain's day room. I managed to turn the storage capacity from essential minimum to maximum, but had to withdraw; mental communication with the Core was too demanding. Our days continued in similar vein, occasionally we would stay connected for slightly too long, but the after-effects lessened as we progressed. The length of time of our interactions with the Core also increasing slowly, if steadily.

n'Gnung was also included, although a long way behind us. His aim was simply to learn the ancient language, as sometimes Kay and I unintentionally spoke in the tongue of the Ancestors. He stayed under for seconds at first, but by concentrating solely on the language program we had discovered, he came on quickly.

I am sure whatever Fates exist, must collude to stymie us at times of greatest inconvenience. One such time was our final preparations for remodelling the habitable parts of the craft. Others may have thought us withdrawn, but we were merely focused. Everything was finally in place, but our energy had been sapped by the last interaction.

Kay and I rested, before the final phase began: remodelling of the spacecraft. We had enough power in storage, and several drones had been renovated and reactivated. We were at the point of pushing the button, but just needed to rest for a short while before instigating the final series of commands.

n'Gnung brought us drinks, and we all took coffee, he having worked out how to make the device in the kitchenette provide it.

We relaxed; it was chill-time before the big event. n'Gue entered, "Guardian, Queen Elect, the Empress and your mother have requested your presence at the Imperial Palace. As I speak, both Sar Tan clones are being prepared for trial in public, and will be executed forthwith. You must leave within a few minutes, and I will return for you shortly to escort you."

My eyes locked with Kay's, and we gulped hot coffee. We both knew that once instructed, repairs would continue in our absence. It took us about twenty minutes, but we set the Core to begin full restoration, working from the control room outwards, section by section, module by module.

n'Gnung had strong, sweet coffee cooling for us when we came out, and we drank it as quickly as possible, knowing time was short. As if on cue, n'Gue again came to the door, "Guardian, Kay, your presence is required now on the Imperial ledge."

We hurriedly finished our drinks, transported to my home to change into our official costumes, and moments later appeared for the trial and execution. The Sar Tan clones spat at me as soon as I joined the party, and proffered a seething torrent of verbal vitriol in my direction. I smiled contentedly back at the bitches, and knew I could instinctively tell them apart. That was the strangest feeling—they may have started life the same, but real life had happened to them since. Knowing most about the clones from Elven interrogations, the Queen of the Eleventh was given dispensation to act as prosecutor.

The clones were irascible, challenging and evasive by turns, both claiming to be the real one. I'm not sure where my insight came from, probably from within, or was it the Core? There came a pause and I felt emboldened to rise and state, "You are Sar Tan's clone number two, the one that interfered with our transporter."

Turning on the other, I said angrily, "You are clone one, the one that I know, the one who murdered the Empress. You replaced the real human Sar Tan years ago, didn't you?"

The clone rose to the bait, and openly mocked everyone, elaborating on her deception of the Second into believing she was the original person. She gloated on her poisoning of the last Empress, and extolling details hitherto unknown, or only surmised. Ælthrelntheine encouraged her in her outrage.

Chapter 13

The clone finished her outburst by saying, "You will not live long, any of you. Soon the Great Ogre will awaken, and when he does, he will kill every last one amongst you. However, he will bring me back to life!"

Her cackle chilled the air. Her eyes darting, maddened with glee, in full view of the population. They booed, calling for blood.

The Empress walked to the front and raising her arms, declared, "Sar Tan's clones, by their own admission, rejoice in the murder of the last Empress, my mother. And also the crime of treason, by working and colluding with our enemy. The penalty for each is death.

"Bring them before me!"

No execution had been carried out for decades, although Sar Tan clone number one had almost contrived to have Jien Noi executed. The sentence was usually carried out by slitting the throat, as with an animal. Beheading was rumoured to have been have been used in the past. The crowd waited expectantly for the Empress to speak, on tenterhooks of an execution.

"Clone number two, you wilfully compromised two of our transporters, and allowed the enemy access to our homeland. You are responsible for the deaths of one thousand, six hundred and thirty seven Islanders. You actively supported the enemy by transporting them to kill our people. I pronounce you guilty of high treason. Tomorrow you will be beheaded and your remains thrown to the scavengers of earth, air, and sea. So-be-it decreed!"

Cursing, the clone was led away. The Empress smiled as she rounded on Sar Tan, the clone we all knew.

"Sar Tan, you have revelled in the murder of my mother, and were solely responsible for initiating the anomaly that allowed enemy forces to breech our island defences. We now know you were cloned many years ago, and lay in wait like a serpent, ready to strike and devour your host, our nation. You are despicable!

"You wilfully tried to deny me my birth right, have me executed! But most unforgivable is the fact that you murdered my mother, the Empress. I pronounce you guilty of High Treason. I will now begin your execution, although it may take a while. Like for like! Guards, bind her, open her mouth. Sar Tan, you will drink this draft in celebration of your timely death!"

We were all stunned. At her signal, the King of Forest Meade stepped forward and handed a bottle gourd to the Empress. She undermined Sar Tan's remaining sanity; "You forced my mother to drink this, which ended her life. It was a hideous death, one I now submit you to endure as recompense."

The clone screamed, knowing exactly how agonising and prolonged death by mercury poisoning was. Her mouth was forced open by the guards, and her head yanked back. Jien Noi looked into the witch's eyes, as she slowly poured the silver liquid into her mouth. There was a lot of it, the remains of what we had rescued from the latrine. Sar Tan was forced to swallow it all.

The Clone was led away, cursing all and sundry as she resisted. We all knew her death would take a while. Jien Noi stood with arms raised to face the cheering crowd, "People. Sar Tan's clone inflicted on my mother this same death. It will take until tomorrow until this wretch becomes enfeebled. Any that hold a grudge, please sharpen your blade, for tomorrow, both worthless lives will become extinct.

"Tonight we celebrate the justice of these vile creatures' execution. Tomorrow, I will remove their heads!"

Jinnie immediately turned her back, and walked resolutely away. That evening she was filled with rage, venom I had never known before. She would wander out to check on the slow progress of her adversary's death. It became a fixation for her, one only Ræm was capable of breaking. I banned her from taking our daughter to watch the clone's death throws — it was ghastly.

The next morning it completed. The bodies of both clones were carried down and strapped to two large wooden blocks in the middle of the square. Their heads were secured upon another. A gap of several inches in between, exposing their necks: throats. They were both still alive, one foaming at the mouth, the other manic with hatred.

The Empress withdrew the Imperial Sword from its scabbard, and played for the crowd. Everyone close enough to see, knew that each Sar Tan clone was conscious, one struggling against her bindings, the other remaining alive if only by the feeblest of pulse.

What happened next, few will speak of, even in deepest confidence. With one swoop of flashing blade, then a second, Jien Noi removed the clones' heads. The execution was complete. The heads were propped to look at the body, and left for the population to show their disdain. I am not sure if this was fact, and I do not want to know. But I was told ever single islander, plunged a blade into whatever remained of the corpses.

The mood was sour. There was no worth in the act, or the day, except the bittersweet of revenge, complete. We did what was expected. I plunged my ancient dagger into both hearts, and walked away at once. For the population, it was redemption.

I had been so preoccupied; I had failed to notice a newcomer amongst the throng. I turned back at once when I heard someone declare, "That's what ye get if ye cross me and my friends."

I turned around to see Aroweena plunging her sword into one clone, as Owain was removing his battle-axe from splitting the other's torso open. He looked up gleefully, "Ahhh, Guardian, me wee laddie, the

Chapter 13

Ddwyrth needed to see this one off, personally. I'm headed off to the shore of the Outlands. Anyone care to join me? Killing always gives me a large thirst, and I fancy shark steaks today."

In my lifetime, I had only ever met two people who could change a moment, simply by their presence. One was Da Phai Nai, and the other, Owain. His hearty smile and call to action, instantly changed the mood, and so, to the shore we duly followed.

Chapter 14 ~ The Whispering Wind

That night the release was bounteous. Owain and Rambling talked aside for a long time, whilst Aroweena and Gung Loi resumed their female fighting intrigues. Llwydd of the Seventh was as bad as Owain regards drinking, and excellent company.

The following morning began slowly, the true purpose of Owain's visit becoming apparent. They had at last broken through Theodosius Quinn's mental defences, and garnered useful information. In particular, the Himalayan complex could only be entered using the Ring of the Warrior. The Eleventh that had looked into his mind arrived near midday, and the stage was set for drawing up battle plans to return the Giants to their long dispossessed homeland.

The conjecture was the stronghold was likely unmanned and defenceless, but we could not take the chance. Quinn had disclosed information, which varied each time his mind was probed. However, his words had been catalogued, as had a plan of the Himalayan headquarters. The Ddwyrth were talking tactics to anybody that would listen, the Eleventh were concerned about using higher powers, and many others joined in the round to add their pennyworth.

Kay metaphysically knocked, and I allowed her into my thoughts, I was getting much better at mental communications. "Jackie, we need to go and check on the Core. We may have missed something. Come with me, it will not take long, and anyway, these people will talk themselves to death over good intentions. Let's do something that matters."

I agreed at once, but before I could rise, I heard a new voice, one I had never heard mentally before. It said, "Me too."

I looked at n'Gnung immediately, and congratulated him. He replied, "Guardian, we usually talk without words anyway." His eyebrow rose in emphasis before he concluded, "This is simply another way, but I will never be any good at it."

I replied, "We'll see about that." I took him over to the Queen of the Eleventh, and asked her to assist my closest friend. They touched brows, and I knew, in time, my brother would get it. Kay and I checked on progress, but the Core and associated systems had little for us to attend to, and we did not tarry. Nevertheless, the exercise had moved us away from the distasteful events of yesterday, allowing our emotions, our perceived reality to move on.

We returned to the village on the shore, just in time to witness a shark-fishing competition between Owain and Rambling. People were laying wagers on which would be first to bring a shark to shore. The betting was in fruit and for fun, and the trophy, a tankard of ale. Gelar and Myuna of the Third had joined our socialising only occasionally, but were there that evening. They were given the honour to stand on the beach, the distance between them marking the start and finish line.

Da Phai Nai stood to one side, and dropped her arm, signalling the competition had begun. Rambling made the early pace, but was later hampered by his great size. Cheers erupted when it became evident Owain had caught the first shark. He battled back through the water, still with several hundred yards to walk before gaining the shoreline.

Farther out into the lagoon, Rambling had finally managed to secure his prize, and used his long strides to close the gap on Owain. The cheering of onlookers grew more intense, each rooting for his or her favourite. n'Gnung and I watched intently, knowing it would be an extremely close call, but we both thought Rambling would make it to the finish line first. We had not counted upon Owain turning to look behind him. He started to run immediately. n'Gnung observed with his customary paucity of spoken word. A raised eyebrow, a deft flick of the head were all we needed to understand each other's deeper thoughts.

Owain's pace increased as his body came clear of the restricting water, and he began to inch away. Rambling increased his stride, and continued to close the gap. It was going to be too close to call. Technically, Owain's foot landed across the finish line first, but Ramblings, stride was well in front of Owain's mark. The sharks were both large, and about the same length. Ælthrelntheine was asked to adjudicate, having returned from an Elven meeting. She diplomatically declared a tie, which was most befitting.

Rambling sank to his knees in the sand, having clearly enjoyed the competition. Owain gave him a brotherly hug, seemingly mindless of the sharks' ravening jaws just inches away from their embrace. One snapped a little too close to Owain, who immediately stepped back and bashed it on the snout several times, before it stilled amid a rhetoric of Ddwyrthen curses.

The morrow brought with it rain. The dismal feel of damp discomfiture muted what I had hoped would be a great morning. Diluting with raindrops a day of consequence, to be less than what it truly signified. Breakfast was hushed and quiet, as we all allayed our mood to the weather, which increased with antipathy as storm clouds rolled and lightening began to target our island slopes.

I felt a mental tug, and instinctively turned to look at Rambling. He was sitting with his wife and child at a table we had made for them. He was looking at me, and I went over to speak with him. His demeanour matched the weather, dark and gloomy. A wound that festered within them un-assuaged, had replaced their laughter of the previous evening.

"Rambling, tell me what is bothering you. I would like to help."

The corners of his mouth creased with a rueful smile, and with a look to his family, he said, "Thank you Guardian. Know we are trapped here. We cannot leave because the spies and devices of the Great Ogre search for us. We were almost caught several times on our way here."

He stared wistfully at the sea for a few moments before continuing, "We need to return to our ancestral home, reclaim the long-lost Ring of the True Heart, and rebuild our civilization. Once we are in full control, the Great Ogre will have no purchase on our land.

"There has been much support from all tribes, but we deeply yearn to see our homeland for the first time, and come into our true heritage. You are aware we have all spoken openly about this, even last night we worked on invasion plans. What I need is to set a time for the invasion, and make this real. Otherwise, we will all still be talking about it in years to come. My heart cannot take that strain any longer. Please Guardian, help us to help ourselves regain what was lost."

I returned to my table, full of worry and understanding. I spoke openly with my companions, Owain being the first to realize the need for words be replaced with action. We arbitrarily set a date for the invasion to begin — the summer solstice, which was only two months away. The Giants gracefully accepted. We were waiting to gain more information from Theodosius Quinn. The man was broken, but had not revealed all he knew, we were all certain of that. The invasion would begin as soon as he had told us everything about the Himalayan complex, the one we knew he had used to foil our shield.

I heard Kay speak into my mind, and looked up to see her eyes staring at me. It was time to leave, and do what we alone could accomplish, on this most miserable day. n'Gnung rose with us, and we three transferred to the control room to make preparations.

Ælkræleinnoire began the session by taking her usual chair opposite my console in the ready room. She took a deep breath to draw in qi energy within herself, before beginning work. After five minutes interfacing with the Core, her face looked up in shock. She stated, "There is something here I have never known before, but have suspected for a long time. Guardian, I can sense the original design of this structure, nevertheless there is something hidden from me yet."

We watched, observing her face as she tensed, and later, relaxed within her mental review. Abruptly her white eyes flared wide, "Where is the rest of this place? It is my belief that this is only one half, of one of the original craft of the Ancestor. There are inconsistencies, leading to only one conclusion. The rest of this spaceship is somewhere else.

"What if the spacecraft had split in two during the crash landing on Earth, say for self-preservation? Another concern is that if the craft was crewed by thirteen people, why did only one, the Captain, survive?"

I replied, "Excellent, our answers lie elsewhere. Come."

We went to the Halfway House, stood at the bottom of the slope and showed Kay and n'Gnung. I said, "At first presumed this gorge was channelled by a meteor strike. The Ancestral doors that lead nowhere are relatively nearby. The Corridor of Knowledge is just over there."

I pointed in the general direction, before completing my statement, "If this gouge in the surface were caused by a spacecraft arriving, then the rest of it lies inside those rocks. I have no idea how that could occur, shielding perhaps. Any ideas?"

We came up with many explanations, but the clue itself remained indented, like a livid welt, enduring and vital. We entered the farthest cave and walked the corridors once more, this time focused upon our temporal understanding of the 3D relationship. Our presumed schematic matched my hypothesis.

Once certain of our interpretation of events, we walked and exited the fourth cave, coming into the Valley of Knowledge and across to my home. We used the woodpile transporter to enter the high observation cave, and I pointed at the plateau above the control centre. "That lake and the hill nearest us are not natural features. They are like the divot of the Halfway House, but this time masked by a river and lake."

n'Gnung spoke into our new understanding, "So, the control module ends up over there, near your home. The rest of it, whatever *it* is, was, ends up buried within the rocks over there. I know you both want to put 'it' back together again, but how?"

We adjourned to the shore, where the Ddwyrth were in fine form. Owain took every opportunity to banter with Da Phai Nai. Behind his back, we concluded there could be something beginning between them.

Kay was full of mischief the next morning, and choosing her time to perfection, when Da Phai Na was serving, she voiced our thoughts. "Owain, you unscrupulous blaggard, did you sleep well last night. I looked for you, and you were missing."

I think Owain blushed, before he regained his equilibrium and answered, "Well you see now, me pretty, I was a little concerned about one of them there serving wenches—so being a true gentleman, took it upon me good sen to escort her to her bedchamber, for she was not feeling at all well. I thought it my duty to attend to her needs."

"Your needs more likely Owain, you old goat." Everyone turned to look at the speaker, Aroweena, who was chuckling knowingly.

We burst out laughing, increasing his discomfiture. He received a clip round the ear from Da Phai Nai. She stated quite emphatically, "Ladies, Gentlemen … and Ddwyrth, that is none of your business!"

She pirouetted and sauntered off with her head held high. Owain's eyes lingered on her retreating frame for longer than they should. We withdrew, believing our suspicions confirmed. I raised my glass to him, and although it was only water, he returned tribute in kind.

Before our tankards were returned to the table, Ælfreisia, the High Queen's sister appeared nearby. Her manner was gracious, but also overly endearing, fawning even. It was plain to see she was after something. In due course, we learned this was access to the ancient scripts of the Ancestor, written indelibly on our island walls.

We agreed to welcome her party, without fixing a definite time, or day. After Ælfreisia departed, Ælkræleinnoire was elusive. She was long withdrawn, her head in a cosmic world. Elucidating after completing her thoughts, she offered with a sweep of her hand; "With the return of the Twelfth, she is up to something. Please know she is not evil, but a true supporter of all our causes. It's just that she, like many of my kind, is seeking an impossible grail."

Rambling agreed at once, and confided, "There is a game being played here by some of the Eleventh, which we should monitor."

Ælkræleinnoire was nonplussed, unfazed by his comment and replied languidly, "That would be them, the so-called learned of our society, seeking the Tablet of Enlightenment, which is not here."

The statement piqued Rambling's curiosity, and he enquired, "You know where it is?"

She stopped momentarily to look at him, lock his eyes to her own. She uttered sincerely; "No. But I have an idea how to find it."

For the others at the table, she looked up and added, "It is an ancient stone, one rumoured to explain the steps to enlightenment. Nonetheless, it is also written that, within the true heart of every creature, the kernel of revelation resides — would we but acknowledge it. Many of the Eleventh have dedicated their lives, their entire existence even, to its discovery. I consider it a ploy, one a parent may play on an inquisitive child. The truth will out, but from within, in this instance."

Rambling concurred, and it was plain to see, his respect for this most unlikely Eleventh grew appreciably. "Kay," he enquired, "Please indulge me a moment. Tell me what you think of this stela."

He motioned us to follow him to the beach, where in untainted sand, he proceeded to draw a mass of runes within a rectangular frame. He focused Kay's attention on one particular grouping of characters, which Kay thought about for some time, before elucidating, "The meaning is not clear." She read the marks with a purpose, before weighing the significance in her understanding.

"This would appear to say that the Ancestors came from the stars. Yet, it does not make sense within the context in which it this written. I would guess it actually means the Ancestors knew a world of one star before coming here. But I am not quite sure as this is a most complex script. I have the impression this was not our sun, but another." She stilled, and looked around.

Rambling had been watching her intently and said, "And?"

"And, indeed," Kay replied. "I often work in the Elven Observatory, and am revered to be gifted in the ways of the cosmos. There is a disturbance in space, but not in time. No doubt, that will come later. The Constant fluctuates outside of normal parameters, meaning change is coming. It is related to Gaia, but how I cannot tell.

"I discovered the epicentre to be a small star in Alpha Centauri, the slight incongruity appears adjacent to Proxima Centauri, the very same solar system ancient legend infers as being the origin of The Ancestors. I'll say no more at this point, at least until I have an identifiable time-shift, or confirmation from the Corridor of Knowledge, or the Core."

Rambling replied, "Thank you, this is what we perceive also, but not in the way you do. Some of our kind hear distant, obscure voices, both those of pleading for release, and others nay-saying rescue. That is until recently. Please accept my apologies if I insulted you. That was not my intention. I simply wanted a second opinion.

"Our learned believe the Ancestors original home world may be under threat by an alien race, and that some of their cousins may be headed our way. This, even if it is revealed to be the truth, will take decades to become reality." His great smile engulfed us and it became evident Ælkræleinnoire had told the whole truth, as she best understood it. Rambling congratulated her, confirming their mutual understanding.

"Thank you Rambling, later we will talk in depth. My only question is, do we set out a welcome party, or take up arms, all knowing one?

"Guardian, n'Gnung, for the moment know these are side tracks full of obfuscation, traps set to bewilder the foolish. Come, let us focus on what we do best, unravel the deeper meanings, and restore the spacecraft of the Ancestor. If my intuition is correct, we may have need of it, sooner, rather than later.

Ambling around us she added, "We are not alone within this galaxy, and neither are we the only sentient beings. I foresee, some will come to us in 'a short while', and most definitely, within our lifetimes'."

A few days later, the Core informed us the crews' quarters had been restored. We raced through the internal corridor and found a new motif set to the far wall. I opened the door, and we discovered twelve bedrooms, six to each side. The wall nearest us housed several bathrooms, and opposite was a small galley and relaxation area. n'Gnung took the room that was next to the rear of my day room, and Kay the one on the other side. I assigned the first four rooms to the day and night controllers, leaving the rest to be determined later.

Chapter 15 ~ The Himalayan Expedition

As the Summer Solstice drew nearer, Kay, n'Gnung, and I continued to restore the ship. Others were equally active as plans for returning the Giants to their homelands progressed. Representatives of the Eleventh and Seventh joined us with increasing frequency, arriving from their homelands near Lake Titicaca, and Lake Baikal respectively.

Ælthrelntheine came to us one day, having just discovered a key piece of information from Quinn. "Most of the mercenaries died in the assault on this island, meaning we should face little if no resistance. It is time to finalise our battle plan. I will convene our war council."

Agreement was reached, and preparations confirmed. The day of attack, the longest day was less than one week away. The Giants were greatly relieved, their mood light and cheery that evening.

The armies of the allied Tribes mustered and co-ordinated the time of attack. We were scheduled to arrive in the Himalayan stronghold just before daybreak. We already knew to expect only light defensive corps, mainly the few remaining mercenaries of Quinn's security detail, but would be alert for Ogre guards also.

The Elven interrogators had finally managed to prise a piece of knowledge from Theodosius' mind, the Himalayan defence shield was intact, and the only point of entry was via the transporter. This in turn was sealed, and could only be overridden using the Ring of the Warrior.

There was no other option but to use the Ring. Many believed Quinn when he said he would use it to allow us entry, in exchange for his freedom, I did not. Neither did my closest companions. We knew he planned a double cross. I retrieved the Ring of the Warrior, and even from where it lay in the pouch on my belt, I could feel its brooding malevolence. I carried it only as a key to gain entry to the homelands of the Giants, and despite the fact Ælthrelntheine had cleansed it, I needed rid of its malignant influence at the earliest opportunity.

The transporters of the Eleventh, Seventh, and Second were on standby, armies readied, and the Twelfth were impatient—over-eager to reclaim their heritage. I put the Ring of the Warrior on my finger, leaving my true ring with the Gatekeeper. My mind warped as the cold metal coalesced and congealed, as if becoming a part of me. I felt it trying to seek purchase within my being. I wanted, needed this intrigue done with as soon as possible. The transfer circle was packed with allies standing with me, as Jien Noi made the transfer. The white light engulfed us.

We reconstituted and immediately charged forward, only to discover we faced our own people. We were still within our own transporter. Even with the correct ring, we remained locked out.

Chapter 15

There could only be one conclusion, the transporter of the Twelfth was not only locked to the Ring of the Warrior, but double-locked with the DNA of Theodosius Quinn. Magnus was brought to us moments later, and he looked a woeful shadow of his former self, a man broken and eager to die. He duly confirmed my suspicions, and we had a problem on our hands, Theodosius hands, to be precise.

We had little idea of the strengths of the Ring of the Warrior, but knew it was extremely powerful. Theodosius was brought before us, and we suspected intrigue and subterfuge. He was shackled by heavy Ddwyrthen irons, and appeared downcast. His face wore that mask. But his body told a different story, his posture upright and alert. He was blindfolded and warned he would die at the first sign of deception.

Again, we assembled within the transporter, but this time with Quinn. Again, the transfer failed and Quinn laughed, "The Ring has to be on my finger, Guardian."

"One false move and you are dead, Quinn. Do you understand?" I put the loathsome ring on his finger and it swirled with brooding, bloody blackness. I held Quinn's shackled hands in my own, n'Gnung to one side, and Kay the other. They drew their swords and Kay's burst into searing bright blue flame.

I stared at the blade, and then her. She smiled mischievously and said, "This is an ancient runed blade, the badge of my office. It was made specifically to tell if there was an Ogre present. The blue flame confirms Quinn is an Ogre clone."

We transported immediately and arrived in what appeared to be the same room, except none of our companions stood watching.

Elated, I knew we had made the transfer. I removed the ring of power from Quinn, and put it back in my pouch, not wanting to touch it ever again. It was disgusting. We cleared the transporter ready for our reinforcement to follow. None came. We expected the need to unlock security from the control console. I realised I might need Quinn to do so.

We raced to the doorway, which opened automatically, and ran into a brace of guards who were quickly felled. Rambling raced to the fore, being the first to spill Ogre blood, Owain beside him taking the second Ogre's life with his battle axe. The enemy were as hideous as they were large. Grey skin covering bulbous muscles, hands held medieval weapons of menacing intent: maces, flails, and large sharp blades.

The room we entered was not unlike our own control room, larger, but with only one console, which I ran towards. Our small force turned to battle mixed troops of the Ogre and the Last. Fortunately, they were unprepared, and those that did not fall, fell back. The door closed and our forces could not follow, locking us inside; some form of security system was in place.

With Kay and n'Gnung at my side, I brought systems online, forced to use the loathsome ring. However, it was patently clear the console only partially activated. With a nod, n'Gnung brought Quinn to me. The prisoner, although still bound and blindfolded, struggled manfully, the gigantic hand of Rambling coming to assist our efforts. Again, I placed the Ring of the Warrior on the clones ring finger, and at the press of a button, the console came fully to life.

With lightning speed, Quinn twisted free and activated a command rune. A sealed door flew open and the room flooded with enemy troops. Kay reacted quickly, severing the hand with a slash of her sword. I removed the hand, and ring immediately, but the prisoner drove backwards knocking us off balance, and flung himself towards the cover of his arriving troops. Kay whirled after him, driving her blade through his back, rupturing his heart. Aroweena had read the situation, and guarded her as the Eleventh made it back to us safely.

Again, the enemy were a mixture of Ogres, and Ogre clones in human form. Our meagre force was immediately stretched to the limit. Our only recourse was to open the transporter gateway, allowing our reinforcements to come and assist us. We had strength in numbers, but they were in the wrong place and locked out.

The hand to hand fighting was intense, as Kay and n'Gnung stood one to each side of me, their flashing blades a blur of intensity, as I worked the strange control panel, which I discovered to my chagrin, was in the language of the Tenth. I screamed in frustration, as more soldiers of the Ogre flooded through doors. Quinn had sounded an alarm, which was being answered at the expense of survival. I could not seal the doors and the transporter remained locked out.

Ælkræleinnoire beheaded someone, and turned with a flourish, handing me her cherished blade, urging us to swap places. I rose to smite the next attacker, as she swooped down into the controller's chair. I tried to look back and see how she was progressing, but the enemy horde seemed without end. No sooner was one dead, than two more replaced the corpse. Most of our force had grouped to protect the central control station, but I noticed Owain and Rambling fighting back to back in the centre of the room, taking on challengers, from all quarters that spasmodically, continued to flood through the open doors.

Short staccato bursts of machine guns fire rang out, but Gung Loi and Aroweena saw the danger, and took out the interloper with a daring pincer movement, capturing the weapon. The Ddwyrth was unsure of how to use it. Renewed automatic fire came from one doorway. Gung Loi grabbed the weapon and aiming quickly in the general direction, pulled the trigger.

Chapter 15

Several of the enemy fell dead or wounded, but her strike was not enough to prevent the RPG launcher, which sent a shell directly into the massed mêlée. Bodies of both sides were torn and flung asunder, and I knew we were done for. An Ogre guard strode forward, demanding we surrender, a heavily spiked metal ball swinging menacingly on a chain. He lunged towards us swinging the Kriegsflegel, and we dove for cover.

Ælkræleinnoire could have dodged aside, but she stayed to make one last key press, and although quick, took a wound to her temple, and crashed to the floor, unconscious. My brother and I leapt to protect her, but the Ogre was enormous, and far stronger than we were. His arm flung us aside with distain, and he swung his weapon to extinguish Elven life. As if out of nowhere, Gung Loi stood over Kay, and used the empty machine gun to ensnare the Ogre's deadly weapon, which circled around to strike him in the stomach. She tried to attack him with her dagger, but he cast her aside with ease.

At that moment, the door to the transporter room opened, and our reinforcements flooded through, at first unprepared for the raging battle they were hurtling into. The Ogre guard momentarily distracted, n'Gnung made a foothold of hands, and I sprang, him impelling me to save the life of our dearest friend. Kay's sword proved true, and I guided it to its target unerringly, the right ride of our tormentor's torso. The blade reverberated as if in euphoric lust, as it appeared to drink the blood of the now dying Ogre, its thirst seemingly unquenchable.

The battle had turned on just one keystroke, one press of a rune. Our forces swarmed through, and I took up station as we regrouped and took the battle back to the Ogre host. I saw Aroweena take a slash to the cheek, one that would debilitate any normal person.

Amazed, I watched as her eyes snapped to a steely focus. Her swords took on new life, as if becoming extensions of her body. Her arms rose and fell with regularity, ending lives wherever they struck. She was berserker, and a most fearsome sight to behold. Her strength and daring, irrespective of her own life, brought cohesion and impetus to our floundering troops, as they mustered to her side, and gained courage from her wanton bloodlust.

The initial battle for the control complex raged for several hours, and the mop up operation, for several days. Eventually we held sway and returned Rambling Longshanks to his rightful inheritance.

Once the plague of Ogre was dispelled, we helped Rambling come into his power. Forces of the Eleventh, Seventh, and Second stayed to guard and rebuild. The city was in dire neglect and much was derelict. Renovations would take years, but the most important were begun first.

Junior worked out where Furlong Fourgay might have hidden the Ring of the True Heart, and in due course, it was reclaimed from the ruins of their now dilapidated church, a secret vault within the ruins providing ruse of protection and concealment, similar to our own.

Representatives of all three Tribes stayed to effect repairs. Farmers replaced troops, and healers, corpses. Rambling sent out a call for long lost brethren to return to their homeland. Many answered his entreaty, but as many did not. In time, we left them to their own devices.

The Giants were bitterly scarred as a race, and needed time in unity to heal. Our own troops also needed time to adjust. They had been exposed to a different world and different culture from the only one they knew of. Under Lo Si's guidance, what started out as an adjustment centre became a school, and then several. Understanding and knowledge grew, in time to flourish throughout the lands of the Second.

One evening before we departed, I asked Aroweena about her going berserker, and she explained it thus. "It is as if a red mist comes over me, and I simply react. I am conscious of every part of my body, at each, and every moment in time, and that of my swords.

"It is hard to explain to one who has never experienced it. I remember watching myself as if from a distance, orchestrating what my limbs did, simply observing as my body exacted its toll of the Tenth. As my blades swept the air before me, I knew how to make a minor adjustment to make each a killing blow. I knew one Ogre had a shoelace undone, and this I used moments later to trip him into his death. At the same time, I was aware that another was slightly off balance. But then, I also was aware of a small colony of bats sheltering in the eaves, and the sound of a mouse desperate to hide under a fallen bench. It was like being between this reality and another, yet totally aware of everything.

"I hope you never know this feeling; warm, flowing blood lies heavy on the soul, even that of the Ogre. Mind you, you must admit, their hearts are awfully tasty, don't you agree."

She reached out and took another bite from the pile of fresh, raw hearts in front of her. I had no reply. The ways of Aroweena were especially singular. Fresh blood ran down her beard, which she used to twirl into a point. I offered her a toast of ale, before seeking out my wife. I returned to Jinnie's side, seeking, I don't know, solace? She summed it up by saying, "She's a girl, but not as you know of."

The first evening after returning to our home, we settled on the Outland shore. It would be one of the last nights before the Tribes went their separate ways. I was plagued by a doubt, one I could not define. Strolling along the sea strand helped settle my soul, but my mind was wandering. The persistence of the Ogre hordes, and presence of Ogre clones had deeply unsettled my psyche. Given tales of myth and legend, I was fine. To actually meet them, slay them was disconcerting. They proved a most fearsome enemy, one we would doubtless fight again.

Chapter 15

I came to the sentry rock and climbed, seeking to lose myself in the stars. I was surprised to find another already there. Without looking at me she said, "I knew you would come here seeking salvation in the heavens. Or should that be absolution, for we are so alike, you and I."

I did not reply but sat nearby and let my mind wander between the stars above. At length she told me a story of unrequited love concerning mortals and gods. It was absorbing, and her storytelling excellent. I in turn replied with one of Chinese myth, Chang-e, the Lady of the Moon. She listened intently to my rendition, and clapped when I finished.

She advised me, "This is actually a tale from the old religion of the Second, because Chang-e was a real woman and this did in fact happen long ago, though not quite as remembered by the masses. It is interesting that you chose that particular tale this night to relate. Know that her husband, Houyi, was a Ddwyrth, not one of the Second."

It seemed the heavens moved around me, as a sliver of ancient truth came to me unbidden, and I knew the words she had spoken were true. As if coming from a swoon, I turned to her, only for her to have me quiet. She finished, "Guardian, Jackie. Know the heavens hold many wonders, secrets, and truths. Also know that of all those that seek to find a truth, most often end up with a lie.

"I have seen you here before. 'Known of you' is a better phrase, for this is a place of unique power. It is an up thrust of Earth power, one the Eleventh revere as protectors of Gaia. It's the same power that always draws you, and sometimes your wife here. It is unique on this planet. I would tell you that only those who seek to understand the mysteries of the stars come here, and you are their foremost patron. In your world, this would be called *star gazing*. So that makes you 'The Star Gazer'."

Ælkræleinnoire left me with questions rising on the metaphysical wind, and within the cosmic embrace that enfolded my small self. I knew in my heart and soul her statements were true. It was not long before I followed her back to the warmth and companionship of my friends, but from that moment on, I always had an ear extended, a sixth sense, for a bigger picture, one I had been missing.

Some months later we would all return to the Himalayas for the marriage of Junior and Constance Merryweather, a princess from another fork of the Twelfth's lineage. It was a political alliance, and in due course, the bride's parents and greater family returned to their ancient home, and the Twelfth's number multiplied overnight.

The celebration was doubled, when Rambling announced his wife was with child, a most rare occurrence for the Twelfth. Their unbridled celebrations were as large as their bodies, and their hearts.

Chapter 16 ~ Restoring the Old Religion

Some days later life returned to its normal metre, and our fields prospered. We continued to introduce new husbandry techniques and crops, all according to the original islander's design. I did not lead them, but offered my advice when asked about new plans. I would indicate if they were good, or not good. I occasionally let slip a small clue, which fired their interest.

Da Phai Nai seemed quieter than usual one morning in early Autumn. She was distracted, but I put that down to Owain leaving us a few days before. She was talking with Lo Si, and he gave her a cuddle. I realised there was more to this than my presumption.

I spoke with him a little later, and he confided, "She is fine. She misses Sun Kist. It is almost half a year since she left. Da Phai Nai worries about our daughter, as do I. It is what parents do, as you will soon discover for yourself, Jackie."

I nodded my head, "I have already had these thoughts. I suppose it only gets worse as they grow up."

I grimaced as the reality settled within me. "Lo Si, do you know where the Shaman lives? I have a mind to pay her a visit."

He beamed back at me and said, "You will not find her if she does not want to be discovered. The rumour is that she lived somewhere in or near the Badlands, one or more leagues west of the old capital. We now know where that used to be, thanks to you. In ancient times, an old Master of Knowledge was given the location by the Shaman herself, or so the story goes. This is what I was taught, although the passage is short and rather strange, as indeed, are the ways of the Shaman.

'Seekest thee a cave for me,
a sign where one should never be.
Within the darkness turneth thee,
the entry clear, but will you see?'

Oh, and there should be an offering of worthy plants, medicinal perhaps, the advice is rather vague."

I looked at him and humphed, "Another riddle. Why can't she use normal language like everybody else?"

Lo Si patted my shoulder in a fatherly way and advised, "Take your closest with you, the young ones, but make your number few." I was about to rise when he put a restraining hand on my arm, "Wait. Regards the Shaman, I have an indistinct recollection, all numbers should be prime numbers, so your party should be three people, possibly five, but not too many."

Chapter 16

I thanked him and went about my business. My first task was to pinpoint a possible location for this mysterious cave. With prime numbers in mind, I spent several days searching the presumed general vicinity, and discovered several red herrings. My closest companions helped, but we had reached the point where we only looked for the place when inspiration stuck us.

I had written the riddle down and was staring unseeing at it for the umpteenth time. I had been interfacing with the Core, but had not removed the interface device. I said mentally, 'Where the hell is the cave the Shaman mentioned?'

A thought came to me, as if from the ether. I zoomed in on the location. Above the cave opening I made out a mark, two circles, one inside the other, and a line running behind them. Weathering had made them almost invisible, unless you knew where to look.

The cave was one we had already discounted. However, I knew the thought came from the Core, not my own mind, or was I being driven insane? I looked back at the words, and reread to glean any hidden meaning. I had been in the cave, and it was dark inside, even in daylight. I had turned around, and there was nothing to see. I called n'Gnung to my side, and we set off in the gloaming. Intrigued, Kay said she would follow in a moment. We entered and turned around, as night-time's shadows stole the world from view. There was nothing to see.

I stalled, because it was not yet fully dark. The air shimmered nearby and Kay appeared. Turning and looking before pointing delightedly, she exclaimed, "Jackie, you found it!" She gave us both a hug, her excitement contagious.

We both stared at her, as we saw nothing. However, I remembered the Elves had exceedingly good eyesight. She pointed to a particular spot, and I could just about make out what appeared to be a waxing and waning halo of lesser blackness. It was extremely difficult to determine, but she was sure. We transported from the cave across the gorge that separated us, and arrived within a whirl of fireflies.

We were elated, we had finally discovered the entrance to the Shaman's domain. If the secrets of the Ancestors were hidden three and four layers deep, then those of the Shaman appeared to be hidden within walls of obfuscation. I was beginning to get the hang of her riddles, as they also had many levels, and a choice of obtuse meanings.

We returned the next morning, our group consisting of n'Gnung, n'Gue, and myself. We stood where the fireflies had been the evening before, and walked through a natural break in the trees. It resembled an arched gateway, branches overhead entangled, but we followed a clear avenue through a short, dense woodland. It gave way to a tranquil meadow, set within a peaceful valley. To the north, I saw an impossible cottage. It resembled no building I had ever imagined; it was so diverse in aspect and design. It appeared to be woven from the roots and branches of one or more trees. Windows fashioned like portholes within the demi-spherical structure, which in turn was moated by covered veranda. We approached close to her home before stilling below a large oak tree to prepare for our audience. Along the way, we had gathered likely looking herbs and flowers as gifts for the Shaman.

Unexpectedly, a gust of wind chilled us resolute. We looked at each other with concern, but no words were spoken. The world turned deathly quiet and seemed frozen in space and time. The eerie silence was broken by a cackle from above, followed by the words,

"Seek me to creep up upon wouldst thee?

What treasure wouldst thee steal from me?"

Startled, we all looked up to find the old crone chewing a stem of sweet-grass between her few remaining, blackened teeth. She watched our discomfiture with a steely grin, a look of haughtiness shrouding her demeanour. I reacted, reckless of the consequences:

"Wise woman, know your Emperor and Guardian comes before you this day as an ordinary person. I seek your advice. I am sorely troubled these times. I have brought you these flowers and herbs as a token of my good heart."

She leapt impossibly down and peered at my offering, soon inspecting those of my two brothers also before asserting,

"These weeds are of no use to me.

But flower nice to bring, to see;

the wort of healing also free,

and oh, the bonny sweet of pea."

She took one from each of us and stated, "Goest now ye may."

"Good woman, I also seek to speak with your new daughter. She is a dear friend of mine. I need to know if she is happy here."

As I spoke the words, I also walked to come in front of her, and between her good self and her strange cottage.

With unreasonable alacrity, she danced to the side, outmanoeuvring us, and laughed as she skipped away like a sprite. We watched her receding form. If this was a game, we were losing badly. And then she was gone.

I was tired of being toyed with, and told my companions to wait for me. I strode purposefully towards the unusual home, beating loudly upon the door and asked the occupier to admit me.

I stood still and heard the whirring of gears and the clanking of metal upon metal. Then more gears turned, followed by a chain pulling, before a catch snapped loudly. Slowly the door creaked open. I was about to walk through when a feather-like aberration touched my conscious from the side, and I noticed a rocking chair set on the stoop.

Intrigued I sat down to wait; confident I had made the correct choice. It was as if my mind was a separate entity, one not fully under my control. I banished the crazed perception and reasoned these people did not have metal, so whatever I heard was in my mind only, a deception. Perhaps the same was true of the strange house and even the old woman herself.

All of a sudden, it seemed a veil lifted. I was in company with two women who were smiling at me in wonder. One was Sun Kist, and the other a woman in her late-twenties, one I had met before at the blessing of our child, but looking slightly younger. I already knew that speaking to the Shaman was like talking a riddlesworth of riddledom, and she did not disappoint.

"Between the veils of time to see,
the world of secrets meant for thee."

"Oh no learned one, I simply made a lucky guess, that is all. Sun Kist, how are you? Are you well, enjoying life here?"

"Guardian it's fantastic, although that first day I was terribly scared. I have learnt so much already and find the days spin within the circle of life so quickly that I lose track. How is my mother?"

"She is fine although her age is becoming a burden. However, know that she misses you greatly, but yearns only for your happiness, as does your father.

"Shaman, would it be possible for Sun Kist to visit her mother occasionally?" I left the question to hang between them.

She considered this an odd request, but elicited, "
Barrier I see not.
Promise never sought;
Prior warning never got.
Future made from this or thats.
Hopes created, measured, tapp't;
Plans hang on hooks like bats.
Journey now if you see fit.
By eve in rocker must she sit
All her soul and most of wit."

I immediately gave my promise and Sun Kist was overjoyed, rushing to get a present for her mother. Left alone with the Shaman for a few moments I thanked her for her dispensation, before asking; "Shaman, I have a mind to learn more about your ways and the old beliefs, the old religion especially. Is this possible?"

"My student do you wish to be?
Know then this: I cannot see."

"Shaman, please know that was not my intention at all. I would be a hopeless student."

"That, my gallant, t'was truly said.

What then? All choices being dead."

I countered immediately, "I am interested in preserving the old ways for posterity as part of these, my people's culture. It is my intuition that only a few traditions linger, such as marriage rights, and attending the birth of a child.

However there must be so much more that you can share with them. What of the mysteries of healing both the body and the mind? The people's common identity through what you teach and practice. A resurgence of interest in the old religion driven by your knowledge and guidance."

She looked long at me, fixing my eyes before replying, "

Then know O Stranger, O Friend from shore,

This can never be as was before.

Banished in darkness, unto darkness more;

The weight of knowledge, Gaia's lore.

Rites few were to carry on, to wend their way, to set in store.

Shaman old sent marching out, alone to live, a beacon tor.

Banished I ceremonial rite, when knock-ed I on bless-ed door.

Know, O Foreign, O Native Son, this can never be no more."

I replied at once, "And what if the banishment were rescinded and the old religion made legal once more. I see no reason why this cannot come to pass within the time of my suggestion to my wife, the Empress."

Her shock was palpable. She studied me intently for several seconds, her eyes sparkling with intrigue and mischievous intent.

Sun Kist came back to us, but I signalled her to be silent while I waited in anticipation. The Shaman closed her eyes and at length her features relaxed. Abruptly her eyes flew open, becoming alive once more.

"Sun Kist, bring the ancient bones,

I must listen for the Angels' tones."

Totally ignoring everything without her being, she focused inwards, as the old bones were brought to her hand. She began chanting an ancient mantra, building in tempo as her request formulated. Time passed as her momentum built up to her final act, which was exclaimed in the ancient tongue, "New paths on old, where none should be, were this true, then show to me."

Chapter 16

The Shaman cast her wish, her spell, throwing the bones to the wind. Still in a trancelike state, she swooped like a maddened raven to study the bones, before rocking back on her haunches.

She rechecked one bone several times, before talking from within her reverie, "Jack Barleycorn, your sister dear, a modern Shaman, let's be clear, is known to Angels present here."

Before I could reply, she returned to her thoughts. I informed Sun Kist she was correct. This was quite unnerving under the circumstances, because she could have absolutely no prior knowledge of that fact of my heritage.

The Shaman spoke again, though more inwardly, "
Once foretold, be long ago,
Third Path to tread for heel and toe.
This way be nary clear nor slow,
and passage doth, like child to grow.
From past to future bravely go,
unscathed for all, the truth to know,
of mind and soul submit no blow,
enlightened from the heart below."

This peculiar statement was followed by silence. She rocked back and forth from heel to toe, as if mimicking a journey, her arms locked around her knees in a parody of the foetal position. As the moment passed, so she stilled and swooned.

Sun Kist rushed to comfort her. Only a few moments passed before she came back unto herself, and asked her young aide to fetch a particular tonic. Hurrying back, Sun Kist placed a worn wooden cup in her hands filled with herbal tea, which she sipped.

I never expected her to speak in clear and measured tones, let alone what she said; "
At next false darkness of the Moon,
Earthen spirits return for boon.
By then thee must have cleansed the wound,
honoured us, or forever croon.
One of your number attend me soon,
a learned one of lore in tune,
for him with knowledge I would festoon."

She cast about within her mind before continuing; "
Of this moment within a group,
he speaks in tongues to teach his troupe,
with waves of knowledge his acolytes poop,
his master watches from the stoop.
Hasten both to me from teachers coop,

Time comes to stir the knowledge soup,
These learned men, as pupils whoop,
When Shaman teaches, teachers swoop.
O Stranger, O Son, true then for answers snoop,
if true to task and does not droop,
by Sun and Moon be set one hoop,
Thus end thy task — return the loop."

With that statement the veil shrouding her returned and I was left alone, except for her puzzle. I walked down to my brothers, who were quite agitated, not being able to see me for some time and wondering whether to mount a search and rescue operation.

They stilled quickly as they saw I was unharmed and in a cheerful frame of mind. I thought to explain to them that I could see them all the time, but on reflection, thought better of it, and simply told them our meeting was most constructive.

However, instead of leaving we waited until Sun Kist came running down to join us, overjoyed to be able to spend a little time with her mother. We walked back to the entrance of the Shaman's realm and transported to the shore. Upon seeing her daughter, Da Phai Nai dropped what she was carrying and rushed over to greet her, holding her close before examining her features in detail, running her fingers over her daughters face.

Their reunion was happy and turning to me she mouthed, *Thank you*. I gave the elder the rest of the day off, so they could enjoy time together. My next task was to report on my day to my wife, who was preoccupied with affairs of the realm. Harvest Home was due in two weeks' time, and everyone was working in the fields.

At first, the Empress was convinced that my concerns were groundless, before I said, "The Shaman told me she is still banished. The old religion has been outlawed since the depths of the Dark Time, when it was blamed for the cataclysm."

This was a great surprise to Jien Noi. She said, "Those laws were repealed long ago. Surely there is some mistake?"

"Maybe they were, except nobody bothered to inform the Shaman, or practice the old religion. With your sanction, I will make this right, although she will need to hear the pardon and reinstatement from your own lips."

I had one thing left to do, and that was take Lo Si and Ju Lo to meet the Shaman. Ju Lo was taking class in the city, and had obviously been there all morning. Lo Si was resting on the veranda outside, but keeping one eye on the students, and another on his own pupil. I wondered once more, how the Shaman knew this?

Chapter 16

It would be a reasonable guess for my closest friends. But she was extra-worldly, and could not have known in advance.

Therefore, it was with a curious smile that I sat at on the veranda and waited with Lo Si until class was done. When we three were alone I said, "I met the Shaman this morning. She wants to teach you both about the old religion, and restore it to this society. Is there anything you need to do before we leave? I would like you to meet her as soon as possible."

We departed moments later, and I left them sitting expectantly upon the rocking chairs of the stoop. They waved when I turned around, and I left the rest to the chances of destiny.

Chapter 17 ~ The Ring of The Earth

The following day began brightly, but for some inexplicable reason, my mood remained mired in contorted lethargy. I simply sat to stare at the heavens, as if trying to understand the infinite.

The Sun was bright in his arc above, as if challenging all to submit to his formidable glory. To the west, the object of his pursuit, La Luna, hurried as if trying to escape his all-consuming embrace, as their chariots raced across the sky above. I concluded there were perhaps only an earthly hour or two, between the heavenly arcs of their daily escapades, as the primordial protagonists sought the crescendo of their unearthly play.

Lo Si and Ju Lo did not return until late that evening. Ju Lo needed to attend the Empress at once, and debrief the main points of what they had learned. Lo Si gave his understudy his head, and stayed with me to speak of his experiences, "I have a lot to learn, it is like being back at school again. I wish I were as able a teacher as the Shaman, she is brilliant."

After taking a drink he said, "Guardian, we sat for some time after you left that day and wondered if it was a stupid trick. I must admit, I was on the point of leaving when there was a shimmer of the air, as if a curtain was lifted, and next to me sat a charming young woman of similar age to Ju Lo.

"I remember that she spoke quite strangely. Her talk of Spirits and Angels was most confusing, but later made sense within the whole of her art, as I now understand her teachings to be. The Shaman told me the world we know of is in flux, and she left me with this message to give to you just before we departed.

'Whence hearts of light become one dally,
Great Mother Earth to witness'll, rally,
To intrigues of their immortal ballet.
When light and dark become love's ally.
If sign returneth to my tally,
Then pure of heart may seek my valley'.

"I don't have the vaguest idea what it means. But it is word perfect. The Shaman stated you would understand and honour the request, or be damned all for eternity."

I stared back, my mind agape, as was my mouth. I wrote the riddle down, and cursed loudly. "Another damned riddle!"

I looked up towards the heavens as my curses subsided, and the more I watched the heavenly bodies at play, the less at ease I felt. I knew I was missing something, but what?

Chapter 17

Above where I sat, the Moon wore a wisp of crescent bonnet, as if to protect her integrity from Helios' ardent advance.

Turning back to look at my friend, he now appeared noticeably wiser, if simply by the way he held himself and spoke to others. He said one last thing before going about his business, "Guardian, whatever it is that she bade you do, you have only two days, this one and tomorrow, in which to do it. She is expecting you on the morning of the third day."

I cursed again, and tried to pick the clues of her seemingly impossible riddles, but enlightenment once more eluded me. However, he was able to put a smile on my face before he departed. "Guardian, I thank you for enabling Sun Kist to see her mother yesterday. Both are buoyed by their meeting, as my daughter explained to me last night when she returned from the shore.

"Now I must attend Da Phai Nai, but I'll see you this evening."

The next morning at our home, the Empress called a breakfast meeting closed to all except our most learned and trusted. Lo Si encouraged Ju Lo to speak, and he began, "Much of our knowledge has been lost to us. The Shaman told us that during the Dark Time, the Keeper of Knowledge died, and his successor was only partially trained. She knows of what was lost, and will teach us full knowledge of the old ways.

"Our ways, our beliefs are ancient, and handed directly down from times immemorial. Times of when the Ancestors arrived on Gueir. We represent the original and unbroken line of Druidæ or Druids, of which the Shaman is the most learned of our time.

"Our duty is to respect the great Mother Earth, and protect her, not exploit her resources. This is not a religious worship of any god. It is caring, showing due honour and deference to the bounty we see all around. This is defined as fertility, and is represented by the sign of a tree."

Kay spoke up in astonishment, "The One Tree."

Ju Lo smiled, "Yes, The One Tree symbolises fertility, mercy, and harmony. It also represents the feminine, the creators of life."

Animated talk followed this revelation, which Ju Lo could not quell. Lo Si rose and commanded silence, "There is much to learn, far more than the remaining number of my days, but enough for Ju Lo to become a true master of knowledge. Unknowingly, perhaps unwittingly, we have remained true to the path, as the ways of the Druid are interlinked with philosophy, theology, cosmology, astronomy, the passage of time, the study of Gaia, and the ways of the world and nature. Seeing, divination, and augury are also part of our heritage, as represented here by Won Long and Weid Noi. I now understand why our daughter was so named."

Won Long spoke, "I gave her an ancient name, one revered in our work; 'Weid' means Seer in the ancient language. You, husband, are entitled 'Deru', meaning tree. The roots, trunk, branches and leaves represent the paths of knowledge, and you are supposed to be their stalwart keeper."

The barb was passed over as Lo Si spoke once more, "Indeed it is so. There are many paths, all interrelated. Those of Seer, sage, bard, and magus, to name but a few. I will not speak long, because our knowledge is incomplete, but would ask you to look at this valley. To the northwest is a large circle of standing stones, which is related to cosmology and the passage of time. Directly west, the strange monolith with a hole near the top, you have all seen it I am sure. At dawn on Midsummer's Day, the sun shines through the hole, and appears to sit atop a smaller stone near the fourth cave. If seen from the entrance of that cave, they all align perfectly."

Lo Si and Ju Lo shared more with us, but he closed with a statement, "The Shaman has requested we restore the fertility rights, and for that we need a High Priest. This will become Sun Kist's job, but in times to come. Today she needs to learn her craft and come into her power. Ju Lo has offered to take the role for the intervening period, with your permission, Empress."

Later that morning I took Ju Lo to the Corridor of Knowledge. He had been many times before, but this time I asked Ælkræleinnoire to accompany us. n'Gnung led the way until we reached the panel in question, it was one few bothered to study.

Kay read the ancient text and translated the meaning. It described the old religion in great detail, but as an observer would, not a practitioner. I realised it was not a controlling religion as such, but a way of living within Gaia's bounty. Natural elements were honoured, like streams providing water, but the focus was on the fact that water was essential for life. There was no associated god or *Naiades*. I came to understand the religion was about respecting and honouring Mother Nature, but definitely against the worship or empowering of human or ethereal beings.

Ju Lo became enlightened, and learned the entirety of Kay's translation by heart. It dovetailed precisely with what he had recently learned. I, in my turn, wondered just who, or what, the Shaman was.

By luck, one of the first things Ju Lo did was to encourage the people to say a small *thank you* before each meal began. It reminded me of saying grace, but was not beholden of any god. It was simply a form of reverence for nature's bounty. In time I reflected, the ethos resembled Doaist philosophy more than any other I knew of.

For my part, I returned to my day room in the control centre, and n'Gnung enquired, "Guardian, have you unlocked the mystery of the riddle yet?"

I replied in all honesty, "No I have not, but I think I know what it means. We seek a sign, brother. What I do understand is that before midday tomorrow, this world will turn once more. We must prepare to fearlessly stride upon the third and windy way; wherever, or whatever, that may be?"

The day passed into late afternoon, as Kay and I worked with n'Gnung to try to solve the riddle. All we understood was that I had to return a sign to the Shaman. We didn't even know what it was or looked like.

We had planned to spend the evening enjoying the quietness of the shore, but Fate cast her die as we prepared to leave. Jien Noi required my presence at the evening meal. It was a trifle, but the Emperor was growing older, less able at times, and sometimes, increasingly more often, I needed to step-up.

This was one of those occasions, and I attended as decreed. During the meal, I went to the latrine, and was surprised to find n'Gnung and Gung Loi loitering within the breath of an embrace. There was clearly something happening between them, so I attended to my business in another area, and made my way back towards the throng inside.

The area was dark, although faint light shone beyond from the fires burning to light the evening. I turned back to look at my best friends, wondering what they were actually about, when my foot caught on a tree root. I could have sworn the way was clear, but I went flying, and ended up on the rocks, grazed and cursing.

My hands and knees stung from the unexpected rasp of landing, as I continued to issue expletives liberally. I heard my friends approaching from the night, and turned my head to look at them. My prone position only allowed me to turn my head so far, and then I saw it.

My voice stilled. My scrapes negligible, except for my wounded pride. I stared at the mouth of the old church. Within the flickering fire-cast brightening of stone walls, I saw a sign, one I had only seen once before. I stared at two circles, one within the other, and a line crossing behind them. It was identical to the one above the cave that showed us the way to the Shaman's domain. I no longer believed in coincidence.

My friends reached me at that moment, worried I was injured. I looked into n'Gnung's eyes and pointed. He grasped the significance at once. I sat upright to contemplate any deeper meanings, but they eluded us. Within time n'Gnung said, "There is no resolution here. Guardian, what we seek lies elsewhere."

Gung Loi spoke into the vacuum, "That is correct, Guardian. Apart from this Shaman, there are perhaps only three, maybe four, who can unravel this bizarre intrigue. I suggest you begin with your wife, because the Empress is key to understanding the treasures of times past."

I rose and clasped her to me like a sister, for in essence, that was what she was. I knew I was searching for a key, one that would unlock the Shaman's weird conundrum. I also realised that time was limited, within another's hand of play. I unthinkingly spoke a children's rhyme aloud, "'Jack be stalwart, Jack be sleight; Jack be nimble, or lose the sight'."

I went to sleep as those words of an old rhyme my father spoke to me, many times, came to haunt my dreams.

A person knows when the time comes. I can't explain it in words — a person is *called*. Come that new dawn, I knew I had been called-out, and was expected to deliver in full, or 'be damned for all eternity'. I went outside and arbitrarily looked up to the sky. Helios was almost upon his Pagat. The time was nigh.

Jien Noi was preparing to leave for court, when I claimed her for a moment. She indulged me, and we stood before the entrance to the church. I pointed above and said, "Have you any knowledge of this sign. Please? It is of the utmost importance, this day, this morning, this moment."

It took her moments to focus, but when she saw it, she replied, "What that? It is a child's toy. I have one somewhere. What of it?"

"It's not a child's toy. It is the signature of the old religion. Show me."

Between her hesitance and reluctance, we returned to her private chambers, where she opened a safe in the Imperial room. In moments, she came to me with a ring. As she offered it to my hand, she said; "This is a keepsake of no worth. It is pretty in some ways, yet strange in others."

She wilted, realising a part of the significance. "Before today, I did not know it was the same design as the one above the door to our temple. Jackie, what does it mean?"

She became distracted as Ræm demanded breakfast. I looked down at an awesome ring, and examined it closely. It was made from a band of finest blue jade. It was marked with white blemishes, and further round, had distinct and curiously defined patches of green. I knew the rock was not of natural occurrence, as it reminded me of pictures of the Earth, as seen from space, the land masses were mostly in the correct position, given æons of times passed — as if the island were the focal point.

The crown was a circle of a more vivid green, upon which sat a thin ring of a beautiful yellow gemstone, which sparkled in the light. I thought it might have been yellow sapphire. This in turn held an orb of moonstone within its capture. They were layered one atop the other with no sign of any join.

Profound wisdom engulfed me within that moment, and I knew this was what the Shaman sought. I realised she could have taken it at any time, but what mattered to her, was that it had to be given back to her, by the Empress herself. I held it aloft and said, "This is the key. Hurry, we have little time to return this to its rightful owner. Wait. Wear your entire official trapping of office. This is vitally important."

Before Ræm was fully fed, we rushed outside, our daughter oblivious to the motion. The morning was getting darker. I looked up at the heavens above, and Helios had almost caught the object of his ardour. We were completely unprepared, but the riddle, as my mind understood it, made perfect sense, if this were about to become a full eclipse of the Sun.

Giddy with haste, we arrived at the Shaman's gateway, Ræm finally finishing her breakfast. We hurried through the forest avenue to the Shaman's homestead. She was in the guise of a young girl waiting expectantly for us on the stoop, rocking back and forth in her chair. The daylight darkened more to welcome our approach. Only the stout of purpose walked onwards, others stopped to gawp as the Moon increasingly obscured the Sun. The Shaman rose to greet us without speaking: Waiting.

Jien Noi and I came before her, our companions tactfully behind. I whispered to my wife, as a piece of the puzzle came back to haunt me, 'the pure of heart'. There was only one amongst us. The day was getting darker quickly, as if closing for all time to seal the path we sought.

The Empress decreed, "I herewith rescind the banishment of the Shaman, and gladly welcome her fully once more into the bosom of our society. I reinstate the old religion, and hereby remove any and all impediments to its practice. Please attend the Capital on Harvest Home, as I would have the ancient church renewed. This is my will as Empress of the Second."

Jien Noi smiled and spoke directly to the Shaman, "I apologise for your inconvenience, and hope you will forgive my misguided ancestors. Please accept this token in honour of your reinstatement."

The Empress looked at me, and I duly placed the Ring of the Earth into Ræm's small hand. Jien Noi handed our daughter to the Shaman, who accepted the child gladly. She made a mark on her forehead. She took the ring and looked lovingly at it, before returning our daughter to us.

It was getting difficult to see. When the Shaman put on the ring, she turned to the north, and spoke quickly in the language of the Ancestors. She addressed all four cardinals, before speaking to us in the language of the islanders, "

The mysteries of time and space unravel,
The third and windy way to travel,
Union of Moon and Sun to marvel,
Rarely; honour'd knees to gravel."

We knelt in respect, but it did not feel like any form of sun or moon worship. It was an honour to Gaia. The Shaman switched back to the ancient language, and I understood more than the words themselves, as if enlightened by a higher power. It was not telepathy, but something akin, and far older in time. I duly and dutifully thanked the great mother Earth for providing for us, and putting up with us — Hominina. An inherent cosmology shrouded her short speech, one that at first eluded me, but later that day, it made sense, but one I could not voice as words.

The day was almost night when the Shaman pronounced, "Rise up for cheering and rejoice, the Earth renewed, we must give voice."

We watched above, the Moon was fully within the embrace of the Sun. It was like the dead of night, except for a dazzling halo encompassing La Luna. She wore it only for a moment, before slipping from her suitor's grasp, their play to return unto the daily round.

The Shaman came to my side and slipped something into my palm. She then proceeded to whisper her last, smiling directly into my confusion as she compounded my discomfiture by disclosing,

"For favour done, completed task,
there is one more that I must ask,
dusk becomes the third way's mask,
new dawn a moment soon to bask,
tread quickly, fear of overtask,
fall waters aide you from a flask.
This One Tree's seed you must enmask,
And plant anew when old in cask."

No sooner had she spoken, than she moved aside, her ministry to perform. I was left with one more of her thrice damned, gnarly riddles. The Shaman had a gift of hæmorrhaging language into a paradox of riddles and multiple meanings, my task to try to unravel once more. I looked at the seed in my hand, which slightly resembled an acorn. It was most curious. So was the associated riddle, because it appeared to be simple—keep hold of the seed and plant it, but where and when?

Awe became manifest, as daylight diligently returned, and I cast my eyes to the sky, before closing them, sending a short wish of thanks to Serendipity, or whom, or whatever was responsible for me seeing the sign. I heard a childlike, indulgent giggle on the waft of wayward wind, or was that just my imagination at play?

For the first time I seriously considered whether it was possible to change our lives, the preset course of our existence, our future. Was all pre-written in the stars? I already had my answer, it was, and it was not. I looked down at the seed clutched in my hand, and left at once to write the riddle down. Another unwanted chance for me to change the future, should I make the right call?

Chapter 18 ~ The Sword of Destiny

Ju Lo continued his training with the Shaman, who attended Harvest Home in her guise of a noble, middle-aged woman. The old church was returned to its former splendour, the black stone transforming to white at the Shaman's command. Sun Kist was there as official aide, and when not required spent much time with her parents.

The Shaman officiated at the subsequent festival, a celebration of bounty. Blessings were said for the earth and streams, for the produce of our fields, and the animals. The Empress encouraged her people to repeat the blessings when they returned home.

During the following feast, Ju Lo came to sit with me, and told me of his relief, "Guardian, I am released, at least in part. I am a teacher, a man of knowledge, not a priest. You have no idea how happy I was when the Shaman said that in future, Sun Kist would attend our festivities as High Priestess; this is a matriarchal society after all. My role is to retain full knowledge of the religion, ensure all priests are fully aware, and pass this knowledge on to my successors. It is simply an extension of what I am already doing.

"Guardian, I am so happy. Once I learn everything, I can return to my normal work, festivities excepted of course. Priests will likely all be female, and the Shaman has already indicated to Sun Kist who would make likely adepts. We will visit them tomorrow, and I will begin their training. There will be five in all, one for the city, one for each town, and one roaming as needs be."

Ju Lo was delighted, and drank more than usual. Small things changed after that. The people increased in their respect for Mother Earth, and demonstrated a growing value for the gift of life. For instance, when an animal was killed, it was done with respect and courtesy. The religion became known as 'The Ways of Gaia'.

The Shaman stayed with us for the following feast. She appeared to enjoy the fruits of our labours, and our company. At one point, she proposed a toast to Mother Earth. Afterwards she took Jien Noi to one side and they spoke at some length. Once their discussion concluded, the Shaman left, well, vanished.

Jien Noi returned to my side, "The Shaman and I have agreed to rebuild the old temples of the towns, and recreate their main church on its original site at the old capital city. There will also be a Temple of Fertility, a convent of sorts for training a new line of priests, mostly female. Apparently, the site of the old capital was most auspicious, and a place of significant Earth Power.

"She also wanted shrines erected around the island, and I said 'no'. However, she explained, the shrines would be wells of drinking water to replenish travellers, and aid fertilisation of crops. The Shaman will construct all herself, but check with me before restoration begins. Jackie, keep an eye on her. I think we should expand the colony at the old capital like this..."

We met with the other Tribes some weeks later. Discussion turned once more to the Tenth, and we worried that with their expertise of DNA manipulation, they could present themselves as any race. There was only one certifiable way to check whether a person was an Ogre, and that was to submit them to test by the blade gifted to Ælkræleinnoire, the Sword of Deception.

The Seventh proposed they fashion new swords with the Eleventh. The idea being the blade would manifest as blue flame in the presence of an Ogre or Ogre clone.

The Eleventh thought this a divergence from the real threat we faced, the Wrath of Gaia. I insisted we needed to be able to identify the enemy immediately, and we reached an impasse.

The following day, Kay spoke to Elven practitioners of the ancient arts, who stated they would be happy to work with the Seventh to create such a blade. We met soon after with smiths of the Seventh. They agreed that making such a sword was possible, if the Eleventh knew the secret runic code. The Eleventh confirmed they did, but that the enchantment had not been cast during forging for millennia. The process was recorded 'somewhere'. They added that the location of casting must be a place of great Earth power.

I asked if it had to be a blade, as an amulet would be better in most situations and arouse less interest. The metallurgists of the Eleventh thought it might be possible, either as a bracelet or ring. But everyone thought my suggestion stupid, and the Eleventh were on the point of throwing it out.

I reacted at once. "You do not know me. We have never met before." I pulled my dagger and advanced towards them, pointing it at people's throats with implied menace.

"You all pulled away because this dagger represents a serious threat. It would also let an Ogre know we were looking for them."

I took off a pendant and approached them again. "This time you are curious and want to see the design. A ring would be even better, if we were to shake hands in greeting. What say you now?

"I am the Guardian. It is my duty to protect this civilisation. We all need to know who our true friends and enemies are. We need to recognize the Tenth immediately."

I returned to my seat and rested my case, the immediate effect of my impromptu theatre still lingering. I felt a breeze in my hair, and looked around, but there was nothing of note. However, the hairs on my neck and back were standing up, as if they perceived something I could not.

Kay said, "The Guardian is correct. Masters of the Seventh and Eleventh, perfect your skills in preparation for casting the blade."

The next meeting of the tribes occurred early in our winter, but took place in the Himalayan summer, the Giants being the first off-island hosts. Sun Kist joined us just before we departed, "My Mistress will join us there, Guardian. I hope you don't mind."

The meeting got underway as soon as we arrived, and Llwydd the Bold strode forward with Brynllyn, the master forger of the Seventh, and Algrenguer, master of the ancient Elven sciences of metallurgy and associated spells. They presented their first offering to me. It was an exquisitely manufactured long dagger of Eleven design and proportions, crafted by the finest smiths of the Ddwyrth. It was light, perfectly balanced, and flawlessly formed. Could it detect the presence of the Tenth?

I offered the blade to Kay, but was startled when the old and bony hand of the Shaman wrest it from my grasp. I had no idea where she materialised from, but there she was, peering intently at the dagger. She mumbled, stared at us and said,

"Sorely missed, if made not be;
a blade of power? No not thee.
The smithy fine, the casting true,
The runes are wrong, there is no blue.
Maketh this blade once more to do,
On shortest day, I comest you.
With power of Earth, your witness true,
Elvenholme, with power, imbue."

Ælthrelntheine rose and bowed formally to the Shaman, "Princess of the Third and Windy Way, Renegade of the Rune. Are you willing to help our meagre attempts to recreate this lost art, and form the Sword of Destiny?"

"Know me not I thought ye do?
Inside you of I see is true.
The Grey and Green you would espew,
when knoweth this will cometh due?
Of what you seek, I cannot tell,
excepted I will cast the spell,"

Silence fell as we considered her words. I shook my head, as did others. The dagger was back in my hand, the Shaman gone. Kay took the knife, and wheeling aside, threw it with force at a wooden door. It went through the hardwood to the hilt. "I hate it when she does that!" We all chuckled in acknowledgement.

Gangling Shortfalls, sage of the Twelfth, arrived at my side in a personal flurry of expectation. "I will assist you understanding the words of the Shaman, Guardian," he whispered surreptitiously.

"That means *Yes*," and nodded his head most knowledgeably. I had kind of guessed as much already, and I nodded back intimating great sharing of his wisdom.

Encouraged, the Giant further expounded, "The grey and the green refer to the Tenth. Ogres are grey skinned, whilst the Trolls are slightly smaller and green of hue." I thanked him for his most generous information. He informed me it was his great pleasure, before moving-on to his next victim.

Sun Kist spoke up; "You do not understand, it is her way to be contrary. Gangling is correct, but there is more. Just so there is no mistake within her words. The new sword will be cast on the shortest day, at the centre of the female world, in Elvenholme. The Shaman has foreseen a far greater threat, not only to ourselves, but the existence of this solar system. She knows so much you know."

Kay said, "I too know of this threat from the stars, and it's very real. First, we must slay the Ogre, reunite the Twelve Tribes, before we look to the heavens. Time escapes us, we rally in action."

Sun Kist curtseyed to the Queen of the Eleventh, her daughter, and then into the round. She smiled her winsome smile, and was gone. My mind was shrieking in clamour, as I muttered words aside, "How can she do that? It is impossible, but we all saw it, yes? Am I going insane, or is there something I am missing?"

Ælthrelntheine said, "The Shaman is an enlightened being, one who still keeps watch over us. We should give thanks for her perseverance with us. She represents the strongest force we have on our side in the wars ahead. The blade will be forged in Elvenholme. Owain, ready the Ddwyrthen smithy, there is little time to prepare. Daughter, Guardian, remember, all is not as it appears to be. Rambling, we will make good your door."

The King of the Twelfth chuckled and said, "As you quite rightly implied, all will come to pass. The dart is fine where it is, adds a sort of obsequious harmony to this chamber, don't you think. Every time I look at it, I will remember you, all of you here today. Thank you, Kay. Your gift is most timely. Regards the Great Ogre, what is the latest news…"

Our days passed quickly, and on the morning of the Solstice, we performed a revived ceremony in the Valley of Knowledge. Sun Kist officiated, attended by the five priests and Ju Lo. The islanders would feast that day, but we had other work to do.

Sun Kist spoke to us afterwards, "Empress, Guardian, please celebrate the Sun's shortest day with your people. The sword must be cast when the Moon is at midday over the lands of the Eleventh. This is most propitious."

Prince Angkrelguer came to us moments later, and invited us to attend the Eleventh that evening, adding, "Owain and the Ddwyrth will be coming in our late afternoon. Please honour us with your company, for none other has set foot in our homeland for many millennia. Tomorrow we will cast the blade, but tonight is for celebration and friendship."

We enjoyed a most pleasurable evening, amazed by the magical beauty of the faery realm. Babbling brooks ran through flower-enraptured meadows, sheltered by almighty trees, many of which were used as arboreal homes. Our hosts were gracious, showing us some of their treasures, and introducing us to the ordinary people. We were shown their High Council chamber, and library, both of which looked out over the largest tree I had ever witnessed, it was unworldly. Ælthrelntheine said, "That is the One Tree. Remember, there is only, ever, one of its kind."

I patted my pocket and was about to tell her of the seed I carried with me, before thinking better of my impulse. We dined in the grounds of the Royal Palace, and it seemed the whole nation was with us. The entertainment was exceptional, and later we slept in leafy bowers lined with gossamer, such a peaceful sleep I had never known before.

The Shaman appeared as we were completing breakfast the following morning. She was accompanied by Sun Kist, and our party left a short time later, and entered the Temple of the Moon. This was not some recent Mayan construction, but clearly of Ancestral design. The walls shimmied with a silvery sheen, almost as if touched by the radiance of the Moon.

Ælthrelntheine led us to the altar, but the Shaman walked away, studying the walls intently, as if to get her bearings. She chanted with closed eyes for a moment, before coming alive and saying, "Good be-it." She brought forth an ancient dowsing twig and walked the round. She obviously found what she was looking for, "The power sought is down below, suffer us the crypt to go."

Ælthrelntheine stared knowingly at the Shaman's back, one already walking towards the holy of holies. We hurried to keep up, and through the crypt, where every ruler since time immemorial was entombed. Coming to the far wall, graced by an ancient frieze, she swept the panel with her bony hand, revealing a motif. "High Lord attend us please, the lock with key you must release."

Chapter 18

Ælthrelntheine looked startled, but did as requested, her ring finger sliding into the motif. The fresco disappeared immediately, being replaced by an eerie dark corridor. The Shaman spoke one word and her staff lit with light. She led us down a very long way below. We eventually came into a vast, circular cavern. The floor was convex, the Shaman leading us unerringly to the centre, which I had presumed to be a hole. It turned out to be a small depression, one made from the blackest rock. She spoke,
    "Centre of female exposed to see,
    for what has being, is yet to be.
    To make new life come here will ye,
    time runneth short, bring all to me."
The Shaman stamped her crook to endorse the command, and immediately Ælthrelntheine touched her return bracelet. Within moments, the smiths of the Seventh and the metallurgists of the Eleventh joined us. Kay knocked my hand and we wandered aside. "Jackie, we thought this place was a myth of legend. This discovery has come as a great shock to my mother, she … we, never knew it existed. The true centre of the female world. Wow!"

The smiths of the Seventh brought forth their finest raw materials, and began the hand-powered smelting process. It would be several hours before the heat of the furnace was hot enough for us to begin casting the sword. A second Ddwyrthen team arrived moments later with extra bellows to fire the furnace. The Shaman stood statuesque looking on. Time passed, and the Eleventh drifted off to explore the cavern of ancient folk law.

Outside the Moon was rising, her midday majesty an hour or so away. Below, we took our turns to man the bellows, encouraging blisteringly white-hot temperature to grow within the forge. During a rest period, sweat dripping off me from the heat and physical exertion, I thought to ask, "Why this place?"

Kay offered me a towel and answered, "Guardian, the ancient ways honour the will of Gaia. Our Mother Earth is female, and she wields the power to bring forth new life. Today, we bring forth that power into the world, in the form of a new blade. One with power to conquer not only our enemies, but hers. Believe! For this is the will of the world."

When the heat of the forge glowed whiter than white, the Shaman nodded her head, her first movement for hours. She watched as Algrenguer and Brynllyn attended the finest ores of creation, by turns hammering the blade flat, only to remake it once more. They folded and refolding the almost molten metal, again, and again, and again. Every single one of us had put our hand to a bellows. The Shaman began muttering in the ancient tongue.

I witnessed symbols, words of an unknown language, as they danced in the air about her. Within a trance, she began to grasp them and toss them into the fire. She teased one rune apart from all others, and sent it to create the future. Instantly, the fire became blue flame. "Smiths insert the blade. Hurry now, make the blade."

They waited, until the blade glowed white with blue hotness.

The Shaman selected runes from the air, and cast them onto the steel, adjuring the smiths to enfold them within the blue-hot blade. And so it continued. Sometimes the glyphs writhed or smelted, at other times they lay peacefully along the shaft of molten metal to be enfolded within. A bluish-green hue began to emanate from the dark depression, where the anvil was placed.

When the final rune was cast, Ræm was called forth, and given in trust to the Shaman. She pinched a finger so a single drop of blood wept from the scratch. The blue-hot blade became the host. We all watched transfixed, as the impossible occurred — the single drop of blood landed on the hilt, and slowly rolled its way towards the tip of the blade.

There it hung within an impossible heat, before the Shaman released the hilt, and the blade turned by its own force, vertical and true between the Moon and Mother Earth. Uncannily, at that instant a beam of moonlight centred on the tip of the blade, and it co-joined with the green energy of Gaia emanating from below.

These forces whirled and bound around the blade, as all the time the drop of our daughter's blood bore witness to their union.

Their unearthly carousel collided in an explosion of kaleidoscopic colours, before being absorbed into the blade. The small drop of blood still hung impossibly from the tip, before rolling back and cleansing the blade, until at last it was gone, the sword made whole, complete.

As the Shaman handed Ræm back to Jien Noi, Sun Kist whispered to us, "The blade must be pure and innocent. Your daughter's blood offering made it so. Thank you. This sword is now your daughter's destiny and you are its regents until that time comes. Use it wisely. I know you will."

The blade remained floating above the exact centre of Earth power. The Shaman produced a pouch, and teased new runes from the contents, as if blessing the hilt of the sword.

"True of heart can only be,
Excepted one who cannot see.
Regents please, not turn to flee,
And Dæmōn slay appropriately."

Sun Kist explained, "Shaman blessed it with power for good at the exception of evil."

Chapter 18

The sword seemed to dance before our eyes, as if captured within a hologram, except this was no modern deception. The blade hung in the air before us all. The Shaman was not quite done. She came to me and removed a ring from her right hand.
    "This knowing ring I cast for thee,
    though ye were all a'busy bee,
    tell it can and evil see,
    wearest this most suitably."

Chapter 19 ~ Powers of The Ancestors

Time warped on, as Kay and I tried to expedite restoration of the craft. Time was interminable. Late one afternoon, disconsolate, I asked the Core "How can we speed up reconstruction?"

"Turn on the main power supply."

"What? Which supply are we using?"

"You are currently using emergency power."

Turning on the power was not that simple. The area needed restoring and renovating first and, the Core informed me this would take several days. Kay and I rose in congratulations. I said, "I'm done for today, let's pick this up tomorrow. I feel so stupid."

Kay looked at me and said, "No Jackie, we were both stupid. Give me five minutes and I am done. While I finish up, invite Owain over, I fancy some fun tonight."

Later, the island was blessed with MacDonald's song, and the hearty companionship of the Ddwyrth. The next morning the Core informed us, "The observation deck has been refurbished."

We went to the lift, and a new rune had appeared at the top. I said, "Observation Lounge," and the device transferred us.

The door opened to a big room. There was a large sweep of glass-like material to the fore, presumably for watching the stars go by. The area was strewn with tables for eating, and easy chairs for relaxation. I turned around and froze. There was a strange looking man standing behind what appeared to be a bar. Across from him, a young woman stood behind a servery. Neither of them moved, or even acknowledged our presence.

Kay drew her sword, n'Gnung and Gung Loi their daggers. I took out my blade, and we cautiously advanced on the two people; neither moved. I stopped just out of range of the man and asked him what he was doing there. He made no sound or movement. Nearby Kay inspected the female, with her sword ready to strike. The blade did not turn blue. She asked, in the language of the Ancestors, "Who are you?"

The woman came alive, looked at her, and said, "I am Chef. What would you like to eat?"

Kay put her sword away and we all chuckled, the automatons were so lifelike. I enquired similarly of the man, and he replied through moving lips, "I am Steward, may I get you anything?"

With growing excitement we checked out the rear, discovering other rooms for keeping fit, games, and a hot tub, to name but few.

Over the days that followed, other areas became available to us, and existing ones were transformed. The pace of renovation increased dramatically when full power was restored. The floor below was dedicated to engineering and technical control. Departments included science labs, engineering control, shields, tactical and weaponry, navigation, communications, and medical. Most of these were essentially control rooms for ship's systems, containing screens and dedicated control panels.

The medical room was different, having beds and strange looking equipment I could not even guess the purpose of. It was staffed by an android nurse, who answered my query, "I can attend to minor issues today. The medical facility is not yet complete; droids are still working on systems and scanners. Specialist nurses are being reconstituted as I speak."

Moments later we saw our first droid, a sort of spider. It looked strange and purpose built. But not as strange as a larger one, built like a man, but looking like some wild imagining Frankenstein built from Meccano. Delighted with progress, our new challenge was to understand everything, and how to operate it.

This was to take us on a new and steep learning curve, and we pressed our minds to the limit in order to learn as much as possible, as quickly as we could. We systematically progressed through Engineering and discovered the shields had an infinite array of interlinked settings, even down to atomic level. We could allow or prevent rain entering, and could also control the amount of ultra violet, and other radiation that entered. Kay had been working on a related issue, but jumped up and enthused, "Jackie, that room over there contains toys and treasures, come see."

Inside we found personnel shields in the forms of bracelets or rings. Kay put on the former, and I the latter. n'Gnung's first strike hit me square in the chest. Fortunately, the projectile was only a cloth. We turned them on and tried again, and they withstood all he and Gung Loi threw at us. We reversed, and the same held true for n'Gnung, but not Gung Loi. They only worked for ring bearers. n'Gnung gave her his ring, and she was protected, but he was not. We tested the devices away from the ship, and the same held true.

Later we investigated Weaponry, which was even more impressive. The Core detailed usage of some seriously disruptive radio-magnetic pulse beams, and plasma bombs. Moments later I made a significant discovery. "Kay, come and have a look at this."

I went to a nearby door and opened it with my ring, "Welcome to the armoury of the Ancestors." We were like kids with new toys, and immediately took ourselves to a distant location to try them out. The premise was the same as for the ship's armaments, but these were hand-held versions, ray guns and plasma grenades. Once we understood the weapons, n'Gnung and Gung Loi took their turns, again only being operable by ring bearers.

Days later, we learned how to make specific rings, and created a zero access ring that was accepted by the weaponry and personal shields. From this small beginning, a new corps was formed. It initially consisted of Horovitz' troops, who by trial and error, became skilled in the use of Ancestral weaponry.

Training went well until break, when one of the men took a mango and was about to eat it. The fruit exploded when another fired a beam at it. The soldier reacted impulsively, vaporising the top button of his attackers camouflage trousers. Many laughed, but the soldier doubled over, clearly in pain. The strike had also vaporised part of his lower belly and we rushed the man to the medical unit. Horovitz collected all weapons as we departed.

The head nurse was not impressed, and repaired a slight rupture to his gut, remodelled the skin, and bawled him out as she did so. The surgery and reconstruction took only a few minutes, and he was left under a strange machine for the healing to complete. The nurse informed us, "This device speeds up cell metabolism and reconstitution. He will remain here for a few hours, but should be fine by this evening."

After training completed, we returned the weapons to the armoury, and made another discovery. A room between Tactical and Comm housed a dozen more return bracelets, and I gave one each to n'Gnung and Gung Loi. We found location transponder rings, and minute communicators that were injected into the cheek, at the back of the jaw. Again, the wearer had to be a ring bearer.

Work had progressed relatively quickly over the course of several days, but then faltered. We did not understand why. Acknowledging another puzzle concealed within the current one, we finished early one day and retired to the shore. We were both frazzled. The lure of discovery stymied by the contrary and sudden stonewalling of progress. n'Gnung and Gung Loi were at our sides, as if protecting us from the intrusion of others, at least until we had recovered our equilibrium. I smiled when Da Phai Nai brought us a beer unbidden, and without retort.

As we recovered, we began to chatter freely, and I knew we were well again when Da Phai Nai felt free to reassert her ribald tongue. "I'll presume you'll be requiring the hogshead this evening, although the sun still hangs high in the sky. Never mind me and those who work around here, enjoy your leisure time."

"Excellent idea," n'Gnung replied. We chuckled, before talk returned to the current problem. We were conversant with the new systems, and had progressed as far as we could with renovations. We could do little else without knowing the next step, "What's holding us back?"

Later, I noticed n'Gnung speaking quietly to Gung Loi, as they had been that night at the latrine. I whispered to Kay, "Do you think it's their personal or professional liaison that is moving on?"

"Perhaps it's both."

"You don't think they're... you know."

"Maybe. They make a good pair. Shhh, they're coming over."

n'Gnung proffered a wry smile and looked at us for a moment, before toasting our good health. He said, "Tell me the problem once again, from the top."

"We've restored all habitable areas that are accessible to us, and brought most ships systems back on line. The schematic shows related and nearby areas, but the Core informs us they are inaccessible. What of it?"

"Do you think that is because they are not part of this half of the craft, but in the other half, presumably buried near the Halfway House? Perhaps you need to put the two halves back together and make it whole again, before restoration can continue."

Kay and I froze. We instinctively knew he was correct. As if a double act, we turned to look at one another, and rose immediately to return to our work. n'Gnung gulped to finish his beer, and grabbed a shark steak as he got to his feet. Gung Loi was already coming to our side, her refreshments left behind in an instant.

Back in the Captains ready room, frustration quickly surfaced. We discovered that if the craft were whole, a complete renovation would be underway. Instead, only the habitable living and working areas of the part we were in were being transformed. We learned that these amounted to a small part of the whole.

We were in the detachable Command Module, a short-range spacecraft in its own right. Main ship systems were interlinked across both parts of the craft, and must be renovated concurrently. Hardware like engines, weapons, long-range scanners, and main batteries were in the other, part of the ship.

We realised everything would have been returning to the way it was originally designed, but for the fact the vessel was in two parts. There was nothing for it but to interface again, and this time set in motion reunification with the rest of the vessel.

I brought up the schematic of the entire ship, which the others immediately inspected as a holographic projection. Using finger and thumb, they were able to pan and zoom in on details. With the engines in the other part of the craft, we would have to use the shields to accomplish the feat.

There was a lot to understand, and we broke to rest and re-gather our thoughts. In time, Kay and I talked of what we had to do, deciding to attempt it in the morning when we were fresh. She needed to check something, so I said, "Brother, Gung Loi, thank you, but we are done for today. Go and order the beers, and see if Da Phai Nai has any beef steak left, we will join you shortly."

Not long after, they departed, Kay said, "Jackie come quickly, you must see this."

The assembly process appeared to be quite simple, but we worried about the others on board becoming entrapped by the changes we were about to instigate. I sent the night crew to the city for refreshments, while Kay made her way down to engineering. We would need to use both interfaces in concert, and directly with the Core at the same time. I discovered that if the ship were in space, rejoining the two parts could be done simply. On terra firma, we each needed to monitor of one half of the ship. We began as soon as Kay was settled to control the missing part of the craft. We both presumed the initiation process would take a few moments, working in tandem…

Somewhere from the distance, I heard the words, "Jackie, break the connection. Come out … Come back now!"

It was a voice I knew intimately — my wife's. I wondered what she was doing there. The voice of my brother added, "I cannot break the mental connection, both he and Kay are locked to the Core. I have removed the interface, but they do not respond."

I was drawn immediately back within the Core, and knew Kay was also there with me. I became engulfed — my essential essence was but a small island floating impossibly within something of truly massif proportions. I would run, except my only form was consciousness. I would hide except there was nowhere to shelter.

Wallowing helplessly within the unknown, I sensed an angelic clarity that felt like pure light. I headed towards it and there was *nothing* for a timeless age. It was like being cast adrift once more, after the wreckage that brought me to the island, but consummately more overwhelming. I was powerless.

Later, much later I knew I existed and that I was somewhere within time, and space, and thought. The moment slipped and I floated once more in *the nothingness*, but this time within my own comprehension of René Descartes *cogito ergo sum*: I know I am *I*.

It seemed æons flashed past as I became aware of something, a world and a people outside of my own core of being. I did not know them. It was just a primordial sense of companionship. The mutuality, the combining, the exceptions all came fleetingly to my grasping

121

comprehension, before leaving as if before they even arrived. The pace quickened, and I became completely lost in a history that was not my own, nor of my known Earth.

There were futile battles with an alien race seeking domination of the known universe. The resultant decimation of their home planet, lead to a desperate escape to Rhea, the remains of which now formed our asteroid belt. All prayers for survival of a great species, left to the whim and reaction of a few who were not chosen, but just happened to be spared, the colonies of Mars. The species survived, before a mighty meteor threatened their survival, and three craft fled the immanent destruction of their meagre atmosphere.

One craft was damaged and crashed upon entry, but another landed safely. The spaceship we were in was badly compromised. I learned the points of containment and leakage, the ghastly threats to the life within, the crew sent to the escape pods. The spacecraft separated in order to survive, and possibly preserve the life within. The landing was heavy. Captain Taris set the emergency beacon with his last conscious movement.

It seemed as if the images slowed, my comprehension swiftly becoming a blur of crazy design of deeper understanding, as I gave myself up to the future, by accepting the history of the Ancestors into the heart of my being.

Chapter 20 ~ In-between Times

"Baba! Baba, wake up!"

The pull on my hand was unmistakable. My daughter was calling me. I held the idea and strove to reunite with my body, held in stasis by a gossamer veil that prevented passage back. I centred my thoughts, and thrust with all my willpower to break through.

The rupture was severe. I was instantly cast adrift from my shackles, and opening my blurry eyes, found I was in bed with my wife, our daughter between us. n'Gnung was the first upon us, I heard the shout, "He's back!"

I made a sign, before falling immediately into a proper sleep."

I heard it again, "Ba — ba!"

There was monkey crawling all over my body. I tried to defend myself from the welcome invasion of my daughter's curiosity, with limbs that did not work. But how, she was … but months old? I felt Jinnie touch me, as n'Gnung came into my blurred line of sight, "Guardian, welcome back! Five hundred suns and more have passed since you were with us last."

By twitches and toads, I came back amongst the people I loved. I tried to sit up, but found my muscles had wasted away to almost nothing. I was skin and bone, my strength, feeble. Jinnie helped me to sit up, as food and drink was brought immediately. I was encouraged to eat as much as I could, before needing to rest almost without delay. As I lay down I croaked, "What of Kay?"

"Guardian she is like you are, were. You have no idea how worried we have been for the pair of…"

Knowing she was the same comforted me. I knew she would be OK, and drifted off to sleep. Several days passed with a regime of regular feeding, light exercise, and sleep. Da Phai Nai insisted I drink a special potion twice each day, and it helped. I thought she winced as she leaned over to press the cup to my lips, but my wife distracted me before I could mention anything.

I quickly grew stronger and managed to walk a short distance on the third day. I went to see Kay, and she lay there like a corpse, but one that retained the colour of life.

Her brow furrowed, I knew the extremes her mind, her essential being, were being subjected to. I held her hand, and wiped her brow. Her expression relaxed and a slight smile appeared as I spoke soothing words to her, both mentally, and verbally. I brushed her hair back from her larger than life face, before I stilled and looked intently. "n'Gnung, look at me. Am I exactly the same as I was?"

"Yes Guardian, I can tell no difference. What is it?"

"I don't know. Humour me. Give me Kay's crown, you know, the one she keeps for official engagements."

He handed it to me, and raised her so we could place it on her head. It no longer fitted. The difference was not much, but it was clear to see. "Her head has grown, which is impossible. Did you take us to the medical unit?"

"Yes. The Matron insisted you both went there once a week, as she was worried about you both, and someone called Meg. It didn't make any sense, but we did it anyway. Well, she was very insistent. You were both kept for several hours each time. What is it?"

My mind seemed to be working more quickly than before. "Our brains have grown, no doubt to absorb the heritage of the Ancestors. Physically, our skulls are bigger, if only by hundredths. What have we done?"

"Guardian, Jack, you and Kay look exactly as before to me."

"Hmmm. What about the spacecraft, is it back in one piece?"

"I do not think so, it appears as it was before you both went under. We searched all over, but nothing has changed, not even one new room."

"Damn! I'll need to check this out."

From the door a voice commanded, "Not today, and never again if I have a say in the matter, husband."

I looked up into Jien Noi's eyes, and saw her smiling, almost goading me. She pushed Ræm towards me, who said, "Daddy, Mommy says I need a brother. What's one of those?"

My face creased into a wide smile as I picked her up, searching frantically for the words to conjure a reply. I looked at Jinnie for help, but she retorted, "Your duty as a man is to beget offspring, and until you are well enough to complete that simple task, dearest husband, you are tethered to my bedchamber."

I tried to rise and prove my manly worth, only for Ræm to grab my hand as my enfeebled muscles gave way. She and n'Gnung helped me totter back to my bedroom, Jinnie chiding me, if playfully. Her time would come, but I realised she was correct. I needed to heal properly before doing anything rash, like begetting another child, or interfacing with the Core.

By the fifth day, my strength was returning, and I instigated a series of short meetings, talking with everyone in turn, as my strength allowed, and catching up on events. n'Gnung was my guide, "Guardian, the Ogres tried to reclaim the lands of the Giants, and failed. We stood with the Twelfth, the Eleventh, and Seventh to ensure they did not circumvent the Twelfth's shield."

Gung Loi added, "They also struck here Guardian, but our shield easily repelled their attempt."

Afterwards I talked with Barph, "We now have a large army, with many more people skilled in all forms of weaponry and combat. I promoted Horovitz with the Empress permission, and they are now a dedicated Blitzkrieg unit, serving a role between our main army, and Gung Loi's Special Forces. The idea was Horovitz', and they form a mighty weapon."

I spoke to many others as my strength and stamina increased, and the days passed. Nevertheless, I remained troubled by Kay's catatonic state, having expected her to wake up shortly after I did. Once I felt fit enough, I went to the control centre determined to bring her back to us as quickly as possible. I needed to discover what the problem was, and there was only one way to do that, interface.

I went to my day room intending to free Ælkræleinnoire from the clutches of the Core, despite protestations from others vehemently opposed to the idea. I connected effortlessly, and knew immediately this was not like before. I quickly assimilated and felt at ease. I interfaced with rapid thoughts exchanged like probes, and soon realised I was now doing so directly in the language of the Ancestors, which I appeared to comprehend fluently.

I discovered that in order to put the spacecraft back together, we both had to become fully trained crewmembers. This meant we had to learn the language and technology, as in the history of the Ancestors. Some of their customs were odd, but understanding necessary to operating the craft. It appeared I had been imbued with all their knowledge, and especially the skills of the previous crew. I knew instinctively that was true.

The Core revealed Kay was trapped within a safety loop, one designed to stop her brain being overloaded. I ascertained that each time the protective loop cleared of the information download, the mind-training programme resumed, until the next loop was encountered. It appeared the full download must be completed, or it could be manually over-ridden by another person.

I was now able to act as that control, and set about to interrupt the download. I merely had to think it, and it would happen instantly. The Core cautioned me, 'The download is virtually complete, one day more, maybe two'. I decided to let the download complete.

"Core, why is the download taking longer for her?"

"Because she already knew much of an Ancestral dialect, but not the way we use it. Her learning is also relearning, preserving the extant, and adding a new language layer is more complex."

"Thank you, that makes perfect sense. Now I understand."

"In time, I am sure you will."

The others were greatly relieved to know Ælkræleinnoire would soon be restored and they began preparations for her healing.

That evening I ventured to the shore in company with n'Gnung and Gung Loi. I eased down to the beach and made it as far as the Sentry Rock before needing to sit and rest. I felt a curative peace envelop me as I leaned back against the rocky spire and closed my eyes.

I must have nodded off because the next thing I knew, I was being hoisted between my two friends and carried back to our table. I objected, but they ignored me, and if I were truthful, I am glad they did.

Bu Te came to take our order, but I was scared by my recent frailty and ordered vegetable soup, salmon with bread, and spring water. n'Gnung ordered beer and beef steaks and cajoled me to try, but I said, "Next time brother. I am still too weak and need to look after my body."

Bu Te returned with my soup and I asked, "What of Da Phai Nai?"

"Oh, Guardian you will not know. She is resting just now. Sometimes her back plays up and she needs to lie down for a while. She was sweeping up earlier today and must have tweaked something. I'm sure she will soon recover. Now, your salmon will only be a moment. I have some fruit juice if you'd care to try it?"

Before returning home, I checked on Da Phai Nai, but she was sleeping so I let her be. I spoke to others about her and realised she was getting older and suffering the pains that come with age. There was little I could do for her except to make her life easier, offer her retirement perhaps? It was something I would mention another time.

Days later I was working in my ready room when the Core informed me Kay's download had completed. I immediately went to her, sat at her bedside, and held her hand. I was waiting and willing her to come back to the world of the living, rejuvenated. I tried to mentally tell her to push and break through the veil, like I had done. Nothing happened.

Waiting, I casually looked over her form, and felt desire. I admit, were I a single man, this fine woman would make an ideal partner. No sooner thought, than I chastised myself for thinking such a ridiculous thing. I was startled when a soft voice wafted to my thoughts, "Jackie, know I would perhaps seek this also."

I started upright as two white eyes locked my blue orbs, and bored into the depths of my soul. I immediately leaned across to welcome Ælkræleinnoire, the High Lord of Destiny, back into the land of the living. She put her arms around my neck for support as I raised her up into a sitting position, and she kissed my lips with deepest, but fleeting intent.

Stunned, I staggered back. Before I gathered my senses, the moment was gone. Our souls returned unto ourselves, like two ships passing in the night. However, that single moment would by its intensity, haunt both of us for decades to come. I was left floundering, wondering how I could possibly have avoided that kiss. It was not right, not right at all. The devil's voice in my head asked, "Would you have prevented it had you known?"

I had no answer, and chagrined, my eyes flicked to hers before I nodded and turned away, that battle to never face another day. Her voice came into my head, seemingly unbidden, "For friends Jackie, just for old friends' sakes."

I turned in the doorway and bowed to her. It was a stupid thing to do, but also the correct thing. We smiled across the emotional abyss between us. Her eyes closed. I had to leave.

I called others to attend Kay, and once alone, took a moment aside to thank the three sisters for my doom: Ladies Luck, Fate, and Serendipity. Now I had the High Lord of Destiny to contend with. My small *boy-brain* needed release, a beer or three, and the companionship of my wife, child, and my brothers most of all.

Like me, Kay had woken momentarily, and went straight back to sleep. Her recovery process mirrored my own, but I hastened it by taking her to the ship's now fully functional medical facility.

The head nurse ran several scans before pausing, "She will be fine and recover in a few days. I have administered a sedative also, so put her to bed. Feed her lightly when she wakes, medicinal vegetable soup is recommended, and let her sleep most of tomorrow. Her healing is mental for now. Once alert, she will need physical strengthening also, so bring her back to me when she is able to walk and I will administer tonic and rejuvenation medicines. I will also set her a personal exercise program. Next time you interface, she like you will have no problems."

"Matron, what has happened to our brains? I am sure my skull is slightly larger."

"You are correct. Your brain's interconnectivity has been increased. The Core advised us it was necessary in order for your education to complete. Your brains grew in size, so we increased the skull to suit."

"Impossible. Who is Meg?"

The medic chuckled, "MEG is short for Megalencephaly, or an overly large brain. It is usually a birth defect, but in both your cases, we induced it using pur-alpha, a sequence-specific single-stranded DNA and RNA-binding protein. It is responsible for neuronal proliferation during neurogenesis as well as the maturation of dendrites."

"In other words, our brains and skulls are larger than before."

"Yes, but only the cerebral cortex and surrounding bone."

Chapter 20

The Matron, insisted on carrying out a thorough check of us both and seemed surprised when apart from being weak, we passed all her tests. "Matron, if I did not know it was impossible I would say you are quite amazed."

A slight chuckle escaped her speaker as she admitted, "I have only ever known the Ancestor read me as you do."

The Matron quieted for a moment before adding, "The potion your friend administered to you and the Eleventh, please may I study it? Your recovery was far quicker than our medical knowledge indicates.

"You are recuperating well, Guardian. Eat fish, and exercise as much as you are able. These preparations I am now administering will assist. You are free to go as long as you do not overtax yourself for a few days, and no more interfacing with the Core until you are completely healed. I have also cured the small problem with your vision. Return when you are well again and I will perform a full body assessment and repair."

I thanked her and was about to leave when an odd thought struck me, "Nurse, do you mean you can repair a body that is very old?"

"Of course, although we can do nothing about the actual ageing process itself. Once a body has run its course, we simply clone it and transfer the existing mind into it, as such. We cannot do that complicated process here with these facilities. However, we can make limited DNA and RNA correction, meaning the body heals itself, almost instantly. It works best on things like internal organs; traumæ like cuts and breakages take noticeably longer."

I returned Ælkræleinnoire to my home, and leaving instruction with staff, headed for the shore. I was looking for one of three people. Da Phai Nai was the first I encountered, and she greeted me ebulliently, "Ahha! The ringleader has returned at last, no doubt to drive me crazy with incessant demands for beer no less. Here's your first." She put the flagon down and whispered, "Welcome back, Guardian. It's been boring around here with you gone for so long."

I looked back into her eyes and stated, "I need a guinea pig, and you're it. Come with me, this won't take a moment."

Da Phai Nai became less trusting as the head nurse of the spacecraft's medical facility gave her a full examination. There was a long list of things wrong with her, the ones that troubled my friend the most being concerned with joints, especially her knees and back. I ordered a full reconstitution, and left the room accompanied by the demonic revelations of a vitriolic tongue.

Later, n'Gnung spoke knowingly, "Guardian, I remember you once said that certain people make a difference, just regards how the days of our lives play out. You said you knew of two, Da Phai Nai and Owain. I agree up to that point, but for me, there are three I know of. It was never the same with you gone. It is once more, now you are back."

n'Gnung and I raised a glass in brotherhood. Finishing our toast, we watched the others at play on the shore. Some were checking the rock pools and others beach-combing, or swimming. I thought aloud, "It is a shame Owain isn't here this evening."

"A shame indeed. He'd enjoy this evening more than most."

We started, as a noise behind us turned into a familiar rumble of belly laughter, "Would that be so now me gallant young friends. Ye did'ne think I would miss yer wee party here now, did ye?"

The night was great fun, my will to live life to the full returning. Owain was excellent company and kept us amused with his tall tales.

A few days later, I took Kay back to see the medic, and waited for the treatment to finish.

One week passed. n'Gnung and I were ambling towards our table on the shore. Da Phai Nai had been released from care that morning, and she spotted us at once. She strode towards us with her best broom at the ready, and chased us towards our seats. "I have never — [whack] — felt fitter — [whish] — or better — [wallop] — for I don't know how long. I feel twenty years younger, and it is all *this* rascal's entire fault! You'll be wanting a large flagon tonight, what with guests expected. Don't even bother to rise, I can now manage quite ably once again. This is all *his* doing!"

n'Gnung spoke to my side, "It would appear Da Phai Nai has missed you. She hasn't used her broom for a long time. Years."

I smiled ruefully and said, "There was a reason for that, she couldn't. Her back had a progressively debilitating problem, which has now been cured. Brother, we better wear padded pants in future."

We were chuckling and chortling, when I saw Won Long and Lo Si being wheeled over to our table. I learned that walking more than a few paces was beyond them. Lo Si had personal carts to be made for them. Won Long had developed a bronchial cough that was fairly constant, and Lo Si's mind had begun to wander occasionally. I knew just the remedy, and made it so moments later, against their protestations.

After depositing a thankful Lo Si, and complaining Won Long to the medical unit, I determined all our old and infirm would be likewise treated, and I would begin with the Emperor the next day. I returned with n'Gnung to the shore, eager to pick up with Owain, but Gung Loi interjected with a pointing finger, "Look. Aroweena has not been here for a long time. It is good to see her back, I have missed our fights."

I was not prepared for the greeting Aroweena delivered. She was never one given to formalities. As soon as she saw me, she let out a whoop of delight and ran full pelt towards me. She leapt into my arms, sending me flying backwards in the process. I was besieged with hugs and kisses, before she sat up, astride my prone belly, and smiled in joy, before hugging me tightly, dragging me to my feet, and back to the table. I understood within that moment, there was more than one reason why Aroweena was renowned as 'The Keeper of Hearts' — a fearsome foe maybe, she was an even fiercer friend.

Representatives of the other tribes joined us the following day, as did our own dignitaries and friends, in what proved to be a weird sort of homecoming celebration. Ælkræleinnoire arrived and sat to one side quietly. She was still deep within recuperation, but wanted to make a physical appearance. To save her being pestered with well-meaning inanities, I took her to one of the new and secluded gazebo's set along the heights above the shore. I placed her opposite the Sentry rock, and asked if she needed anything. A curious play behind her eyes spoke more than words, but I had noticed one person not pay her any mind, her own mother.

Kay spoke to me mentally, "I discovered something of vital importance concerning the Eleventh, proof of a fact considered myth or heresy. It concerns me personally, the reason why I am considered 'different'…"

I subsequently received an insight into her own kind, and knew I had work to do. The Queen of the Eleventh was disarmingly indulgent, verging on ingratiating as I took her out of earshot, it didn't work on me. Once we were alone, I bawled her out. I probably said some things I should not have said in the heat of the moment, but what was done, was done with — as best of friends.

Afterwards I escorted her to her daughter's arbour, and waited nearby but out of earshot, for just a minute … then five … I departed before ten minutes had elapsed. This was now their business, and none of mine.

Chapter 21 ~ Paths of Providence

Our celebrations of the night before were tremendous with so many people and different tribes attending. Over breakfast, I worried about Kay, but it seemed no one had seen either her or her mother since the previous evening. I excused myself to go to check if she was still there.

I found Ælthrelntheine talking quietly to the sleeping form of her daughter. She quietened as I approached noisily, and welcomed me to sit with them for a moment. It was clear there had been a dramatic shift in their relationship, and one she had no intention of relating. Instead, we spoke briefly about the previous evening, the impending doom, and how changes had already taken place. Later, she surprised me, "I have been such a fool, Guardian. Tell me about my daughter?"

What could I tell her, except the truth, "Kay is highly gifted and a credit to you and your Tribe. She is a fearless seeker of knowledge, and a truer friend…"

Kay stirred from her slumbers and came gradually awake. We enquired how she was feeling and she told us she was weak, but doing well. I left to order breakfast of her choosing and encouraged Ælthrelntheine to join us also. However, it was clear she would stay with her daughter, and subsequently I gave staff two breakfast orders for delivery.

That morning Dawn came to welcome me back to the land of the living. I knew one of my closest had sent word to her. One look at n'Gnung confirmed my suspicion. He shrugged his shoulders and smiled knowingly. Ælthrelntheine returned before we finished breaking fast, and seeing representatives from all the tribes present, called a meeting, cancelling the one due the following week. It made sense to everyone. As others prepared, she took me aside, "Guardian, is what my daughter tells me about Oma the truth?"

I looked deeply at her and replied, "Oma was Captain of the spacecraft that landed intact. The vessel we are trying to put back together again was under the control of Taris. The third craft was heavily damaged. We need to know where Oma's spacecraft is, and who now controls it, although I would think that pretty obvious."

She breathed life within understanding, "The Great Ogre."

"I believe so, but we need proof. It would explain a lot of things, including their power to clone, manipulate races, DNA. It may also explain the Ancestors apparent disappearance, because unlike here, there is no physical record anywhere, except in the known historical testimony, written by Taris.

Chapter 21

To answer your question, Great Queen, I can confirm that Oma had jet-black hair and white eyes. You know their kind always had silvery white hair and blue eyes, just like our androids.

"What you did not know, was that Oma created the first ever Queen of the Eleventh in her own image, but all others of your kind had blonde hair and blue eyes, some green bespeckled gold, like your own. I do not believe this was a coincidence. The order of the world is in flux, and we need to unite as one if we are to have any chance of survival."

She stood silent, unnaturally still and erect for a moment, before admitting, "I have been an idiot. The world turns, and as it does so, my daughter the High Lord of Destiny walks this Earth in Oma's form."

She quieted for a moment before adding, "I hear them sometimes you know, the Ancestors—calling out for release. It is as if they are entrapped within some macabre, alive but held in stasis. Thank you, Guardian."

The subsequent meeting took up most of the morning, and I learned it was mainly a repetition of those I had missed. There had been developments, but nothing of note until right at the end. Rambling said, "Some of our brethren knew of the Sixth a few hundred years ago, but they are a secretive race and not given to trusting others. They live in great fear of the Ogre, and espouse contact of any kind. I know where they were last sighted. It is a place to begin."

The meeting broke apart shortly after, Ælthrelntheine coming to walk with me as we made our way for luncheon. "Guardian, the only way the Great Ogre could wield such power is if he controlled Oma's spacecraft. There can be no other explanation."

"What about your control room, surely it can do the same?"

Ælthrelntheine smiled wistfully and said, "No Guardian, you are wrong. None of our control rooms has the power of a spacecraft, and its Core behind it. That changes everything. As soon as Kay is well enough, you must finish putting the craft you have back together again."

As I watched Ælthrelntheine walk away, I realised she had called her daughter 'Kay' for the very first time. The world as we knew it was indeed in flux.

Dawn wandered over and guided me back to my family and closest friends. Once settled she said, "Jackie, I need to return in a moment, why don't you come with me? You need new clothes, footwear, and I'll treat you to dinner. Tomorrow we can get you a laptop, so you can begin to write all this down for posterity, what do you say?"

I looked at my wife, and she confirmed she would look after Kay, urging me to go. I took time with Ræm, leading her down to the sea and playing with her in the shallow waters. We skipped in the foaming strand and both got soaked. In time, Jinnie ushered me away, although I did look back and waved from the crest of the slope, as she had once done so many years ago. In that moment, I understood why my wife had done that.

London was a blast and we reacquainted with old haunts, Camden Town, Covent Garden, and later, a favourite West End restaurant. We were about to order, when a man came over to us and Dawn welcomed him with a hug. As we left to join his table, she said aside, "He is an old acquaintance, and very well connected. His friends are fun, trust me."

We were introduced to his group and made welcome. I shook hands with the men, and kissed the women's cheeks Hollywood style. The host shook my hand forcefully, and I saw my ring turn blue, the only ring of power I was wearing. I knew instantly he was an Ogre in human form. As he turned away, I looked at Dawn and whispered, "My ring turned fiery blue."

Her eyes flew wide, "What does that mean? … Oh My God!"

Our plans changed dramatically within the knowing look of eyes. The host invited everyone on to a party, and Dawn's friend urged us to join them, "Mr. Barranger has many friends in the City and government circles."

The evening turned bizarre, becoming a game as we tried to keep up with the man's ego. I shook every hand that came my way, and between us, we managed to get drinking glasses correlating to snapshots, of every one we met who turned my ring to blue fire. There were not many, but they were all highly influential people, or their escorts.

We left when most hangers-on did. Once back on the Island I erupted like a verbal volcano, my tongue tied for too long. "My ring was blue, fiery blue. Many times and often. You know these impostors appear to be everywhere. What are we really facing? I'll tell you what, Ogre clones the world over, within the higher echelons of the Last. These are not ordinary people, but the movers of commerce and journeymen of governance. Presidents even?"

Later, we assembled our evidence in my day room, and sat to stare at it. I made provision with the Core for us to interface Dawn's digital camera, and my new laptop and memory devices. The result was like a shelf, where we could put anything down, and a suitable connection would be made. I asked, "Dawn, do you know of any way to run fingerprints on these wine schooners?"

She set about taking professional quality, digital images of the prints, and associated them by filename with photographs of the providers. All that remained was to process them.

I had nothing to offer, but Dawn said, "My only hope is an old friend, John Tredwell. He's Chancellor of Aston University, but should have retired before now; you met him once, remember? Anyway, I would not expect him to help directly, but he may know people, or of a University that has a forensic science faculty."

It turned out he did, and some days later our information was used as a support project by Staffordshire University. The only problem was they had the processing skills, but no access to the databases we sought. I got a tip off one of the students, and later that day, we found ourselves in New York meeting a computer geek who worked the black market. I had to pay the nerd several thousand dollars, but eventually he agreed to run the prints. The results proved to be quite interesting. One set of prints matched those of a deceased CIA operative. The file he gave us had a photograph of him with some of his known CIA operatives. The problem was, I had one of those other faces on an ID card back in our control centre. He was one of the militia who attacked our island under Quinn.

Some days later, Dawn got an email from the geek. He had made a link between one set of prints, and a second guy from the Central Intelligence Agency. This was getting nepotistic, and also piqued our curiosity. We attended the meeting early in the evening, but something was off. The guy seemed genuine and gave us a file that had a couple more faces I recognised from our massed ID collection back on the island. I wanted more information, and he worked his array of computers, complaining about the internet connection. I got the impression he was playing for time, but why?

I asked him what was going down, and he must have sensed our unease. His phone bleeped and he received a message, dismissively swatting the intrusion away. "Annie wants to party tonight. I hope we are almost done here? She's great in the sack."

All of a sudden, his computer got hits, and we both leaned forwards expectantly. He copied a folder to a pen drive and said, "This is straight off the Agency server. It will include a tracker when unzipped, so I cannot open it now, but I know it is what you want. Time for you to leave, Annie is waiting."

We left immediately, but in the event, the only things that went down that night were the torsos of Dawn and myself, hard onto a Brooklyn street, cuffed, and taken into custody by NYPD.

We came to rest in holding cells of the FBI field office, Queens. For hours I gazed around, noticing the room was bare, apart from the table, a few chairs, and what must surely be a two-way mirror opposite. They wanted me to fret. I started to nod off. I was almost asleep when the door banged loudly, and two men entered the room, but only one spoke, "Sorry to wake you, but I need to know why you were running fingerprints illegally."

He looked at me expectantly, and I yawned as I came fully awake. I knew this could be fun. I smiled and said, "First, tell me who you are? FBI, CIA, NBA?"

The man gave me a strange look, as if trying to catalogue which type of felon I was. He replied, "I am not CIA, and neither am I a basketball player, nor NSA for that matter. Henry Walcott, FBI. And you are…?"

"Thank you Henry, I need to shake your hand before I say anything more, and that of your colleague, indulge me please. I was expecting CIA. Are your supposed security services double-dealing once more, or are you the real deal?"

He did not proffer his hand to me, so I crossed my arms and stared straight ahead. They harangued me, but in time left the room, only to come back a while later. Entering, Henry held out his hand, which I shook, and that of his associate. My ring remained as it should. I looked up at the mirror, wondering who was watching, and how far a chance I could ride on my luck.

"Sorry, my name is Jack Barleycorn and you can check out my history if you wish. You will probably find I was lost, presumed drowned in wreckage somewhere east of Fiji in August two thousand and ten."

He nodded in confirmation, "That is what we have, and then your trail goes dead. Which terrorist group are you working for?"

"Let me assure you that Dawn and I are in no way terrorists, and neither are we a threat to the USA, or at least anyone who is honest and law-abiding. We have recently discovered the two may not be the same."

"So why were you running fingerprints illegally?"

"One set of prints you enquired about belongs to a dead CIA operative. We met him socially in London a couple of days ago. Do you have the folder I was carrying?"

"You mean the man in this photograph?"

"Yes, but there is another shot of him with some others."

"This one, what's so special about it? Why were you interested in this man?"

"If I told you, you would not believe me."

"Try me."

I shrugged my shoulders and looked back directly into his eyes, "He was a clone working for forces allied to a foreign power, which we call the Tenth … Column. No doubt, his mind was altered during the process. Their aim is to enslave all humanity."

I sat back and waited. Henry belly-laughed, before issuing threats, and ridiculing me about the absurd hypotheses. However, he did let slip the CIA man was known to be alive, and was being investigated. I waited until his tirade tailed off, and said, "See. I told you that you wouldn't believe me, but it happens to be the truth. You see the man standing next to him in this photo?"

"Yes, what of him."

"He is dead."

"You murdered him?"

"Yes and no. He was a mercenary who slaughtered innocent civilians, women and children — with a machine gun. I did not kill him, but I would have done. They waged war on a peasant village because they could make money. I also have the fingerprints or information about several others in his group. I will go and get them if you promise to process them. It won't take a moment."

It was clear I had touched a nerve with Henry. He looked at me as if deliberating. His partner spoke for the first time, "There is no way we will let you leave here until you tell us the truth."

My fingers rested on my return bracelet, but before pressing the button I said, "Not all is as you understand it. Let me get the other wine glasses for you to check out. This rabbit hole runs awfully deep. What do you say Henry?"

"Jack, say I were to indulge you, believe your preposterous story, how would you proceed?"

"Run the prints, and once you have the results back and analysed, I will say more."

"OK, you can make the call from this phone."

I stood and touched my return bracelet. Moments later, several wine schooners and a pile of photographs appeared on the interview table. I did not return, but watched them scratch their heads, before examining the evidence. I would see how this played out. We got Dawn back moments later, and continued observation until they knocked-off for the day, following Henry back to his hotel. I presumed he was either not local, or in marital dispute.

That night Ælkræleinnoire felt strong enough to join us for the main meal, but she ate little, and little often, and soon departed for the gazebo. I took time to be alone with her because I was coming to believe the immediate future hinged upon us alone to a great degree. She confirmed this was her understanding also, and we spoke in tongues for our amusement before tiredness overtook her. I brushed her hair aside and settled her, before rising and attending my own true love, our daughter, and our companions.

The next evening, New York time, I went to see Henry. I had agreed a series of outcomes with Kay, who monitored us. I had expected him to have a house and family, but he was using a hotel near the field office.

He was alone, and knocked on his door. A shout came from within, "Go away, I don't need anything."

I replied, "I thought you wanted to see me, Henry."

I heard him moving, and in time the door opened, a Glock pointed at my heart. I said, "You can keep the bullet, but I'll take a beer if there's one going begging. We need to talk."

At first wary, distrusting, he pressed me to explain how Dawn and I escaped. I gave him a brief demonstration, apparating behind him as he peered through the door ajar. "Now, the beer if you please, Henry, and I will tell you a little more. I am easily bought."

He spun round in disbelief, prodding my torso, making sure I was real. He went to the mini-bar as if on automatic, retrieving a beer for me, and a large bottle of bourbon for himself. I said, "Thank you Henry. I promise I will explain how I do that, show you perhaps, but first level with me. We are on the same side, you and I."

With little commitment, he started to open up. "We analysed the prints you gave us, and they matched the mug shots you took. These were all powerful men, but one of the lady escorts from London appears in a terrorist database here in the U.S., one we have been tracking. It is high-brow, politicians and the like. She's linked to a group that hold great interest for us. I initiated a tail on her, and we have just discovered links to a previously unknown underground cell."

Refilling his tumbler he said, "This does not leave this room, Jack. Your host, Mr. Barranger, is in cahoots with someone we have been trailing for several months, Mr. Hunter. He is why we became interested in you in the first place. Hunter's company Envirotech is simply a front. At first, we thought he was aligned with the State Department, but our latest information contradicts this. He has fingers in many pies and a network of offshore subsidiaries mainly associated with armaments and computer intelligence. Our official investigations got absolutely nowhere. Even our Director and the ODNI…"

"What?"

"The Office of the Director of National Intelligence, they had little on Hunter. So we set up this team to infiltrate their organisation and find out what was really going on.

"I simply put the two together and came up with the fact that his likely sphere of operations is counter-intelligence, espionage, and state of the art weaponry. This includes sales to the highest bidder: Russia, China, disenfranchised countries, terrorists, you name it. There appear to be leads to all of them, until they go cold. So rather than looking outside, I thought to bring the investigation inside. But yet again, his trail goes cold at the doors of the White House, and the Senate. However, I do not think the President knows exactly what is going on."

Chapter 21

I reflected on his words and took a long slug of the cool beer. "Henry, you have shown great confidence in me and I thank you for that. I can tell you that Barranger works for an alien power, and I would by inference, suspect the same of Hunter. They are a group of people, but as powerful as any country. And believe me when I tell you that they do not have your country, or my country's best interests at heart. I would show you everything we have. Tell me, who do you trust with your life?"

"Jack, I basically trust no one. No, that's not true, but outside of my team, my director, my wife and family there are very few others in my life. What about you?"

I smiled and chinked his tumbler, "That's fair, about the same here. I have one last question for you, and as an American, it will be far simpler for you to answer. If anyone wanted to subvert the United States of America to their own will and use a few people; which positions would those people hold?"

"Holy shit! Stop screwing with me. The Presidency of course," he flashed back as if I were stupid.

"His power and personage change every four years, Henry. What of the journeymen, this Director of National Intelligence perhaps. What if he worked for the Russians or Chinese?"

"Jack, I ain't some newbie, you got that. Conspiracy theories come and go. We remain, simply because occasionally one of them adds up. Most turn out to be government diversions targeted for the press to mislead the public, whilst something much bigger passes unnoticed. Either show me what you got, or assume the position, hands behind your head."

"I have an extremely good reason why it is not only possible, but has already occurred. Will you trust me Henry? Indulge me please with a trip into my fantasy if you will, and I will rest my case."

He looked at me before laughing and downing his shot, "OK, show me, and don't disappoint me."

No sooner had he replied, than there came a loud rap to the door. "Henry Walcott, this is the CIA. We know you are in there. Open the door and come out now with your hands held high."

Henry hurled some abuse back, before I made him listen, "Henry, focus. Stall for time. I will get us out of here before they break the door down. Gather everything you need from this room, and be quick. Keep talking to them."

"I guess it's time I trusted somebody, everything here in NY stinks to high heaven."

Henry cleared his table come desk, whilst I gathered the rest of his things together in a pile. We were about done when the man outside the door got fed up with waiting and put shoulder to the door in warning, they had tried the keycard, but were held back by the deadbolt. I said, "Time to go. We got everything?"

Henry nodded. I gave the signal to transport. It looked like his eyes popped out of his head when we reanimated in the control room of the shore. Waiting for us were Kay, n'Gnung, and Gung Loi. Henry stuttered to say, "He's not human."

"He is my best friend, and a close cousin of our kind. I will explain more later."

n'Gnung came forward and proffered his hand, "Hello, how do you do," in his best British English.

He spluttered, "An Elf," before his eyes focused on the screen, and gawked at his hotel room, just as his bags disappeared into thin air, arriving moments later in the transfer circle. "Impossible!"

On the screen, the door splintered open, and four armed men rushed into the room. "Henry, do you recognise any of these people?"

He gave me a strange look, and turned his gaze back. Moments passed before his rationale kicked in. "Two are CIA, one I do not know, and the fourth is with the NIA. What's going on?"

"You tell me, why were they after you? Did you get too close to something?"

"It must be to do with you, but I cannot see how?"

"Time I got you out of here."

I took a moment to mentally link with Kay, "See to it all four are tracked by the control room. We need to know who they are and where they are based."

We cajoled Henry to the transporter, arriving on the shore moments later. Word had been sent ahead, and Dawn welcomed us as we walked towards my table, "Hello Henry, so good to see you again. It is so lovely here, don't you think? Come, let's go for a walk on the beach. Dinner will be a few hours I'm afraid."

It was obvious Henry was in a state of shock. We skipped in the sea horses and stripped off for skinny-dipping. He joined us, although kept his boxers on. I remain sure it was the feel of physical nature that made him realise what he was experiencing was real. Sand between his toes, salt water and coughing as he swam, the warm sun, and later the meal.

His education was severe. He met with Dwarves, Elves, and others of humanity that evening. I explained about the Twelve Tribes, and of the Ancestors, whose technology we were using. I proceeded to tell him about the Tenth and our suspicions of their infiltration into his real world. He took it all in, and I wondered if by doing so, I had made a

Chapter 21

grave error of judgement. Time would tell if he believed me, and if we could trust him.

Chapter 22 ~ A New Alliance

The next morning n'Gnung shook me gently. I came awake and he told me Henry had woken already. I found him talking quietly with Dawn and strolled over to where he was sitting.

We chatted, and generally soaked up the feel of the new day in the most idyllic of places. He espied others eating breakfast and I asked him what he would like eat. He replied, "Strong coffee, black."

In time I ordered a beefsteak for him, I wanted him to experience familiar things, ones his mind and body could relate to.

Henry seemed to relax within the familiarity of smells and textures of food he knew. He was almost done when a shadow passed behind his eyes. He thanked us for the food, and stood to wander along the shore. Later he climbed the sentry rock, gazing out over the sea for a long while. Afterwards he walked in the surf, and clambered over rock pools, delighting in our seafood larder.

Meanwhile, we decided what to do with him, and what to show him. The control centre was out of bounds, but most places were open to him. n'Gnung and Gung Loi cleared one of the huts, we needed information from him also. When he returned, he stood with chest proud and said, "OK. Hit me, show me what you got."

"Come, I'll show you what is really going on. The walk to the transporter is not far, and it will give you a view of this headland."

My closest companions accompanied us, and a little later, I showed views of the island on the screen. We visited places of interest. We showed him around the palace and Grimwaldi Rinns; Kay stayed behind to personally manage transfers.

We finished late morning, and as the tour concluded he said, "This is impossible. Yet, it is real. If this technology fell into the wrong hands, it … I dread to think of the consequences."

"I hope you are sincere Henry, and not just saying what sounds good. I doubt there is any force on this planet that could take control or overrun us, now we are in full control of it."

"Where am I?"

"Somewhere in the South Pacific near the tropic of Capricorn."

"This island is large, and has never been charted. How come?"

"It is shielded from all eyes and satellites. It can withstand a direct nuclear blast, several actually."

"OK, you have won my trust. I promise I won't breathe a word of this place, or these people to anyone."

"I already know you won't Henry. Nobody would believe you. You have no proof regardless. Say anything and they will lock you up as a delusional madman."

Henry acknowledged the truth of my words by grunting a mirthless chuckle and nodded begrudgingly. "So, what's next Jack?"

n'Gnung said, "All is prepared, Guardian. Let's go."

Henry said, "Jack, I will walk back, I need the fresh air, and time to think about what you said last night, let's all take a stroll."

As we departed, I fixed him intently in the eye; "I know there is another one of these somewhere, and it is under the control of the Great Ogre. A war coming, one *homo sapiens* know nothing about. I'm taking a big risk trusting you Henry, don't let us down."

"Yes, the Tenth. Jack, I'm a man of facts, proof. You show me the impossible, perform the impossible, and I distrust it is real. Yet, I know it as physical fact. The Captain Slog transporter trick for instance — impossible, but you do it all the time. What is this place, who made it, the Ancestors?"

I gave Kay a knowing look and replied, "Yes Henry. I feared for my own sanity when I first arrived here, and later when we discovered this place. Remember what we talked about last night? The Ancestors arrived on this planet several million years ago. They created the Twelve Tribes … this technology is older still."

I was going to say more, but Henry's mind engaged inwards, doing the maths. We began walking as he deliberated, and in due course, he seemed to reach a conclusion. Looking around, focusing on the old banyan tree we were nearing, before turning to look at me. I added to his confusion, "So there is no mistake, the Second, have lived here for thirty thousand years, and until my arrival, had been left undisturbed by the outside world. Their culture is stone age, yet they know how to work the ancient device."

Dawn spoke up, jerking the moment around, "Jackie, why don't we show Henry what you collected after the invasion by Theodosius Quinn. This is real sharing we can all benefit from."

Henry immediately snapped out of his malaise, "Theodosius Quinn. He was the ringleader of a group we were after, but he disappeared a few years ago. There's been no sign of him since."

I looked at Dawn, but she gestured to me. I said, "That's because we defeated his invasion plans, and later executed him. He was a senior Ogre clone, and a nasty piece of work. We have a hut full of his militia's paraphernalia, care to take a look?"

The room was a goldmine of intrigue, and Henry filled his boots with a tactile reality he could comprehend. "This stuff is all state of the art, look at this one, it isn't even on the market yet. These were serious people. How on Earth did you defeat them?"

"All was lost. We were armed with stone daggers and wooden spears. Even with our control room, they managed to run disruption of their own. Had not the Eleventh and the Seventh come to our rescue, we would all be dead or enslaved right now."

I wheeled away as the bitterest of memories caught me unawares. I gabbled, "They killed over one and a half thousand of this unique culture with modern weapons … women and children, stone-age peasants, just for the money. I can never forgive them."

I heard Dawn say, "He needs a moment, Henry…"

I had withdrawn to where the dog tags and ID's were piled, but I found no solace there. I grabbed a handful and slapped them into Henry's hand, "You may know some of these murderers."

I had no idea what I was going to do next, but Henry became animated, "Jack, this is incredible. We have been after some of these people for years, decades in one case. You have more?"

I ushered him over to the pile, and he went through each one quickly, his enthusiasm bringing me back from the brink. "Jack, I need to check all of these out, personally. I need to take these back with me, and in return I'll not only believe in what you have shown me already, but swear never to breathe one word about this place to another. Do we have a deal?"

He was acting like a kid in a sweetshop, vibrant and full of wonder. Kay sent her calming thoughts into my mind, with a way to move us all forward. I interpreted her words and said, "Henry, we have our deal, or at least, a place to begin."

Dawn photographed every ID for posterity, while Gung Loi took charge of bagging the identification. Time passed quickly, before we made our way back to my table for late lunch. After we had eaten, Henry asked me to check a couple of locations for him.

I used my return bracelet, and duly transferred Henry and my team to the island transporter. I brought up several locations at his direction, but all appeared to be in order. He seemed pleased, but also hesitant, before asking, "Jack, could I check on my family? I haven't seen them for a while. It won't take a moment, promise."

Now I understood the true heart of the man, I obliged willingly. I reasoned that if he did not trust us, then that was the last destination he would reveal. I was surprised to learn he lived near Washington, D.C.; "I usually work out of Pennsylvania Avenue. However, I am heading the task force in New York, my team were established for this particular case."

His home was in a nice residential area, but there was no sign of life. "Jack, can you check the refrigerator. Good, there, can you zoom in on that note, or bring it back?"

I did as asked, and he was relieved to show me the paper, 'Hon, Mom's unwell again. Same old thing. I'm taking the kids and will be gone a few days. Call us there...'

He seemed relieved, but there was still a worry within him. "Where does 'Mom' live, we may as well do this right, eh, Henry."

He gave me a big smile. I felt a dam had been breached, and we were now committing to trust one another. He guided me to the place, way out on the coast, and was relieved to see them all laughing and having fun. His heart calmed, he turned to me and said, "Thank you. I need to repay you. Time I got back to work."

"Henry, some of the mercenaries defected to our side, and are still with us. I could arrange for you to talk to them, as long as it does not turn into an interrogation. I do not know if they can offer you useful information, but they may know something about the others we killed."

We left moments later, Horovitz and a couple of his men offering Henry some deeper insight into their dead associates, and how Quinn had set up the operation. This was augmented later, when we introduced him to Magnus. We had kept him alive and he worked as administrator in the court of the King of Soi Long. The information he revealed went a long way to persuading Henry what we postulated about the Tenth was the truth.

When we returned, I brought up his destination, their temporary offices in New York. The place looked like it had been ransacked and his team were missing. So was most of their equipment. Henry wandered aside for a moment, before saying, "I need to clear out all our evidence and files from our main New York Field office, that is if it has not been taken already. This is not the work of the CIA, they don't do this. The more I see of this, the more I am coming to believe in your tales of the Tenth. Let's do it now."

Henry was transferred to the office where he worked quickly, making distinct piles of documents and evidence, which we transported back to us. Kay was monitoring the greater threat from the control room and hurriedly transported back to us. "Jackie, that CIA guy you wanted tracked, well, he's just pulled up outside the building Henry is now in."

I gave Henry a few moments before pulling him out. Once back with us, he asked me to remove a few other things from their suite of offices, before the CIA guy knocked the door, in company with the head of the field office. The latter opened the door with a master key, and they set about searching the area.

Henry watched them intently, before saying, "I have no idea what we have a handle on, but someone very high-up wants us shut down. My team is missing, and I have no idea where they could be. There is no current deployment, so they should be there in those offices. Jack, we got a problem"

It was time to start putting the pieces together. Kay had spent time with Langnor, tracking where all four intruders had been over the preceding days. She had logged every physical contact and stopover, which made our task much easier. Kay ran through the destinations for Henry at the transporter on the shore.

Henry briefed us from the accumulated footage; "The CIA guy hassling me is local to New York, and I will follow this up as soon as I get back. The NIA agent returned to Washington, D.C., and disappeared into the governmental security woodwork. The other two attended to seemingly normal business, before they caught a private jet to Los Angeles. The unknown guy went to a naval facility in West LA, El Segundo. It's more than secure, and even more secretive. The CIA has several highly classified operations running out of there, meaning he is CIA. What of the other?"

I offered a cheeky grin. "The other guy headed south to a place called March GlobalPort, and entered this building here. I cannot see inside because the building is shielded from my scanners, which is highly irregular. We suspect this to be a transfer point, but we do not wish to transport there for fear of being taken."

Henry stood back in contemplation. "March Reserve Air Base is where they used to fly the old B52's and refuelling aircraft from. Today it is still home to the air force reserve, and also active units from all the armed forces. GlobalPort comprises two adjacent areas, one designated for military use, the other for civilian and commercial use. However, the high military presence means that it is only used by defence industry contractors, although DHL did try to run an operation from there for a few years, before relocating due to military disruption of their commercial schedules.

"This would make an exceptionally good base of operations for those working in military hardware and intelligence." Looking up momentarily he asked, "How sure are you this is the Tenth?"

"I cannot be sure, but they are the only people who would have the capability to create a shield, apart from ourselves of course."

It was clear to see Henry was rolling his options, before hitting us with his next question, "Could you do this? Create one of these shielded places?"

Kay replied, "We'll try making a shield tomorrow."

I smiled my irascible smile, and shook my head; "No. Maybe in two or three days' time, when you are fully well again."

We mentally agreed to disagree about the spacecraft reconstitution timetable, but we both knew it was imminent. "Henry, excuse me for a moment, I need to check we have all the necessary, before we fix a timetable."

I interfaced with the Core, and discovered that creating transfer circles was in the other part of the vessel. I ran through what we would need to create a new transporter, and it seemed reasonably straightforward. I checked the supply chain, and was informed we had no 'Singularity Crystals', we would need to manufacture them.

The Core informed me "Singularity Crystals are identical pairs of the same crystal, inversely opposed and of the same unique whole. They are grown as an identical pair from a starting point in the middle, one nanometer wide."

"I said to no one, I need a beer, this is crazy chemo/physics. We cannot begin to make them until the craft is put back together."

I returned to the shore, "Henry, apologies. Tomorrow we will do as you ask, although it may take us several days to accomplish."

n'Gue appeared at that moment, "The Empress has requested Henry attend a banquet in his honour at Grimwaldi Rinns."

I added, "Trust me, it will be fun. Come, share our table."

The next day, we devised a simple contact and messaging system before we sent him on his way. As he prepared to depart Henry said, "I'm not sure what awaits me, or who I can trust. I will return to work at Pennsylvania Avenue, let me show you where to put me."

Some days later, Henry entered the shielded Envirotech building at March GlobalPort, and never came out again. He disappeared without a trace. Our priority became to find him. As a precaution, we ripped out any pertinent files from his office, and took his home bureau, an antique wooden desk. This was self-preservation, denial of information to the enemy.

Chapter 23 ~ Rebirth of a Starship

As soon as Kay's strength returned, we initiated reassembly of the spacecraft. A long time had passed since Kay and I first began the undertaking, and we were both keen to finish it. Once set, Kay headed down to Engineering control, accompanied by Gung Loi, n'Gnung stayed at my side as a safety precaution. We were the only four people on board.

"Beginning isolation of outer body Jackie, this may take a while, this craft's outer surface is anything but smooth … Done."

"Got it, locking points located on main craft, aligning with our own … Lock set. Confirm. Configuring mass of rock beneath and behind us to transfer out. You will need to activate transfer of main craft into the space, there can be zero time lag."

"Stasis shield in place, secondary parameters … Ready."

"Let's do it. Three, two, go!"

There was not so much as a jolt or shudder. The Core reported, "Main craft transferred intact, first objective achieved. Initiating initial docking sequence … pairing now … spacecraft reunified."

I whooped with joy, and was sure I heard Kay's similar release from below. I wanted to rush down and hug her, but instead, jumped for joy with n'Gnung. There were two more stages to go, the next set of clamps being activated by Kay from Engineering, and the last activated by the Captain from the control room.

The Core cautioned, "Suspected hull contamination, seal degradation identified. Nanobot inspection and repair necessary before full docking and reintegration."

One hour later we activated second and third docking clamps. Finally, the craft was back in one piece, the crew returned, and we wanted to celebrate, but it was not to be. The main craft had lain dormant for millennia. Whilst contamination had been contained, no repairs had been affected, except for basic safety and integrity support. Batteries were critically low on power, all but dead.

We immediately ran a series of diagnostics on the other part of the ship, before initiating the restoration of standby power. Several drones were sent to accomplish this, some of them checking the environment for potential internal leaks or other hazards.

Without the knowledge of the Ancestors, we would not have understood the deeper concepts of Ancestral engineering principles, and advanced robotic repair parameters. We learned that several of the sub-space engines had malfunctioned before impact. A high-density containment field shielded the intra-galactic Boson Drive, and required complete overhaul. No repairs could be effected without the Captain's explicit order, which I gave at once. Without containment shields, we would have been exposed to irregular and fleeting bursts of deadly meson radiation.

The reintegration process progressed as we invigilated and reacted; "Main power supply connected, status OK. Bringing the greater Core back online: three, two, now."

"We are rebooting from our known Core Jackie, I have a power fluctuation down here, correcting. Phew, that was close."

"Thanks Kay. I have one hundred percent structural stability of habitable area, initiating detox and biohazard removal of main craft. There is a glitch…"

"Jackie, the power supply is now stable, faulty modulator replaced by bots. Main Core coming online, we will need to interface together, be prepared…"

Once the ship was reunited and stable, we took a break and celebrated restoring the craft. It felt like a living organism was now complete once more. That was the strangest of feelings. Time dissipated to such a degree, we returned to the world outside expecting dinner, but instead took breakfast at my home. Despite the rising sun, it was time for us to sleep.

We woke to the setting of the sun and I was ravenous. After we ate, Kay took a walk in the Valley of Knowledge, whilst I spent dedicated time with Jinnie and Ræm. The therapy suited us both admirably, but all too soon, we returned to our labour once more.

Work on repairing the entire spacecraft was coming along nicely, but a few directives required the attention of Kay or myself. We instigated the manufacture of Singularity Crystals as soon as we were able, followed by the creation of a transfer circle. This required us to fix many parameters, which we did and saved the resultant design profile, as we finally came into our power. I reasoned that if each pair of singularity crystals was unique, then they would have a specific signature when used. I asked the Core if it was possible to identify each transporter, and determine usage.

I was informed, "Each transporter has a unique signature that can be traced, and logged when in use."

A plan was forming in my mind. I tasked the Core to begin cataloguing all transporters on the planet, beginning with the USA. I watched the visual display of progress, as a double spiral of lines on my screen, which slowly began working out from the centre. I knew this would take several hours, but we needed to be thorough.

I spent time with our controllers, checking they were comfortable with our upgrades, plus the people and places we were monitoring.

There was neither hide nor hair of Henry, but a curious thought struck me. I went to my ready room and zoomed in on his wife's parental home, surprised to find them enjoying Christmas leftovers. Asking my closest to back me up, I transported.

Within moments, I was standing outside their door and knocked instead of using the buzzer, as was my preference. I waited and was about to knock again, when sounds from within indicated someone approaching. I straightened myself out of habit, and composed the persona I wished to project. A man answered the door and I said, "Seasons greetings. Sorry to intrude, but I am a colleague of your daughter's husband, Henry. I would like a private word with her if possible?"

He gave me a serious look of appraisal. Answering stiffly, "Henry has forsaken his family duty and left Bryony, my daughter, to bring up his children on her own. I cannot help you. Good day."

He made to slam the door in my face. Thinking quickly, I said, "Sir, please. I believe the Russians have him imprisoned. I need to speak to your daughter urgently in order to save him, to bring him back to share your lives."

The door stayed ajar, "Sir, you have no reason to believe me, but know his life hangs in the balance. Without our help, he will die serving his country and preserving it from a terrorist threat."

The door opened a little, hesitantly as the information was absorbed. "You are English, MI6 no doubt?"

"My father is English and my mother is Irish. I have been working as an associate of Henry for some time now. I'm worried about him. Please. I need a moment of your daughter's time."

"How did you find us?" came the abrupt response.

"Henry had someone check on his family before he was captured. I was there when he received word that Bryony and the children were here with you, about two weeks ago that would be. It was school time, but they took a few days break because your wife was slightly unwell. That is how I knew how to come here. You, Bryony, are my last hope of ever finding him alive."

"You better come in then I guess," was his gruff reply.

"I don't wish to intrude upon your lunch. Perhaps I could see her for a moment out here and away from the children. There is nothing secret, but I do not wish to alarm the youngsters unduly."

"How do you know we were eating, spying on us were you?"

"No Sir. I presumed because of the serviette at your neck."

"Serviette?"

"Napkin, sorry."

"What, ah…" He looked down and felt the cloth just below his throat, although covering my slip was a lucky call.

I perched on the bottom step as time dragged by, considering whether I should cut my losses and leave. However, a noise behind disturbed my thoughts. Henry's wife opened the door and came towards me. I rose and proffered my hand. She ignored it and railed at me immediately, "Why are you looking for Henry?"

I was ill prepared for such direct affront, but I guessed it was only to be expected. I repeated to her much of what I said to her father, elaborating on some points as she hovered close to catch my every word. I took a chance and informed her that I lied in one small way. "Our mutual enemy is not the Russians, although they do have Russian operatives. We are actually fighting the Tenth Column, which is hell-bent of destroying all modern society. Henry had just identified a lead in Los Angeles and went there. I have not seen him since he entered the building we were observing. I am most worried about his safety. Can you help us?"

She nodded and asked more gently, "How sure are you that he is alive?"

What could I say? I told her the truth, "I do not know. He has vital information, and is probably being tortured as we speak. Until he breaks, they will keep him alive, I am sure of it."

"How can I help?"

"I need to know who he trusts implicitly: work, friends?"

She considered before saying, "Dean and Colin, Figaro, and Ellen. There are a couple of others I have seen once or twice, but do not know by name."

"Dean and Colin, yes, they are missing also. We think they are all being held together at the same facility. Would you recognise them or the others if you saw them?"

"Of course" she replied, "Do you have them on video?"

I was about to reply when I felt a tug, and my ring glowed with intense blue fire. There had to be an incoming transportation. I grabbed Henry's wife and transported back with her immediately using my bracelet. She was befuddled as the shock hit her, doubly so when the Tenth appeared on our main screen.

Bryony screamed when she saw the Ogres materialise out of nowhere. They were grotesque, and fanned out with military precision to surround the house. They cocked machine guns and set an RPG ready to blow in the front door. Bryony screamed, "Do something, get them out of there!"

I had to get a fix on the people inside, but they kept moving. It was now or never, so I focused on the entire structure, and transported the whole lot out, just before the RPG was released. We saw it hit and destroy a tree behind where the house used to be.

I had no idea where to put it down, but decided upon inclusion, at a safe distance. I settled the house a little distant from the old Banyan tree on the interior of the Outlands. Bryony was out of her mind with worry, confounded by impossible technology straight out of science fiction. I transported with her to the building, accompanied by n'Gnung, Gung Loi, and Aroweena. There we greeted a confused older couple and two inquisitive children. I spoke immediately, "Please accept my apologies for having to do that, but you were just about to die, and I could not allow that. Please trust us all here, and come with me. Your luncheon was ruined this day."

I turned and started walking towards the shore immediately, and soon two children were matching my strides, or rather Aroweena's. They look up at her and said, "Are you are a Dwarf."

She chuckled amiably and corrected them, "In your language I may be, but know I am a warrior of the Ddwyrth, and that sometimes I eat naughty children."

They quietened immediately, still too young to perceive Aroweena's wit, although I would not put eating overly inquisitive youngsters past her appetite whatsoever.

Behind me, footfalls told of my other companions accompanying the oldsters and their daughter. The man was a bluster of outrage, and I left it for Bryony to explain what she had witnessed, as we headed for early lunch. I hoped this would instil a sense of normality within their shocked minds. It was already clear the kids perceived this as a great adventure, one that was manifest seconds later when they saw the sea, and ran full pelt to play on the shoreline.

As I waited for the others to catch up, Bryony's father said, "These people, they are not human."

"They are my brothers and sisters, my dearest friends. You saw the creatures that came to attack your home, kill all of you. They are Ogres, and they are real. You have been transported to a new location, just like on TV, except this is now a real fact of your lives. Remember, I just saved all you from a fate far worse than death. This is why I am exceptionally worried about Henry. He was here with us a couple of days ago, just before he disappeared. I am trying to find him. Perhaps now you will lay down the cold-shoulder and help us. Come, let's enjoy lunch."

As Henry's family acclimatised to life on the shore, I returned to check with my team. The Ogres were not thrilled but thwarted, and the video recording was amusing. They were chasing ghosts. We had shown our first hand, and that was a worry.

Chapter 23

My main concern was their destination, which came as a great surprise. It was nowhere near where any of us expected. I tracked the receiving transporter spike to an unshielded area with a high concentration of Ancestral rock formations, situated in the southern heartlands of Kazakhstan, just east of the Aral Sea. I searched the precise location, finding Bayqongyr located nearby, a city servicing the main Russian cosmodrome.

I backtracked to see where they originated from, and that was an even bigger shock, a small island in the middle of the Indian Ocean, a Black Site known as Diego Garcia. I knew it was another version of Guantanamo Bay, only more secretive.

Chapter 24 ~ The Tenth Column

During the afternoon, I showed Bryony views of the island and her known world from the transporter on the shore. I transferred all of Henry's things to their home, and left Bryony to rifle through all of her husband's effects and papers; she would be busy for some while.

Kay asked the unspoken question, "How come the Ogres arrived where you were Jackie, in the middle of nowhere? Was it information from Henry, or a target already set? "

"Do you think they are monitoring our transfers, like we are theirs, Kay?"

"No, Jackie. It is too soon. If they were doing that, they would have already taken you when you went to London, or Wales. Think. What was different?"

I had no idea, so we scrutinised the video. "There, you were wearing the Ring of the Ancestor, see," n'Gnung pointed.

I hollered both physically and mentally, "You mean they tracked my ring."

My friends deliberated, but the Core answered, "Affirmative. The logged residual scan signature of Captain Oma's craft is unmistakable, they picked out Taris' ring when you materialised."

"So they are not logging our transportation signatures."

"No, not yet."

I cursed my stupidity, but my friends buffed and buffered my battered ego. Later, n'Gue came with a message, "Guardian, Bryony is walking towards the shore transporter and wants to speak to you."

We transferred some minutes later, and in due course, I became aware of a presence nearby, at times looking around the room, at the main screen, and in time locking eyes with my own. She began, "I … we … this is all such a shock to us. I did not even know what Henry was working on. I thought that perhaps he had a lover somewhere, as that would explain why he was away so often.

"He never discussed his work with me. I mean, he was forbidden to by the rules anyway, but he hardly ever mentioned anyone, anything, any place during all our years of marriage.

"Apart from Dean and Colin, there are three people I know he would trust with his life: Ellen an agent from LA, and the one I suspected him of having an affair with. Bob Martin whom he trained with. He is still at Quantico I think, but I have not heard about him in ages. Lastly, there is Philmore Ballard, although I am sure that is not his real name. He is a shadow character who had been in touch a lot recently, according to the desk diary. There is a recent reference to him in Henry's notes made just before he left for GlobalPort.

Chapter 24

She handed me his rough and almost illegible notebook and pointed out the line PMQ. I stared at it. My guess was an afternoon visit to Quantico. I queried that it should be PB, to which she smiled. "Philmore had the same middle name as John Wayne, and PM was a nickname that stuck over the years. Henry would always write p.m. in lower case if it were a time of day."

Henry had planned to meet someone called PM at Quantico the day after he disappeared. I needed to speak to Bob, and asked Bryony to assist me by pointing him out at Quantico. She was uneasy, scared of the science we used, and kept looking around, as if searching for a means of return to her known world. I was supportive, but firm, "Bryony, please help us, help find your husband. It will only take a minute of your time, and afterwards I will return you to your family."

Unfortunately, it took far longer than one minute. We checked every face at Quantico, and there was no sign of either Bob or Philmore. Neither could we find any trace of them, Dean, Colin, or Ellen in Washington D.C., New York, or Los Angeles, all of them seemed to have vanished into thin air. Meanwhile Kay was checking Russia, and there was no sign of anyone at all where the Ogres had transported, except for a large shielded area. That left only one destination open to us, the Indian Ocean.

Bryony was getting edgy. I needed to calm her, but also press on, "We have drawn a blank. There is only one place they can be, Diego Garcia, a British / U.S. base in the Indian Ocean north of Mauritius. Bryony, we must check it out, and if Henry is not there, we will finish for today. It's almost dinnertime."

I zoomed in using the Core's map, and found the small island with ease. We spent time searching before finally coming across a complex that was quite distinct from the rest of the base. We searched the prison, drawing a blank, before discovering a second containment area, which was more open to the elements.

Bryony let out a whoop of joy and pointed to Ellen, whom Kay immediately locked-on to. Bryony was excited, and I hoped she would not be disappointed. I continued my grid search, but before we even saw him, Bryony was leaping up and shouting, "That's him, it's Henry!"

How she knew I had no idea, because all I saw was a pair of shoes, but she was proved correct, as his jaundiced face came into focus on our screen. The two other agents were recognised a short time later. They were pretending not to know each other, and keeping well apart. The transporter locks were quickly set and we initiated transfer of all our targets simultaneously, to the transporter on the shore. I would see if the Ogres were tracing our transporter signature, or my ring.

Within moments, Henry, Ellen, Dean and Colin, were back with us. We saw the lights go on in their eyes. Henry recognised where they were, and that they had been saved. Bryony flew into her husband's arms, whilst Ellen and the men were naturally confused by everything.

I greeted Henry heartily like a brother, and shook hands with the others, before asking him for the team's eyes and focus. I scanned everyone left in the prison. We were searching for Figaro. The nerd was hard to find, but eventually we tracked him down to a small and distant secure section with lighter guard.

Figaro was the last we transferred back, although Henry suggested that if a certain group were transferred to the other side of a particular wall, there would undoubtedly be a riot, which would cover discovery of their own extraction, at least for several days. I did so immediately, and also removed a couple of doors at his direction to make the revolt far easier for them. It took moments for total mayhem to ensue, and soon the captors became the captured. More importantly, no Ogres appeared, they were not as yet tracing our transporters.

I broke contact fast. Our visitor's shock was beginning to be replaced by curiosity. I had each of them attend the medical unit, and when they checked out, they were transferred to the shore. As we waited for the last to clear, Bryony came to me and put her hand on my arm. She said, "Thank you Jackie," and gave me a peck on the cheek.

I was eager for the debrief, and Henry did not disappoint, "Our missing agents, the four here now, had been taken in the swoop we escaped from. Dean was with me when I initially interviewed you, the others watching from behind the glass. They knew nothing, the supposed CIA were looking for you, Jackie."

"That's what we figured. So how come you all ended up in Diego Garcia?"

"When I returned to Washington, I recalled the team as soon as they were released from CIA interrogation—my Director had lodged a formal complaint. I wanted to follow up your information, and either prove or disprove your theory. It is an occupational hazard. We set on a plan, and I entered the Envirotech building you identified at Globalport with Ellen, the others were monitoring us from the SUV—our cover was investigating arms shipments.

"We were welcomed and a meeting called with their bosses. We waited moments in a meeting room, before being transferred somewhere, I don't know where. We were interrogated, they wanted to know why we were there, and if we had backup. We stonewalled. Someone entered and whispered, and we were left alone. Jack, I caught a glimpse of something monstrous, large and grey, maybe nine feet high and rotund."

Chapter 24

"An Ogre!" I exclaimed. We now had confirmation, and so did Henry, that the foe existed. "The humans, they were likely Ogre clones, Henry. Go on, what happened next?"

"The next thing I knew, we were transported and incarcerated in Diego Garcia, the others having been found and transferred with us. Interrogations resumed, but what could any of us tell them. They wanted to know if I had met you, and I was effectively puzzled. Nobody else knew anything. The days passed in similar fashion, until you rescued us. That's about all there was to it."

I thanked Henry, but later worried that too many new faces were appearing, coming into knowledge of the island. I took Jien Noi for a walk that evening, once the celebrations were well under way, and she calmed my fears. "Jackie, I know what worries you, but what else can we do? We will soon be at war with the Ogre hordes, and this is but the prelude. We need to keep these people safe, if only because they will be of great value to us in the future. They can check things I cannot even imagine, and with the ability to set our own transfer circles, we can protect them when they are on the other side."

When we returned to our table, the first strains of Old MacDonald had been uttered, the kids loving the play-acting. I wanted to hold a more serious discussion, but realised the moment was already passed, for the night at least. It was time to make new friends, and define any threat they posed to us, which appeared negligible. I answered toasts and became one with the flow.

After breakfast the next morning, I called a meeting, and was delighted to see Lo Si striding towards us. He no longer waddled, but walked purposefully, his mind likewise directed, sharp, and incisive. The FBI newcomers were still playing catch-up, but accepted that the Ogres existed, and were a definite threat. Our talk was a mixture of debrief and looking for ways to strike back.

Henry and his agents became focused on how far the Ogres, or The Tenth Column as they preferred to call them, had infiltrated the agency, government, and other institutions. At one point Ellen said, "I wish I could take all this directly to the President. If he is not an Ogre, then that is where the power to fight this lies."

I replied flippantly, "Why not? I'll bring him here so we can have a little chat."

I was joking, but as their eyes turned to look at me. I realised they were not. When I woke up that morning, I had not considered kidnapping the President of the United States of America, but that was what I was faced with. I asked n'Gnung to see if Dawn was available to join us that day. I needed her advice and knowledge of current affairs.

A little time later, Dawn joined me and said, "Jackie, what you propose is stupid, and incredible. By doing this you will show they are not rulers of this world, but answer to a higher power. In this case, that will be you. I love you, but you are no world leader … Can't say that you'd be any worse at it though. OK, talk to me, convince me."

Talk to Dawn we did, all of us had a voice. In some ways, that was the problem. At the end of it we were little further ahead. n'Gnung had the final word, "If you are going to do this, then act, do it. Now!"

I needed to reinforce our hands', both generally and personally. We scheduled a meeting of all the Tribes for the following day, the day after being set aside for a meeting with world leaders, and leading lights of current affairs. We would see what developed.

I kidnapped my old friend Neal Podmore in a similar way I had Dawn, meeting him in person and transporting him to the island. I realised that for most people, the short, sharp shock of experience was the best way to go. He had also met Dawn before, if briefly.

He proved to be a good choice because during my absence he had been elected to Parliament. Once over the initial shock, he became highly proactive, on condition his wife and child could come and visit. The Gatekeeper agreed, and so it came to pass.

Dawn remained adamant, "We need outside, objective assistance. Let me bring John here; remember how he helped us find somebody to run the prints. Jackie, he is a very clever man, and knows all about petite politics. He is currently overdue for retirement, but can't let go of being useful. He needs something new to thrust his energies into. Empress, let me go and talk to him, you won't regret it, I'm sure."

During the subsequent meeting of all the Tribes, we analysed the information reported from the Core, Ælthrelntheine supporting with what her spies had discovered. Ogre forces were already mustering to attack us, no doubt the Great Ogre wanted the Ring of the Warrior back. It was clear we needed to attack first, and I had presented a list of targets. Although scattered throughout the world, they had three things in common: transfer circles, power, and money. We spent the rest of the morning discussing invasion tactics. We needed to strike decisively, undermining the Great Ogre from the outset.

During the break for luncheon, Ælthrelntheine departed, and returned shortly afterwards. She had company, and introduced the Sixth, a hairy, scary looking race of similar build to myself, but taller and wider of girth. They were the epitome of the fabled Yeti, Bigfoot, or Sésquac. Apparently, the Fourth had found their whereabouts. They were a highly insular race of humanity, but had been persuaded to join our war council. The first time the Tribes had known them openly, for fifty thousand years.

Chapter 24

Ælthrelntheine said, "Guardian, all comes into being as prophesised, for now we are seven of twelve discounting the Last. The Twelve Tribes of Humankind will come together, although I do not understand how the Ogres can be a part of us. That is the most puzzling element."

Hogar, King of the Sixth, stated, "We have a deep-seated hatred of the Tenth. They have tried to exterminate us for all of our existence. We stand with you, if only because we want vengeance. I have full revenge in mind for the Ogres, and although we are few in number, we need to be a part of it; the overthrow and total annihilation of our oppressors."

I was sure the introduction would have gone badly, given Hogar's hostile, yet reclusive disposition, had not Owain and Rambling come forward. Their respective outgoing and calming natures offered parity and comfiture. They distracted Hogar by taking him for a walk into our hinterland, later reappearing on the shore. Hogar appearing Kingly for the first time, as we welcomed this most unusual cousin into our cohort.

While Hogar was being given the tour, John arrived, but his initial shock soon turned to one of amazement and open inquisitiveness. Before long, one of the Eleventh offered to act as translator, because he wanted to speak to everybody, to understand everything. As soon as he learned of our plan he came rushing over, "Jack, thank you. This is amazing. You may not know, but in three days' time there is a meeting of the G20. You can get hold of all world leaders when they are all sat around the same table." And that is what we did.

In preparation, Kay and I created several transfer circles with specific parameters, which included a large shield. However, issues of security remained high as our plan was actioned on the third day, when the world leaders, their teams of ministers, and support workers were in closed session. Our first move was to place a transfer circle inside the meeting room and activate the shield, locking the room out. We then transported everyone within.

Our island shield was set to bar transfer of weapons, electronic devices, and Ogres or their clones. In the event, no delegation arrived complete—'The United States of' Europe was by far the most infiltrated, except for Russia who had no representatives at all.

Our job was to convince those who came to us, just how badly world governments and financial institutions had been compromised. The meeting started badly, and got worse. What I had hoped would be a constructive discussion concerning the menace of the Tenth, quickly decomposed into salutary threats and petit squabbles.

In order to win our cause, I transferred everyone to the transporter on the shore, and showed them the enemy for the first time: footage of Bryony's parental home invasion by the Ogres. We were denounced as fakers at once. That was until Bryony stated that the creatures they saw on screen really did exist. I was not sure they believed her, but she was convincing enough to allow us to move on.

After the recording finished, I led them outside and stated, "Gentlemen, Ladies, these creatures are now a fact of your lives. The house you witnessed disappear is currently over there, see, near the old banyan tree."

Henry spoke up, revealing his official identity, and briefly, how he came to be with us. "They are called the Tenth Column or Ogres if you prefer. They have another one of these control centres, and can do the same things these people can. They aim to kill or enslave every human being on this planet. Your own governments and corporations are already coming under their control, because they can take human form as virtually undetectable clones. They include all those people in your secret meeting room who were not transported here today. I suggest you run DNA tests on everyone. Know the CIA and FBI are already deeply compromised."

Returning inside to emphasise the point, I pulled up the image of the meeting room, which by then was in a state of pandemonium, as people tried to get out, or understand what had occurred. Our serious negotiations finally got underway when we returned to the hinterland, Neal proving to be an excellent conciliator. The outcome was that both the U.S. and China were now aware of serious infiltration to their security services and systems of government. They wanted more information, meaning access to our technology — no chance.

Other countries offers of support were more equivocal. We needed troops and modern weapons. I left others to talk up our cause and play word jousting, speaking my mind clearly when required. We were promised support before the meeting broke up, and would wait to see what that amounted to in due course.

After they departed, we talked about the meeting. John, Neal, and Dawn revealing things I had missed. Consensus was they were afraid of us, and would steal what we had, given the slightest opportunity. Overall, we had made a good start, and had garnered promises of the support we so desperately needed. Time would tell.

Neal left as soon as our business concluded, but John was enamoured to understand more, especially our technological capabilities. He represented no threat, and at Dawn's urging, we showed him the control centre. He became the epitome of a child agog within new secrets of understanding.

"Jackie, there are others who must come here, leading lights in their fields. Penelope Pendleton is the first. I know her quite well, and we first met when she headed CERN" … he mentioned others of due worth, and it felt to me like we were being bullied into welcoming camels and tents to our island oasis. Jinnie supported me. She now understood my concerns. She decreed that only one person would be allowed to visit us.

Of John's great plans, we only allowed Penelope to come to us. Kay and I had downloaded the subatomic knowledge from the Core, but that did not mean we understood it.

Penelope Pendleton was the world's leading sub-nuclear particle physicist, had written dissertations on space-time, space travel propulsion units, and was a leading light behind Rainbow Gravity, which had led to disproving the big bang theory.

She was hyper-motivated, and quirky with it, oddball. She had insisted on seeing the engineering section of the ship. "Dearest Jackie, I love this place, it's a fairy tale full of Elves, Dwarves, and Giants. Since I was a little girl, I always knew they existed. Anyway, know you can kidnap me anytime, except right now. It's my sister's Birthday, I think, or is that next month. What month is it? Never mind, time is a quantum phenomenon, you do understand? Being there at the right moment is all that matters."

"That would be a Heisenberg moment, no doubt."

"I didn't think you were that clever, a man of many talents indeed."

During her visit to engineering, she asked questions both Kay and I had difficulty understanding, let alone answering. The brief tour concluded with her being returned to the transporter. Readying to depart, she said, "Anyway, I need to see and understand all of this. You did say Boson Drive, right? I've been working on that for years, but it's a dud. Mesons don't behave properly, just like most men I know."

She looked askance for a moment, and I said, "You are welcome back, because we need somebody who understands all this particle science. You do. Could you help us?"

"Why yes, this is right up my street. It's all to do with Higgs, The Standard Model, and the god particle. I've been following developments of Longshot and the recent Project Prometheus. Then there is the EM Drive, which is quite intriguing. Damn — bosons. I can see there is a lot to learn. It is truly fascinating. Now, how do we get in contact?"

"Why not hang a disc on your back door."

"Oh good gracious no, that will never do. I'll put an alarm clock in the window, set the hands to twelve, and then you'll know how long I have been waiting. Au revoir."

n'Gnung came to my side and raised an eyebrow. "Most females appear seemingly unfathomable by the male of the species, The Eleventh doubly so. This one appears to inhabit a parallel universe. Come brother, time for a beer."

Chapter 25 ~ Eight of Twelve

The fallout from our meeting was palpable, it became clear the Ogres had infiltrated the governments of many countries, and had people in powerful positions, not only within the ruling body politick and associated national security services, but within industry, global companies, and world financial institutions. In particular, the United Nations was badly compromised. I dreaded to think about how deeply that web of deception went.

World leaders urged us to take action on their behalf, we demanding troops to support us in return. We were left with promises, not plans for deployment. During one meeting Neal confided, "This is diplomacy. Troops will come, but first you must identify targets and prepare invasion plans, then they will take you seriously."

I returned to interface with the Core, define targets, and work on assault strategy with our military. We identified the main targets from Ogre transporter signatures, and honed our plans to strike first, fixing the day and time of attack.

The Tribes mobilised to stand against our common foe. The assistance of the Last was limited to advisors and reconnaissance. We had little use for either. We felt used, but more secure for their lack of physical presence, which often felt more akin to intrusion.

Several major world powers entrusted communication with us to special envoys. For instance, the U.S. deployed Don Phillips as our dedicated liaison, and we got along very well. He was an undersecretary from the Office of the White House Chief of Staff, known by the acronym POTUS. By contrast, the Prime Minister of China committed a young woman called Huang, a Mandarin speaker who was also fluent in English and Cantonese.

Neal had many commitments, but came as often as he could. By contrast, John became engrossed in what we were about, especially regards the other Tribes. "Jackie, the world of science demands answers, investigation not only by palaeontologists, but linguists, botanists, and other experts. We need to create a small centre of study and bring in the right people, what do you say?"

I reasoned he wanted to recreate his university life as an all-embracing research project on our island, and the Empress saw no reason why not.

I had misgivings, but was amenable when his wife, Cynthia visited; "John told me so much about this island, I just had to come and see for myself. He is such a good man, but he needs to be preoccupied. You also need to record every detail relating to these Hominidæ, correctly, they are of the genus Hominina, and they are quite fascinating. This information is priceless," she leaned forwards and patted my hand.

"Jackie, I, we have had enough of Birmingham and all this modern world now bestows, wanted or not. Our only tie is the grandchildren, and our home. John should have retired last year, but found a means to stay on. He is overdue leave and could start here today, officially retiring at Easter. Could you bring our home here, like you did for Bryony?"

"Yes. My worry is that this island and its unique inhabitants will be turned into a theme park…"

I took a deep breath intending to say more. Cynthia grasped my hand. "God Forbid! I'll ensure he has the smallest possible team, and they can work from some place out of the way, so as not to interfere with the natives. I have read Heisenberg you know."

Something in her eyes, within her delivery soothed my disquiet. We spoke about the implications, for everybody, and I was virtually won over.

n'Gnung came to me at that moment and interrupted, "Guardian, the war cabinet assembles, your presence is required. We are mainly of the Second, Eleventh, and Seventh. Other tribes will add a few token soldiers, but we are it regards numbers. There has been nothing from the Last."

I rose to leave, but Cynthia said, "Jackie, I'll have a word with John. I'm sure he can get you the reinforcements you need. Let him talk to the Americans and Chinese, prove himself to you. All we ask in return is our home, and a place to study from."

"Oh, how come?"

"He has a past, one he cannot speak about, but he is very well connected with the military, and in related political circles."

"Intelligence?"

"Classified. That's where we met and fell in love."

I cast a curt look back, and uttered, "If he pulls this off, your wish will be granted. So-be-it!"

Oh, how the wings of providence empowered upon such little wind as a casual word cast aside.

Some days later, I watched my screens in the morning, just before we took the battle to the Tenth. Owain came to us with his armies at the ready. The Seventh were soon joined by the Twelfth, Eleventh, Fourth, and Third. Barph assembled our own armies of the Second. He was supported by Gung Loi's guerrillas and Horovitz' Blitzkrieg Corps.

These were greatly enhanced moments later via an aide, when we were given control of three SEAL platoons, one from the British SAS reserve in Hereford, and two platoons from the French Foreign Legion. John had indeed worked miracles, and I knew I owed him a large debt.

Our teams assembled in the hinterland of the Outlands, where the Marine's commander offered us great insight into attack strategy and subterfuge. Timely, Ælthrelntheine arrived with three of the Sixth, led by King Hogar in person. Whilst their number was small and their demeanour *scary*, they came to offer their kindred spirit of support freely and to stand with us against the Tenth.

As the hour of our attack approached, I took time aside to scan the valley below, and it was a remarkable sight. There were thousands of people representing eight of the Twelve Tribes. Some races provided far more soldiers than others, but what was undeniable was that we were standing together against a common enemy. As we were making final preparations, a surprise came from the Orient. A whole division [one thousand] Chinese troops were made available to us, and they were not simple foot soldiers, but those with highly advanced skills and weaponry.

And so it began. Joining our forces for a moment, I raised the Sword of Destiny and borrowing a line from my culture, shouted, *"All for one and one for all."*

Immediately the leaders were transported to the control centre, and assembled in a war-room specially prepared earlier to be our base of operations. Located deep within our craft, it was secure. They could not access other parts of the ship.

I had previously made a personal provision via the Core, allowing Dawn and I to interface digital devices like my laptop and memory devices with what amounted to a personal database. We had made a similar provision for the War Room, and in turn, we got a snapshot of the memory of each device that was attached.

I watched as waves of our troops were sent to all of our identified locations, beginning with Lesotho. Many of the smaller transfer circles were secured and it became apparent we had taken the Tenth by surprise. We took many of the outposts and minor positions meeting little or no resistance. I was aware that some of the locations might not be under Ogre control at all, but simply legacy circles. We quarantined each with a transfer circle, the associated shield annulling any possible future threat.

However, the major locations we had identified proved to be great obstacles. They were like small towns similar to a modern-day fort or prison. Most fortresses were ringed by guard towers and walls that enclosed open ground, dotted with occasional buildings. The main structures were heavily fortified, and protected. We could not presume

Chapter 25

this was where the control centre was located, as many voices considered this would likely be underground.

Ogre Shields activated once we were inside the complex, as we expected. Our ploy to add our own transfer circles broaching their shield perimeters worked well, allowing our reinforcements to enter hotly disputed locations. We took out the guard towers, and sent in the second wave. Ingress had stalled in three places and was being repulsed in New York. Regiments of Chinese troops were sent to each prime location in support.

I took the loathsome Ring of the Warrior, preparing to wear it with dread, issued weapons and protection bracelets to our team leaders. Kay took with her Gung Loi, Barph, and half of his best troops, one platoon of SEALs, and Llwydd with his most trusted. They transferred to the fiercest battle of all in New York.

I called n'Gnung to me, the rest of Barph's elite, one platoon each of SEAL's and SAS, and Aroweena with her Ddwyrthen corps. And so it began in earnest.

I was still convinced their major stronghold was Lesotho, and we duly arrived to bolster penetration. There had been a stalemate, until I activated the protection of my bracelet and strode forwards, holding the flaring Sword of Destiny within my upraised hands. I drew fire from the enemy, and we made swift and steady progress, penetrating deep into the heart of the complex.

We met stern resistance when we entered their lair proper, and I was forced to drop my protection and wield the Sword of Destiny in its first battle. I could not use my weapons with the shield active. The sword seemed to drink the blood of the Tenth, as beside me the berserker Aroweena came into her killing frenzy. To my other side, n'Gnung choreographed our elite corps, their Ancestral weapons making a decisive difference.

With sword in one hand, the ancient dagger in my other, and the most ferocious of opponents to my side, we decimated the opposition, and quickly took full control of the main complex. Special Forces covered our flanks. This was neither their battle nor strategy, but they secured our progress.

We broke through into the nucleus, we had a coup d'état and took charge of their control centre. Two of the Tenth cowered in a corner, they were green of hue, and smaller in size than the regular greyish-brown Ogres. We killed the Ogres, but I tested the two strange beings, who caused my sword to flare green, not blue. They were put under arrest, and later, after making specific exception with the Core, under confinement in our cells.

I removed the controller's ring of power, and their control flared to life under the power of the Tenth's Ring. I had access to their entire worldwide schema, and discovered the main location of their military and offensive capabilities was New York. I glanced at the screen, which showed our troops under heavy bombardment; sending n'Gnung back to supervise reinforcements.

Meanwhile, I needed to disable the control I sat at, and reboot it so it would only respond to the Ring of the Ancestor. To do that I would have to interface with the mainframe, and wear the dreaded Ring of the Warrior for a few minutes.

Aroweena stood guard as I set about the task. At first it is easy, but then I became swamped by gibberish, as the device reset to only understanding the language of the Tenth. It took a seemingly long time to over-ride the aberration, as there was trickery and deception involved. Eventually I set the basic default language back to Ancestor and closed down the control. I reset the Core by rebooting. I had disabled all overrides, and finished by locking out the entire Lesotho complex so it could only be reactivated with my own ring, the Ring of the Ancestor.

I began disrupting communications between all the various sites of the Tenth, which put all of their simple sending circles out of action, which we quarantined. In time, I was left with eight centres that I could not over-rule; only internally from their respective control centres: New York, Washington, Kazakhstan, Nizhniy Novgorod, New Delhi, Sao Paulo, Kyoto, and Brussels.

Leaving a guard detail of SEAL's, SAS, and Second, we regrouped back at our control centre. We were greeted by worried faces, as the other remaining battles all started to go against us.

Following a short conference with the commanders of our tactical units, we sent in reinforcements, supported by a small task forces of our crack troops carrying Ancestral protection and weapons. Quickly Kazakhstan, and soon after, Nizhniy fell to us. I locked the bases out, as our shielding was placed to do likewise.

Meanwhile, the Eleventh and Seventh took Sao Paulo and Kyoto respectively. With more support troops, I transferred directly to our battle in Washington, supported by the Twelfth, leaving Jien Noi in control of our headquarters. The assault on Washington was a mess. It appeared to be an interlinked station, where adversaries came and went at their whim, leaving us chasing shadows. We made progress, but it was slow and costly. That changed when Hogar appeared at my side, "Shield me Guardian, there is more afoot here than you realise."

Chapter 25

He strode gallantly forwards as I shepherded him. Our SEAL's used diversionary tactics to confuse and befuddle the enemy. It took me a while to determine Hogar's plan, as there appeared to be no logic too it.

As I began to despair, he jumped aside and secured a hidden sending circle. It looked like a low, flat rock, just like the one in my home. I realised the scan I initiated had only revealed the whereabouts of transfer circles with a control panel, and I sent word back at once using the jaw inserted communication device.

Hogar broached a broad smile, saying, "Do your kind and the Tenth always fight like this? All I had to do was find the source of trickery. There will be another on the other side of this area also. The ways of the Great Ogre are not those merely of the seeing, but understanding. Know your enemy, Guardian."

Hogar was actually a timid person by nature, although meeting him properly under those circumstances, I found it hard to believe. His actions and perseverance, his words gave us the clue we needed, to stand firm and secure the area. However, we had still not taken the main control centre, or even breached the central structure. I got the feeling we were being herded in one direction; it was time to break pattern. I left our best platoon with Hogar, their mission, to hold the existing, and take the other suspected, hidden, transfer circle within the Washington perimeter.

I pressed forwards with leading SEAL's, the ease of our ingress increasingly becoming more worrisome. Broaching the main building perimeter at last, we came to a large hall that was completely sealed except for the entrance. Forces of the Tenth, who drove us inside, immediately swarmed the entrance. I used my protection bracelet to block the doorway and prevent them following, but fighting our way out of the prepared killing zone was going to be tricky.

I dispatched n'Gnung to reconnoitre the room. He confirmed we were trapped. Then his eyebrow rose with indicative eye movement, he mentioned, almost casually, "Guardian, there is a motif set into the far wall. I find this most intriguing. Swap places with another, let's go and investigate."

Rambling took over from me, and I inspected the motif. It was like the ones used on hidden doors, and inspection revealed it was a good match for the Ring of the Warrior. While n'Gnung readied our troops, leaving a few with Rambling to hold the entry, I tried the motif, and it locked. We had a way out, although I cursed the ring that empowered it. I knew it was draining my essential essence every time I used it. I acted for the greater good, and held fast as n'Gnung led our troops through the doorway I held open. I was last through and felt drained, until I removed the hideous ring.

We followed the corridor on the other side, and the layout was similar to that of Lesotho. We came to another door with motif, and I wasted no time activating it and holding it open for our shielded troops to pour through. Aroweena and n'Gnung were ferocious fighters, although the SEAL's had far better strategy. We were in a main access corridor, the light enemy presence being pushed relentlessly back, and eradicated. Moments later we burst into the control centre, a large and heavily defended area. Our troops were becoming skilled at the intricacies of ingress, needing no orders to group behind shield bearers and advance quickly. The key was to use our element of surprise as momentum.

I scanned the room, looking for the control console, noting it was unoccupied. My side vision caught a door across to the rear of the room closing. Aroweena must have noticed as well, because she ran towards it. I worked the control station, disabling shields and unlocking doors. This allowed Aroweena to burst through the secured door, and I saw her come face to face with one of the most malicious creatures I had ever witnessed. He was a step away from a transfer circle, but touched his wrist before wheeling to face her.

Her strikes were solid, and would have despatched any ordinary Ogre, but this one appeared to be wearing a protection device, similar to our own. He was larger and more ugly than any Ogre we had so far encountered, appearing like a sumo wrestler compared to an ordinary man. He was almost as tall as Junior, but wider across the shoulder; his muscles bulged and rippled like those of a bodybuilder.

I acted quickly, noted the destination, and gawped. The location was unknown to us. I did not understand—all locations should have been revealed to our scan. I concluded it must be hidden somehow, and would resolve the problem later. I deactivated the transportation in progress, ensuring the monster could not escape.

Glancing up, I wished I had not. Aroweena's blows were bouncing off the monstrosity. He stood square and mocked her with a leery grin. His demeanour changed within an instant, his movements impossibly quick for such a large creature. He struck, presumably dropping his personal shield. Aroweena staggered back after blocking his first mighty blow.

n'Gnung rushed to take her place, as the unequal battle unfolded. He fared little better, the Ogre's parry sending him flying across the room. I rushed heedless to their assistance, as the blows of the Seventh and Second made no impression. The Ogre laughed as a man would at a tempestuous toddler. I was several paces away, when he delivered a telling blow, badly wounding Aroweena's arm. Maintaining the sweep of his arc, the Ogre aimed a fatal blow at n'Gnung.

I could not get there in time, and despaired as the broadsword descended towards my brother's heart. Within that instant, Aroweena swivelled and kicked n'Gnung out of the way. By doing so, she saved n'Gnung's life, but the blow cleaved her legs in two.

Her pain was obvious, but her spirit remained unbroken as the Ogre wheeled his massive arm to deliver the blow to end her life. She swung her sword instinctively, almost removing the Ogres leg. Without thinking, I leapt and swung the Sword of Destiny with all my might aiming for the midriff. At first, I thought I had missed, or my sword passed straight through, and yet there he stood. A malicious laugh rumbled from deep within the Ogre's chest as he turned to look at me.

Unfortunately for him, only the top half of his body moved. His hips and legs stayed firmly planted for a moment in their original position. The sight was bizarre. His torso swivelled and fell off his planted body, before both halves crashed to the floor with a mighty thud. I cut off his hands and took his rings, bracelet, and anything else of value I noticed. Turning back, I found n'Gnung tending to Aroweena. She had a mortal look in her eye, and a glow of pride knowing she had fallen in battle to a most fearsome opponent.

I ripped cloth from my shirt, and used two strips as a tourniquet. I picked her up, n'Gnung collected her severed legs, and we interlinked for immediate transportation. Flicking my return bracelet, we arrived in our main transfer circle.

I spoke the command, "Infirmary,", and were instantly sent on to the medical centre. I knew Jien Noi had been looking out for us, and sent a prayer of thanks.

I lay Aroweena down on a bed, my brother giving the robot medic Aroweena's legs. I said, "She is a Ddwyrth, save her. I would stay, but we have work to finish, we battle the Ogres this day."

We left immediately to rejoin the fray. I had no idea if Aroweena's life could be saved, never mind restoring her legs, but I had to try; it was the best I could do.

We had been gone seconds, but in that time, Rambling had battled through to us and taken over the mop-up operation. I found Hogar interrogating frightened operatives of the Tenth and despatching them regardless of whether they talked to him or not. My timing was perfect, as Rambling has just stopped him from killing three who had human form and were holding up badges in their defence. The Sword of Destiny fired to life and confirmed they were Ogre clones of the Last.

Dismissing Hogar, I discovered something of great interest; two of the badges they brandished had CIA emblazoned across them, the other identified the host as Homeland Security. I had the feeling Henry, and even the President himself, would be especially interested in this discovery. I sent them back to our base immediately with orders that they be completely stripped, searched, and kept in our highest security confinement. Ju Lo was tasked to summon Henry and tell him they were Ogres in human form.

Finally, I was able to return to the Washington control station, locking it out so only the Ring of the Ancestor, could reactivate it. This took time, but less than before, even though the control centre was more powerful and complicated. It appeared I was improving, although the finger that wore the Ring of the Warrior was bleeding so badly, I worried that soon I might lose it completely.

Meanwhile our troops had done a most impressive job, and worked as a team to secure the base. Hogar and the Sixth went from body to body, decapitating every single Ogre they found. I knew what he was doing, we all understood how deeply they resented the Ogre's continued existence, but I could not watch.

As before, we annexed the base, quarantining it with our own transfer circle and accompanying shield. We removed all rings and devices from every one of our victims, and left a squad with orders to secure the site, and strip the enemy of anything useful, especially regarding weapons.

The SEAL Captain took me aside, "Guardian, my people are wasted here, and at other objectives we have overrun. There are other battles ongoing today. My advice is to leave one member of my team, or an SAS in charge, and staff these sites with others of … how can I say, less military experience."

I chuckled conspiratorially, "You are wise, and also correct. Thank you Captain Stewart, I will make it so immediately. Horovitz…"

This suited us well, because it freed up more of our highly trained troops. I put Horovitz in charge of deployment because I wanted to control it with our own personnel, and also see how he measured up. The policy was actioned immediately, and I left it up to Horovitz' discretion to enact in all locations under our control, without committing him or his elite corps to man the positions.

n'Gnung joined me as we prepared to move on. He was aghast at the state of my finger, insisting I take off the Ring of the Warrior immediately. Some skin and puss-like yellow fat came off with it, and so much so he asserted I go to our medical centre for treatment without delay. He would hear no argument, so I was sent on my way, leaving him in charge of our troops on the ground.

Chapter 26 ~ Lairs of the Great Ogre

I arrived in the medical unit where a team were working on the unconscious form of Aroweena. The head nurse answered my enquiry, "The Ddwyrth will make a full recovery, and should be able to walk a little in a few days' time. Light exercise will be prescribed, but full healing will take several weeks. Now Guardian, what can I do for you?"

I showed her my finger and explained about the Ring of the Warrior. She wanted to examine the ring before seeing my finger properly, and took it to be scanned. She returned a short while later and stated, "This ring is not one of Taris' crew. It belonged to the Warrior on Oma's spaceship, yet the Core already knows of it. Had this been Taris' ring you could countermand it, but not this one. Now I will examine the damage it has caused."

Although it looked bad, the injury had only compromised skin and underlying fatty deposits, most muscle sinew was intact. My finger was taped with strange gauze and covered with paste. The nurse said, "This will repair the skin, you could liken it to a skin-graft. Just hold still a moment while I remodel the tissue ... Good. This other device intensifies the healing process by accelerating stem cell proliferation, and regeneration of natural tissue."

She used a thin, pen-like instrument with a glowing red end moved it closely above the wound. I watched as miraculously new skin appeared, and my treatment completed quickly. I departed with orders not to wear the ring again, something I knew I would be doing several times in the near future.

She appeared to read my mind, "No doubt I will be attending to your wounds again later. You are much like the last one that wore the Ring of the Ancestor. Now be gone, I have a lot of work to do in order to restore your friend's legs to full function."

I didn't even know this robot could talk, as in conversation, but she seemed to already know us intimately. I bowed to her/it, which brought forth a chuckle within metallic form. I patted Aroweena's shoulder, before bending to kiss her forehead, and with a squeeze of my fingers, I left wishing her a speedy recovery.

I went directly into the war council, where I was surprised to find we had guests from several leading world governments watching the battles unfold. I talked quickly aside with Dawn and John, who were keeping an eye on things in general.

John had been playing games, and garnered a whole division from the US Army, "They don't want to lose face to the Chinese by providing fewer troops. They are sending in the Marines, whilst Canada has sent us several dozen Mounties. They arrived with rifles, swords … and horses Jackie, it is most odd."

"They are standing with us in battle, John. That is what is most important. Any other news?"

"I have other irons in the fire, but it's too soon to tell, mainly Commonwealth, but not exclusively. Burnam left on a mission."

"Thanks John, we need all the support we can get. Send any soldiers through as soon as they arrive, the controller will transfer them to where needs are greatest."

I spoke quickly with representatives of the war council, before departing hurriedly for the control centre; I needed to catch up with the real battles of the day.

Ju Lo called out as soon as I entered. I stared at the ferocious battle in New York. The buildings we sought to take were surrounded, but by more enemy defenders, than our troops. Jien Noi battled bravely alongside Kay, but it was clear her shield was gone, and the Eleventh's shield and weapons were weakening, they needed support immediately. They were supported by Foreign Legion and Chinese troops, but not enough of them.

Ju Lo said, "The Gatekeeper went to Kay's aide, I could not stop her. Reinforcements have not broken through to their exposed position. We have few troops, and there is precious little time to act. Due to the Ogres shield, we could not get a lock to transfer them out. Their return bracelets do not work either, probably for the same reason. However, our shield still compromises theirs, so we can send people in, just not to the right location."

I shouted, "n'Gue, I need everybody except our defence force, out of Washington, and in New York now. Ju Lo, send all our uncommitted troops to New York, and send the Mounties here. We may get more allied troops, if so, send them to rescue Jien Noi. I am headed there at once" I pointed at the screen, issued a quick-fire stream of instructions, and raced for the transporter.

Arriving at the battle, I wanted to rush to my wife and dearest friend's aid, but n'Gnung arrived with reinforcements; they did not know the battle situation, and I did. I laid it out for n'Gnung, Stewart, and Horovitz. The briefing took seconds, n'Gue staying to relay my orders to the next wave. We ran with our teams to support our troops.

Horovitz headed towards Gung Loi, who was secure, but her forces were trapped. Barph's elite forces headed to relieve their general, who was similarly pinned down, their troops Ancestral weapons and shielding also spent. Platoons of our recently acquired U.S. marines augmented both forces.

I knew my orders were being supported and carried out, glancing occasionally around for confirmation. I noted the Mounties charging across open ground assisted by Rambling and a corps of Giants. The latter were not good fighters, but they were taller and had longer reach than the Ogres, plus Ancestral weapons. They distracted defenders, and drew the enemy's fire.

This gave Horovitz' Blitzkrieg troops the edge to forge a division deep into enemy ranks and attack from the rear. US Marines, who consolidated our gains, took the attack forward, filling the space Horovitz' force had created, securing it.

n'Gnung and reinforcements caught up with me as I battled forward to a different part of the field of conflict. We were using our rings of protection to gouge a channel through to the most important women in my life. Our new tactics had distracted many of the enemy, but some remained entrenched around the pair, somehow knowing the importance of the two women we sought. Their attack remained focused, but too few of our troops plus the *Légion étrangère* stood between them and their quarry.

Our presence caused many to break and face us, stalling the final assault. The Ogres we faced were large, mean, and battle hardy. n'Gnung shouted, "Guardian, ahead, slightly to the right side, see them? The Ddwyrth, Llwydd."

We veered immediately, no other words necessary between us. It was a longer route, but quicker if Llwydd's forces were liberated from their corral to assist us. With the aid of the Ancestral weapons, our assault became a mighty weapon in its own right. Time slowed, I noticed things I had missed before, the din of battle receded, and I became acutely aware of my body, and everything immediately around me. I seemed to watch myself disable the protection, and wield the Sword of Destiny in anger. I took machine gun fire, deflecting the bullets with an almost casual shift of blade. It was surreal. I knew I was berserker, and felt invincible.

The fighting was fierce, but we liberated the Ddwyrth, and made slow, if steady progress towards my wife and Kay, who were by then fighting back to back.

I was near to despair, despite my determination, when a strange thing happened. The Ogre I fought turned to look with horror in his eyes. I slew him before following his gaze. A small herd of Indian War Elephants were marauding across the battlefield, with Apache braves on appaloosa horses in support.

They were headed directly for Jien Noi, the head of the herd having a shield bearer aboard. The momentum was decisive, not because of the small number of Ogres they killed, but by the panic they instilled in the

Ogre psyche. The elephants were trained to toss the enemy aside with a wrap of their trunks, and then trample them under foot.

Our soldiers rallied as breach after breach appeared in enemy ranks, and we slaughtered them unmercifully. I looked up and saw Jien Noi and Kay battling for their lives, a thin ring of our troops encircled them. I ran to them, heedless of the risks.

I was aware of n'Gnung and Llwydd behind me, their troops answering the call and driving into enemy ranks. We had taken them by surprise, and had impetus of battle. We broke through and we became three, then four, five, and many.

Our progress did not stall, but grew. We engulfed Kay and Jinnie, sweeping them up in our momentum, as with a snowball rolling down hill. And then there were no Ogres left to kill.

I came back to reality, my arms slowing as I realised the enemy were all dead. We had broken through, and were now behind enemy ranks, taking the fight to their rear.

Jinnie came before me, and into my scattered thoughts, to the side I heard Llwydd say, "He is berserker, he needs to come down. Let him rest a moment and recover. n'Gnung, we head for Gung Loi, you go left, I'll take the right flank."

I rose to follow them, but my wife smothered me with kisses and admonishments. My pulse slowed and my eyes properly focused. She said, "Llwydd said you should drink this. I think it is Ddwyrthen spirit, but it will calm you. I am so proud of you, and so angry with you also. What am I to do with Jack Barleycorn?"

I only took a small sip, coughed expansively, and was soon returned to my equilibrium. One glance around and I knew the battle was almost won. But we were still outside the main complex. A stared for a moment without understanding the enemy intent, as all the Ogres rushed towards the main building. I realised they were retreating, and hollered for the Mounties, sending all forces able to hear me to rush the building, before they locked us out. We had to be inside, or this day was already lost.

Rambling ran with his troops, they had the longer strides no other race possessed. A horse skidded to a halt nearby as I tried to keep up with the others, failing. "Sir?"

I leapt on the back and said, "Charge that doorway, we must get inside at all costs."

The Mountie drew his sword and pointed forwards, as if re-enacting a cavalry charge. I activated my protection bracelet. Other Mounties followed us, each bearing a passenger. We beat all of the Giants inside, except for Rambling, who was already flashing his broadsword in earnest battle, and heavily outnumbered. We did not stop by his side, but drove deeply into the defenders ranks, as our supporting troops flooded through the brink.

I remember the battle within the complex as a series of snapshots, my body and mind aware of every nuance at the time, but few stuck for memory of recall. I was berserker again, and I was not the only one. I was aware of a flick or feint from Llwydd or n'Gnung. I realised the Ogre blood was caustic, and started avoiding it. I think I told the other's, but cannot be sure. The red mist of killing was upon me, and it became a most joyous, yet heinous burden. The evisceration of one life for another became my addiction, as humanity, our constant and contradictory histories played out in the round.

That episode felt like a remote lifetime, a divergence from the normality of life. Our diversity and courage conquered a far larger and more warlike foe, and I was at a loss to feel any empathy for the Ogres, they remained an anathema to humanity's existence.

Like a recovering drunkard, I came back with a second wind when we broached the control room. I cannot think of the thousands of enemy we killed to get there, nor our greater losses, it was abject annihilation, eight races verses one. We won.

I closed out the complex with our own transfer circle and shield, locked out the control centre with much more ease, and in so doing, returned within my own equilibrium.

The berserker moments felt like divine intervention at the time, but I needed my innate humility, something the killing frenzy denied me. I mentioned this to n'Gnung, who responded, "Guardian, this is a new phenomenon. I am certain it is the influence of the Ring of the Warrior."

His suggestion carried great merit, and I came to understand Aroweena a lot better. I knew her eating of the fallen's hearts was but a salve to dress, and redress deeper wounds within her psyche.

As soon as we were done, I checked on Aroweena. Medics were still operating, so I moved on to the control room.

I knew we had already struck a decisive blow, deep into the heart of the Great Ogre's domain, but our work remained unfinished. Other battles still raged elsewhere on the planet. I took a brief review. All objectives of the day had fallen to us, except for New Delhi and Brussels. Several control centres needed to be locked out and I departed at once for Sao Paulo.

I was becoming much better at locking out enemy control centres, but it took great toll on my ring finger, and a larger one on my soul. Once my mission was complete, I returned to the island, and we resumed our war cabinet.

News came. Ælthrelntheine and Owain had taken New Delhi, people celebrated. I headed for India, and locked out that control centre as well. It was a joy to reunite with the leaders of the Eleventh and Seventh, both sporting new scars and covered in Ogre blood. Nearby stood the Chinese commander and I spoke to him in turn, congratulating his troop's fine work in Cantonese. I'm not sure if it was my presence, or my speaking one of China's two official languages, that brought forth an endearing smile, and new warmth of brotherhood between us.

I turned and walked away, there was one objective left. I spoke to n'Gnung at my side, "Brother, I have the strangest feeling the main battle is about to be joined. We dismissed Brussels, but it has not been taken. This is the Ogres influence, the EU, the UN at work. Come, sharpen your sword, a'hunting Ogre we will go, once more."

Chapter 27 ~ The Fall of Brussels

Brussels was proving to be impossible to take. It was time to regroup and formulate new tactics with our war cabinet. We decided Ælthrelntheine and Owain would lead files of their combined forces in a pincer movement. The War Elephants had proved decisive in New York so would drive into the centre, supported by Horovitz Blitzkrieg troops. The vacuum they created was to be filled with our remaining ground troops, mainly American and Chinese, mounted units to be sent as support where needed. Hogar was put in charge of annulling Ogre transfer circles.

Jinnie was put in charge of our control room, and she began transporting our reinforcements as soon as they were battle-ready. I was called away. The corridors of the medical centre were littered with the bodies of the mortally injured and dying. It was chaos. I spoke quickly with the Matron and took immediate action. I set a transporter ring on the headland of the shore, near the lake, and sealed a large surrounding area with a shield. She had requested an environmentally controlled atmosphere.

I returned to her moments later, n'Gue walking with me from the control room and offering a verbal update of our overall situation on the way.

The Matron said, "This is a great help, but I need another area. One area for incoming and initial diagnosis, and another dedicated to recovery. Serious treatment will be conducted here in the medical unit. I need a dedicated controller working closely with me and more staff. Hurry, we are losing lives."

I placed a second secure and interlinked transporter unit and said, "n'Gue. Work with your team of messengers and as many of our healers as can be spared, and take any fallen ally to the new area. I need you to control this, work with the Matron and use the transporter on the shore." I was about to say more, but he had already turned and was leaving. I called after him, "Once set up, delegate, we may yet have need of you. Send John to me."

A short time later, we committed all of our remaining troops to the battle in Brussels. There were fewer of us, the Second had already lost two-thirds of our number, roughly one thousand brave hearts at arms, either killed or maimed. Other Tribes casualties echoed our own. John came to me and I showed him our field hospital, where our healers and robotic medics worked in tandem; it was surreal. "John, I need field hospitals from the military, see what you can do. I'll place another interlinked, shielded compound for them to work in. Be quick, people are dying."

Chapter 27

It was the best I could do, and I returned my gaze to the battle, we had a war to win. I rallied the remnants of platoons and other groups on the hinterland of the shore. Those left standing were determined to prevail. Quickly new teams were forged and readied to renew the fray, as a regiment of Australia's finest joined us.

They saw our medical units and the efforts we were making to save lives, engendering respect within our forces. I greeted the Captain of the Foreign Legion, and thanked him in pigeon French for their stalwart efforts in saving the lives of two of the most important women in my life. He was duly deprecating, but in a forceful way, "It is why we are here Monsieur. Where to next?"

I led our remaining forces into the thick of battle. Only Special Forces were not committed. We supported the momentum of the Elephants, and turned the tide of battle to our favour. With a determined push, we broke through to Ælthrelntheine and Owain's forces and were soon in control of most of the compound.

We held most outer grounds, plus a few outbuildings of strategic importance, but there remained no way inside the main complex. Every other site had ways in, doors we could break through, motifs. This area had nothing and appeared to only support movement via transportation, controlled from inside the complex. Stymied I said to n'Gnung, "My brother, what are we missing? There is no way inside."

"If there is no doorway, then this is a trap."

As if to confirm his wisdom, the enemy fired canisters that exploded, releasing vapour. Troops started clutching their throats, rushing from their positions seeking air to breathe. I signalled an immediate withdrawal, but the American, Chinese, and Australians donned gas masks to maintain our presence. They dug themselves in and were set to stay for the duration. They were giving us time to find a way inside, time we must not waste.

Our withdrawal was hasty, but we got everybody else out. Many went directly to our field hospital. I forewarned Matron of the medical emergency. I sat back in my chair and cursed.

It fell to n'Gnung, as so often before, to offer us the insight that everyone else had missed, "Guardian, could we send our people in from one of the other Ogre outposts we took, perhaps New York?"

"We have no time to lose." Immediately Kay, with her Mother and Owain came to stand with n'Gnung and myself. Within moments a band of thirty leaders and fearsome fighters assembled in our transportation circle. I insisted Jinnie stayed behind to operate the controls. We tried to transfer directly to Brussels, but could get no lock. It was shielded from us, as we expected.

We arrived in New York, where startled guards were surprised to see us return so soon. I opened the main control panel and reactivated the transfer corridor, but could not get a lock on Brussels. I had feared as much, because the control centre was now under the control of the Ring of the Ancestor.

I altered the parameters once more so the control again responded to the dreaded Ring of the Warrior, having to wear it during the process. I could only get a lock when I was physically wearing the loathsome ring, and knew I would again be attending our medical unit in the near future. I fixed a lock within moments. However, I could not get a visual due to the high level of protection, so we would go in blind in two groups.

The Eleventh and Seventh were already waiting for transportation in the nearby sending circle. I dispatched them at once, followed immediately by the second group. Again, I was forced to stay behind as the only person that could wield the Ring of the Warrior, but not knowing what was happening started gnawing at my mettle. Then I wondered just why I was waiting behind, as I couldn't actually do anything to help them from my current position, or even bring them back.

Determined to fight at the side of my brothers and sisters, I set the transfer lock once more, and strode towards the transporter, accompanied without asking by two of the elite Chinese troops. I was surprised when five of the Third ran up to join us. They were led by Gelar and sported wooden spears and blowpipes. I cautioned them to drop behind me when we arrived. I prepared to activate my protection as soon as transference was complete.

My caution was wise as we arrived into the centre of a maelstrom. My shield was up the moment we materialised, immediately being pounded by enemy fire. Most of this came from normal weapons, but there were several Ogre Captains using Ancestral shielding and weaponry. Troops from both sides had fallen and there appeared to be a stalemate, as they sought to isolate us either side of the automatic door, which was forever opening and closing.

I had expected the next room to be a control centre, but it was an anteroom. Corpses lay everywhere, and more Ogres appeared as if transported in from another sending circle. n'Gnung beckoned me to him with a flick of his eyes. He motioned to a motif on the wall adjacent. I hollered for all to protect my position, and dropped my shield. The Ring of the Warrior locked with the motif, giving us a way out, and a fighting chance.

Our troops poured through, leaving only a few shield bearers to frustrate the Ogre presence. Kay was already atop the stairs by the time we were all through, and it seemed by the dust, the staircase has not been used for many centuries. I inserted the dreadful ring into the corresponding motif at the top of the stairway. Almost before my finger had made full contact Owain and Ælkræleinnoire were through the doorway, closely followed by our mixed militia. n'Gnung and I were last through and spread to the side establishing our bridgehead.

Our speed was such the Ogres were completely taken by surprise and their control centre became mayhem. None of us had activated our protective bracelets. We were intent upon taking the battle directly to our foe, and defeating them this one last time. Kay's blade danced with blue fire, as did the Sword of Destiny. An Ogre lieutenant in full armour stood laughing to bar our passage before the Captain's control. I swung my blade, as did Ælkræleinnoire to my side. Owain's trusty battle axe striking a serious blow to the Ogres arm. He began to laugh, his armour appeared to be unnaturally protected. His smile wavered and he held his neck, a main artery, where a wooden pin of poison lodged deeply. To my side Gelar said, "The power of the blowpipe, watch him fall," and he did.

Then we saw *him* at last, The Great Ogre; he was larger than any, bigger and meaner, somehow emanating pure evil. His haughty demeanour brought down to size as he watched his lieutenant fall, and we rushed him. There was a split second where I could have lunged at him. I aimed the Sword of Destiny to strike and cried, "I have you now Great Ogre."

"Not this time. I'll see you in the future, Guardian." The Great Ogre smiled maliciously and disappeared within a flick of his giant wrist; his hand rising to his neck. Both my opportunity and his death thwarted within an instant, he obviously had some sort of return bracelet, but to where?

To my side Princess Myuna of the Third said, "Guardian, I know I got him when he dropped his shield. He was big, far bigger than we ever imagined. I doubt my hit will be fatal."

We controlled all known transfer circles, except for the one we were in. I was distracted for a moment, which proved just long enough for another Ogre to swing his blade at my neck, fortunately the worst was deflected by Owain's timely intervention of blood axe. I fell. I felt a searing pain, which was quickly masked by trauma. As our forces began to annihilate the remaining soldiers of the Ogre, n'Gnung dropped to my side and pulled me upright into a sitting position, concern etched deeply within his brow.

"I'm all right. Help me to stand; I must lock this control out."

He half-carried me to the main control station, where I opened all doors and barriers, and locked the place down. It was only a matter of time until the few remaining Tenth fought to their death, supported valiantly by their meanness and bravery. The end of the Tenth in Brussels came swiftly. With their control centre breached, the rest of the complex fell quickly. I felt my consciousness drift, and remember being carried by strong arms.

I came to in our medical unit, and the scathing company of the robotic nurse who was not surprised to see me again that day. She castigated me for being so reckless. I made a note to have the Core give her a more caring disposition. As soon as my treatment finished, I departed to lock out the New York site again, and finally get rid of the malevolent Ring of the Warrior.

A short time later our victorious troops returned to a hero's welcome. The magnitude of our accomplishment would take many days to sink in. In my absence, Kay and n'Gnung had ensured all our advanced weapons and protective bracelets had been returned and accounted for, as several took a little finding. However, they also ensured parameters were set just in case we missed anything, so that when people transported out, they could only leave us with what they came with. The system was already in place of course, but Kay set it as a double and specific security threshold.

That night a great celebration was held for everyone on the shore, but this time centred upon the lake, as it was a larger area to hold the massed corps, minus those that were either injured, working, or due to take the next watch. Farther across the caldera, our improvised medical facilities were a frenzy of activity.

Jien Noi spoke at my side, "Your call for field hospitals was answered, Guardian. I had to place two more shielded compounds so all medics could be used to their full potential. Due to your decisive action, our losses should be much less than we feared."

I continued the initial debrief, Kay, n'Gnung, and Jinnie all adding their own perspectives and concerns. Our battles left us with several dozen rings and other devices fashioned by the Great Ogre; I labelled them and placed them all back with the Ring of the Warrior in our safe.

My one problem was that we did not find the real headquarters of the Tenth, something that troubled me greatly. I remained sure that it must be where the Great Ogre transported to, but where was it? Neither had the search revealed Oma's spaceship. It must be highly shielded and invisible to our regular scans, just like other sending circles the Core appeared to miss, "Were the search parameters correct?"

I went to join the celebration party, and played *the Hero* for as long as I could stand the onslaught, knowing our larger work had just begun. I was still healing and needed rest. I settled with my most trusted companions at the village on the shore, taking Da Phai Nai's tonic instead of beer. I spoke openly about my concerns, before leaving to action them.

I returned to interface with the Core, learning, "The previous scan only logged primary transfer circles at ground level."

"Set a new search in motion immediately. I need to cover the entirety of the planet, underground, inside mountains, in the air, wherever they are. I also need to know where Oma's spaceship is located. Please add all new locations found to our log."

"This will take days, Guardian."

"It takes as long as it takes. Begin with the U.S. and Europe."

I left to check on my dear friend in the medical facility. I entered to find a very bright and chirpy Aroweena, complaining that she was missing all the fun. An invective of Ddwyrthen expletives followed, as she verbally accosted the medic that would not allow her to leave. She was duly sedated.

Before I departed, Matron gave me a brief update regards Aroweena and all of our injured. She thanked me for the extra field medics. Her work was far from finished, but she told me to stay. As I lay down beside Aroweena, I looked at her two legs in new plaster. I wondered about her heart. She was a rare and truest friend.

Chapter 28 ~ Gaia Wakes

We had battled the Great Ogre and won, yet that was not even the beginning of our nightmares. Our victory celebrations were well underway by the lake of the Outlands, when the earth shuddered. Ælthrelntheine rose from her seat, a look of horror in her eyes, "Gaia wakes! I must know what this portends; Daughter, check the power of the Sentry rock."

We knew something of worldwide significance had occurred. Dawn left for her home and came back to us with the answer some time later. "As a best-case scenario, it couldn't get much worse. Jackie, you know Iran and Israel have been at it again, for some months now actually. It's all to do with the recent UN sanction for the partitioning of Iraq, Syria, ISIL, and all that stuff.

"Anyway, yesterday there was a concerted attack and disruption of the sum of world's key routers. I very much doubt this was the work of the Great Ogre. It was more likely continuation of the centuries old war between the West and the Middle East, Christianity versus Judaism versus Islam, if you prefer.

"However, this is what took up my time; almost unnoticed was a cyber attack on a key Iranian nuclear facility. Several online sources believe Mossad launched another cyber attack, this time on the Bushehr nuclear facility on the Gulf coast of Iran. What should have been a serious risk was compromised because of a test in progress, one that left many systems out of the safety loop. This in turn led to a core violation, resulting in a major breach of containment much worse than Fukushima. The Iranians were incensed and launched several nuclear missiles against Israel. These inflicted widespread damage and resultant contamination. That is confirmed in news broadcasts from across the world.

"We know the Israelis responded, meeting force with greater force, as is their way. Nobody knows what actually happened yet, but the earth shudder we felt here on the other side of the world, occurred several minutes after the Israeli nuclear retaliation. Currently, scientists believe it was an atomic bomb dropped on an oil or gas field, but confirmation will take days, if we ever discover what actually happened. Jackie, this is more than serious."

Our victory celebrations became muted, and were dampened further when Kay returned from the Sentry rock. "Gaia's power is stronger than I have ever known, she has awakened. The red Earth dragon begins to stalk the land once more, and we should be very afraid. Do not expect to be spared this wrath. Drink with me, I'm in need friendship. Cheers!"

Chapter 28

The next morning, Phillips, our dedicated U.S. envoy, came to me and introduced the head of the CDC, Dr. Janet Hopewell. The Doctor was gawking at my companions scattered around our round table. Acknowledging her introduction she said, "Guardian, what an unusual name, is it your first, or your last?"

"It's my title. We're done here. Hope well Doctor. Good day."

"Guardian, apologies, I meant it as a joke. Seriously, the DNA from the three agents does not fit with our databases. Their records check out on CIA, Homeland, and IRS databases, yet they are not homo sapiens. Can you enlighten me?"

"They are technically termed *Hominina*, and are clones. Do you know this already, how come? DNA testing takes days, weeks for a full assessment. Are you after the use of our technology?"

"No Guardian, I am not. I cannot speak for others, you do understand. Phillips?"

"Jackie, this is serious. She doesn't understand. Show her what happened if you must, but we need her on board. She is in charge of federal U.S. response to health threats, including worldwide pandemics and cataclysms. She is here at the President's personal request. You need to understand their 'Zombie Apocalypse' strategy; Guardian, this is very important."

I sighed with resignation, "Let us begin again, Doctor. Come."

Using the shore transporter, I showed them random recorded scenes from the battles, the excessive bloodletting ran against all her instincts, until we convinced her of the deadly threat the Ogres represented to all life on Earth. As emolument, we transported to the still overcrowded field medical facilities, where redress and rebalance was encapsulated.

Her interest swiftly focused on those that were not homo sapiens, she wanting to run DNA and other tests. I was forceful, but friendly, "I am sorry Doctor. I cannot allow that. However, we may allow you to work with us in the future. That's the best I can offer today. I do not intend to let these individuals become part of some freak show circus for the modern world, as you perceive it."

"The title suits you, Guardian. Now I understand. Please forgive my ill-considered words of earlier; this is all such a shock."

We returned to the village of the shore, and I asked John to join us. Speaking privately before he took a seat, "After I introduce you, I need you to assess the threat versus the opportunity this meeting represents. John, nothing leaves here, not even one drop of blood, understood. Also, discover what 'Zombie Apocalypse' is."

The meeting that followed was verbal jousting, John understanding the thrust and parry with words far better than I. The upshot was a mutually beneficial relationship. They wanted access to our technological capabilities, the current CDC concern being worldwide nuclear contamination. We needed access to independent DNA processing of highest laboratory specifications. I came to realise that had we been in contact before our war, they would have provided a full emergency response team and all the medical facilities we required — lives would have been saved.

Doctor Hopewell rose to depart, "Guardian, again I apologise for the initial misunderstanding. This place, this technology, these peoples have come as a great surprise to me. We need dedicated contacts and a signalling system — I will hand liaison over to Doctor Sylvia Steele, she also is unconventional, but the best at what she does."

When Hopewell had left, Phillips came to the real reason for his visit; "Guardian, we need to understand just how badly we are infiltrated, how the new President will be compromised when she duly takes office in a few weeks' time. The President tasked our Office with clearing the Tenth Column from the White House before the next President takes office. Only you can do this. Can you assist me, Jackie?"

I considered his request, knowing its importance, and that we owed his Country a great favour. "I will come as soon as I can. There are pressing issues I must attend to first. Perhaps tomorrow."

Phillips hurriedly departed and I returned to the control room, taking the Captain's chair. The scan of transporters I had initiated would take several more hours, days to fully probe the deeper layers of the Earth's crust. The Core assured me new locations had already been added to the database and were being monitored.

I was idling by in thought, when from the corner of my eye I noticed a spike appear, and it disappeared from my screen a fraction of a second later. "That was odd," I said to myself.

My eyes snapped to the display but saw nothing. However I was sure the source was somewhere in eastern Europe, well to the east, and possibly in Russia. I was about to turn away when there was another spike and this time in eastern Germany. I was greatly intrigued and studied the log until a pattern began to emerge; there was a great deal of activity centred upon Germany, and another in what I would term as Olde Prussia, nowadays the wilds of Poland near Belarus. I considered calling a new meeting of the Tribes and another war council, but decided to think upon it first.

Seeking a distraction, I realised our two green prisoners had not yet been debriefed. I went alone and was surprised to find two exceedingly large and meek individuals wondering when we would kill them. I had not considered their demise, although it was an option. I pressed them to tell me why they thought I had come to end their lives.

Chapter 28

"We work for the Ogres," they blurted out in unison, "And you have already killed many of them."

I sat down nearby and smiling, stated, "No. We have killed every single one. I would take your lives now, unless you have anything useful to tell me?"

They both spoke at once, as if a second were enough time to convey a hundred words of understanding. I discovered their names were Volkar and Stoltvar, and asked a series of open and leading questions, hoping to elicit information from them.

"We are slaves of the Ogres. We, our race survive because we do their bidding without thought."

"What Tribe are you?"

"We are the Ogres half-cousins, The Thräœll."

It sounded like they said *Traull*. I realised why we all called them Trolls, their enunciation was impossible to repeat. "How did you become indentured to the Ogres? Tell me about your lives."

They begin by describing their childhood, family, and village, which I determined was somewhere near the borders of Kazakhstan and China. Like most of their kind, they lived as a reclusive society in hiding from the ever-powerful Ogres. They stated, "At that time the Ogres controlled an area of great importance far to the west of us, but the Great Ogre instigated war amongst the Last, which destabilised their world. It was an experiment in mind control of pre-programmed clones. The Ogres moved east to observe, and scouts found our community.

"Our men were either killed or enslaved. Our women, our own mother's, were used for genetic experimentation. We were school friends back then and taken as trainees for the Great Ogre, the one we have served ever since on pain of death, or much worse."

"The Great Ogre. What is he? Have you ever met him?"

"Oh no, the Great Ogre has never been seen by most, even the Ogres themselves only know of him by reputation."

I knew my European history, but genetic and DNA experiments? "Where and when did these experiments take place?"

"Oh that's easy. They took over one hundred years to perfect, but eventually they created a great leader to rule the world, and he was the first Hob Goblin, one of their first in human form. That would be eighty or ninety years ago when he came into power. The Great Ogre created experimental camps and the clone provided an endless supply of human subjects for genetic experimentation and manipulation. It was horrendous, as any that were not considered pure and wholesome by the megalomaniac, suffered much like we ourselves have done for millennia."

I was considering re-writing the versions of The Napoleonic Wars and WWII, when Stoltvar said, "It was only an experiment to control a clone. The Ogres had already perfected their DNA technology to a highly advanced and manipulative degree. They just wanted to pre-program a clone and see what happened. They celebrated for many years afterwards and were exceedingly happy, even though we suffered even more abuse upon their success."

"Where is the main base of the Tenth?"

They tried to explain, but I had them show me on a screen. And so it came to pass that on the morning of Friday, 13th January, I learned the location of the secret base of the Ogres. Given world history, the city was not a surprise.

The information mapped perfectly with my first observations of transfers we could not account for, and was certainly a major hub of coming and going. I returned the Trolls to their cell and was about to leave, when Volkar elicited, "There is a secret way in that few know about. We could show you. Would you give us our freedom in return?"

The Troll fell silent and covered his head. Stoltvar stared at him disbelievingly. Cowering, expecting my wrath. I squatted down and asked them to tell me how, which they did.

My formulating plans changed instantly. I called out, "Guard, bring us three thick steaks and three beers from the shore without delay."

n'Gnung joined us minutes later proffering three trays, and he had included fresh bread also. He set the trays down and stood to one side.

Our prisoners grabbed their steaks immediately and savoured the flavour, commenting that they had not eaten this most delicious of foods since they were very young. The beer was weak, but a welcome wash for the rich meat, and they were done before I had taken one bite or sip of my own.

"Guardian, your presence is required on the shore," stated n'Gnung. As we walked away he said, "Will we kill them today?"

I laughed and replied, "No brother. We may have discovered two most unlikely allies. Convene the war cabinet immediately; we need to take the Ogres real stronghold: Berlin."

The meeting was brief and to the point, we already knew what lay ahead of us. The hiatus of celebration had confirmed new unity and alliances, at the expense of the momentum of battle. King Ruaidhrí of the Fourth spoke up, "It is time the Fourth showed their true worth. I have a wee plan of my own, Cayden and Cayleigh will leave for Berlin immediately, and surely be captured by the Ogres…"

We considered the Red King's plan, and it appeared to be stupid. He was insistent, and so the two were sent ahead and were duly captured by the Ogres. We left to rally our troops for one last push, our timetable set for our evening, dawn in Europe.

John spoke to the Americans and Chinese leaders, most of whose remaining troops were still with us. They demanded special deals and inclusion regards key Ogre locations in their respective countries. What they really wanted was control of the transfer points we had taken. I was not a politician, and said, "No way!"

We did agree that I would attend the White House before we attacked, and the Chinese wanted preferential information regards Kyoto and Pyongyang in return for further assistance.

I returned to the control centre and detoured to ask the guards what happened to the food and beer I left with the Trolls. "They left it untouched, Guardian, before I told them you had gone. They divided the remains of the meal exactly in two and had half each."

I was surprised. I had expected them to fight over it. My growing respect for these strange creatures was fortified. Conversely, we had learned nothing important from the three clones in human form. Henry had worked on them, gaining a little insight into how they had compromised America, but this did nothing to assist us. Needing immediate answers, I asked Kay and Aroweena to interrogate, but not quite kill them, just yet.

As I had suspected, but did not want to watch, they broke when the Second Warrior of the Ddwyrth began massaging one agent's heart directly with her talons. I listened to their report, and learned many things that would help us in our next battle. They confirmed Berlin was a main centre of operations, but not the Great Ogre's home. The agent's did not know where that was, except it was in the far north, somewhere white with cold. And the place where they were born, as hobgoblins.

I stopped by my station and added the information to the Core's search. I left seconds later to attend the war cabinet, but was distracted along the way. Phillips was with us again, determined to speak to me privately.

"Jack, Guardian, I need you for a moment, please. There have been grave repercussions from the strike on Bushehr. It was much larger than we thought, how much larger is still unknown, but the President must react at once. He needs to contain political fallout, you do understand. He needs to instigate a state of emergency across the whole of the USA. This will cover what we do whilst we root-out the Tenth. I now know they are behind this.

"Jack, please spare me a few minutes to check his immediate staff. We need to know who can and cannot be trusted. The President will move from the White House to our reserve facility, a secret bunker, immediately I leave here."

I considered momentarily, as our time to attack the Tenth drew ever nearer. "No, but I will ask my wife to go in my place and bear the Sword of Destiny. We can send you directly to the new base of operations unless you wish to return to the White House?"

Phillips replied, "Thank you, but no. He will pronounce this from the War Room beneath the West Wing. Guardian, I need you to accompany me now, to check everybody present, as with no disrespect intended, you alone have normal human form. Then he would have us all transferred to the secure war headquarters, although he asked for his wife and children to be brought here for safekeeping. We need you to run an initial sweep of all the staff currently in the War bunker, and once done transfer this duty to your wife. We will keep her safe from any misfortune."

Phillips had made a good point and we transported a few minutes later. We found the President in a secure conference room where he was calling for emergency powers, and meeting opposition from those within, and The Observatory. There appeared to be a power-struggle going on as I arrived by his side. Conversation stopped as he began to introduce me. Two agents immediately rushed me, and my sword glowed brightly. I flicked my wrist, and stood defiant as automatic fire bounced off my personal shield. When their clips emptied, I struck them down in a rage of the whitest blue flame.

The President chuckled, "That's what happens to the enemy. Lay down your arms, and mobiles, all communication devices, and submit to inspection, and that means everybody in this room."

My blade only flared once; the permanent undersecretary to the Head of DNI. He drew a weapon, but froze when I pressed cold steel to his throat. Secret Service took him away for questioning.

The President spoke, "Ladies and Gentlemen, it is already plain to see we are deeply compromised. I therefore declare a nationwide State of Emergency, effective this instant. Guardian, President Elect, you're with me. Everyone else, please wait a moment while we ensure your safety is secured. Thank you." The President Elect gave him a whiney look as she fell in step behind.

With time against us, we transported to the secret bunker and I checked out personnel in the main secure complex. Noteworthy; there was an ever-present pull to the Sword of Destiny, one I did not understand. I confirmed with the President that all was clear, but I had a problem with *something, somewhere.*

The main staff were cleared, but my time was pressing. I arrived back in our control centre as Jinnie and Kay were marshalling forces for the attack on the Tenth, and donned the mantle of Guardian once more. We would take battle directly into the heartlands of the Tenth.

Chapter 28

I handed the Sword of Destiny to Jinnie, imploring her to make time to find the anomaly. I was convinced there was a weakness in the place that we did not understand, yet. She kissed me, and we made a date for drinks and dinner later when we got back. I took a moment to watch her leave, and smiled as she turned to capture my eyes within her own. With a wave, she was gone.

Chapter 29 ~ The Battle of Berlin

Jien Noi

The Gatekeeper arrived at the secure compound, and was greeted by the President, "Everybody inside has been checked by your husband, what do you need?"

"Where, how do people enter?"

"Follow me … This security gate has X-ray screening. To the side is a curtained-off area. We would need you to stand inside and check everybody that enters."

"OK. That sounds simple enough, but I must check it works."

"Thanks. Bring the former undersecretary here immediately."

The ruse worked perfectly, the sword flared, and she set to work. Behind him were thirty people awaiting scrutiny. They were all clear, but moments later a convoy of troops arrived, several of whom were compromised; a Captain and two Sergeants. They were immediately taken into custody.

The next arrivals would be by helicopter, about thirty minutes later. Jien Noi started looking for the aberration Jack identified, and felt it too, a distinct pull on the sword. With one of the regular staff, she followed the direction of the sword to the rear of the building, and down into the depths of sub-basements, and subsequently the caves below. The house manager had never been down so deep before, and was amazed at how far the tunnels ran.

Finally, they reached the lowest levels, where several tunnels led off in different directions. They were about to follow the pull of the sword into the central corridor when the sword flared to life. The Gatekeeper activated the protective bracelet, just before machine guns fired. The putter of heavy calibre resounded in the caves, and bullets bounced off her protection.

She pulled back to where the tunnel led back up, "Go. Raise the alarm, and send troops down here. Hurry!"

She blocked the way as the bullets became fewer, her attackers had realised they could not penetrate the shield. Time passed, Jien Noi hoped the shield would hold until assistance came. She was brave, but not a trained fighter.

Ten minutes elapsed before she heard a slight sound behind her. A voice close to her whispered, "Do not turn around, Gatekeeper. Pretend we are not here. Walk to where the tunnel divides and we will be behind you. Use your shield to protect us."

She did as instructed, edging forward into the central corridor, her heart beating loudly. Bursts of gunfire rang out from the tunnels either side, SEAL's deploying for containment.

Chapter 29

She recognised a face, "Empress, we must move forwards quickly. Use your shield and run. We need to take out whatever lies down this corridor. Go!"

She crept quickly at first, until gunfire bounced off her shield. She ran headstrong, and headlong towards it, knowing that by doing so, they were closing the gap.

She slowed as they approached the enemy; a SEAL rolled a grenade forward from under the protective shield. It exploded moments later, maiming the forces operating the machine gun position. The noise was excruciatingly loud, and even with covered ears, they could not hear for a few minutes. Despite her temporary deafness, they killed the Ogres and moved on. They came to a transfer circle and looked at one another in astonishment.

Moments later three Ogres apparated, and were quickly dispatched, almost before they fully materialised. Adams, the leading SEAL, wiped his brow and examined them. He looked up and enquired, "Where to next, Empress?"

"Onwards! Let's see where this wormhole leads."

Staccato bursts of machinegun fire came from behind and they dived aside for their lives. An Ogre captain strode boldly forwards, laughing at them, his prey. They fired empty, their bullets spent, bouncing off the Ogre's shield. Jien Noi shouted, "New clips, go. Into the sending circle, now! Wherever we end up, start firing."

Jack

Our attack on the Tenth started discreetly. The two Trolls guided our team into the depths of the lair in Berlin. The team were wading through an underground river and had breathing apparatus should it be required. Kay and Aroweena shadowed them on the lookout for the first sign of deception. I had argued with the Ddwyrth, but she insisted she had been repaired.

Before agreeing to her deployment, I had checked with the Matron, "The Ddwyrth is a feisty one. Her legs are fully supported from heel to knee. The extended cast she wears is like an artificial limb, but on the outside. She should be fine, although there will be damage to repair."

The ingress went well, and they infiltrated deep into the interior without being discovered, before I lost visual. They had with them squads of SEAL's, SAS, and a contingent of the best Chinese troops. Handpicked soldiers of the Eleventh, Seventh, and Second accompanied them.

After the agreed twenty minutes head start, we sent in our main troops. As expected, the enemy's shields were raised after our first troops arrived. However, I continued to send in more through our transportation circles that I had placed to bridge their shields.

The battle in Berlin was intense, with Ælthrelntheine leading the attack. Some of the opposition also had personal shields and advanced weaponry. Meanwhile, Owain led our other assault on the base in the hills of Olde Prussia, ably supported by Rambling.

Both groups had support of marines, Chinese soldiers, and assistance from the corps of the other tribes. The Trolls had informed us the Berlin control centre was set deep underground and was heavily guarded. Our troops were still above ground, looking for a way inside. It became clear that the only way we could advance was to keep firing at the Ogres personal shields until they ran out of power, when we could make small advances before the next was encountered. Ælthrelntheine closed on the central building, but progress was slow.

They reached an area that was sealed off with doors sporting the typical motif. I had resigned myself to having to wear the Ring of the Warrior once more. I transferred to the President's security bunker in order to return with my wife, as without her assistance, I could not open the secret safe where the ring was kept.

I left n'Gnung in charge, and arriving swiftly, was pleased the guards and aides recognised me. I was looking for my wife, but I bumped into the President in a corridor. He was looking slightly odd. I did not know why until I went to shake his hand, my ring flared with searing blue flame. I covered it immediately, and knew instantly that something was wrong, and went on my way.

I gave Don Phillips a telling look, who guided me away to another room. "There is something wrong, the President has just adopted a UN resolution he was directly opposed to, and ordered a complete review of all our security services."

I stared at him in disbelief. The magnitude of this would potentially empower the Great Ogre, not the United States. Phillips said, "I think he's not the President, does this sound crazy to you?"

"Don, that is not the President. It is an Ogre clone. However, even as a clone, the President will be difficult to move against."

I asked after my wife, and he said, "She went in search of an anomaly some time ago, entered the underground caves, and has not returned. We sent marines after her, and they are overdue."

My initial reaction was to chase after her, but my duty lay elsewhere. I asked to be shown where she went, and Phillips obliged. Having moved deep into the underground complex, Phillips showed me a tunnel leading downwards and pointed, "She went in that direction." I thanked him for his efforts and enquired about the President's family.

"Ah yes" he remembered, "He wanted you to keep them safe. They are in their private quarters. Come now and I will take you directly there. We should act before they are compromised also."

Several minutes later we were admitted to the bunkers version of the East Wing. There I was introduced to the First Lady and her children, and I shook hands with all as a precaution. She was personable at first, and until Phillips asked the children for privacy, whereupon we told her of our suspicions. She looked at us and stated quite categorically, "The man in there is not my husband."

"I know, and so do several others loyal to the real President. It was his wish you come with us for safekeeping, will you come with me now please?"

Phillips confirmed, and with a little apprehension, she agreed, calling the children back to her side. "My cases are not unpacked, so can come with us. Now where do we meet the flight?"

"First Lady, this is no ordinary means of transportation."

Their bags were brought and positioned in front of us. Two members of staff accompanied her, as did Phillips. I flicked my return bracelet, and moments later, transferred them directly to our war room. We were standing in what appeared to be a normal military command room, although the layout was rather weird. The First Lady made the mistake of asking me where they were, and I casually replied, "Somewhere in the middle of the South Pacific ocean near the Tropic of Capricorn."

Her eyes never left me until John welcomed us. I said, "John, Dawn, please ensure our guests are well looked after, perhaps after they are briefed, they could visit the beach. The President has been cloned since I last met him. I must leave at once, the Gatekeeper is missing and I must find her. First Lady."

I returned to the control room and after a brief review, scanned for Jien Noi, following the tunnels deep into the dark using a drone. I found her at the end of a tunnel, and watched, helpless, as she turned off her protection and stood to face an extremely large Ogre. He also disabled his protection and pulled back to strike a deadly blow. The Gatekeeper feinted, and was quicker, rupturing his heart with the Sword of Destiny. She reached down and removed a ring from his finger, before jumping backwards onto a sending circle, and disappeared from view with a group of SEAL's. Bullets ricochet around where she stood moments before. It became clear the corridor was under the control of the Tenth.

"n'Gnung, form an elite squad now and go to the rescue."

I hurried to my day room, "Core, why didn't we know about that transfer circle?"

"Guardian, underground scans have not penetrated that deeply yet." I added the location to the database and log at once.

I examined the battle in Berlin. Our troops began returning for new protective bracelets and Ancestral weapons, the used needing recharging. I delegated the task to n'Gue, after showing him what to do, and he delegated in turn, instigating messenger teams to supply charged equipment on the battlefield.

Dawn came to me and said, "The First Lady is unhappy and wants to know what is going on. I think she needs to see this control centre, Jackie."

I gave permission as n'Gnung returned, having pulled together a fine team. They were led by Gung Loi with a platoon of her guerrillas, accompanied by mixed troops of many Tribes. I relayed my instructions to her, our troops were to clear the corridors where the Empress disappeared, and kill all resistance. Once the area was cleared, they were to set guards at the entrance to the level from above, and again at the transfer circle. "Remember, Ogres could come through at any moment, as well as our own people. Stay sharp."

Dawn arrived within moments, accompanied the First Lady and Phillips. She gawked at our screen, consoles, and the hominina operating them. She shook the aberration aside with a flick of her head, and took it all in her stride, and so much so I began to feel she was harder-headed than the President.

She joined me at the Captain's console, where I began the search for her husband, where she grew into knowledge of our powers, and the true power of our enemy. However, I was sad to report there was absolutely no sign of the real President, so asked, "What actually happened before you realised he had changed?"

"From the first moment I saw him there, I knew it was not him. Each contact we had since has only confirmed this, and d'you know what? I thought there was nobody that would understand."

Phillips spoke, "When he left you, Guardian, he was the real person. About thirty minutes later, he was not. I was not with him for most of that time, but I do remember he had changed clothes before meeting the Joint Chiefs, which is highly unusual."

No sooner were his words spoken, than urgent news came from Olde Prussia. I panned to the location, where a celebration was in progress. Owain's forces had been victorious, taking the control centre, and they had annihilated all the Ogres. Hundreds of bodies lay lifeless before my lens, including many of our own and a few Trolls. However, several hundred Trolls had been captured, and were severely shackled with weapons pointed at them.

I changed view to find the fight in Berlin was going against us. They needed reinforcements urgently, or the Ogres would break through our ranks. I recalled Owain and after brief, but hearty congratulations, showed him the battle for Berlin. "The Ddwyrth will leave at once. We'll leave behind a few men at arms to baby-sit the Trolls. They turned on the Ogres and assisted us greatly."

"I'll set a shield to cover the entire area and prevent any more Ogres entering. I intend to commit every man at arms to the battle in Berlin. Go, give your instructions, and rejoin me in a minute. n'Gnung, ready the War Elephants, then…"

Our controllers acted at once, sending reinforcements into the heat of battle at my direction. It was plain to see the impetus, the renewal in belief this brought. The First Lady said, "I can't believe any of this is real, yet I just saw Owain in the flesh. He is not quite human, is he? Those are Elves—and monsters. Oh My God! … Your friend mentioned the beach?"

I sent her and her party to the shore. No sooner had they departed than Owain returned and said, "Shall we dance the macabre once more brother?"

We arrived just before the Ogres extended their shield, locking out our transfer circle, but after our reinforcements apparated. War Elephants rampaged into the midst of the Ogres, cleaving a route as we followed. I drew enemy out with my shield, as Owain's berserker became a killing machine of mayhem and death, and we ploughed a deep furrow into the heart of Ogre ranks.

Ælthrelntheine came immediately to bolster our drive, ordering our holding defence to reform into an attacking wedge that cleaved its way deep with death into the enemy ranks. Predictably, the Ogres rushed to defend the centre, falling back in support as they did so. This allowed Angkrelguer and Ælfreisia to form a pincer movement of the Eleventh to our flanks, breaking through with fleetness of foot to bring the battle back to the Ogres at either side.

However, the Ogre leader proved experienced and countered, setting his troops with reinforcements that never stopped coming, such were the enemy's depth in numbers. Our advance faltered against sheer numbers, but still we pressed forwards, then sideways, and eventually linked-up with the Elven pincer movement, killing those trapped within.

From his secure position, the commander of the Ogres used a communicator. Fresh troops arrived to our rear moments later, and soon we became encircled, fighting for our lives defensively once more. We sought to break out, and succeeded several times, only to be driven back as fresh troops of the Ogre transported in to stop our progress, and return it to defeat.

The ground was slippery with fresh blood, the stench of death lay all around, and dismembered bodies multiplied, as we pushed forward once more, and yet made no progress. Our number was slowly, but continuously being reduced against a mighty foe whose numbers only increased, in spite of the hundreds we had already slain. It was as if they rose up from the depths of hell, there was no end to them.

I saw a weakness and we broke sideways to our left, reaching a small rise, and in the process took one of their secreted transfer circles, thus being able to kill reinforcements before they could act against us. From there, we were able to hold off our attackers, as their bodies piled high around us.

I was nicked as my protection began to fail. Beside me, Owain offered his own protective bracelet, as I remained the focal point of our shield for the others to fight behind. However, the injury I received was minimised because the Ring of the Ancestor reacted in my defence, something I had never known before. I realised all I had to do was to wish it. It was like the protection of the Ogre Captain from before. My body was protected, but I could also wield my weapons. Owain and I feinted, probed, and searched for the slightest weakness in our massed enemy.

We continued to hold and grew stronger within our own communal belief, as for the first time the enemy forces ceased coming. I presumed they had finally run out of reinforcements.

The bodies of the Ogres stacked so high before us that the time came when the pile of their dead was level with our mound of earth, and subtly the battle changed.

The Ogres only attacked us directly and I saw the chance of counter attack. I spoke briefly with Owain and Ælthrelntheine, before running across the mound of dead Ogre bodies to our right, and somersaulted over the advancing troops, causing a distraction, and killed as many as I could with Ancestral weapons.

Troops of the Eleventh and Seventh were beside me moments later, and we headed for the Ogre's commander. At first progress was swift, we had completely wrong-footed the enemy, but their troops regrouped to come at us again. We rallied our forces for one last stand, placed our backs to each other and fought for our lives.

Then something truly bizarre occurred. The Ogre commander fell, his life ebbing away as the Sword of Destiny cleaved him in two. What had appeared to be our certain death of a few moments before, turned into a rout as we watched Jien Noi and Kay, ably assisted by their soldiers, take the fight out of the Tenth.

Chapter 29

I realised the Ogre's main shield was down. Reinforcements encircled the remaining enemy and cut them down with ferocity. The end was quick and forthcoming. The last of the Ogres tried to surrender, only to be cut in two by the Sword of Destiny.

As the last head rolled across the ground, I watched as my wife fainted from the exertion and I rushed to her side immediately. I had no idea how she managed to even be there, let alone be wearing a powerful Ring of the Tenth. I swept her into my arms, and directly to our medical centre. I removed the dastardly ring, which was weeping blood and swirling with bloody blackness. Her finger was a total mess and I wondered if it could be saved?

I stood aside as the robotic nurse tended to her. After a brief examination she administered medicines and turned to me, "She will be fine. No doubt I will be attending to your wounds again later. Are you two competing to see who will lose a finger first? Now be gone, I have too much work to do, and need another field unit. I will also restore your wife to full health, Guardian."

Chapter 30 ~ The West Wing

While our troops celebrated and mopped up remaining pockets of resistance, Jien Noi regained her strength and unlocked the safe. I took the Ring of the Warrior, and transported directly to Berlin. Once that control was locked out, I did the same in Olde Prussia. I returned to base, needing time with my family, but n'Gnung came to us with a report.

"Guardian, all targets were taken successfully, and are now under our full control. I have assigned guards to each location under the direction of Horovitz, as before. Your faith in the two Trolls was entirely justified. They saved the lives of many, including Kay when Ogres surrounded them and they were out of ammunition and protection. The Trolls used a ploy to make the Ogres believe they had lured our army into a trap, and having gained their confidence, took weapons and killed their former masters. This allowed our troops to regroup and strike back.

"It seems the mischievous Fourth had gained the Great Ogres pleasure, and instead of being incarcerated, were allowed access to him personally, and even places normal Ogres were forbidden.

However, when the battle turned fierce they were able to surreptitiously monitor a vacant console, and were the first to discover the secret advance of Kay and the Trolls, which they alone knew about in advance, of course. They quickly switched focus, turned off the screen, and *borrowed* a ring of power from one of the Ogres, before making their way towards the only access point our secret forces would arrive at.

"Without their subterfuge it is highly unlikely Kay would have been able to negotiate a motif sealed door, but they were on hand to let the party through and guide them into the heart of the lair in Berlin. Once they had reached the outer corridors of the control centre complex, they were startled when a door abruptly opened in their midst, and our Empress came through with her small force."

n'Gnung finished there as Jien Noi picked up the story, "I found the aberration beneath the secret bunker. We were cut off deep underground as Ogres trapped us. Had it not been for my protective bracelet I am sure we would all have died. Adams and his men stood in the sending circle, but it did not transport them. I reasoned there needed to be an Ogre ring bearer with them.

"It was horrific Jackie. We were forced back by one bullish brute, and I took a great chance, ridiculing him for being scared of a woman, hiding behind his shield, and not fighting like a man. I dropped my protection, and called him out. Fortunately, he responded likewise. I tricked him and managed to kill him with the Sword. I took his ring and the transporter worked."

I smiled and said, "I sent a drone in search, and saw you on the screen. I sent in reinforcements, but the last I saw of you was when you transported. I was so worried for you, you have no idea."

She cuddled into me and continued, "We found ourselves in another transfer circle, a major one, accompanied by half a dozen Ogres. Our troops opened fire as soon as we arrived, taking the Ogres by surprise and killing them. Adams deserves special praise because he is highly skilled—not only in weapons, but in deployment of troops and tactical warfare. Several Ogres followed us through from the caves and we despatched them before they could react.

"I used the Ogre's ring on the motif of a secret door we discovered in the transportation area. We went through and found a passage that lead up and we followed it hoping the design was similar to most others. Clambering up, we reached an anteroom, where several Ogres were staging. We prepared to fight them, but they received a communication and left via what I presumed was the main door. There was another motif to the side. I used the ring again and we came out right in the middle of our own troops.

"We combined forces, and the leading SEAL with Kay, Captain Stewart, advised us correctly as we took ancillary positions and cleared Ogres, before making a twin assault on the main control centre. It was quickly taken with our element of surprise, and I collected several more rings and tokens of power. However, the main control station was empty, so I think we missed capturing the Great Ogre.

"Holding the control room, Kay managed to interface and lower the shields using one of the operator's rings we had taken. She opened access corridors, as we pressed forward and fought through towards the outside. Along the way, we were ambushed and our weapons ran out of ammunition and power. That's when the Trolls tricked the Ogre captain, and when he turned back to us, they killed him. We regrouped and fought our way outside, where we were able to take the enemy from behind, and thus relieve the pressure on Ælthrelntheine and Owain, and you, my love."

I congratulated them both, amazed at the courage all our troops had shown that day. We had struck a mighty blow at the centre of the power of the Ogre. However, with the Great Ogre still at large. I knew we still had a lot of work to do, and were not yet safe from counterattack.

Neither had we located the real President, nor completely dealt with the threat facing us. With these thoughts uppermost in my mind, I returned to the control room.

The Ogres were clever, and devious. They had left us a mystery: 'where does one hide the President of the United States of America so nobody could find him?'

I check the false President was still in his bunker, noting he was deeply involved with what appeared to be a clone and replacement exercise. I focused on the Chief of Staff, a man I had come to know quite well and respect, and found he was younger looking and was wearing a slightly different uniform with a lot more badges on it. I had an idea he was also a clone, so where were the real people?

I scanned below using the drone, and found Gung Loi holding an alcove deep beneath the secure bunker. Her troops were set against fearsome odds. Ælthrelntheine, Owain, and Rambling answered my call immediately. Although battle weary, they responded proactively to the new situation, the Queen of the Eleventh leaving at once to augment Gung Loi's forces, by using the Berlin transporter. Owain, and Rambling would attack from above, trapping the Ogres between them. That was the plan, and their troops transferred to action it.

My mind returned to wonder where was the least likely place you would seek to find the President of the United States of America? I threw my question open to all, but it was n'Gnung who, as always, came up with the most leftfield and plausible solution. "Have you looked in the White House?"

The White House had been evacuated due to the threat. Yet the answer became dreadfully evident, once we looked in the most obvious place. Knowing the President left the White House earlier that day, this was indeed the last place any of us would have looked for him. And yet as the words were aired, so they became the most prophetic. We found the real President in the Oval Office, and under restraint. He was entertaining the Great Ogre. It appeared he was signing papers, much to his apparent dismay.

I immediately tried to get a lock on the real President, but there was a shield in place. We would have to go in and rescue him, and to do that I needed insider information. In answer to my request, the First Lady arrived, and she clutched my arm when I showed her the presidential clone, followed by her real husband. She watched aghast. Her eyes flew wildly open as her fingernails dug deeply into my flesh, her mouth agape. Nary a sound came to our ears. She froze like a petrified tree, mortified.

Phillips tried to gentle her away, but her children finally distracted her, "Mom, what is going on. Which one's our real dad?"

I was already running a reckie, when Phillips spoke, "You will need me to go with you, and others. The Secret Service may have been cloned. Oh My God! Where does this end?"

Chapter 30

I replied distractedly, "It ends here, and it ends now. n'Gnung, assemble our best, we leave in moments to right this wrong."

Phillips, spoke to the First Lady, "The Guardian needs all of us to go, Ma'am. Between us, we know all of today's passwords, and can recognise the real people from the clones. Madam, as is your wish?"

We transported into the White House moments later, the Presidential family, Phillips, and I. My team watched us leave, ready to come to us once we had reconnoitred the vicinity: n'Gnung, Kay, Aroweena, and the best of our uncommitted troops.

We transferred close to the Oval Office, but I knew most of the few staff remaining would be Ogre clones. Flares to my ring confirmed as much, but we needed to know what we were up against, something I could not tell from the control room. Powerful though the Ancestral technology was, it was not perfect. Some things had to be done by people and in person.

The First Lady rose to the occasion, and walked formidably towards the Oval Office, but was courteously declined entrance. I walked with her and everybody I encountered, turned my ring to blue fire. She remonstrated outside her husband's office, and a more senior Secret Service agent came over. He spoke sincerely with her, taking her aside. The First Lady introduced him as Bob Samuels, head of security. I shook his hand, and my ring stayed mute. We required an ally on the inside, and he was to be it.

I needed to show him what was going on, and took him to our war room. At first disbelieving, I am sure this most practicable of men thought he had lost his mind when he looked at our screens. He witnessed impossible things and I pressed our advantage. There was no other recourse.

We garnered his support and returned with an ally, and Kay, who insisted on coming with us. When the Great Ogre sent out for refreshments, we went in behind the waitress, once the shield to the Oval office was dropped. We set interlinked broaching shields, and caught the Great Ogre off guard, for the second time in as many days.

Entering the room, we rushed to kill him. He raised his personal shield, as did we, and we had a standoff. He mocked us, castigated us, and threatened us with fates far worse than death. We advanced on him, but Ogre guards barred our path. I realised my mistake. In our haste, we had forgotten to set our own shield to lock out the Ogre's shield.

The head of the Joint Chiefs transported in, and presented the real President with a raft of documents to sign. The President glanced at the contents and cursed. The Joint Chief looked older, and I had the feeling this was the real one, not the clone I had seen earlier, supported by some of his comments that implied as much.

Three henchmen transported in at that moment, one forcing the President at the point of a sword, to sign the documents. He spoke out, and the First Lady rushed to him, only to be restrained. He looked up at us, helpless but to comply. Deep within the heart of this new Ogres lair, we needed a new plan. Whispers later, we attacked

I advanced on the Great Ogre, and when within striking range, dropped my shield, activated my ring's protection, and struck with full force. The Sword of Destiny did not penetrate the Ogre's shield, but neither did it not. It locked, a power struggle ensuing, and it became as much a mental struggle as a physical one.

I was aware of my companions beside me, more of our own troops transporting in, as did more Ogres. They were shielding me from the raking blades of death by Ogre broadsword. Kay feinted to attack the nearest Ogre, but spun to add her blade to my own. Both became enmeshed within the Great Ogres protective shield, which weakened imperceptibly, and then, slightly more so.

I flicked my eyes at Kay encouragingly. I heard her voice in my head, "Deeper Jackie, we must kill this abomination."

I twisted the sword, seeking leverage within the shield, and it gave slightly. The Great Ogre stumbled backwards, bringing his arm across his chest, as he sought his return bracelet. We pressed our advantage, badly wounding his arm, but within a jot, he was gone.

Kay cursed, "We almost had him, you and I. But he ran like the coward he is. Damn him. Damn his ilk. I swear to any god that can be bothered to listen, I will kill him, and all of his illegitimate spawn!"

I am sure she wanted to say more, but her words were cut off as we were transported out, and before the Ogres could lock on us. This included the President, his family, and Chief of Staff.

Once secure, the President said, "I now believe you Jackie, Kay, all others. You all spoke the impossibility of truth, in a land where I find it rare, more so as the days linger. Those documents I signed were an abomination, but they are not official. My signature is not, quite, correct, and they do not have the official seal. It seems, this Great Ogre is not as clever as he thinks he is."

In due course, we held council. We needed to plan our next moves and the removal of all hobgoblins, as Ogre clones of the Last were known. Eradicating the cloned president and his associates was a matter of the utmost priority.

The true President's mind was set on direct confrontation with his clone. He gathered his resources and those he trusted who were cleared by my ring. We would support the intrusion with our weapons and technology. Kay had instigated continuous production of transfer circles to act as shields before she departed, which we now needed. We were discussing placement and soldiers when n'Gue arrived with a message, "Guardian, you are needed in the control room. The fighting is far heavier than we imagined. Come quickly."

I sat at my console and saw hordes of Ogres arriving at the mountainous retreat where the Presidential war bunker was located. n'Gnung said, "Guardian, I tried to close them out, but the area is too large and rugged for the shielding we have. We would have to make a new and specialised transfer circle, and that could take hours. I have isolated areas, and the Great Ogre has tried to compromise us by copying what we have already done elsewhere — shields overlapping, or within shields. The bottom line is, this is a mess, and they have soldiers on the ground."

Chapter 31 ~ The Presidential Bunker

There was little time to prepare for our assault upon the Ogres infesting the Presidential Bunker. I held review with our war cabinet, and aside with our best tacticians. Time was pressing and we needed the latest information to pinpoint our best points of insertion. Although nearing exhaustion, our controllers had been monitoring the current situation. I received their intelligence as I scanned their screens, working my way around the control room until all were done.

I scanned to find Ælthrelntheine breaking through to the higher reaches of the secret bunker complex, Gung Loi and her battered troops swelling their numbers and battling gallantly at her side. Ju Lo called out, "Guardian, Ogre reinforcements are appearing in a concealed part of the outer courtyard."

I set a transfer circle nearby and quarantined the area surrounding the Ogres transfer circle. However, hundreds of Ogres troops had already made it through and were invading the main building, oppressing our overly tired defenders. They were entering the complex via one main doorway. I could not set a shield, because that would hinder us as much as the enemy, and prevent us reaching Ælthrelntheine.

Captain Stewart assessed the situation beside me, and left with his forces at once, determined to take the Presidential bunker, a separate building set to one side. I held Horovitz in reserve, not knowing where we would need reinforcements, nor when.

I left at once to block the doorway to the main complex with my own body and a fully charged protection bracelet. There were no words spoken between us — Kay following me through. Soon we were scything down the Ogre's forces with n'Gnung and Aroweena at our side.

Our group swelled as others came to reinforce us. Corps were deployed to fight to the enemy already inside, and break through to rescue Ælthrelntheine and Gung Loi. I held resolute to bar the passage of unwelcome intruders, letting only one or two pass at a time in order to be killed by my accomplices.

Behind me dozens fell, until Kay reported that she was finding real humans amongst the Ogre battalion. The massed cohort outside began to push hard against me, and although the protection held, the ground I stood upon was slippery with blood beneath my feet. Rambling unexpectedly appeared at my side and said, "Return to your control centre, recharge your weapons and protection bracelet. I saw the situation and came at once, Guardian."

With a loud laugh, he activated his shield, and set his ground to hold the onslaught at bay. Many Ogres lost their footing as he took over from me, becoming our bulwark against further intrusion, an impassable force facing insurmountable odds.

My instinct was to rush to Kay's side, but instead I returned to the control centre via my bracelet to reassess the situation and recharge. The courtyard still contained many hundreds of Ogres, and a similar number of enemy Last, or clones. I sent in the remaining Mounties and Apache to help Owain take the open space. Ju Lo said, "No reinforcements have arrived for some time, Guardian. I think they have finally run out of troops."

I examined the complex. The Presidential bunker was set to one side, the small and heavily defended entrance being a security device. I knew most of the bunker was underground, but interlinked with the main building by a few subterranean corridors. The main building was a decoy for the unwary, and almost square. It had a central grassed area exposed to the elements, marked with helicopters pads. Offices without windows were set to both inner and outer walls, with a main corridor connecting all internal areas, again in a square layout.

Rambling was holding an entry to the west end of the front of the building. Troops of the Tenth had found another entrance set to the east side, and were pouring through. This led directly to where Ælthrelntheine would arrive within the complex, when she emerged from below. I sent out a call for Junior to blockade the second entrance also. He was delighted and thought this is a great day for the Giants. I could not disagree, as without them we would have been badly compromised already.

However, the fact remained that we needed to clear the internal areas of the complex, kill all the Ogres, yet preserve the lives of those of our own. I set transfer parameters and arrived with Junior at the second doorway, along with Horovitz forces, the Foreign Legion, and all the troops we could muster. Only Kay and I had blades that could tell an Ogre or clone. I wielded the Sword of Destiny as Junior began to let a steady stream of the Tenth pass by his defensive shield and into our flashing blades. Behind us, Horovitz used modern military, and Ancestral weapons plus shields, and began to make progress against the rear of the enemy already inside.

In time we prevailed, Kay and n'Gnung had battled through from Rambling's position to support us, and drive forwards. The onslaught from outside withered to a dribble, and the few that remained outside formed a defensive arc. I told Junior to hold the doorway as I rushed inwards to assist our beleaguered troops fighting upwards from the lower reaches. However, I stopped dead at the sight before me, it was unworldly. Ælthrelntheine clambered over a mound of dead bodies, and looking in awe at her daughter, embraced Ælkræleinnoire. This was the first time I had ever know the Eleventh to touch one another in public, yet alone show any recognisable form of human emotion.

After congratulating our troops, I spoke up, "We have taken the lower reaches and secured these two entrances. The central complex is secure and under our control, but every room needs checking."

The sound of several helicopters grew louder, "Quickly, secure the helipad within. Horovitz, your team and your pick of any others. Go! There may be Ogres in the inner courtyard that need despatching. Every one of the enemy left alive needs to be checked by either Kay or myself. All of the Ogres are to be killed. n'Gnung, please detain all of the Last who fought with the enemy, until we have personally checked them. Is this clear? "

A voice at my side interrupted, "Well now me young and gallant Guardian, to be sure the Fourth will gladly check out the rooms and see what we can find, isn't that so brethren."

Ælthrelntheine replied, "Thank you King Ruaidhrí. I accept your kind offer, and know that this time I may allow you to keep some of your findings. Angkrelguer, please keep a watchful eye on our diminutive friends, and see they come to no harm."

She bent down to face the King and added, "I would hate for an Ogre to eat you."

King Ruaidhrí blanched, and I watched them depart, a mixed group of all tribes followed the Fourth, and began checking every room. Without being asked, another group assembled and departed in the opposite direction to do likewise. Ælthrelntheine shocked me by saying aside, "I need a beer. All this bloodletting comes with a price. My complexion is ruined! Look at my fine robes, blood spattered and torn. Oh woe is me."

Kay brushed victims' blood from her mother's cheek and said, "You need to wash all this Ogre blood off you. Jack is correct, it is slightly corrosive. I'll drink with you tonight, but for a party, we will need Owain. Come ah-Theine, the Ddwyrth are still fighting in the outer courtyard."

Again, no words were necessary. We turned and departed intent on finishing the day of killing. Owain's troops assisted by Giants, had corralled the remaining Ogres, who were in a strong defensive position.

I ran outside with the others, and noted all but fifty of the Ogres had been felled. I was wary. I could not quite believe that after two days of fighting we had almost won. Something felt wrong. Too easy, but what? The Great Ogre would not have given up so easily, even if he had finally run out of troops.

I watched others overrun the last stand of the Ogre, and felt no pity. We still had one more task to complete. Take the presidential bunker. I turned to check on Stewart and his team.

Entering the bunker, I was greeted by a pile of bodies, and several of Stewart's men who were guarding both entry and exit. No word had come from below, and occasional sounds of gunfire filtered from the depths. I went outside to call for reinforcements, when I felt a tremor come from within the main complex, followed by several more. A helicopter rose in the sky, its missiles discharged, but our forces took it out. A pall of smoke appeared, rising from a central location to the east.

Moments later, many of our finest troops emerged from the far door, spluttering for fresh air. I turned in horror, and took a step in their direction, before realising this could be another trick. The Great Ogre appeared to have run out of foot soldiers, so had he decided to blast us to smithereens instead?

Horovitz was first to report, "Guardian, we suffered few casualties but need extraction of our wounded, one of the Fourth is in a bad way. There was only one helicopter, but I heard at least one more close by. Yet there is no sign of it."

Kay ran over to join us, hearing the last of our exchange, "Jackie, I saw the other chopper. It disappeared behind the main complex. We need to find it."

I waved n'Gue and the Mounted units over to us. "Kay, one of us needs to join Stewart and check for clones. Take Gung Loi and support troops. Horovitz, you're with me, at the double, there is no time to lose."

We separated, Horovitz collecting his men on the way, and the remains of the Foreign Legion ran with us. The Mounties joined us. I yelled, "Captain, gallop ahead and locate the other helicopter, and whoever came with it. Don't engage, we need information."

n'Gue was with us moments later, "Full search in control room for missing helicopter and payload. Information as soon as you have it. Go."

Chief Iron Claw, of the Apache galloped to a stall in front of me. "This is a great day for our nation. Where to now, Guardian?"

I and others hitched a ride, and arrived behind the main building just as the helicopter took off. Horovitz, yelled to his man on point, who fired a missile and took the craft out. A call came from the Mounties, "Over here in the ravine, a group of Ogres and a large box—they had trouble carrying it, Guardian."

Horovitz went left, The Foreign Legion right. We that remained went directly towards our prey. We closed quickly, aided by shield bearers, Apache arrows, and set upon the group of one dozen Ogres. One was working at the box, the others forming a protective shield, and using Ancestral weapons and shields. We had numbers on our side, and managed to take them out one by one, leaving only two with raised shields. I was only a few strides away, when one dropped his shield and dove for the box, seeming to press something before he was badly injured.

I dodged aside and looked at the box. I didn't know what it was. Horovitz joined me moments later, and yelled, "Atomic bomb!"

I looked back in dismay, but heard a sound, "Tick tock, tick tock, tick tock…"

My eyes locked on a countdown clock: 9, 8…

I pressed my return bracelet as the countdown continued in my head: 7

I took my console, my fingers danced so slowly as my mind worked at far higher speed at the controls: 6; 5

I got a lock but needed to define a destination: 4

I remembered Jien Noi's problem with sending from extant Ogre transfer circles, and locked on the last Ogre defender, as well as the box: 3

I locked on the Ogre circle that first allowed them entry: 2

I send the bomb and dying Ogre, and instantly hit the transfer button: 1

Zero.

Silence.

Zero plus 1; plus 2; plus 3…

Eyes turned to look at me, but were drawn back to the main screen. It switched from the bunker complex to show a security threat. A large nuclear bomb had just exploded in the middle of nowhere, mid-Greenland. The Core informed us, "The detonation took place well above ground. Guardian, initial indications suggest this can only be the approximate location of Oma's spacecraft — the only thing on this planet able to withstand a transported, nuclear device, except for us."

My mind awhirl, I replied without thinking, "Core. What is your name?"

The reply was enlightening and chilling by turns. "Taris."

I was still in shock when Kay put her hand on my shoulder. "We are tying the place down now; this is a major victory, Jackie. I left the sword with my mother, because you and I have but one small task remaining. Attend me. We must lock the entire area out."

I was led to my day room, as Kay went below. The new transfer circle we created took all of fifteen minutes to locate, and would have saved many lives, had we placed them hours before. We were not to know. We locked out the entirety of the complex, securing it from the clutching reaches of the Great Ogre's machinations. I heard a great cheer erupt from the control room, and went through to find out what had happened.

n'Gnung offered his initial report, "Horovitz discovered the other helicopter delivered a second nuke to the helipad, but the Ogres were taken out before it could be activated. Various factions of the Last want to take it for safekeeping."

"I bet they do. No, we will do that. I do not trust them, that much. What else?"

"We've won!"

I punched my fist in the air, as I watched the real President of The United States appear in the courtyard with several staff. Kay and I returned to verify everyone left alive, and subsequently many clones were put in chains. The real President retook control of the bunker, and later, as we watched the mopping up operation from the control centre, he transferred to us. "Congratulations. This is a momentous victory for the true of heart, the land of the free. Thank you, all. However, I need to speak with you urgently regards another matter.

"I have just been made aware the Great Ogre may not be the largest threat humanity faces. You will remember Iran deployed nuclear missiles that exploded in Israel. The Israeli response was swift and damning, with five larger nuclear warheads hitting prime targets, including the Bushehr plant once more. Their aim was to cause a catastrophe. Instead, the nuclear explosion unleashed a cataclysm. One warhead exploded deep inside the already compromised, and previously unknown Bushehr nuclear weapons warhead assembly and storage facility."

"You mean the nuclear warhead exploded inside a nuclear bomb factory?" I asked incredulously.

"Yes, that is the sum of it. The strike was at best a one million to one chance. This set off a chain reaction that magnified the blast ten thousand fold and shook the entire world.

"I now know the resultant explosion, which has been classified as an impossible 10.0 on the Richter scale, caused a major rift to appear on the northern rim of the Arabian Plate. This in turn propagated gigantic eruptions to occur at several points around the plate, including near Bushehr, way to the north in Turkey, and to the intercontinental rift that is represented by the Red Sea.

"Thank you, Guardian, because of you, and our meetings here, our nations are aligning against any larger threat. China registered this explosion at point of source, at 2, 385.4 gigatons, or large enough to remove a State the size of Maine from the world map. However, due to providence perhaps, something strange occurred at Bushehr. The surrounding rock of the bunker was deep within the crust and highly valenced. That in turn acted as a shield, driving the main force of the explosion downwards, and through more yielding rock strata. As we currently understand the implications, we believe the Arabian Plate has, or will, fracture along fault lines, plate boundaries, and become fully detached from the rest of the world.

"Several dormant volcanoes in the area southeast of Bushehr reactivated as a result. Nevertheless, with the Arabian Plate destabilising, this has led to a dramatic shift. The world has been rocked and the plate is adjusting. Within days, renewed volcanic activity became apparent in Turkey, Israel, Europe, Sinai, and Abyssinia/Somalia: areas that ring the plate. I have no idea where this will lead, but I am told this is a most ominous threat to all life on this planet.

"We already have as many scientists and specialists as possible working on this. Guardian. Jackie, would you be so good as to monitor the area with your advanced science? You may find clues we are unable to detect. Early indications are that the Bushehr side of the Arabian Plate is going down, and the western side is rising along The Rift Valley through the Gulf of Aqaba. I cannot impress upon you how serious the repercussions of this could be."

The President returned to the White House, leaving me with a landslide of worries. Had the Wrath of Gaia already begun? I immediately informed the Core, asking for the Arabian plate to be monitored, and a projection of likely results made. I knew the timeframe was open-ended, and initial results could take days.

Deeply concerned, but with minimal understanding, I transferred to our home, and wandered down to the pool to soak my feet in the cool and flowing waters. I looked up and witnessed a cosmos yearning to share its secrets. Yet, as if the heavens were weeping, I saw the stains of ash clouds begrudge the sky, like a plague of finite aggravation from the West. I dreaded to think what else this forebode. The Earth's natural and unnatural forces appeared to steal the valour of the day, and that night from us, Star Gazers all.

In time, my thoughts turned to the ordinary people, and I returned to my screens to observe Iran. With growing horror, I watched as the midday Arabian sky darkened, and the fires of hell arose to conquer the poorest of nomadic peoples. The only good thing was that there had been no further nuclear missile attack, although I presumed the whole world had gone into nuclear crisis and lockdown.

Chapter 32 ~ Slaves of The Ogre

The third day after our victory, Owain called a council of all the tribes. The situation regarding the Trolls needed to be resolved, and quickly. Llwydd had been controlling them in Olde Prussia, and realising they posed no threat, had taken it upon himself to release their shackles and allow them to live ordinary lives. Only a small guard force remained. The Trolls were monitored within the shielded complex that enclosed their ramshackle town, but that was proving to be a waste of time and resources.

The meeting was held in the Trolls' new homeland. It began with Owain making an impassioned presentation in favour of granting them Tribe-hood as *The New Tenth*. He recounted, "During both the battle for Berlin, and again here in Olde Prussia, the Trolls never acted against us. In Berlin Volkar and Stoltvar led us deep into the lair via secret underground passageways, and also saved many lives by their resourcefulness and swift actions. Without their assistance, we may well have lost that battle.

"I led the assault here, and can tell you the Trolls never once raised a word, never mind a weapon against us. They did wait to see our strength I will grant you. But once they knew we could defeat the Ogres, they rose up to kill their former masters, and made our victory easy in countless other ways.

"I call on this Council of the Tribes to grant the Trolls freedom to become a nation in their own right."

Owain sat down as cheers, and some boos echoed around the large hall. Hogar immediately rose to challenge the proposal, "I deeply reject this proposal. Have we not endured enough already? The Sixth speak for all those that have suffered at the hands of the Tenth for æons. The Ogres and Trolls are the same. They merely seek their strength before they will turn on us."

Hogar expressed a deeply fixated and vehement loathing of the Ogres, and saw no difference between them and the Trolls. A quarrel broke out, although people did speak in turn. The Fourth, represented by Ruaidhrí Ó Riáin, sided with Hogar. They let us know some things best kept within the secrets of darkest unknowing. However, I noted that these were either atrocities committed by the Ogres, or events where the Trolls as slaves, had been acting under strict orders, and no doubt under pain of death if they refused.

The Third saw things from a completely different perspective, and Burnam proved effectively articulate in pursuing a different tack, completely countering the arguments of Hogar and Ruaidhrí. During the ensuing exchanges, we also learned a lot more about our disparate band of brothers.

The bizarre day turned surreal, as both Volkar and Stoltvar were called forth to speak for their people. Their presentation was amateurish, but it gave everyone an insight into the thinking of this large and imposing race that had lived in slavery for millennia.

I had been keeping my own counsel, as had many others, but was surprised when during a pause n'Gnung at my side rose to address the entire hall. "Would it not be wise to ask these people what they want for their own future, before we decide it for them?" That was all he said, whilst throwing his arm in a wide loop to highlight the Trolls present in the room.

Immediately the Twelfth and Eleventh rose and left to speak to the ordinary people present. I looked to my side and wondered why n'Gnung always found a path towards the solution of intractable problems, and wished I possessed his insight. But then again, to see with the eyes of other's — would that become a blessing or a curse?

John came to me and offered his advice on how to move forwards, but wanted to know if I was in favour of giving the Trolls statehood or not. n'Gnung already knew my answer, as did Jinnie and Kay. I was formulating my response when Dawn interrupted, giving us many valid reasons to support the Trolls. John offered counter-arguments, not because he believed them, but because he needed to understand the opposite viewpoint. It reminded me of debating class at University; he was acting as agent provocateur.

n'Gnung caught my eye and imperceptibly flicked his head towards the door. I turned my own to follow, and saw Owain, Kay, Aroweena, and Gung Loi looning at me expectantly. John and Dawn were enjoying an exciting difference of opinion, although I knew they were on the same side.

And so it came to pass, n'Gnung threw a brotherly arm around my shoulder, and guided me unresisting towards the bountiful mercy of the Three Sisters of Destiny. We swept Jinnie up in our wake. Owain welcomed us, "Let's see the real people and hear what they have to say. Come, time to fully explore this nightmare."

Images of a lightning struck tower briefly crossed my mind as I was led willingly to meet this nation's fate, because upon the few of us present, hung their future, and even survival. Our group was deep in conversation, as unbidden, we roamed deeper, and yet deeper still into the darker recesses of their town. We had no idea where we were walking to, but there was an area of ramshackle homes set to the far side of the prison-like factories and workplaces we passed.

It was dire, and made more discomfiting by the deepening shadows of evening. I am sure we all felt uneasy, but to meet the ordinary Trolls, we were definitely headed in the right direction, straight into the heart of their clan. A group of burly men in ragged clothes watched us as we came towards them. They were loitering outside a workshop and observing us intently.

They thanked us for saving them from slavery, but I noticed one of the Troll's hands clench and flex. They obviously wanted to know our intentions. Our swords and daggers presented a threat, yet they stood their ground and were obviously relieved when Owain spoke to them. "Friends, we mean you no harm. We want to learn about you, the real people. Help us understand your lives under thrall of the Ogre."

The woeful tales were virtually the same for all. Lives spent in complete servitude to the Ogres, who beat them and denied their families food upon the slightest error, or sometimes just because they felt like it. One Troll removed his shirt and turned around, letting us run our fingers over the deep welts caused by years of continual beating and lashings. His skin was rough and felt more like that of glacier scoured rock, than something part of a living being.

At my side, Jien Noi turned to speak to me, but instead tears of horror ran freely down her cheeks. I held her close. This was grosser than she could ever have imagined. She was not alone; it was clear we were all deeply shaken by the atrocity. In time, we learned he was not as badly scarred as some and had not been permanently maimed, although others had lost the use of limbs, or the actual limbs themselves.

The revelations of these men only served to spur us on in our quest to uncover the depths of these poor people's abject desolation. Despite the revulsion ingrained on her face, Jien Noi held up her head and stated firmly, "I have to see the all of it. I must understand the full gloom and gruesomeness of their lives. This is despicable."

All present agreed, we were deeply moved. The man who had shown us his back overheard us and offered to show us around, an offer we gratefully accepted. Our guide led us fortuitously to his meagre home set in the deepest depths of the ghetto's poorest quarter.

We felt eyes watching us as we strode deeper and deeper through a shantytown beset with abject misery. I remember one curious child standing to watch our approach, as if witnessing a miracle. His eyes were shining with wonder. A large green arm grabbed him and he was gone, his presence being replaced instantly by the slamming and bolting of a door.

Flickering fires appeared as the signs of evening meal were being assembled. These were left unattended, although we caught flickers of dread eyes watching from the blackness beyond. Twice I caught the unmistakable smell of rotting meat and wondered if these people liked to eat carrion, but we were informed; "It is a necessity, even though it makes us ill."

After twenty minutes, we arrived before a collection of rubbish that had somehow been conjured into a small abode. The lean-to of our guide was a hovel, but spotlessly clean. His prematurely aged wife made us welcome. I had reservations, because nobody else knew where we were. But then, we were actually meeting the real Trolls for the first time, and not their more fortunate representatives, all of whom appeared to have presence right of that moment in the great hall. Where we were resembled Chernobyl, repopulated after the meltdown.

We were greeted with a soupçon of spirit, it being the last they had, and they talked openly about their lives under the Ogres. A slave is too kind a word to put on their utter squalor. Their son and daughter, both less than 14 of our years, looked as if a mad scientist had played with their bodies in some hideous and ghastly way. Apparently, this was the fact. Their eyes were alive as they moved on faltering, deformed limbs to serve us. They smiled at us because we had taken the time to honour them with our presence.

I'm not sure just how small and insignificant they made me feel. I rose and had them stand with me, as lesser beings would for taking a snapshot. My finger hovered over the return bracelet, and all heads of our company nodded to me in turn. I did not know if our medical facility could fix their bodies or not, but it was something I had access to that they needed, and so desperately.

I had imagined being away a long time, but surprisingly the immediate treatment was swift, and the robotic nurse even put a metallic extrusion on my shoulder and patted me. Alarmed I wondered what she knew that we did not. But her reticence returned before illumination was born, as are the ways of true enlightenment.

In spite of Owain's presence, the mood had turned sombre when I returned fifty minutes later, with two agile and bouncy teenagers. Shattered does not even begin to explain their parent's response. Their pure joy was all that was needed to make a grown man cry. I was guilty of that crime. We all were that night.

After the sobbing release came happiness, followed by astonishment, not just from their family, but for us also. Word soon spread about the miracle I had performed, although I only tried to do the best I could. That evening in the worst backwater of the town of the Troll, they came to us and welcomed us into their dingy midst with dignity. Not as saviours of their kind, nor new rulers. They welcomed us as being people they respected and wanted to share their meagre lives and sustenance with.

The food was awful. The beer watered down, and watered again. Nevertheless, they shared what they had with us willingly, and even to going hungry themselves the next day. In the process, we became more horrified by their previous existence and determined to put it right. We confirmed the Trolls had been created by the Ogres as their slaves. Most had never known freedom, except for those few who managed to escape, and those such as Volkar and Stoltvar who were born free, and captured.

Rather than ravage the meagre remains of their cumulative larders, I sent n'Gnung to raid our stores. Moments later, he came back with an irascible Da Phai Nai, who insisted on taking over provisioning, and later went missing. I rose to find her, and she was standing outside the door near our transported supplies, staring at nothing. I scuffed as I approached her, and she turned to me, a tear forming in her eye, "They…"

Her eyes swept around as she stifled a cry, her emotions almost engulfing her. I put my hand on her shoulder and patted her gently. She recovered and looked up at me before continuing, "They don't have enough to eat."

"Do what must be done."

She flew into my arms, and as she quieted, I comforted her until she stilled. In time the brusque lady we all loved reasserted herself, "Try to take advantage of me would you, Guardian. Dream-on."

I watched her march away with purpose and knew she would leave supplies that would feed an army for one week. As I watched her go about her work, bringing in others to assist, Owain came and stopped beside me. We did not speak. We watched and waited engrossed, as our eyes drank in the wretchedness surrounding us one more time. Da Phai Nai was busy cooking as we looked on.

"That there wee lassie," Owain broke the silence for the first time, "I would take her for a wife."

I put my arm on his shoulder and replied, "You have my blessing, although we would be lost without her, as you have just witnessed. To take her would bring her untold joy, but destroy something else that is unique."

"Aye me young and gallant brother, therein lies the rub."

With a heartfelt sigh, we turned as one, and with our steps aligned, eased ourselves back into the companionship of other's. The evening became a matchless party, and *Boy* did we learn about humanity, humility, and the gift of life that evening.

Chapter 32

It is not *life* itself that is of paramount virtue, but what you do with it of your own free will that matters.

Chapter 33 ~ Return of The Tenth

The next day, the Council reconvened. After a long and eye-opening discussion, which included our observations from the previous evening. Owain called for a vote that was taken almost at once. The Twelfth, Eleventh, Seventh, Fourth, Third, Second, and I, all voted for the motion. Hogar stood isolated and voted against, but did not use his veto.

A cheer erupted from the Trolls, which quickly spread outside, and throughout the town. Word of our adjudication multiplied exponentially, their freedom at last. We were mobbed and it took a long time to reach the outdoors, where a celebration was already in full swing. A feast was being set, with supplies coming in from other Tribes. And wouldn't you but know it, Da Phai Nai was in the centre of the chaos ensuring everything was just perfect.

We had been watching the gambolling fun of dancing, Troll style, with some weird singing thrown in on occasions, when I heard a familiar voice to one side. "Now where are my useless boys hiding? They'll be up to no good I shouldn't wonder. Ahha, there's the ringleader, idling with his principal mischief maker."

I turned to greet Da Phai Nai's advance with a wide grin, and felt my party hat move a little. I grabbed it and standing to attention, swung it into a bow, as a musketeer might greet a Lady in knightly honour. I rose to ask, "You called Mi'Lady?"

To my side n'Gnung raised one eyebrow and looked at me intently for an instant, before copying my motions. Imitating, he proffered his best boyish charm.

I swear Da Phai Nai almost laughed, but caught herself in time and proceeded to berate us. "Just who is in charge here, because at the moment I am, and I already have more than enough to do!"

We gawped at her, grappling hopelessly to understand her question, and failing miserably.

She swept her hand around the multitude present and asked again, "Who is their leader? Their chief must sit at the top table with all these fine and dandy people, plus you two I suppose. So tell me, who is their leader? How many Trolls do I set places for?"

I turned and looked directly into n'Gnung's eyes, as he did likewise with mine. We stayed like that for several seconds as if waiting for a duel to begin. Eventually both his eyebrows rose in tandem. I turned to our mother hen and instinctively said, "Two. I will tell you their names when I find out who they are going to be. Thank you wise Mother."

With that I reprised my courteous bow and n'Gnung followed likewise. I gave Da Phai Nai a brief nod, before I strode off with my brother to find Owain and the other leaders. But time was against us, as people were already forming to sit down for the feast. We would have to do this at table in the round.

The leaders came together at the top table, and we ensured two central chairs were left untaken. n'Gnung leaned into me and whispered, "Guardian..." and we formed a cunning plan.

I knew Owain was about to rise and propose a toast, so I jumped to my feet to forestall him, "Ladies and Gentlemen, loyal friends of old, and our latest friends — The New Tenth. All known Tribes are represented at this table, except for The New Tenth. I would ask the Troll for your leaders to join us in brotherhood."

I had expected muttering and indecision. My words were greeted by deathly quiet. The concept of having one of their own lead them, was alien to their millennia of slavery under the Ogres.

We waited a few moments before n'Gnung stood and said loudly, "Guardian, these people have no leader. May I suggest that for this meal, they be represented by two of their number that have already shown great worth during our battles against the Ogres. I would call on Volkar and Stoltvar to come and join us at the high table."

I knew that Owain was itching for a drink, and he rose immediately to second the proposal, holding his goblet high and looking directly at all the other leaders in turn. To my side Jien Noi was rising also, as were all the Eleventh and Seventh. Within the time, it took to say *Jack Robinson* all were on their feet, and Hogar was not the last to stand and applaud.

Cheers erupted, and this time n'Gnung could not quiet them. The chosen were too shy and needed to be cajoled and pushed to the fore. Kay went to take their hands, and extricating them from the crowd, seated them centrally at our table.

Astonishment and great pride were evident as they stood with the rest of us. They raised their beakers in unity, at last to take their rightful place amongst the Twelve Tribes.

After the festivities, I left quickly, but John returned many times. The Trolls had no official leaders, nor any conception of how to create their own. Neither did they have a moral or legal code to guide them through their daily lives.

They did have a rough set of family rules but that was all. John worked to understand them as a nation, and gift them a set of basic laws that would become their Commandments. There were not ten of them, but less than twenty, as suited their culture and needs, although perhaps not my own.

John asked me to attend one morning, and began by thanking us for coming so quickly. He was always so polite. He added to the knowledge we had gleaned from our wandering of a few nights previous, by explaining in some depth just how difficult his task was, and asked for our opinions. Unusually for him, I think he actually wanted somebody else to approve what he was working on, because creating a new nation is one thing. Giving a race of perpetual slaves a moral code, and functioning identity in their own right was something completely different.

He was still finalising The Commandments of The Great Troll, as he had been asked to call their new constitution. Many were obvious, and biblical references abounded, several found also in the Quran and Buddhist scriptures: Do not kill, do not steal, do unto others as you would have done unto thyself, *et cetera*. He surprised me by admitting, "The Trolls have a special way of honouring their dead, which would be horrific to ourselves, and I mean all of us present. However, to the Troll it extols the highest of reverence, Jackie, they eat their own dead — as in parents and siblings."

"What? You cannot be serious. Gross!"

"The Trolls believe that when a family member dies, their spirit stays with the body and will be consumed by evil spirits that lurk within the earth if buried. Like us, they also believe that fire can cleanse a body of harmful influences and purify the spirit within. Our cremation rituals are based in similar beliefs.

"When a body is pronounced *dead*, they cleanse it, including internal organs, of all evil, and by that I include the gut, discarding the contents thereof. The deceased is marinated externally, and internally with special herbs and spices. The carcass is barbequed on a ceremonial altar, bestowed with gifts, keepsakes, and flowers.

"The cooking temperature is critical, because it must cleanse the spirit without consuming it in the flames; possibly where we get our own references to *being consumed by the fires of hell*? Once the body has been cooked properly, it is offered to the family, in order of age and closeness first, then extended relationships, and honoured friends.

"The greater a person's worth, so the more Trolls accept the honour of eating this blessed flesh. They even cook the bones into a soup afterwards, they consider it a life-giving tonic, and hence no remains can be found in the fossil record. I am told the Ogres do similar. I know what you are all thinking, but bear with me and learn something.

"By eating the person, the accepter takes into their own being, the purified essence, spirit if you prefer, of a dearly loved person of greatest esteem and importance to them. Through consuming this, they themselves move to a higher plain and can become more enlightened. It sounds bizarre to me, but the logic is actually infallible, once you open your mind to their beliefs."

Chapter 33

John squatted down in Indian style, and rocked backwards and forwards on his haunches, arms wrapped around his knees, his bottom resting on his heels. His forehead banged onto his knees, repeatedly, and began to knock on them in rhythm. He sought guidance, release from within this most extreme of revelations.

We greeted his revelation with dumb astonishment. None of us had an answer. Eventually n'Gnung broke the silence, "It is repulsive to us, but is the belief of these people and should not be interfered with, no-matter how objectionable we may find the practice. Would you mould them to your own image? If you do, isn't that simply a different form of slavery?"

Immediately John stilled and looked at n'Gnung, saying, "I was thinking to ban it because this is the Devil's work. And yet, it is the highest honour these people know. They have nothing else by which to judge their own worth.

"If we ban the practice, then we interfere and impose our own will upon a sovereign nation. I won't touch upon the hostility and deepest resentment that may follow, allowing seeds of discontent to flower over the course of decades. Therefore, I have left it as is, being one of their central customs. I just wanted to check with you first. It is something no mere mortal should be asked to rule upon."

John had tears in his eyes, and I knew he was a deeply religious man. He was advocating something so alien to his version of God that in some ways he was seeking absolution.

I needed to act, "John, thank you for your excellent work, and for sharing this with us here today. You are in an impossible situation.

"If this is their way, then it must remain and we must accept it, if only for now. John, perhaps over time, we could gently educate them to other ways and beliefs in the future. But remember, once they come into their nation-hood, there will come a time when they by turn judge us, and what we have done this day. I say, let it stand. Raise your hands now if you approve because, know that if we do not, we have taken the first steps towards making new slaves of these people."

The response was unanimous. And so the disgusting wake of the Trolls was approved, but our sombre mood remained slow to leave. It was finally broken in a most auspicious way, when n'Gnung nudged my arm and tilted his head. I followed his gaze, and picked out our guide and host standing with his wife from our strange party some nights before, and their two bouncy teenagers.

I went to greet them and chatted, but they were jittery, hovering, and not speaking their minds. Others joined us, including John, who talked to them for a short while. In time he said, "They are far too shy to ask, but could this woman look at Ræm?"

As with all races, Trolls were no different and loved babies. This was the telling difference for me, because I recalled Ramblings anguish as he described the Ogres eating Furlong's still unborn child. In this case, Jien Noi presented Ræm to our party, and she was duly handed to the wife of our guide. We all moved away slightly as the woman tried to pass her back, like one would be scared of handling the most highly valued bone china.

The Troll looked and wondered at the hopelessly small thing in her massive green arms, and held her close in tears of joy and disbelieving. For her part, Ræm settled into her alien, yet motherly embrace immediately, and grabbing a handful of the woman's long body hair, used it to climb like a monkey.

I cast a look to Jinnie, but she was in awe and completely focused upon this treasure of sharing. The Troll could have easily crushed our daughter's skull with a simple reflex of her massive arms. I gulped when the woman hefted our youngster and threw her high into the air, catching her safely, Ræm eager for a repeat. Our daughter became the star of the show.

Over the coming days, we organised a vote for leader of the New Tenth. I was not surprised when I received the results and presented them to the new nation. "As Guardian of The Twelve, and The One, it is my honour to announce Volkar..."

No one heard another word I said. Poor Volkar was immediately enveloped within a carnival, and never did reach us for his official inauguration. Instead, he was hoisted high on shoulders and paraded around for all to party with. The band struck up. Trollian dancers appeared, green and larger than Sumo wrestlers, and fireworks lit the midday sky.

Ælthrelntheine sought me out during the ensuing festivities. "Guardian, I could never have imagined this result. The Prophesy is being fulfilled, and the Tenth are once again a part of our number. Thank you. I am confident the Twelve Tribes can now be reunited."

"What of the Thirteenth?" I enquired. It was a throwaway line, but one that brought undue creases to the High Queen's brow. She appeared frozen for a moment, before remembering something important she had to do.

I stayed for as long as I could, but events were happening elsewhere that eventually demanded my undivided attention. I did learn that during the celebration that followed the announcement, John finally managed to present Volkar with their new constitution. It was received with rapture and did become their own Commandments.

Chapter 33

We had given them their nationhood, and later, full use of their control centre, but with handicapped powers. As bearer of the Ring of the Ancestor, I was tasked with creating a new Ring for the Trolls to use. Its powers were quite limited and specific. The New Tenth received it with great joy. It represented our acceptance of them as a nation.

What Kay and I actually did was to create a neophyte's Ring and an acolyte's Ring, the specifications of which all the tribes agreed too, including Hogar. They were presented with great ceremony to the two Trolls we first captured: now the President and Vice President of their formative nation. The leaders could only use the rings personally. Their combined power was minimal, yet contained inclusion and means of contact.

Reflecting, I concluded we had given a race of perpetual slave's identity and freedom. We did not demand their subservience as repayment, but shared our wealth and knowledge for the greater good of each and every one of us.

All that remained was to adjudge how they repaid our generosity.

Chapter 34 ~ John Gets a School

The evening John returned to us from his stay with the New Tenth, Cynthia joined us and we dined at the shore. John's wonder and excitement was infectious, as he waxed lyrical about his experiences. He bided his time, before enthusing about how useful it would be to have a dedicated place of study. Everybody agreed with him, and Cynthia obliquely reminded me of the promise I had made to her.

Given our recent exposure to other cultures and their technology, my objections were largely irrelevant. Time had moved on. So did our conversation, as we tried to define the perfect location for the new research centre. Several places were discussed, but all those mentioned had drawbacks, either being too remote, or too close to existing towns.

John was keen on the region of the old capital city, remarking, "If we were based there we might be able to find archaeological remains of the old settlement. You already have storage facilities there with associated housing, and a canteen for the workers, plus the Old Religion is based there. They even have a sending circle so I could commute from our home on the shore. It sounds perfect. I may keep unusual hours. Is it possible to make a transfer circle that works automatically?"

The thought had never occurred to me and I was searching for a reply when n'Gnung spoke up. "Guardian, this is a great idea, and we already know they exist. We could do this in many places, thus saving the controllers a great deal of unnecessary work."

Kay added, "That's brilliant n'Gnung. Why is it always you that comes up with the obvious? I can't believe we haven't done this already. Jackie, I think I know how to do it, but do we make one circle with many destinations, or several circles with only one preset? Thank you John, we will look into this as a matter of priority."

"Kay, John, I will deal with this new establishment tomorrow morning, but remember, this will be a small and dedicated team, not a grand design. What about buildings?"

John smiled, "I have already been working on that. The University has acquired land to build a new satellite campus. We have outline planning permission, and are currently waiting for formal plans to be approved. The site has several existing structures that will need to be demolished before building can commence. This is additional expense. Why don't we just take them?"

It felt like stealing to me, but John assured me we would be doing the University a big favour, save them money, and that he would cover the paper trail.

The next morning John guided my scanners to the location, which looked like a Victorian school. It had since been used as offices, after local schools were amalgamated into the new comprehensive. I placed a circle to shield us and we went to take a look.

Despite several years of disuse, it turned out to be in reasonable condition. The slate roof protected a red brick construction that employed beige, almost yellow bricks, standing proud in relief, and alternating to highlight doors, windows, and building corners. The overall design was attractive, in a dated sort of way.

It had originally been built as a primary school, having different entrances for boys and girls. Later this had practice been abandoned, but left us with a dozen classrooms, an assembly hall, kitchen, and adjoining dining room. Within reception were several offices and a staff room. Outside were a couple of additional prefabricated classrooms, several small utility buildings, and a separate sports hall. I had to admit it appeared to be perfect for our needs.

When we returned I interfaced with the Core, I was worried about building foundations and pests. I had noticed a recently dead rat during our foray. The Core informed me, "The shield only permits homo sapiens to enter, all other life, down to bacteria and microbes, are excluded unless an exception is made. Any DNA of the Tenth is specifically excluded, unless individually overruled, or the directive cancelled."

This probably explained why there were no flies or mosquitoes, and other nasties like rats, snakes, or spiders on the island. However, the reply gave rise to several questions, "Define homo sapiens."

The Core replied, "Homo sapiens refers to Taris and the Ancestors, and includes all of their creations, such as yourself."

"How were the animals that are on this island allowed to enter?"

"Taris approved the exception. They came through rid of infestations like fleas and their eggs, ringworm, and foot rot, so only the fit and healthy were allowed to enter. However, they were allowed to retain specific and essential bacteria for life, such as those from the stomach and gut."

I understood and it seemed probable, except, "What about the fish in the lakes?"

"Fish are allowed to pass through the shield. Taris did not specify where they came from, so some fell from the beaks of birds and landed in the water."

I shook my head, I hadn't found a flaw so far, but queried, "What about the houses of Bryony and John. Were they cleansed before arrival here?"

"The buildings were completely free from infestation when they came through, including all living and dead biological matter, excepting *homo sapiens*."

I had one last question, and addressed the practical aspects of the new building's footings. The Core informed me that was already accounted for, the existing houses had been transferred with footings intact, the corresponding soil removed, being replaced where they originated.

We were set. All we needed to do was define where we would put the new buildings. John identified three locations, and I transferred him to each in turn. He decided upon an upland meadow that had deciduous trees to one end, and a stream at the other. It was a harmonious spot, and with night falling in England, I transported the entire school complex.

The team transferred immediately to inspect the buildings for integrity. They appeared to have survived transit with no sign of any shift or damage. Wandering back from the gymnasium to check out the main building in more detail, we stopped and stared. Two dishevelled people rushed out of the entrance and almost ran into us.

They froze as soon as they saw us. The girl's eyes flicked back and forth between us, clearly disbelieving what she was seeing. The young man at her side moved protectively in front of her, casting his eyes warily around, checking for danger. He took a defensive posture and demanded, "Who are you? Leave us alone. Where are we?"

The girl had become fixated with Kay, and finding her tongue stated, "You're an Elf."

John recognised the girl and moved towards her, "Cathy?"

I flicked my return bracelet, and within moments, I transferred them back to Birmingham. I laughed with relief knowing that if they said anything, no one would believe them. From their state of undress, it was clear they had been making out. The Core confirmed they were the only two transported, and I had learned to specifically exclude humans from similar transportations in the future. As my view returned to the new building, Kay walked outside carrying the girl's bag, n'Gnung following with an assortment of clothes. I returned all to our uninvited guests, before rejoining my colleagues.

John returned to the lands of the Last later that day, intent on recruiting at least four members for his new team. I left with my closest, and we idled the remainder of our day away on the shore. Our bodies were bruised, and all of us sported fresh wounds. In time, we tried to remember what we had been doing before the war with the Great Ogre began, was that only a few days before? It felt like half a lifetime.

The following day Kay and I resumed our work on the restoration of the spacecraft, which was almost completed regards hull integrity and major systems. The engines and weapons would require more time, but we were pleased with progress.

As the second week of freedom from the yoke of the Tenth drew to a close, we all begin to realise we had not seen the sun or the moon for a long time. The days were overcast and continued to darken, the skies above became laden with ash from a resurgence of volcanic activity. The debris from seven nuclear warheads helped cloud the world, and it became colder, raining all the time; it was irradiated acid rain, and caustic. Kay and I adjusted the island shield to keep out all the nasty particles in the air.

Ælthrelntheine and Hogar joined us one afternoon, buoyed by great news. They had contacted the Eighth, although the Tribe were not ready to meet. Hogar had spoken to their leader and they could not believe the Ogres had been defeated. Understandably, they remained quite wary despite Hogar's personal testimony. Hogar added, "They let slip that they know of a small community of the Ninth, and they are renowned as a nation to be even more distrusting of others, especially the Ogres. I am determined to find them as quickly as possible."

I cautioned him, "Hogar, I know you have the best intentions, but be careful. When you meet them, let us know in advance and we will shield you and watch over everyone. The Ogres are still a powerful threat."

Ælthrelntheine said, "I agree, Guardian. Be on your guard King of the Sixth. Nevertheless, the Prophesy is coming true, this is so exciting, isn't it. Now we only need to find the Fifth. The Fourth were the last to have contact and are searching for them as we speak. The Third are also trying to locate them. They also volunteered to go to all their cousins the modern world and tell them about the coming world catastrophe. Many they have so far seeded did not heed the warning, but some did, especially those tribes with strong links to history and their roots. Jackie, could you spare the Third a day or two? They need somebody with native English."

"It will be a pleasure now everything is quiet once again. I've never been to New Zealand, come n'Gnung, it will be a holiday. I know the Denisovan's lineage is scattered all around the Pacific Rim, so we will be travelling a lot. It seems their tribe were too good at inter-species marriage and their line became lost, mixed up with yours and mine."

"Good," replied Ælthrelntheine. "I have adjusted the shields of the Third so you will both be quite safe. Burnam suggested you arrive for breakfast in two days' time."

Chapter 35 ~ Hogar's Humiliation

Hogar

Being Lord of his own destiny, Hogar had completely disregarded the advice of the Guardian and continued to pursue contact with the Eighth. He hoped eventually to contact the Ninth, which he had long wished to do. An ancient relic of theirs had come into his possession when he was still a young and impressionable kid, and he intended to offer it back to them. His search was driven more by the lure of myth and legend, than based in logic.

But things had gone wrong, the Ogre had invaded, and he now admitted the error of his ways, in more aspects than one. His was no longer merely a battle for his life, but the existence or extermination of at least one, if not two tribes of humanity. He waved goodbye to the Leader of the Eighth, and knew he must divert the enemy from their true purpose of killing them all.

He took a drink from a nearby stream and stopped to remember how he had attended their village for a prearranged meeting at midday the day before. He had spoken at length with their leader, King Keos, and several of their wise men and warriors, upon a mound near the outskirts of the community.

Unusually, the villagers had gathered to watch them and talk about what may be decided, because Hogar understood that many of them wished to return to the protection of the allied tribes. Others, including Keos did not. The air shimmered ominously. A horde of Ogre warriors appeared and set about a killing rampage. The screams of the community broke up the meeting, and Hogar stared from behind cover, aghast.

Normally they would have been ready and few if any would have lost their lives. However, out in the open and lying exposed without weapons, most could only run as the invaders came after them with killing blows. In the mêlée a young mother tripped and fell, clutching her baby protectively to her bosom. The Ogres made play with her distress, and many stopped pursuit to come and toy with her and her child.

She was cut at first by the sharp blades of the Ogre's swords. Slowly, as a large gang gathered around her, she was cut deeper and deeper until her arms and legs were awash with her own blood. Her screams of agony echoed long and loud as she fought desperately, and in vain to protect her offspring from certain and horrific death.

The gang took pleasure in shearing off her clothes with their swords, reckless of any bodily injuries or loss of thumb that might be inflicted. She quailed as fresh cuts were inflicted deep into her arms and legs, as they not only removed her clothing, but also denied here the use of her limbs. Her tendons and veins were cut for fun, and in time, she crashed to the ground unable to hold her baby, which was also covered in cuts and bruises. Unfortunately, her ordeal was only just beginning. Hogar could not bear to watch, but neither could he tear his eyes away from the atrocity.

An Ogre Captain picked up her baby and looked at is curiously, trapping it under his massive left arm. She was hoisted onto a suitable cart and pinned with her legs under her armpits, her feet quickly tied behind her head, linked via a noose around her throat, locking her head back. Her earth-shattering cry was not because the leader violently entered her, but because once inside, he stopped, brought her child to his mouth, and took a giant bite out of his belly. He kissed her roughly with bits of gut still drooling from his mouth.

Hogar quailed. This utter savagery belonged only to the Ogre. They were inhumane.

The Ogres plundered her body as no male had any right to do, whilst handing the baby, still alive, around for others to share. The invaders group swelled to enjoy the fun. Hogar believed she died of a broken heart. The evil of the Ogres' knew no mercy. Hogar wondered about humanity, what differentiated humankind from the beasts. He believed he was watching the devil's work. Tears rolled down his cheeks in open horror and penitence.

Keos sent two warriors to assist his people, not to take battle to their mighty foe, because that would soon result in their grotesque deaths. Their purpose was to lead and organise an escape, to bring survivors circuitously, to a chosen destination when all was once more secure.

Keos and his small group left instantly, and by the time extra Ogre troops arrived to kill them, the parties to the meeting were long gone and extremely well hidden. The Eighth and Hogar hid until nightfall, before trying to escape properly and regroup.

The Eighth possessed excellent night vision, almost on a par with the keen sighted Eleventh. Therefore, during the hours after sunset they carefully wove an obvious and confusing trail for the Ogres to follow the next day. By turns, they slipped away over rocks, and at convenient points where their passage would remain undetected.

In due course, a volunteer was required to continue the trail for the Ogres to follow, and Hogar claimed the right. "Brother Keos, if I had not come to you alone, against the strong advice of the Guardian and the other allied tribes, then you would have been spared this massacre.

"I am undone and humiliated by my carelessness and gravest error. I of all people should have know better. I would ask your forgiveness, but know I am unworthy. My heart bleeds for your people who suffered this outrage. I will make amends in my own way by leading this monstrous horde away from you."

"Hogar, know we also misjudged the situation and should have done what we always do. It is I who should take the blame. We know the ways of the Great Ogre so very well. It was of course obvious he would track us and find us by your visits. I feel so stupid and share your humiliation, brother."

Keos thought deeply for a few moments, the time of their parting swiftly approaching, as the sky lightened imperceptibly. "Hogar, I think that if this Guardian was so against our meeting, then another time we should meet with him. I make no promises. It is simply a new and serious consideration I have.

"Let us make a trail of many people together before I leave you. Come now, together we will make footfalls for our survival, because once the Ogre knows you are but one person, they will hunt you down and return with greater forces to search for you and us."

With great cunning, the King of the Sixth and the King of the Eighth ran forwards and backwards many times to make the sign of a multitude fleeing. At times they deliberately stumbled together to amplify the spore they laid, so the perception of a mass of people passing was carefully represented.

Both were skilled at this ruse, due to years spent evading and confusing the Ogre and the Last, their races masters of diversion and subterfuge.

Completing their final pass, Keos led them back to the place he had chosen to leave the trail. Gripping Hogar in a manly hug, Keos said, "Go now with God's speed brother. Keep your wits about you, and know you are always welcome. We will meet again."

With that statement, Keos turned his back, and Hogar hefted him up onto a rocky ridge leaving no clue as to their deception for others to follow. Hogar took another drink from the stream as his memory was reviewed, and returned once more to the present.

By daybreak, Hogar has laid more trails that ceased at the water's edge. He took care to make tracks at several obvious exit points from the river, which all led in turn to barren rock. Satisfied he made his own personal escape, Keos having told him where to shelter from the eyes of the Great Ogre.

Chapter 36 ~ Trials of the Eighth

Ælkræleinnoire

Kay had been monitoring the renovation of the spacecraft from engineering, but was becoming increasingly distracted by fleeting thoughts of the Eighth. There was no logic to her uncertainty, but there it remained. On impulse, she went to the control room.

Kay took a report from the Empress, and relieved her at the Captain's station so she could spend time with Ræm. This was followed by a more detailed debrief from Gung Loi, who was standing in as First Officer during n'Gnung's absence.

Once she had been brought up to date, Kay checked the scanners on the Guardian's console. Her orders flowed freely, "n'Gue, I have prescience that something terrible has happened to the Eighth. They are not where they should be on my scanner. Contact Hogar and find out if he knows anything about this. Do this yourself, but send others with messages to the Twelfth, Eleventh, and Seventh."

She sat and thought for a moment before cautioning, "Due to time differences, some may be asleep, but leave word, go now with haste. The Eighth are my main concern as of this moment."

Kay took a detailed report from Bufor, who had been monitoring the Ogres. She became concerned when she was informed about two spikes in the log, indicating transportations. She returned immediately to her terminal and tried to define them; one was an outgoing transportation by the Sixth. The other was indefinite, but originated somewhere in Greenland. She swore, "Damn! The Ogres must be after them. Gung Loi, prepare your troops for battle immediately. Inform Barph and Horovitz at once, we may need them very soon."

n'Gue returned with news that the other races would come for dinner whenever suitable, and they all thought the next evening would be ideal. Kay agreed, but would confirm later. Regarding the Sixth, n'Gue stated, "It appears, Hogar ignored our advice and maintained contact with the Eighth. He left for a routine meeting yesterday midday, and there has been no contact from him since."

Kay was immediately unsettled and asked him to bring the person in charge to her right away. In due course, Hogar's son, Hollybrand, arrived and was introduced. Welcoming him into their midst, Kay quickly dispensed with formalities and demanded a full report.

Hollybrand said, "I do not know a great deal, but I do have the transport co-ordinates. Our equipment is limited, we can transport, but only with great difficulty and without scanners."

He gave the Eleventh the location and Kay entered the co-ordinates. They all stared in horror, as the pillage of the Ogres became clear for all to see. She scanned and found forty bodies ruthlessly hacked to pieces and a couple despicably raped. "How many were here?"

"I know this was a major village of about two hundred people. They usually meet somewhere nearby on a rock or hill."

Kay zoomed out and identified the scattered layout of the hamlet. She discovered a few more dead bodies, but remained certain the majority of the tribe escaped. In time, she found a rocky rise with obvious signs of recent occupation. She set three interconnected transfer circles as shields, and sent Horovitz to search for survivors.

Nearby was a trail that crossed wild country, but showed obvious signs of recent passage. She followed this for a long way until she reached a river, where the trail disappeared.

Leaning back, she thought about the situation, and considered what little she knew of the Eighth, acknowledging they were indeed masters of evasion. Her dread somewhat mollified she said, "It is my considered opinion that most escaped from the Ogres, including Hogar. The Eighth would probably circle around under nightfall, and regroup in an entirely different location. I need to find them as quickly as possible.

"Hollybrand, without scanners, how do you return Hogar?"

"Oh that is simple. Our King activates an ancient device that sends a signal and I know to return him once I receive it."

"Why have you not received this signal?"

The Sixth looked at her with apologetic eyes and said, "High Lord, our equipment is nowhere near as sophisticated as your own." He stopped and waved his hand around the room before continuing.

"I have a small plinth to work with, a location, and if the signal is activated within the field, I can bring a person back, in this case Father. If he is outside the zone, I receive nothing. The device must be activated within a small range of my locked co-ordinates."

"What nonsense is this. Damn!" The Eleventh breathed a heavy sigh, but thanked Hollybrand, as he was doing the best he could under the circumstances. He was desperately worried about his father. They were indeed stuck, and she was about to dismiss the Sixth, when an odd thought struck her. n'Gnung always had a way of offering strange, yet pertinent advice. On a whim, she sent his brother to bring him back.

n'Gnung arrived within moments and first Kay asked about Jack. The First Warrior informed her, "The Guardian has spoken to many people, leaders of their clans. He is making a big difference, but many want proof. We decided to hold a party here in the not so distant future. Kay, you look tired, have you eaten? Now what may I do for you?"

Ælkræleinnoire smiled and stated, "You are so intuitive my brother. Yes I had forgotten to eat, and will attend to the matter shortly. That is exactly why I called you here to assist me, because we are in desperate need of your wisdom. Hogar is missing."

Kay related the situation to n'Gnung, who paced nearby in consideration. He came back to the group a minute later and said, "You are looking for a man in a mountain range. This is not compatible and a complete waste of time and effort, unless you prove very lucky indeed.

"Hogar's ring must be like our locators, but perhaps with an added signal function. Therefore, if Hollybrand were able to supply us with the signature of the device, we should be able to locate it."

Before he had finished speaking, Kay whirled into action. Taking Hollybrand by the arm, she attended the Sixth homeland moments later, and was surprised to find the dark of late evening encroaching. Taking Hollybrand's ring of power, she reset the shields, activated their scanners, and adjusted their transportation criteria. Satisfied she returned to her main task.

It soon became clear she required Hogar's Ring of power to reveal the returning locators signature, so instead she asked, "Hollybrand, how powerful, how alike is your ring to Hogar's?"

"They are almost identical, but mine is not quite as powerful."

They returned to the control room using her return bracelet, and submitted the ring to the Core for examination. Immediately she set a search for another ring of extremely similar design and functions, beginning at the river, near the Eighth's former base.

Once the search was underway, she handed the ring back to Hollybrand and said, "We are now searching for your father and the results may take minutes, or days, depending upon his current location. I think it will be of the order of minutes."

The Sixth bowed deeply to her, and waited patiently for the results. He was amazed at the power of the Eleventh commanded, and what she and the equipment could do. Moments passed before an alarm sounded, indicating the Crystal Ring of the Sixth had been found.

Ælkræleinnoire zoomed in immediately, and found Hogar in dire distress, having fallen from an impossible incline and lying prone, as Ogres sniffed out his location some small distance thence. She gave Gung Loi instructions to deploy, being aware the Great Ogre would also be watching his troop's quest.

"I will set a protective shield there once the Ogres discover Hogar, I would taste their blood this day. Aroweena, sharpen your blade, Gung Loi, we are a go in seconds."

The screens revealed Hogar was aware of his exposed position, and he edged away in order to find reprieve. He was aware the Ogres were imbued with one sense lacking in all the other Tribes, the keenest sense of hearing. Looking backwards, his foot nudged a pebble, and that was the only sound the Ogres needed to close in on their prey. The King of the Sixth raced along a defile as quickly as his injuries would allow, but he was becoming entrapped within a conduit-like ravine that extended to a breakpoint atop impossible cliffs, and an ice-covered river many hundreds of feet below.

Realising this was his last stand, Hogar straightened himself to the fullness of his royal majesty, and drawing his sword, stood firm and walked towards the Ogres. He appeared determined to take as many of them with him as possible.

Kay watched as the Ogres grouped together to form their plan of attack. She placed an encircling shield to capture them, and with a nod to Gung Loi, they went to Hogar's aid. Langnor sent them in small groups to surround the Ogres. Taken by surprise, the outcome was very bloody, and incisively quick. Half the Ogre party were killed before they even knew they were under attack, and as the others mustered arms to deal with the new threat, so they were cut down.

Having decimated the troops of the Ogre without a single casualty, Kay returned with Hogar, who was taken to the medical centre. Everybody was pleased to see him alive and quite well, but before she could admonish him, he said, "I have been very foolish, but the Eighth insisted we continue to meet regularly. Upon reflection we all now realise that was a very grave error. The Great Ogre must have located me with a seeing device, because Ogres are not clever enough to track me over land.

"Neither will they find the remainder of the Eighth, because most of them escaped, and will eventually regroup north east in several days' time. I have an idea where those caves are, but only the general location. I will finish by stating that I believe King Keos now wants to meet with us, and many of his people already seek our protection. They are a proud and wary tribe."

n'Gnung had waited until Gung Loi returned safely, and after he welcomed her back, they spoke quietly together in a corner for some moments. Kay returned from visiting Hogar in the medical unit, and watched them for a moment. She became convinced Jack's observations were correct, something was happening between them. They were obviously worried about something, and verging on a quarrel.

Kay determined to get to the bottom of the matter, and would speak to both of them in turn. As her thoughts coalesced into a plan, she said, "n'Gnung, return this evening for dinner and bring the Guardian with you, he needs to be brought up to speed with current developments.

Horovitz came with a report, "Kay, we found five of the Eighth clinging to life and Ju Lo transferred them to the medical centre. Only three arrived. The other two remained with us. How can this be?"

Kay interfaced with the Core. The answer was as she feared. "Horovitz, they did not come through because the shield prevented their transfer. They are Goblins—Ogre clones. n'Gue, please go to the Seventh at once, we have two Ogre clones of the Eighth for them to interrogate. Inform the Eleventh also, this is serious, and explains why they were compromised. I better check the rest of their Tribe, once we catch up with them."

n'Gnung rejoined Jack, but they both returned for the evening meal on the shore. Meanwhile, Kay had taken Aroweena aside, and discovered the root of the problem. Later she spoke to Jien Noi about marriage laws, but refused to say why she had asked her question, adding, "Come to the shore for dinner. Everything will be revealed in due course."

Kay spent time with Jack, n'Gnung by his side as always. They were alarmed by the cloning of the Eighth, but were almost finished in the control room, when Jack sent n'Gnung to prepare for dinner. He looked at Kay and said, "OK, out with it. I know you well enough, you are up to something, so spill the beans."

Kay filled him in on the real purpose of the evening and Jack chuckled conspiratorially. They actioned the plan as the evening meal concluded. Ælkræleinnoire waited until people went their separate ways, before asking Aroweena to ensure they were not interrupted.

Jack took his cue, and looked knowingly in turn at Kay, Gung Loi, n'Gnung, and Jien Noi. "There is a matter of the utmost importance that must be resolved this evening. n'Gnung, walk with me."

None could hear what was said, but it was evidently emotional. Finally, n'Gnung bowed and they returned to the table. n'Gnung went to sit, but the Guardian said, "Now brother, the time is nigh."

Knowing it was now or never, n'Gnung knelt formally before the Empress and revealed their secret. "Your Highness, know that I am unworthy, and yet I must ask the impossible of your forbearance. As you know I was once married, my wife and unborn son dying in childbirth.

"There is another who was also married once before, her husband, children, and parents murdered by mercenaries under Quinn. Our way is that no person can ever be married twice. And yet, I would wed this girl and raise a family, that is if she will have me."

He cast a despairing look towards Gung Loi, before continuing, "Gung Loi is with child, and it is a sin for the baby to be born outside of wedlock. It is also a sin to marry twice. What am I to do? I am aware I have overstepped my position, and am ready to be banished for speaking so forthrightly, Your Highness." He stood tall and pulled his shoulders back, concluding with a formal bow.

Chapter 36

Gung Loi rose and tried to speak, but her emotions muted her eloquence. There was a pure crystal tear in n'Gnung's eye, because the previous monarch would have executed him for his temerity. Instead, he found Jien Noi and Jack at his side, consoling him, and guiding him back within their familial fold.

The Empress stated, "My Brother, there is no law banning a second marriage, it is just that we have never considered it before."

The Empress recollected the laws and added, "You cannot divorce in our society, but if a widow and widower meet and fall in love, then there is no law to prevent their union, except that we have no common law for such an event.

"Henceforth, I formally decree that second marriages are allowed between all single people of age. First Warrior of the Second, stand proud and ask this woman to be your wife, and know I will approve the union immediately. n'Gue, spread the word to our people. There will be an official wedding in the near future."

Gung Loi leapt into her betrothed arms and kissed him passionately. When they parted, Jackie clasped him and said, "Brother, your temerity has just made many others very happy. You will need to build her a home, and know there is a vacant plot near my own, in the Valley of Knowledge, should you wish it. Come, let's celebrate."

The evening turned into an engagement party, as word spread quickly throughout the Queendom. Kay stayed until they started singing, and feigning tiredness, left to check on developments.

Using the daylight in the lands of the Eighth, she narrowed down the probable location to a series of caves. One of them, she had a feeling about, but the Eighth would not be active until late at night. Knowing she possessed the keenest sight of any on the island she said, "Langnor, I must rest. Wake me as soon as dusk descends on the lands of the Eighth."

Later, as she lay down to sleep, her thoughts turned briefly to her situation. She thought about the predicament of the Eighth, and later, about her true title, High Lord of Destiny; such a loquacious expression and implication for being able to do something so very simple — the ability to tell what was right from what was wrong.

She smiled upon her secret. The sword she carried was not a magical weapon, just a runed blade that was in total harmony with her position. Her mind lingered for moments on other High Lords of Destiny that had gone before her, and she wondered briefly if they would have acted differently than she? Kay considered rising to draw on the inspiration of past wisdom, but was soon fast asleep within the embrace of futures passed, and those yet to come.

Keos

The Eighth meanwhile had doubled back via a very long and circuitous passage to the northeast, and into entirely inhospitable lands. They knew other tribes of the Eighth lay to the mid-west, and made it to a series of caves before dawn broke. They were wary of predators, but the caves were empty. They hid in the deepest levels so that the eyes of Great Ogre could not find them. The attack had killed roughly forty of their number, but over three-quarters remained to live another day.

Keos and the Eighth all knew the region well, having avoided detection by the Great Ogre all of their lives. He was sure the survivors would regroup into large and larger groups once the threat had passed. They had done so countless times before, and he was not worried about detection. They were close to the lands of the Ninth, or where they had been recently.

Knowing they were safe for the time being, Keos deliberated. Hogar was a good friend, and yet through the Sixth's, and his own stupidity, they had exposed themselves to the all seeing eyes of the Great Ogre. He began to berate himself, until an elder hand on his arm quelled his distress.

Mentor spoke wisely, "My King, to see the coming with future's eyes — Ah, how many mistakes could we avert and good deeds be a'doing? But know, there is no end to this foresight, for therein only confusion reigns, and madness lures the unwary.

"This is what all humanity seeks, and yet what if it were granted? Would this change the world? It would not, because it would also mean we shared the future with our enemies also. Does not the great Mother Earth do unto one as she does unto the next?

"My Lord, listen to the words of an old and stupid man, because some say that, 'what you will do, for another has already come to pass'."

"I understand, Sage, and yet I remain troubled. This was my duty to my people and I failed them."

"My liege, do not tally blame where none should exist. We are human and we are bent to folly; we make mistakes. Do not dwell on what has been lost, but focus on what has been gained. We have new friends to help our tribe and us in years to come, and though the cost has been heavy and washed with blood, know we will emerge stronger for future alliance.

"Be still now and ease your heart's concerns, they do not become you. All will be well, as you will witness."

Grudgingly, Keos heeded the sage's words and let go of his self-abjuration. Subtly prompted, he focused instead upon the Guardian and the strange Eleventh. He surmised that these were indeed wise people seeking contact with them for his tribe's protection. The other tribes were not seeking to profit, or trying to bring slaughter amongst them, but were there for friendship and forbearance.

With a rumbling belly and an empty heart for the loss of sacred life, Keos curled into a fitful sleep and yet, his dreams were of a bright new world where they and all their kin lived in peace and harmony. His sleep was short, yet unusually refreshing.

Chapter 37 ~ Eleven of Twelve

Ælkræleinnoire

Ju Lo shook the Lord of Destiny awake and said, "Kay, the sun is setting in the land of the Eighth. You have time for breakfast before dusk descends upon their world."

The Eleventh were the keenest sighted of all the Tribes, and Kay's eyesight was extremely good, even for the Eleventh. She took watch from her station in engineering using the largest screen, knowing she would see anything others were unable to perceive. Leaving orders she was not to be disturbed except for an emergency, she began her vigil.

For a long time she saw nothing, and after several hours she leaned back to stretch her muscles and clear her eyes. She had been looking into virtual blackness for a long time and knew the act distorted not only the watcher's vision, but other senses also. Ensuring the watch was maintained by others; she went up and took a coffee, settling at her station in the control room. Thirty minutes passed before she came alert. She asked aloud, "What just changed?"

All faces looked to her and had no answer, not even a clue as to what she may be alluding to. She was about to speak, when the slightest flicker within the darkness of her screen caught her eye. Immediately she leaned closer to define who or what it was within the fleeting and almost ethereal discontinuities. But she knew these were indications of life. She focused on the merest sign, determined to fix as definitive what she knew to be there.

The darkness she stared into was as black as an event horizon. The moon had not yet risen, and perhaps would not that night. But then, it had been several weeks since anyone had seen either sun or moon, and for all she knew, that night could be a full moon.

There came another glimpse of movement, but always with her peripheral vision, not main focused eyes. She had laughed inwardly when Jack related, the Yaqui who had visited the Third, had talked about 'the art of not seeing'. Now she knew, because if she changed the way she looked at the screen, she could almost determine what was not there, and by extension, what should not be there.

There was much movement peripherally, so with crossed eyes she looked again, before moving her focus to infinity. In time, she is able to bring up a pattern of movement, and that pattern was headed inch by stealthy inch towards the caves.

"So?" she asked herself, "What do I know as fact?"

She answered herself, "I know Hogar told me the Eighth might come to a location like this one, or another nearby. I have not seen the Eighth at all, so there is no confirmation. Fact: Many movements are approaching this cave. It could be the Eighth, a pack of wolves, or Ogres hungry for blood. I cannot see because the forest surrounding disguises my tracking ability."

Even with the greatest powers of the Ancestors at her disposal, there was a limit to focus and low-light visibility. The only way she could be sure was to go and look for herself. Ælkræleinnoire wrestled with indecision for a moment, before deciding she had to go and find out what was happening on the ground.

"Gung Loi, I am going to see what is there. It's probably nothing of note, but I need to be certain. My sword will tell friend from foe. Have our troops stand by just in case, but this is likely to be a *no contact* situation."

The Eleventh's mind set changed the moment she arrived, her blade flared to life within the blackness, marking her as a target wherever she went, and whatever she did to try to hide the blade. The broadswords and Kriegsflegels of the Ogre bombarded her with ferocity as she ducked and weaved between trees, and hid within scrub, then somersaulted aside. Her night vision blinded by the sword's intense flare, she cursed, "My ultimate power is now my Achilles heel."

In time, she learned to use her sword as a decoy, but yet there were too many Ogres to fight. Kay knew she could simply return using the bracelet, but as High Lord of Destiny, this would only come to pass as her dying wish. As the game commenced, seemingly hundreds of Ogres attended her play.

Jack

n'Gnung and I arrived in the control room seconds after Kay left. n'Gue had watched Kay transfer and informed us at once, worried for her safety. I glanced at the screen and saw Kay's sword dance with blue flame; she had transported into the midst of an Ogre attack. I instantly set sending circles as shields, and interlinked them across the area of the cave complex. Gung Loi was already marshalling our forces.

"Ju Lo, add more interlinked circles as shields, and keep adding them. I am sure the Great Ogre will try to out manoeuvre us. n'Gnung, send a call to the Eleventh and Seventh at once. Send in our troops as soon as they are ready, I presume seconds!

"Kay is alone and we must support her. I will get the Ancestral weapons and protection bracelets, we leave straight away."

I arrived at Kay's side moments later, giving her a protection bracelet and ray gun, as n'Gnung and Aroweena shielded us from the Ogre's ominous assault. Gung Loi and Horovitz arrived some seconds later, their platoons strengthening our position, but we were exposed, and we were relying heavily on our shields. Kay said, "The best defensive position is to our right, but we need to be between the Ogres and the caves behind us. Follow me."

As we regrouped I spoke to Gung Loi, "Set one platoon in Viet Cong style to cover our tactical withdrawal. After they strike, have them move to flank and encircle us all, and take the Ogres from behind. The enemy will expect them to fall back with us. Set the second platoon in Ninja Mode, remember: Stalk, kill, disappear."

As we fell back, Horovitz was already holding a good position we could defend and use to counterattack. Most of his men wore night vision headsets and they were able to pick off targets before they reached us. However, he had recently become the proud owner of an ancient Gatling gun and was winding a ribbon of large calibre bullets into the rotating chambers with manic ferocity.

The Ogres retaliated by forming a wedge and driving directly at us. We could only take out the leader, who was quickly replaced, as the Ogre army continuously reshuffled to maintain formation. Horovitz' men used flares to light the night. I saw at once the Ogres had night vision as well, and their leading troops wore protection, our bullets bounced off their personal shields. They were closing fast and we had not gained any reinforcements for some minutes. No doubt, the Great Ogre had contained our shields within his own.

The Ogres roared with bloodcurdling glee, when the first of our personal shields gave out through dissipated power. They rushed us en mass and we reacted instinctively, separating as their leading troops powered through our midst. We fell away from the assault, only to attack the unprotected enemy flanks.

The Ogres peeled from the rear, and tried to catch us in a pincer movement, the Great Ogre was a good tactician, and I needed to outthink him. We dummied to shy away from their assault, but drew their lines sideways, spreading their host so we could attack. This we did before falling away again, and drawing the enemy further apart, isolating groups for dispatch by blade.

The red mist of killing frenzy settled upon me once more, and I became aware of a lot more than the Ogre I was about to kill: had killed. Barph had troops covering the caves, and they were fighting bravely, but without Ancestral weapons or protection. I was about to run to support them, when Owain and the Seventh rushed to reinforce the position. They began to drive the Ogre onslaught back. We were not alone. Reinforcements were arriving to bolster us.

I did not need the constant light of flares from both sides, to be aware other enemy were falling to arrows of the Eleventh. One nearby clutched his neck, withdrawing a mote of poisoned wood before he keeled over in the throes of death. I noticed one of the Fourth dancing upon an Ogre's head, only for said head to be removed by Junior with a quick twist of broadsword, the head kicked away in disgust.

The battle turned when Hogar led a phalanx of Trolls deep into the rear of enemy ranks. Between strikes of the Sword of Destiny, I saw an unknown people join them, taking battle to their oppressors of millennia. The thrust split the Ogre ranks, allowing our troops great advantage. We flooded into the midst of the Ogres, who were by then not only surrounded, but being riven through the centre of their war machine.

Groups of Ogres fell back seeking to regroup, but came under assault from above. Even in my heightened state, I could hardly make out our new allies, because they seemed to disappear before they appeared. I knew instinctively they were the Ninth.

Disparate does not come close to describing how the assembled Tribes came together that night. We were very differing peoples, but we stood together in battle.

The Ogres kept coming, and coming for us again. I knew the Great Ogre must have breached at least one of our shields with his own. My blade rose and fell in ballet with those of Aroweena and Ælkræleinnoire. We danced the macabre, becoming one killing machine, so closely did we understand each other within a single jot of time and joust of blade. We fought for hours, and still they came, until as the sky lightened and we killed the last. Then there were no more. As reward, I joined with those decapitating our aggressors. Just like running hard, it was hard to simply switch-off and become normal again.

Having won the battle, I counted our losses and searched with others for signs of life. The mood was grim, so much senseless killing: neigh, needless murder. Aroweena passed round her flask of firewater, and I took a healthy measure. I cast my eyes aside with conviction, and said to my trusted, "I am not letting this opportunity go, we will nail this today — Eleven of Twelve."

I flicked my return bracelet, and arrived in the evening of our island. Jinnie flew into my arms, before sending messages to Da Phai Nai to ensure the Eighth and the Ninth were suitably greeted on the shores of the Outlands. I evacuated all within our sphere of control, knowing I had transported new Tribes. Our troops came back in dribs and drabs, most taking a celebratory short beer, before bathing in the lagoon.

The Eighth were wary, the Ninth were outright distrusting. I am sure the evening would have been a disaster without Ælthrelntheine's timely appearance. As High Lord Protector, she brought with her serenity and acceptance of the diversity of life, of all humanity.

We had only one thing in common, apart from our homo sapiens based DNA. Hatred of the Ogres. I wondered if that was enough glue to hold us together, or would we simply drift apart, again. My aberrant thoughts were quashed when Hogar presented the Ninth with his boyhood keepsake, a rare item of great antiquity they had been searching for, over millennia of millennia.

The mood lightened, and more so when Kay cajoled everybody present to do the *Okay Pokey*, as she determined to call it. From such a throwaway insanity of humanity, was a new determination born. We needed to find the Fifth to complete our number.

Gangling joined us primarily as translator, and with the Sage of the Eighth, Mentor, they were able to tell us what happened. Keos said, "We were waiting until dark before we moved, but became aware of the Ogres searching for us. I knew the caves were interlinked deep underground, and I decided we would leave by a different exit. We were several caves over when I heard the tell-tale call of the Ninth, a bird call, but one I knew to answer.

"We stayed to discuss recent events, because the Ninth were fleeing south to escape recent Ogre raids. They were heading for the place we had just escaped from. We agreed the Great Ogre was hunting all of us, and trying to corral us together. King Groël of the Ninth told us he knew of a way through the caves to the other side to the west, but the way was dangerous and could prove treacherous without light, which the Ogres would see. We had decided to wait until dawn before moving. Then we heard the sounds of battle."

King Groël spoke for the first time; "The Ninth have evolved a mainly arboreal lifestyle, one that hides us from Ogre searches. I dispatched scouts to discover what was happening, and they reported about your battle with the Ogres. I could not believe their testimony, because the Ogres always win. I had to look for myself, and saw many Tribes standing together, and winning. What I witnessed was impossible, and yet there you all were. I knew you had come to the aid of the Eighth.

"King Keos urged us to join the fight, and although few in number, we realised the time had come to rid ourselves of the Ogre dread. I would offer sincere thanks to all who fought for us. I never imagined the Ogres could be defeated. This is the dawn of a new era for us, for all of the Twelve Tribes."

That evening new friendships were formed, and forged deeper over time, aided by a liberal amount of beer. Nonetheless, the fighting had taken its toll; we were all physically exhausted and mentally drained. We needed to recuperate, and the night finished early.

Jien Noi gathered everyone together as we rose the next day. "As host of this auspicious party, I would welcome you all to break fast with us this morning at the Imperial palace. It is fitting that we welcome our new friends, our new sisters and brothers into our bosom this day.

"We now stand together as Eleven of Twelve, and it is my sincere wish that soon the Fifth will also join us and complete our destiny. The Twelve Tribes will stand as one."

Chapter 38 ~ The Twelve Tribes

Two days later, I was waiting for John to return. He had found an anthropologist who appeared interested in our project. John had arranged a meeting to show him a short video that Dawn had taken of our first meeting of the Eleven Tribes.

John was also searching for a linguist and a forensic archaeologist, or someone with similar skills and an adaptive mind set. We needed an independent check of Hominina DNA in a way that would not arouse suspicion. Was Owain in actuality a Neanderthal? We needed unequivocal proof that matched with our known fossil records; more so with the Denisovans. I wondered if we should work with the CDC?

I interfaced with the Core and refined our search parameters regarding the Fifth. We were looking primarily for their ring, the Ring of Honour. During our staccato like bursts of mental communication, I widened the search to include any minor rings with the same signature. I was asked immediately, "What do you want done with them?"

"Send them to the shore, when we find them."

The Core confirmed, "They are on the shore."

I blanched. "What?"

I ran to the transporter, hollering orders in my wake. I can't remember exactly what I said, but I knew I covered all bases. Within seconds, I was standing beside Da Phai Nai, who was facing down an unknown group of twenty frightened and feisty people, with her broom.

I needed to defuse the situation instantly, because kidnapping the Fifth had never been my intention. I asked Da Phai Nai to fetch a flagon of our best beer, and bowed to the newcomers. My finger hovered over my protection bracelet, ready to use it at the slightest cause.

Their leader nodded back to me, but they did not secure their weapons as I had hoped. We shared no common language, so I swept my arm in a welcoming arc, and smiled magnanimously. I went to sit at the nearest table, beckoning them to follow. Da Phai Nai poured beers for all, but none returned my toast. I took a sip from the leader's beaker, encouraging him to share a drink with me. He did not.

I was aware of others arriving to welcome our surprised guests, but there remained a standoff. n'Gnung arrived at my side, "Guardian, come quickly, the Ogres attack the settlement of the Fifth."

Moments later I stood by my console and watched the Ogres begin to destroy the village of the Fifth. They found no one fortuitously. I knew the Great Ogre was monitoring our transportation signals, as we were his. Another game of cat and mouse was in play.

On impulse, I brought the leader of the Fifth to our control room, and left him to watch the main screen as he witnessed the raising of his homelands. At his pointed direction, we rescued a few items, before the village was no more; but his people were still alive.

n'Gnung had been busy, his brother the central figure of many transportations. The leader of the Fifth turned to look at me and nodded as understanding dawned. He realised we were not his enemy, but that we shared the same one, the Ogre.

The Giant's sage, Gangling Shortfalls arrived within moments; he had obviously been woken from a deep sleep. However, he managed to speak to the leader of the Fifth, who I was introduced to as King Xeros.

That night we were joined by representatives of all the other Tribes, who were all ecstatic, and in an enlightened frame of mind. The Prophesy had been proven correct. Finally, all Twelve Tribes of the Ancestors stood together.

Sporting new scars, we were overjoyed to defeat the Great Ogre and foil his plans for world domination and human subjugation. We assembled again some weeks later. n'Gnung had built a fine house for his betrothed, one that added character to our unusual hamlet. I had added an extension to our home to allow Kay more privacy, built a guesthouse, plus improved and enlarged the servants' quarters.

The wedding of Gung Loi and n'Gnung took place in early spring, the new laws allowing them to choose their own date, which equated with the planting of new seed. They were married with full state honours, a holiday being called for the occasion. His wedding was similar to my own, I acting as his 'Best Friend'.

Returning from Gu Long Dux, Gung Loi's parental home, we transported to the road east of the capital, and walked the last yards towards the city proper. A spontaneous fiesta developed all around, but I knew n'Gue and his wife had been planning festivities well in advance. Representatives from all the Twelve Tribes walked with us, as testament to cement our enduring bonds of humanity.

The wedding was held in our refurbished church of the old religion, on the Imperial Mount of Grimwaldi Rinns. Sun Kist officiated and the Shaman made an unexpected appearance, blessing their union in her customary and bizarre fashion.

Afterwards a great banquet was held. Burnam gave the bride and groom a Maori bone twist pendant, representing our growing intimacy, and stoking the fires of enduring friendship.

The new couple spent a lot of time table-hopping amongst the people in the square below. In time, family and friends guided them back to the Imperial Mount, where we had created a new open-air promenade beset with tables and chairs, so the populous could easily interact with us, and us with them.

This, more than anything seemed to breach the psyches of our newer tribal representatives. They witnessed how we as a nation came together to enjoy the laughter and love we shared openly as a people. In time, they also shared more openly with us.

The wedding of n'Gnung and Gung Loi also brought us all much happiness, but other events taxed my patience to the limit.

John had designs to form, what he hoped would grow to become a large research centre full of investigative scientific teams. I remained opposed to allowing a flood of new faces access to the island.

During her inaugural visit, Doctor Sylvia Steel became my ally of limitation, by offering to process DNA and anthropological samples securely, in return for limited use of our scanners.

I fought our corner doggedly during her stay. "Doctor, if you promise these tests and results are privy only to essential personnel, we will offer you, personally, occasional use of our scanners. This relates to epidemics or situations that endanger the entire world, or its population, only — pandemics. Do I make myself clear?"

"Guardian, this is agreed, and trust me when I state that I understand your concerns. I would like to visit sometimes, just for friends and first-hand interaction, if it pleases you?"

"Why not join us now, it is almost dinner time, and we will make you welcome."

"No I can't, sorry, I have to ... no I don't. OK. The other can wait. I have a feeling we will soon have greater need for sharing — Iran. On our way, can I take a quick look at the current situation there, just for friends, call it a pre-emptive scan."

Although we knew she was working her angles, we got along surprisingly well. With her support, I managed to cross several people off John's list. In the process, I secured access to some of the best labs in the U.S.

However, at a subsequent weekend meeting, we did accept the services offered by several scientists from diverse backgrounds and interests; I remember how they introduced themselves in turn.

"Don Prendergast. I'm a postgraduate anthropologist, and wrote a thesis on early Hominina, which was not accepted by the current educational hierarchy, and denigrated by the supposed scientific community. I would offer my services to support you, and also prove my thesis is correct. Or adapt it accordingly with new data forthcoming, using the opportunities offered here."

Faye Wong was next. "I have a Masters in Practical Linguistics, as in verbal translation." She appeared to be fluent in eight languages, switching between any of them in mid-sentence.

Chapter 38

"Guardian, I am fascinated by the diverse languages spoken by these Hominina. Can I stay and begin now?" She was Chinese-American, and by the end of her short stay, had managed to learn a few words and social pleasantries of the Second, Seventh, and Eleventh.

"Hi, Finity Gael. I mastered in ancient scripts, and later gained my PhD. with a thesis concerning ancient Hittite steles. I'm fascinated by your runes and am sure I can translate some of them."

Botanist Julian [Jules] Blanchflower attended with his wife and assistant Jennifer. He told us about himself, "I have a Masters in Botany, and specialise in tropical plants. I met Jennifer at University thirteen years ago."

"Fourteen actually," Jennifer interjected.

"Yes dear, sorry, fourteen years ago, where she was reading Ecology. We are married with two children, but as a family, we are well used to moving around. We would be very pleased to join you, as I already see new species that are undocumented. But, only if our children can join us. Isn't that right, Jen."

Zoologist Nigel Woodcock spoke last, "I have several BSc's, zoology and related fields. I'm greatly intrigued by the evolution of species over aeons, and how this relates to evolution and newer forms of animals. I am especially interested by their adaptation to critical, life-threatening occurrences, such as the last ice age. I can't believe you have antediluvian livestock here. I must see them before I leave. For me, this is a once in a lifetime opportunity. Thank you for inviting me. I'll begin right now if that's OK."

After due deliberation the Empress approved the appointments, and John was thrilled. I knew he would soon be pestering me to add others, but it was another matter he approached me about the following day.

"Jackie, the new people arrive over the next couple of days. We need accommodation, plus computers, and those need power. These people cannot work with Stone Age equipment. It is untenable. How about a water powered electric generator, or a bank of photovoltaic cells. What do you say?"

"No."

"Just imagine, with electricity, we could get the kitchen working properly. How does full Sunday lunch appeal?"

"No!"

"Chinese, Indian? They could do takeaway service."

"Pizza?"

"Of course Jackie, whatever you want, fish and chips, shepherd's pie, sausages."

"Raspberry Pavlova?"

"Spotted dick, bread and butter pudding, apple pie and custard."

"You know how to wound a man, John. This is unfair. 'Fries' you said?"

"We'd need staff as well of course."

"We already have cooks, good ones. You wouldn't want to upset Da Phai Nai now, would you."

"Incorrect. We will increase the feast. They can learn each other's ways, expand their knowledge and culinary skills. There are delicious foods here unknown outside of this island. I have staff eager to come."

"One, a chef."

"Plus an under-chef, and someone to prep, waitress service? A scullery maid. Oh, and a washer up. I'd like a souse chef as well."

"Three people max."

"I was thinking twenty-four seven actually, Jackie, what with the end of the world, and all that. You wouldn't want to go out on an empty stomach now, would you?"

That day felt like fighting a Hydra, because every time I tried to cap expansion and personnel, John came up with good reasons to the contrary. I never regretted the outcome, but at the time, it felt like opening the gates to enemy hordes. After due consideration of the proposal, and subsequent Imperial intervention, John got a working kitchen and staff to suit. He also got a bank of photovoltaic cells, and later, a water mill, which we turned into an electricity generator.

During those days, Dawn came into her own, understanding both my own, and John's wishes and concerns, steering a middle course that suited our needs, the islanders' needs, and our mutual requirements admirably.

We also acquired a Rottweiler along the way, although one of human form. She came in the guise of Helen Crowthyere, John's PA, one who in time became a champion for both John and myself at the learning faculty admin.

The girl we inadvertently transported with the first building, Cathy, also appeared. Supposedly she was a research student, but her role seemed to be that of secretary, and extra hands where needs be.

Penelope Pendleton also became a regular, if erratic commuter to our shores. On her last visit she announced, "Dearest Jackie, I simply have to spend a lot more time here. I must understand the science of the ancients."

"Ancestors."

"Whatever. I'll need to bring my sister Phœbe here, her math are brilliant."

"Maths, the word is a plural."

"Math. She's focused too much on the real world though."

"And you are not?"

Chapter 38

"Why of course not, my works spans space and time. I feel like a raspberry sherbet milkshake. Jackie dearest, that is sometimes an academic or emotional sentiment, but this time I want to drink one — get a bit of fizz into my life; toodle-pip."

Sometimes I felt like a Dutch boy with his finger in a dyke, and while necessary people arrived to support us, I prevented the damn from bursting, and our island being flooded with new people.

I awoke on the first of March 2016, and said "White Rabbits!" ('Rabbits' only, when there was no 'R' in the month). I stretched, wondering why I said that on waking at the first of every month, when the first mad hatter entered my bedroom. Many more would follow as we entered the rabbit warren.

Dawn shattered the moment and her voice was urgent as she shook me fully awake. "Jackie, I am beginning to think this 'Wrath of Gaia' is real. Come, I need your eyes and your instruments all over the Arabian Plate, now!"

Once in the control room, my mind could not interpret what we saw. Neither could Dawn's. I stared at the Iranian city of Bushehr, where the Arabian Plate had obviously continued to descend. The Persian Gulf, almost devoid of water, appeared to have been swallowed by the gigantic crater caused by the nuclear explosion. It was hard to be certain, because clouds of steam and volcanic ash covered the region. In one place, I saw an Iranian coastal road spilt in two, one half being two feet lower than the other. The earth was moving.

Waters were being held back by the Straits of Hormuz, a tsunami gathering force to wipe the northern tip of Oman from the face of the Earth. Dawn shouted, "Aqaba."

I panned left a bit, westerly, and was shocked ashen. Parts of the Gulf of Aqaba were dry! Liquid magma oozed from the fault line, evaporating the waters of the Gulf. I watched, horror struck, as ships toppled hapless into the lava flows, and were engulfed, consumed, incinerated. I watched the Saudi side rise higher. I needed no soothsayer.

Would the Wrath of Gaia destroy all life on Earth?
Would the Great Ogre ever be defeated?
What would become of Humanity?

The End of Star Gazer Book Two

The Chronicles of Jack Barleycorn continue with

The Wrath of Gaia

The Third book of the First Star Gazer trilogy

Imagine the world Jack was born into no longer exists.

Faced with the utter destruction of all life on Earth, can our heroes survive? The Great Ogre continues to wage war with all the other Tribes, confounding chances of survival, when the primordial forces of Mother Earth are unleashed upon a mainly unsuspecting human nature.

In a ripping yarn, *The Wrath of Gaia* depicts a vision of the end of the world, completely original, entirely believable, and based in geologically evidenced fact.

Amid fast-paced, spicy action, survivors struggle with their daily existence, displaying humour, as they are led to question their deepest beliefs: Are religions innately misogynistic? What of the balance between Man the hunter and Woman the creator of life? What greater evil, was evoked within the concept of 'original sin'?

What is the nature of God—a deity, or was humanity created by an Alien race that came to Earth millions of years ago? That hypothesis, as presented in these books, becomes more and more difficult to refute.

Humanity has no common antecedent with the Great Apes. Did a race of star faring Ancestors create the missing link—create us? What is the elusive kernel of 'original truth' when it comes to our shared Humanity? What ties us together might also wrench us apart.

Once we know where we came from,

Once we know who we are,

How will we discover where we are ultimately going:

Star Gazer, Second Trilogy...

§

The official Star Gazer website: http://www.star-gazer.co.uk

Offers a vast array of additional information, character descriptions and images, pronunciation of difficult names, and large scale maps. Sections explain the Ancestral science, while others provide full references, timeline, and much more of interest.

www.ingramcontent.com/pod-product-compliance
Lightning Source LLC
Chambersburg PA
CBHW050024180626
46810CB00002B/564